THE WHOLE TRUTH

THE WHOLE TRUTH

a novel by

ANTHONY ROBINSON

DIF DONALD I. FINE, INC.
New York

Copyright © 1990 by Anthony Robinson

Library of Congress Cataloging-in-Publication Data
Robinson, Anthony.
    The whole truth / by Anthony Robinson.
      p.   cm.
    ISBN 1-55611-202-5 (alk. paper)
    I. Title.
PS3568.0279W4   1989
813'.54—dc20   89-46034
                                                          CIP

Manufactured in the United States of America
10 9 8 7 6 5 4 3 2 1

Designed by Irving Perkins Associates

For my wife, Kathleen

*"Do you swear to tell the truth,
the whole truth, and nothing but the truth,
so help you God?"
"I do."*

PART ONE

Chapter 1

Something about the room—the high ceiling, the pew-like benches, the magistrate's elevated chair—reminded the Rev. Adam Pohl of a church. A small English cathedral, perhaps, or an eighteenth-century abbey. But there was an amorphous similarity too, which he sensed but didn't immediately grasp; then, as he and one hundred and fifty others waited for the proceedings to begin, it suddenly came to him. In both places, the word came down.

Sitting beside him in the second row was the defendant's daughter, wearing a navy linen suit and white silk blouse. Adam turned his head, saw how upset, how terribly anxious Catherine was, and gave her a warm, reassuring smile. Bravely, it seemed to him, she smiled back. Father Pohl bowed his head. First he said a prayer for Leonard, asking the Lord to see him successfully through his trial and to grant his lawyer courage and vision. Then he said a prayer for himself. He hadn't taken a drink since that night of martini madness in Leonard's house some six months ago, and he asked for the strength—the continued daily strength—to hold on. Right now the urge to step quietly out and find the nearest bar was overwhelming.

Adam glanced up. The court stenographer, a woman with

frizzy, caramel-colored hair, was loosening up her fingers at a small desk positioned near the witness stand, while two bailiffs guarded a heavy door in the front. All seats were now taken, and the noise level in the room was becoming higher by degrees. Twelve or fifteen reporters, from local papers, radio and TV, stood along the back wall. Then one of the bailiffs, the heavier, shorter of the two blue-uniformed men, was suddenly announcing: "The Honorable Wilbur W. Cruikshank of the County Court. Please rise."

Everyone stood as the judge climbed the three steps to his chair, giving an easy, well-practiced swirl to his dark blue robe. He was an older man, perhaps sixty-three, who looked as if he'd spent the better part of his life doing manual labor, maybe repairing downed power lines for Mid-State G & E. Judge Cruikshank made a motion to both the defense and prosecution, and Chet Evers and the D.A. approached the bench. Adam Pohl, watching intently, imagined he was giving them last-minute instructions. "No hitting below the belt, boys. I want a good clean fight." The lawyers sat back down; a parrot-faced clerk then appeared and read the indictment in the case now before the court. When he finished, Judge Cruikshank raised and lowered his gavel.

"This trial is now in progress," he said in a flat voice. "I will call on the District Attorney of Cooper County to make his opening statement."

As if receiving a final word of strategy from his seconds, William Woolever spoke for a moment with his assistants, then stood, circled behind his table and walked out to the open floor before the bench and witness stand.

"Your Honor."

He gave a small, respectful nod to the judge, then turned and faced the jurors—six men and six women—seated in a two-row box on one side of the courtroom. "Ladies and gentlemen of the jury," he said, and paused confidently, like one who had all the time in the world.

"First," he continued, "I'd like to commend you publicly on your dedication and civic duty; and for your patience during the long process by which you were chosen to hear the testimony and weigh the evidence in this case, and by hearing and weighing decide the fate of the defendant. Very seldom in their lives do everyday citizens have such a huge responsibility put upon them, as you have now."

He smiled, looked into each juror's face, perhaps letting his striking blue eyes rest a moment longer on the women than the men. "I have not tried too many cases recently, though I have tried many more, in my career, than most district attorneys," he said, launching into his statement. "I work on every case, I spend long hours with my staff, I advise and counsel extensively. But, by and large, it's an assistant district attorney who comes to court. Then why have I left my desk, as it were, to try *this* case? Because its magnitude, its legal implication, its unspeakable brutality demanded that the district attorney himself come to court. Ladies and gentlemen, nothing less than the people's mandate to me— to vigorously fight crime in Cooper County and prosecute offenders relentlessly—brings me before you today."

William Woolever's hands slipped from the jury box railing. Taking a few steps away, he then turned and faced the panel. "What do we know about this case? I'll give you the facts," he said. "Phyllis Bradley was reported missing by her husband, the defendant, Winwar industrialist Leonard A. Bradley Jr., on the evening of September 23 at 7:55 P.M., exactly seven months ago today. Two Winwar police officers responded to Bradley's call. They discovered a ransacked safe in his downstairs office and an unlocked glass top to a display case of classic handguns, Mr. Bradley having one of the finest pistol collections in the state. Upon taking an inventory, an 1899 Smith & Wesson revolver and six rounds of ammunition were determined missing.

"For a week the Winwar Police Department, assisted by the F.B.I., state police and some thirty deputized civilians, tried to locate the whereabouts of Mrs. Bradley—to no avail. Then a local man, a twelve-year veteran of the U.S. Army and a well-known area hunter, in the process of building a tree-stand in the lower Shagg Mountains three and a half miles southwest of Winwar, spotted a badly decomposed human body. He summoned the police on his C.B. radio, other officials arrived, positive identification was made—it was Mrs. Bradley. She had been raped animal-fashion and shot in the back of the head. *Executed.* Some fifteen feet from the scene a revolver was found. The state Bureau of Criminal Investigation ran ballistic tests on the slug removed from Mrs. Bradley's head during autopsy—tests which proved incontrovertibly that the revolver uncovered at the site was the gun that killed Mrs. Bradley; it was the Smith & Wesson .38 special taken from the display case in Mr. Bradley's at-home office."

Woolever inhaled and let his breath out slowly. At the very start of the trial, when the court clerk had read the indictment, the jurors had either looked straight ahead or down at their hands; now, one by one, almost as if the order were predetermined, they glanced at Leonard Bradley and his lawyer.

"Could this be the work of a *husband?*" the D.A. asked rhetorically. "Husbands and wives argue, to be sure; occasionally a marital squabble ends in physical abuse; and from time to time we learn of a fight between husband and wife that terminates with the death of one spouse or the other. But what of rape? Does it seem likely that a husband, with murder on his mind, would first force himself upon his wife? I should clarify: It was impossible for the medical examiner to determine which of the two acts—the murder or the rape—occurred first. But that Mrs. Bradley was raped is indisputable.

"Hardly the work," Woolever went on, "of a husband. Then why is *this* husband in court today? Why was Leonard Bradley arrested and indicted? I'll tell you why, ladies and gentlemen. *Evidence.* When a wife or husband is murdered, the spouse is always questioned extensively; but I'll be honest with you. When I learned that Mrs. Bradley had also been raped, I said to myself: According to standard procedure, the police will question her husband; but it will be routine—nothing will come of it. Because why, I asked myself, would a socially refined and prominent man, such as I knew Leonard Bradley to be, sexually brutalize his wife if his intention was to murder her? Did he want one last taste of connubial bliss before blasting her brains out? On the surface, it didn't fit. Then leads, clues, information began coming in. I didn't consciously change my mind about the case; it was changed *for* me by the evidence."

Woolever slipped his smooth, glossy-nailed fingers into the angled pockets of his suit jacket. "First, there was the gun. Even before it was found, it made me think something fishy was going on; but with Bradley's safe open and some $1,700 in cash and an heirloom string of pearls taken from it, the missing .38 from his collection dovetailed with Police Chief Oscar Flick's initial theory of robbery and kidnapping. Whoever had entered the Bradley house wanted a weapon—not a rare antique but a solid, serviceable revolver. Then this same revolver was found in the immediate vicinity of the murder, as mentioned; but even when tests proved it had fired the fatal shot, that wasn't sufficient. Criminal investigators needed more, and very soon they had it. Footprints were discovered some quarter-mile from the murder site, of a small shoe and a larger shoe, along a little stream called Brenner Heights Creek—you'll be visiting this entire Plutarch Pond/Brenner Heights area in a day or two. Also found close by was a tuft of tan or khaki material, snagged on a bramble. The smaller shoeprint was determined, by police experts, to match exactly the sole of the shoes—or the sole of the *right* shoe—Mrs. Bradley was wearing on that fateful day. But what of the larger print? What of the tuft of material?"

Woolever paced back and forth before the jurors, all of whom appeared completely absorbed, taken in by his argument; he stopped and continued talking. "We didn't know the 'identity' of the larger prints, but if we could find out, we knew we'd have ample evidence for an arrest. Furthermore, it was learned there was another woman in Leonard Bradley's life at this time. For the six months prior to Mrs. Bradley's murder, he had been seeing a Ms. Diane Wirth in New York City. Mrs. Bradley, suspicious that something was going on, hired a detective, whose report documents in great detail what *was* going on. When Mr. Bradley came home from New York on his final business trip— final in the sense that he never made another while his wife was alive—Mrs. Bradley confronted him with the report. A very religious individual and a woman of the highest ethics and moral beliefs, she could not accept his infidelity. Mr. Bradley then said he wanted a divorce, and Mrs. Bradley replied—and I quote from the notes of her lawyer taken on September 23, the day

she disappeared, 'Over my dead body!' No way would she give
her husband over to another woman. Seeing Mr. Bradley's motivation clearly at this point, as a blindly frustrated lover and a
vengeful man, Winwar Police Lieutenant Dave Bock applied for
a search warrant from local justice Titus LaValle—which was
promptly delivered."

With great detail, the D.A. of Cooper County then described
the search of Bradley's house—and when he finished many in
the crowded courtroom were talking. Allowing people a few
moments to vent their emotions, Judge Wilbur Cruikshank kept
his gavel poised. Then he lowered it, and William Woolever
hammered home his point.

"—making it look as if," he was saying, "*as if* a deranged man,
surprised in an attempted burglary, then decided to abduct the
woman who had surprised him—and as an additional false lead
or clue, on the psychologically firm ground that refined husbands
such as Mr. Bradley don't rape their wives before murdering
them, but that a criminal *might* or *would*, Leonard Bradley raped
and shot, or shot and raped, his wife. The evidence doesn't hint
at this, ladies and gentlemen; it *dictates* this. Bradley's motivation
wasn't sketchy or iffy; it was clear, powerful, unswerving. He
wanted his wife out of the way to save himself millions upon
millions of dollars—plus to *make money*, because of his wife's
insurance. His wife's death would also enable him to carry on
his affair with Diane Wirth openly, to pursue her aggressively,
hoping that she would become his wife."

Woolever blew out a breath of air. "It's difficult for a prosecutor to praise the defendant, but part of me wants to tell Mr.
Bradley, 'You came up with a beauty. You just didn't quite pull
it off.' Cops and Robbers, or in this instance Cops and Killers,
is always a test, a game played with real people; the stakes are
nothing less than life and death. Leonard A. Bradley Jr. played
this game, ladies and gentlemen, thinking he could win—only
to find himself a very big loser."

"Objection! This trial is not over, Your Honor!" Chet Evers
said, breaking in. "Perhaps the 'very big loser' will be the district
attorney!"

Judge Cruikshank peered over his black-framed, half-height

glasses. "Counselor, calling someone a loser is not calling them guilty. Anyone arrested and indicted could hardly be called a *winner*, could they? Overruled."

The D.A., head lowered during the brief exchange, returned his attention to the jurors. "I agree with Mr. Evers—this trial is not over; but when it is you will see for yourselves that Leonard Bradley murdered his wife with malice aforethought. By the evidence I shall present before this court, you will see the scales of justice tip, and continue to tip, completely to one side: the side of 'guilt.' I will prove to you beyond a shadow of a doubt that Leonard A. Bradley Jr. raped and murdered his wife on the afternoon of September 23. May God bless you during this process, ladies and gentlemen, as justice is brought to bear in the great State of New York."

William Woolever gave the jurors a last look, of the utmost candor and sincerity, glanced at the presiding officer and took his place between his two assistants.

Judge Cruikshank scribbled some notes, then directed his attention to the table where Chet Evers and Leonard Bradley were sitting. "The defense may proceed with its opening."

Chet Evers moved slowly to the front of the room, recalling, as he did, the story one of his law professors at Michigan, Gilbert Russo, had told the class about "opening statements." It seems a certain county attorney had just finished his comments, finished them so effectively that one of the jurors, totally convinced by the prosecutor's dramatic account of the crime, blurted out as the defense lawyer rose to speak: "Save your breath, counselor. The sonofabitch is guilty!"

The fact is, Russo went on, most defendants *are* guilty, exactly as charged. They're not in court for their health. Add this prevailing bias to a prosecutor's forceful opening, and defense approaches the bench for *its* opening not with two, but with 2.999 strikes against it. Nowhere are a lawyer's skills, imagination, courage so tested as at that moment...

Chet remembered the day well, yet at the time he had taken Russo's comments at face value, as a truism, an academic verity.

Now he felt them viscerally, understood them as he never had before. He had worked hard getting ready for Leonard's defense and he was an experienced trial lawyer, if not recently a practicing one—and the buffed parquet floor was trembling under his feet.

"Your Honor, Mr. Foreman, ladies and gentlemen of the jury," he began, "I have listened with interest to the district attorney's opening remarks. If I were a member of the press or a spectator to this trial, I would think he had an excellent case for himself. Just look at that evidence!" Chet glanced at the table on which it all lay. "Impressive, isn't it?" he said, coming back to the jury. "Yet I can't help wonder if there's any credibility there. One can come across ten dollars in a parking lot; but when you find a satchel of hundred dollar bills beside you on the seat of your car, only a fool jumps for joy."

Chet Evers moved slightly away, noticing, as he gave his eyes a moment's freedom, that Woolever was talking to his assistant, Rhonda Fisch, whose face had the appearance of a scalene triangle. The D.A. had his hand loosely over his mouth; Chet nevertheless saw the smile on his lips.

"Why is it," Chet said returning to the jury box rail, "that a man with such wide knowledge of the law as my worthy opponent, with such great experience as a public prosecutor, doesn't *see* that the evidence he is ready to introduce to this court is phony? And introduce it he will, each piece a new nail, in *his* opinion, to fasten down his case. But *New York* v. *Bradley* won't be nailed down with, or by, the state's evidence. Why? Because it is manufactured, and before this trial is over—"

"Your Honor, I object."

Woolever's words bristled. "For Mr. Evers to say the state's evidence is 'manufactured' is to slander my office. Let him prove this if he can, but I refuse to sit by while he maligns me and my dedicated assistants."

"Sustained."

The D.A. sat back in his chair and Judge Cruikshank focused on Chet. "An opening statement, Mr. Evers, tells the court how you intend to proceed—*not* your views concerning your opponent's evidence."

"I intend to discredit every shred of my opponent's evidence."

"*Your case*, Mr. Evers—state your case."

"I have no case, Your Honor. I only have the truth."

Some spectators smiled, others laughed. Cruikshank banged angrily with his gavel. "Counselor, I hope—*hear me well*—you are not making a mockery of this court."

"I don't see how that would benefit the defendant, Your Honor."

"Good answer," said Cruikshank, glaring at the lawyer. "Remember it. Now continue."

Chet nodded. His gray hair covered the tops of his ears and fell over his collar in back. He had on flannel trousers and a brown herringbone sports jacket with leather elbow patches— not bought with the patches—and a red-and-brown tie. His cordovan shoes, though polished, were old, worn.

"The district attorney has given you," he said to the jurors, "his view on what happened on September 23, but bear in mind he wasn't there—anymore than you were. No one was there, except for the killer and Mrs. Bradley. From the time she left Luigi's Shoe Repair in Winwar at about 3:30 that afternoon, her movements are a mystery. She wasn't seen again for a whole week, when her body was discovered in the lower Shagg Mountains, Winwar Township, by a local hunter and woodsman, Dwayne McManus.

"Then the evidence started pouring in. I mean, ladies and gentlemen, you couldn't *buy* better evidence. Not that my esteemed adversary manufactured it. Like any public prosecutor, Mr. Woolever will go a long way for a conviction—but not *that* far. But *someone* manufactured it, of that I am certain."

Chet Evers looked out at the crowded room, letting his eyes rest briefly on Catherine Bradley—so beautiful, he thought, so worried—as she sat beside the Rev. Adam Pohl. "I would like to review with you," he said, refocusing on the jury, "how Leonard Bradley spent the afternoon of September 23. He left his office at the Bradley Corporation in Winwar at 2:30 P.M., having an appointment to see his attorney—that is, me—in the town of Willow at three o'clock. I have notes of our discussion which I'll introduce at an appropriate time, but in essence Mr. Bradley told me that he was having an affair with a woman in New York City and that his wife had had him followed; she now had the detective's report. Mr. Bradley said he wanted a divorce, even though he and Diane Wirth had no plans to marry. He wanted to continue seeing her and he wanted to do it in the open, as it were. He wanted his freedom. I told him I would start the divorce proceedings. He left my office. After that, only two people know what happened: Mr. Bradley, and the man who killed his wife. The prosecution maintains they're one and the same and has the evidence to prove it. I say they're different people; unfortunately I have no evidence to support this contention."

Chet smiled and said, "Some case! But do you know something, I'd rather have *my* case than the district attorney's. In a story by Edgar Allen Poe, which every high school student knows, the narrator describes a long, narrow fissure that runs through the facade of Roderick Usher's great stone chateau. At first the reader only takes it as an observation, but on the last page of the story when the chateau falls into the dark tarn surrounding it, it cracks along that very line. Ladies and gentlemen of the jury, even as I stand before you now, there is a similar fissure in the house of evidence Mr. Woolever has constructed. He does not see it and as yet you do not see it, but when his case falls, it too will crack at that point.

"Who fired that shot in the Plutarch Pond/Brenner Heights area of Winwar Township last September 23? Who killed and raped Mrs. Bradley? I say someone we are not now, or yet, aware of. Just for a moment follow this line of reasoning. Every man knows, and women should know, that—speaking sexually—the male erection 'happens'; it can't be willed. It happens, usually, at moments of physical intimacy with another person—for the sake of convention, we'll make that person a woman. Now this arousal tends to happen faster in younger men. Some older men, in fact, who have been married for thirty years, experience a phenomenon called 'male menopause'—they lose interest in sex entirely. Last fall Mr. Bradley was having a love affair with another woman; for his wife, he had little if any sexual ardor. And we are supposed to believe..."

Chet pointed at the jurors, "...*you are* supposed to believe that

Mr. Bradley knelt behind his wife with a revolver pointed at her head, tore off her undergarments with his free hand, and bammo, was ready for sex? Do I make myself clear? Ladies and gentlemen, I say it flies in the face of everything we know, have experienced, or read—that a husband in his fifties, under the horribly gruesome circumstances surrounding that afternoon in the lower Shaggs—not to mention with a woman who did not physically excite him—could achieve an erection: the physical state necessary in a male to have intercourse."

Chet Evers bowed his head, giving it a slow shake. Then, looking up again, he spoke quietly. "In this court today we try an innocent man. Not one 'presumed innocent'—whoever stands trial in the United States is *presumed* innocent. But one who *is* innocent. Members of this jury, weigh carefully the so-called facts which the district attorney will put before you; consider well his so-called evidence. Keep asking yourself, 'Is all as it appears?' And if you ask yourself that question conscientiously, then you too, like Poe's character, will eventually see the crack in the House of Woolever—and will watch it fall!"

Chet paused; he waited a moment, thanked the jurors and sat down. Judge Wilbur Cruikshank picked up his gavel, and speaking as if to defense counsel alone—the D.A. stirred uneasily— said, "This court is in recess for thirty minutes."

People drifted out, talking, mingling in the main lobby; but Leonard Bradley did not move from his table. He stayed seated, deep in thought, remembering the day it had all begun...

Chapter 2

Driving down Main Street at 5:20 P.M., he noticed the dark brown pickup drawing away from the curb in front of Stubby's Bar & Grill. He touched his brakes, allowing the truck to pull out. The kid behind the wheel, who had his cap on backward, motioned "thanks," and Leonard continued slowly along. At the last intersection in the village, where Main cut across Chodokee, the light turned red.

While waiting he let his eyes drift. Going up the green-carpeted steps of the Winwar Hotel was one of his executives, Bob Rakower, with two visiting businessmen. The hotel had a surprisingly good menu and a quiet bar. On the opposite corner, the door to the favorite restaurant for local folk swung open two or three times; but as was happening more and more in his home town, Leonard didn't recognize the faces.

The light changed, and he was soon rattling over a steel bridge. Beneath it flowed a slow-moving creek. Immediately on the other side the land opened up and Leonard realized, in his short time away, that the first fall colors had started to appear. It was a rugged terrain with boulder-strewn fields and, in the distance, tree-covered ridges and hills. He put on his directional signal. Forty yards farther along he turned at a rural mailbox; on the side of the box, besides the number 625, were the words "Maple Ridge Farm."

He was now driving on his private road. A big yellow barn and silo stood immediately on his right, and Leonard saw one of his hands working in the fields. He sounded his horn and the youth, a country lad named Jerry Kohler, looked up and waved. The road curved and rose gradually but continuously, following a ridge, then branched left at a vegetable garden—well-culled by now—and entered a grove of maples with a scattering of hemlocks and white birch. At a woodpile of eight or ten cords the road bent sharply, opening to a large parking and turning area of crushed stone, and his house. Leonard touched a button on his visor and the garage door started going up.

It had the same cedar siding as the building proper, which was extremely large, having several long wings, an endless number of roof lines, and a great deal of glass. His wife had always wanted a house that had a cathedral-like quality, so when they had decided—now twenty years ago—to build a new place for themselves, she'd pretty much had her way. Phyllis loved a clerestory and a vaulted ceiling, and her new house would have an abundance of both. Leonard would have preferred less glass and not quite the variety of roof lines. The house was certainly striking and impressive, though, and the property around it, 187 acres of woodland and fields, beautiful. The garage door was now fully up and Leonard pulled his Continental into the right berth, beside his wife's tan late-model station wagon.

He turned off the ignition, staying behind the wheel for a few moments staring at the front wall, where hand tools hung on a pegboard, remembering how in years past he'd always felt glad to be home after a trip, excited at the prospect of seeing Phyllis and taking her to bed. Now he felt nothing; he was a man going through the motions. He stepped out; a brown leather attaché case and a garment bag were in the back and he grabbed the two pieces. A window opened to the ridge and dust was still rising from the road. He passed in front of his wife's car. Beneath the pegboard a maple workbench ran along the front of the garage and on it, among the wrenches, pliers and screwdrivers, lay a chainsaw, partially dismantled; printed on the cutting bar in bold green letters was the word BRADLEY. On the frame to a heavy oak door was a single button. Leonard pushed it, and the garage door started down; then he depressed a heavy brass thumb latch and went inside the house.

She wasn't in. He could always tell as soon as he opened the door; when she was in, the house had a certain feel to it, and when she wasn't in, it had a certain feel; and right now it had the feel that said Phyllis wasn't in. That meant she was out walking. If his wife wasn't in but her car was in the garage, she was out walking.

A long corridor extended from the garage to the main part of the house. On Leonard's left, as he walked along, was the laundry alcove, with a window looking out to the woodpile and the sweeping driveway; on his right, a walk-in cloak room for raincoats, parkas, outdoor jackets. He moved on; the master bedroom opened to his left, and he went in. High up where wall met ceiling, on two sides, was a continuous strip of glass. The room also had regular windows, at the moment concealed behind beige drapes; a luxurious wall-to-wall carpet, a shade darker than the drapes, covered the floor.

Leonard laid his attaché case and bag on the king-size bed, unknotted his red silk tie and took off his suit. He was somewhat over medium height, in his early fifties, with a strong build and dark hair touched with gray. His nose leaned a little to one side, the result of a high-school football accident. His eyes were a warm, a quiet blue. After hanging up his suit he took down a pair of khaki trousers from a shelf in his walk-in closet and put them on with a forest green chamois-cloth shirt.

He opened his attaché case and took out a box of Russell Stover chocolates, just about his wife's sole indulgence, although something she would never buy for herself. For thirty-plus years he'd been bringing her chocolates whenever he'd been away. Holding the white box done up in a red ribbon, he went back out to the hallway and continued along for several steps. Suddenly jumping up on his right was the living room, twice as high as any other room in the house, with a huge hearth, brown leather furniture, brown carpeting and great ceiling-high windows looking north and east. His wife Phyllis would frequently declare that the room took her breath away; it didn't take *his* away but he liked the leather sofa and chairs and the fireplace. On his left was the main entrance, the front door to the house. It was made of heavy plate glass and, instead of swinging open on hinges, slid on tracks. The door was now snugly shut; however, the toe lock on the lower track was in an "off" position. That confirmed Phyllis was out; there were other doors in the house but this was the one they almost always used. It was physically impossible to slide the door with the toe lock engaged, or to reengage the lock from the outside.

The hallway ended at the kitchen. A low ceramic counter ran along one wall; extending its full length was a window opening to a wide lawn shaded by big sugar maples. On a lower level fifty head of beef cattle were grazing, their hides, in the afternoon sun, oily black.

Leonard set the box of candy on the counter, then went to his bar. It overlooked the living room, and standing at it you could see straight down the long hallway to the oak door that opened to the garage. The bar had a stainless steel sink and a chrome gooseneck water tap. He mixed himself a vodka and tonic, opened the small refrigerator for ice cubes, cut a slice of lime and returned to the ceramic counter. His mail was in a neat pile at one end, collected by his wife in his absence; among the letters, circulars and magazines was a cardboard carton about the size of a kid's lunchbox, stoutly wrapped and taped. He picked it up, recognized the sender's name and address; but he'd wait to open it. Four chairs with short legs and brown vinyl cushions—he thought of them as miniature bar chairs—were beneath the counter. Leonard pulled one out, sat down and started going through the rest of his mail.

All business correspondence, of course, went to his office. He had been in close touch with his secretary while away so he pretty much knew what was waiting for him. Here at home—well, most of it he tossed out. He slid three magazines—*Field and Stream, American Cattleman, Fortune*—to one side. Then he came across a card from his daughter, sent from Vancouver, where she was vacationing. He had to shake his head. As if Catherine didn't "vacation" in Santa Barbara, where she lived! Her whole *life* was a vacation. She always wrote in colored ink. This particular three line missive was in green, addressed to him alone.

"Mr. Leonard A. Bradley Jr."

He sat there, trying to remember the last time his daughter and wife had written, spoken on the phone. It was as if the *other* didn't exist. He and Tony, their son, weren't on the best of terms either, but at least they spoke. Leonard took a swallow of his drink. A key was entering the lock in the sliding glass door.

He pushed back his chair and stood up as his wife stepped inside. Her face had a healthy glow; if she didn't work up a sweat, she would say, she hadn't had a good walk. She was a tall woman, with narrow hips, small breasts, a sharp jaw and a fine, perfectly straight nose, and her hair was graying and tightly set. For years he had thought her high cheekbones attractive and had never considered her thin, just sensuously slender. He had loved her long legs and flat hard stomach, and while making love she would often extend her legs straight up and he would take a peek, as it were, thinking it incredibly erotic to see her toes, way the hell up there, arched like a diver's. But now, to Leonard, she just seemed bony, brittle. Sinewy. She was wearing a long tan skirt and a beige turtleneck shirt, and she had on a sturdy pair of brown lace-up shoes.

"Hi, darling," he said, going forward to greet her, an enthusiasm in his voice he wasn't completely feeling.

"Hello."

"How are you?"

"Fine, thank you."

She slid the door shut and he made to embrace her. However, she didn't appear receptive to the idea, brushing past him and walking into the kitchen. Leonard stood by the door for a second, then went back to the kitchen himself. His wife was putting a kettle on the range.

Leonard picked up his drink but didn't sit. "Did you have a nice walk?"

"It was pleasant."

"The leaves are just starting to turn," he said.

She didn't respond.

"Are you okay, Phyllis?"

"Why do you ask?"

"You seem...distant."

She turned off the burner, picked up the kettle and poured the steaming water into a small china pot with a wicker-wrapped handle. She was breathing deeply; her breasts poked at the material of her shirt like acorns under a leaf. "How did it go?"

"Really well," he said, thinking maybe he'd misjudged her mood. "It was our most successful trade show yet."

"What did you do last night?"

"Last night?"

"Yes."

"Let's see. We wrapped up the show at six. Oh, I had dinner with two of our dealers, Al Monica and Frank Winter, in a little Italian place on West 54th. Afterward they went home to New Jersey and I had a drink at the Waldorf bar and went up to my room. I thought you might call."

"'I'm sorry if I disappointed you."

Maybe he hadn't misjudged her mood. Leonard finished his drink and quickly refreshed it. Phyllis filled a light blue teacup, its lip trimmed in gold, and took her first sip.

"What is it?" he said.

"You tell me."

"Phyllis, you're in a very strange mood."

"I just want to know what you did last night."

"I'll say it again. Al Monica, Frank Winter and I—"

"Stop lying, Leonard."

"I'm not lying. What is it you want from me?"

"The truth."

Taking a quick swallow of his drink, he said, "What makes you think I'm not telling you the truth?"

Her thin angular face was glistening, flushed. "Does the name Diane Wirth mean anything to you?"

He did not have a quick answer; then he realized he didn't have any answer. "OK," he said, meaning it as an admission.

"OK, *what?*"

"I know the name."

"The name is familiar to you but the woman isn't?"

"Phyllis, sit down, please."

"Are you going to deny you've been seeing her?"

"Stop this third degree and we'll talk," he said.

"The detective's report I have does all the *talking* I need."

He took another swallow of his drink. "Then why are you interrogating me?"

"What would you like me to do, let it all go by? Sweep it all under the carpet?"

"No, but let's talk like mature people."

"How do mature people talk, Leonard?"

"They try to discuss their problems rationally."

"You've been seeing this woman for six months and I'm supposed to be rational? I could kill her, I could kill you—"

"Then I think we should get a divorce."

She winced, as if feeling a sharp, sudden pain in her stomach. "That's your answer?"

"What's an alternative?"

"You can't think of an *alternative?*"

He saw where he had just hurt her badly. She wanted him to repent, to say he would never see Diane Wirth again. And mean it. To take her in his arms and say he was sorry and say he had slipped, but please, could he have another chance? He understood what she wanted from him and, standing at his bar and looking at his wife, he recalled the years—all the many years—when he would have fallen on his knees, on an occasion like this, and kissed the hem of her dress. He had had girlfriends as a boy growing up in Winwar. Like June Brkich. Saucy June Brkich. On the rocks of Brenner Heights, in haystacks around the county, on the grassy banks of Chodokee Creek—they made love everywhere but in bed. He wanted to marry her and probably would have, in time, if he hadn't met a girl who lived in Virginia, vacationing with her parents on Lake Dunmore seventeen miles from Winwar. A girl who wasn't saucy at all. Who was slender and quiet and didn't drink and who talked of an afterlife and kissed him with sealed lips—when he finally kissed her—and on the last day of her stay he made love to her. It was her first time, and even now, as Leonard thought about it, he remembered how special, how exciting it was. There on the shore of Lake Dunmore at night with Phyllis Clarke, her shapely legs pointing straight up, toes tickling the stars. Best of all, she loved it. Afterlife or no, she wanted more...

He looked at her now, thinking he had it in his power to preserve their marriage, to save the many years they had been together, most of them happily. She would forgive him too. Not today, not tomorrow, but in time. They would go on; only Leonard wasn't sure that that was what he wanted—to go on. He wanted something else. Maybe it was Diane, maybe it was just a wish to once again be free.

"Phyllis—"

She saw it coming. He wasn't going to say what she wanted to hear. In her face he recognized that look that said it was over, that forever wasn't forever at all, that at fifty years old she was out. It hurt him, still he went on, saying what he had to say. "I haven't been happy with you. Something's happened. I can't say what you want me to say. I'm sorry. I didn't come home thinking I'd say this. But now it's all out—and whether you think we should get a divorce or not, I want one. There's no reason we can't do it amicably. Maybe you wouldn't want to stay in Winwar, but I'd still give you the house—"

"You son of a bitch."

He had never heard her swear. His lips suddenly felt warm, and he picked up his glass and drank. "Phyllis, we've had great years together, but I think it's right for us now to go our separate ways. Neither of us is so old we can't start over—"

"You son of a bitch."

"Phyllis, please. You're an attractive, wealthy woman—"

"Who vowed, before God, to forsake all others."

She stood at the range, teacup in her fingers, her eyes burning as she spoke. "You should know something, Leonard—I will never give you a divorce."

"You might contest it, but if a person wants a divorce in this state, ultimately it's granted."

"This one will be over my dead body."

"Come on Phyllis, stop the melodrama."

She set her cup and saucer down, then left the kitchen. He watched her go into the bedroom and come out with her purse, then continue down the long hallway past the closet and laundry alcove to the garage. The door, slamming, echoed through the house.

He stayed at his bar, absently finishing his drink; confused, upset. Then he mixed a new one and went over to the low counter, where he pushed through the rest of his mail. Nothing of any interest. Leonard looked at the stoutly wrapped package. Thinking to keep busy, he picked it up and walked with his drink across the living room to carpeted, down-leading steps, soon coming to a small landing where a door opened to the outside. No one ever used it, but the architect had thought it important to have a door on the landing because the room itself was below ground. The stairs double-backed, and Leonard continued down to his at-home office.

He flipped on a light. A dark brown carpet covered the floor, and the walls were done in a natural toned rice paper. A sofa and two easy chairs, handsomely upholstered in a tan fabric with a light green thread, occupied one end of the room. In the corner, near the foot of the sofa, stood a tall chest with a glass door. Standing in it were five or six rifles and shotguns—also a number of fly rods in polished aluminum cases. A large oak desk dominated the left side of the room; on the right were two glass-topped display chests, as one might find in a museum or jewelry store, also of fine oak.

Leonard sat at his desk, removed a folding knife from the front drawer and sliced open the package. The object inside, nestled among styrofoam pellets, was double-wrapped in thick waxed paper. He slipped off rubber bands and the paper fell away, exposing the handgun he had wanted for his collection for years—a superb 1902 Luger.

He examined it carefully; of all pistols ever made, none had quite so menacing a look. He lifted it, aiming in the direction of the stairs, thinking back to the days when he and his son would test fire every new gun that came in, and routinely fire the others. They had a range in the woods behind the house just for that purpose.

Leonard removed a green legal-sized ledger from his desk and entered the pistol's serial number and the rounds of ammunition included in the shipment. From under the desk he unhooked a small key, crossed to the righthand display case and unlocked the padlock securing the glass top; before lifting the top, however, he raised the Luger a second time, to appreciate again the weapon's exquisite balance. As he extended his arm, Phyllis came down the steps and stood on the landing, facing him—square in his sights.

He lowered the pistol, thinking to apologize—but also to fault her for coming upon him so stealthily. It was a terrible thing to point a gun at your wife—at anyone; but unless people announced themselves, in some manner made their presence known, then—

Suddenly she was gone. Leonard walked over to the stairs. The landing was empty. He took the steps two at a time to the main floor. Nothing. The house was quiet, perfectly still. Leonard stood at the top of the stairs, frowning. Then he returned to his office, crossed to the display case and placed the Luger between an 1847 Walker percussion pistol and an 1873 Colt single-action sixgun, only wanting to finish the job. Using the same key, he unlocked a deep drawer beneath the case and stored the two boxes of 9mm ammunition included in the shipment. Then he replaced the key beneath his desk and, standing, reached for his glass, bringing it quickly to his lips.

Chapter 3

In the executive wing of corporate headquarters, the C.E.O. of the Bradley Corporation was jotting down lines for the keynote speech he'd be giving next week at the annual meeting of the Young Presidents Club. He'd been active in the organization when he had been a "young president," but there were many chief executives today, themselves young presidents at one time, who ran bigger companies than his. Leonard felt honored. On top of the page was a scrawled title for his talk, "Entrepreneurship: Risk & Reward."

He wrote a new sentence, then another; he believed in the free enterprise system and enjoyed talking about it. More specifically he enjoyed talking about the code that had guided his father, who had founded the company sixty-three years ago, and which was still at the heart of the Bradley culture today. *Honesty in All Dealings, Quality Products at Fair Prices, Respect for the Customer.* How well, even now, he could see his father holding forth at those bleak meetings in '46 and '47 when the company was struggling to find its way—carve a niche for itself—and the founder's son had just put aside one uniform, of khaki, for a new one of blue.

His telephone rang. Picking up, he was sure it would be his

lawyer and old friend Chet Evers returning his call. But no. His secretary informed him that Mr. Summersell had the updated third-quarter figures.

"Send him in."

Leonard put the phone down; his train of thought broken, he was immediately besieged by the doubts, worries that had preyed on him so strongly ever since he'd come back from the trade show. Had he spoken too quickly in telling Phyllis he wanted a divorce? He was crazy about Diane but they had never discussed marriage, except as she had told him she could never see herself leaving New York to live in Winwar; and he saw himself out in the cold if their relationship shouldn't develop. Phyllis hadn't spoken a word to him for the past three days. Then there was the image of her on the landing, so vivid still, and still so haunting. Did he want her dead? Is that what his unconscious was telling him? Why else would he see her there? Or closer to it, why else had he *put* her there, dead in the sights of the Luger? There was a knock at his door.

He looked up; the company president was coming in. "Matt, what do you have?" Leonard said.

It was a bright, airy office with Leonard's desk toward the back and a separate sitting area, comprised of three easy chairs and a sofa, closer to the door. A large plate window took up most of one wall, giving a view of the flowing, handsomely maintained company grounds. Summersell, smiling, sat down in a brown-cushioned armchair at the corner of his boss's desk and removed five or six pages of graphs and figures from a folder.

"It's basically the same problem as last quarter," he said, "namely, the less than satisfactory performance of our Consumer Line. People aren't buying, Leonard. Calling what we're in a recession is being very generous. Home lawn mowers, industry wide, are down twenty-three percent."

"Honda's new line is doing well from all reports," Leonard said.

"Their advertising budget is astronomical, that's part of it."

"What's the other part?"

The forty-three-year-old president, who ran the company on a day-to-day basis, didn't answer immediately. He was, as always, smartly dressed; today he had on a finely tailored gabardine suit, a light yellow button-down shirt and a silk, regimental tie. When Leonard had hired him four years ago, he had thought Summersell's Ivy League background would lend a certain air, bring a certain class to the company, which, after all, was located in the goddamn sticks. No doubt it had—and no doubt Summersell had helped attract other good people. Leonard liked him personally, but he was beginning to feel the man, for all his charm and polish, was a bit thin on substance.

"It's a bigger challenge than I ever thought," Matt Summersell said, "to buck John Deere, Toro and Lawn-Boy. The economy hasn't helped, but regardless, it's a tough road. I know we'll make it—there are many good signs this quarter. Our BX-16 chain saw is a pacesetter, 22,000 units shipped last month; that's not what Homelite shipped but it puts us third, just below McCulloch; and the Bradley S-33 Snow Blaster is carving out a substantial share of the market. We're gaining a reputation—"

"We can't pay our shareholders on reputation, Matt."

"I understand that, but—"

"What else?"

"Our industrial division is hot," Matt Summersell said, producing a graph from his folder. "The AGV GreensKing just won't quit. Pinehurst's superintendent, Don Shane, swears it's reduced his cutting time by one-third—and does a far better job than any mower he's ever used. From Augusta National to Pebble Beach, courses are going Bradley. Our T-10 TrapRaker is blowing the competition away. And look right here." Summersell pointed to a bright red line. "Our computerized Sprinkler Queen watering system is showing a five percent increase in market share—"

Leonard's telephone rang and he picked it up. His secretary said his lawyer was on the line. "Excuse me for a minute," Leonard said to his executive. Then into the phone, "Chet, how are you?"

"Yesterday on the Clintondale I took three rainbows and five browns—a couple of 'em fifteen inches. The fall fishing this year has been unreal."

"You really know how to hurt a guy," Leonard said.

"Grab a rod and drive up."

"What are they taking?"

"Hair wings, tied on 24's."

"How can you see a fly that small?"

"Who has to see when they're rising and taking." Chet laughed. "I've rubbed it in enough. What can I do for you?"

"I have a little problem."

"Can you tell me about it?"

"I'd rather see you."

There was a moment's silence. "How's today at three o'clock, in my office?"

"Perfect."

Leonard hung up, his hand staying thoughtfully on the receiver. Then he looked at Summersell. "Sorry, Matt. Go ahead."

"I'm driving to Willow to see Mr. Evers," he said to his secretary, who was stationed outside his office in a large open area where three other secretaries sat at desks; one entire wall was built-in filing cabinets.

Eleanor Chapman was a petite woman who had worked for the company for thirty-one years, first as his father's secretary and now, for the past fourteen, as his. She was pert, extraordinarily efficient, attractive; but she had never married. Except as she was married to the company. Through the years she had also been a good friend of the family, particularly to Catherine when his daughter was growing up.

Eleanor wished Leonard a pleasant evening and he walked out of the executive wing. In the main lobby he said good night to the receptionist, Paula Laidlaw, a forty-year-old married woman from nearby Chodokee Forks whom visiting businessmen were always asking out for a drink; to the best of his knowledge, she never went, but he understood why they asked. He continued on, but before reaching the exit he glanced at the lobby's main wall. On it hung a larger-than-life bas-relief of a man's head. Beneath it were two lines, also finely wrought in bronze.

LEONARD A. BRADLEY, 1899–1977
FOUNDER, BRADLEY CORPORATION

Every morning when Leonard came to work, and every evening when he left, he would glance at the sculpture of his father—out of enduring respect. And a certain lingering fear. For a brief moment, now, he caught the man's hard, steady gaze. In life no one had ever stared his father down; and sure as hell no one was going to now! Leonard looked away, pushed through the center of the three glass doors and walked along a broad stone path to his car.

Willow was best known for Clintondale Creek, next best known for the Willow Diner, and Leonard couldn't help thinking as he drove north on Rte. 21 that he was on his way for an afternoon of fly fishing—and before he was through and heading home he'd drop by the diner for coffee and a slice of home-baked pie. How many times through the years had he fished the Clintondale and stopped by the diner afterward? Frequently with Chet.

They had met on a stream, not the Clintondale but on the upper reaches of Winwar's own Chodokee Creek. He was in the army, home on a week's leave, and fishing one evening he saw a boy casting a dry fly up ahead where the creek curved. Leonard liked the fact that he wasn't whipping the waters with a spinning rig. Then the boy hooked into a big fish and had to follow it downstream, and Leonard got out of his way and the boy—he couldn't have been thirteen—finally landed an eighteen-inch rainbow. He had to rest, so they sat on the rocks together and talked. And even then Leonard suspected that he'd be successful; at twenty-nine Chet Evers became the youngest partner in the illustrious history of Davis Polk. Then, at thirty-five, it had all suddenly, traumatically ended for Chet when his wife—for reasons Leonard had never understood, mostly because Chet had never talked about it—committed suicide. Shortly after that Chet left New York—the glamor, excitement and money of big time criminal law—and settled in a little upstate town not far from Winwar.

It was only a thirty minute drive, and soon Leonard was passing the diner—parking lot packed, as always; he turned on Green Street, went by the famous fly-tying store of Al Darnell, made a right on Main and parked in front of a two-story brick building, circa 1911. The main floor housed an outdoor clothier, windows filled, now, with flannel shirts and hunting jackets and insulated boots. Leonard went up a flight of narrow stairs, knocked on a door on the landing—it had Chet's name on it— and walked in.

Next to a big cherry wood desk was a small table facing the street; the lawyer was sitting at it. On the table were hackles, feathers, patches of fur, hooks, colorful threads and the all-important vise; in its jaws, apparently, was a fly. At least Chet was doing something that indicated he was tying one.

The office was cluttered, a little dusty; on the walls were some paintings of outdoor life—a springer spaniel flushing a pheasant, a fisherman bringing a big rainbow to net, a woodland stream in winter. "Be right with you, Len," the lawyer said, glancing up for a brief moment. "Just thought I'd take advantage of a lull in business."

"I always thought you tied at home."

"Both places now."

"Big investment there, Chet."

The lawyer dipped a toothpick into a small bottle of lacquer and applied a drop to the whipping at the eye-end of the fly, then cleared the eye itself with the other end as a precaution. Nothing more frustrating, Leonard knew, than to choose a new fly while on the stream only to realize the eye was clogged.

"So that's one of your 24's," Leonard said, leaning way over.

"That's what's doing it, on a thirteen-foot leader tapered to 7X."

"I can't fish that fine," Leonard said.

"You wrote the book on fishing fine."

"Ten years ago, maybe, when I could see."

Chet stood up and they shook hands. He was a tall and very spare man with brown eyes and a full, expressive mouth—and his hair, thick and full, was so gray it looked white. He was wearing a pair of old khaki trousers and a blue flannel shirt rolled at the sleeves. "Sit down, Len," he said, pointing to a couple of saggy-looking easy chairs across from his desk. "You look a little worried. It's not the IRS again?"

"No."

Leonard was silent for a moment; it was hard getting started. "I told Phyllis I want a divorce," he said. "It's been something I've thought about for a long time—I know I haven't been happy but I never really saw myself doing anything. Then a couple of days ago I came home from a business trip and she threw a detective's report at me—I've been seeing someone in New York for six months. I couldn't hide it any longer. That was when I said it, when I told her."

"Did you actually see the report?"

"No."

"She could've been conning you."

"I doubt it but I don't care if she was—it got all the cards on the table."

"Who is she, Len?"

He loosened his tie, flipped open the top button on his shirt. "Her name is Diane Wirth, she's forty-two years old and she paints children's portraits and she's wonderful. I'm in love with her."

Chet scratched the side of his face; a shadow was starting to creep across his jaw. "Is she in love with you?"

"She loves me, she says. She's happy seeing me—we're very close."

"Do you want to marry her?"

"I'd like to—I would, but she's got her own life. She isn't lying awake nights dreaming about moving to Cooper County!"

"Does she know you're contemplating a divorce?"

"No."

"What will she think?"

"It won't make her happy; she talks about her divorce as a two-year nightmare. But she's not the reason I want the divorce—she's *a* reason but not *the* reason. I just haven't been happy at home. I need to be free again—"

"Does Diane have any children?"

"A daughter, eleven."

"How long has she been divorced?"

"Six or seven years."

"Is she—" Chet stopped, rephrased the question. "Does she see anyone else that you know of?"

Leonard slipped out of his suit jacket, tossing it across a plain walnut coffee table between the two chairs; on the cuff of his left sleeve were his initials. "She's breaking up with an old boyfriend. I think maybe they see each other occasionally."

"Does it bother you?"

"I don't dwell on it."

The lawyer massaged a bony knuckle on his left hand. "How did Phyllis react when you said you wanted a divorce?"

"It was like I'd kicked her in the stomach. She would've forgiven me, I think—in time—if I'd apologized, said I'd never see Diane again. But then to ask her for a divorce instead..."

"What did she say to you?" Chet asked.

"I'll tell you exactly what she said. She said, 'Over my dead body!' I couldn't believe it... I mean, Phyllis doesn't use cornball expressions like that."

"Anything else you want to tell me, Len?"

He thought of his hallucination, of Phyllis' image—whatever in hell it was—appearing on his study landing. But he was afraid Chet might think he had a screw loose if he mentioned it. "That's pretty much it. We're not talking. No surprise there."

"Maybe you should take an apartment."

"That's a good idea."

Leonard rolled forward and held his head lightly.

"What's the matter?" Chet asked.

"Sometimes the guilt jumps up and grabs me. This isn't exactly my style either."

"It goes with the territory, Len. You've hurt, you're hurting, a person who shared thirty-plus years of her life with you. Guilt's a killer. Keep busy, get a place of your own. I'll start the proceedings." Chet raised his hand. "Unless you'd like me to wait a month, see how you feel then. What's the rush?"

"Then I'd never do it. No, get started."

"Whatever you say, friend."

Outside on Main Street a truck rumbled by. Then quiet again. Main Street, Winwar, compared to this place was like 42nd Street. "Now, I hope you're ready for some really good fishing," Chet said. "I have all the extra equipment. I'll even let you use your old net, the one you gave me when I was a kid—solid ash frame, leather-wrapped handle. It's a thing of beauty, in case you've forgotten. I have a cap, trousers and shirt, boots—water's so low waders aren't necessary. Then after we each pick up three or four nice browns we'll pour ourselves some Kentucky 100 proof bourbon whiskey—"

Leonard had to laugh. But, no, he couldn't stay. Chet asked him a second time. They would even cook the trout on the stream, like they used to. Leonard said he just had too much on his mind. But soon. They would do it soon.

"The season ends next week," said the lawyer.

She had heard of his reputation: out of court, a lamb; in court, a lion. She couldn't vouch for the latter, but sitting with Dudley Wilbraham now, Phyllis Bradley saw him to be, in fact, a gentle, thoughtful, man. He smiled easily; he took plenty of time; he smoked a pipe—she loved men who smoked pipes. His office had a warm burnished look. The desk, the paneling, the shelves—all softly glowed.

"On advice of a close friend I've come to see you," she was saying, "because I don't want to make any mistakes. I am opposed, unequivocally, to giving my husband a divorce. But I still believe legal counsel is important."

"I am glad you are here, Mrs. Bradley. We cannot stop an individual from filing for a divorce, but we *can* make it a most painful experience."

"I want him to pay." She said it flatly, like a sentence.

Wilbraham smiled. "I can guarantee it."

The attorney selected a pipe with a swirling grain. "Would you mind—?"

"Not at all."

"How did you first learn that your husband—"

He spoke extraordinarily slowly. That he was intelligent, thorough, tough-minded, Phyllis didn't doubt; she only wished he would choose his words more readily. They weren't, after all, playing Scrabble.

"—was having an affair, Mrs. Bradley?"

She told him. Coming back from a walk one day last spring, she had heard the noise of her husband's "brush hog." He had been away on a business trip, and the noise told her he was back. Nothing in the world Leonard loved more than his power tools, especially those carrying the Bradley name. He was cutting back the bushes and weeds encroaching on the driveway, and seeing her, as she continued to the house, he waved and smiled. Waved again, vigorously. She went inside to make tea, wondering at the odd sensation she was having. Why was she suddenly ill at ease? She looked at her husband through the kitchen window. He wasn't working *just* to cut back the brush—she had seen him do it too many times. He was giving it "a little extra," as he had given his wave and smile a little extra. Standing at the window looking out, she knew *he* knew she was watching—and thinking what an industrious, home-loving husband he was.

"And that's when I knew," Phyllis said.

"Without telling you, he told you," Wilbraham said. "It's human nature to give oneself away. I believe, odd as it may seem, for reasons of self-preservation."

"Self-preservation, to give yourself away?"

"It's the secret that kills, Mrs. Bradley."

She nodded; it struck her as very astute. Then she produced the detective's report. Wilbraham looked it over with great interest. "Frank Zicca," he said.

"Do you know him?"

"Oh, yes. He's top-drawer."

The attorney was loading his pipe with incredible deliberateness. "Do you have any *other* evidence that your husband is seeing this woman, Mrs. Bradley?"

"Yesterday I found an American Express charge receipt in his suit. For an $8,300 Cartier necklace. He didn't buy it for me."

"Do you have it with you?"

She did, but then she couldn't find it in her pocketbook. Her first impulse was panic. Then she recalled what had happened and immediately relaxed. "I know where I left it. At a friend's house. It's perfectly safe."

"Anything else? Letters? Strange phone numbers on your bill?"

"No. But I've known for months, ever since that day."

The lawyer nodded "Has your husband had other affairs, previous to this one?"

"None that I ever knew of."

The lawyer finally applied a lighted match to his pipe. "Had you ever considered that the detective's report—" puff, puff "—might lead to the kind of confrontation—" puff, puff "—that you and Mr. Bradley had?"

"Yes. I walked on pins and needles for months."

"But you didn't call Mr. Zicca and tell him to cease and desist."

"I *had* to know, Mr. Wilbraham."

He blew a cloud of aromatic smoke thoughtfully to one side. "What did you say when your husband asked you for a divorce?"

"I've given him my life, Mr. Wilbraham. My husband is the only man I've ever known. And just like that, he says it's over. What did I say? I said 'Over my dead body,' and God, I meant it!"

Wilbraham laid his pipe down in a cut crystal ashtray. "I shall endeavor to serve you faithfully and well, Mrs. Bradley."

"Thank you. I count on that."

The lawyer stood up; he was several inches shorter than she, a rotund man impeccably attired in a gray pinstripe suit. They walked to the door of his office. "Please take my counsel to heart. These are trying times. Try to keep a bright outlook," he said, taking her hand. "In periods of stress, it is especially important to do those things we truly enjoy. Do you have interests, hobbies?"

"Walking."

"Yes—perfect!" The lawyer beamed. "Walk—walk and invite your soul!"

"I will. Which reminds me, I have to stop for my shoes."

"Your shoes?"

"A pair of walking shoes, this is the third time I'm having them heeled and soled. I can't throw them away."

"Old shoes are indeed old friends," said Dudley Wilbraham.

As it had done when she had entered, the bell above the door to Luigi's Shoe Repair tinkled when Phyllis walked out; inside her car, parked on Main Street in the village, she put the Great American grocery bag containing her shoes on the passenger's seat, started the engine and pulled cautiously out. Driving down Main Street, she made a quick detour on Mulberry, thinking to pick up the Cartier sales slip.

She had visited with Ruth Pohl just before leaving for Wilbraham's office, wanting the moral support of her good friend, wife of the rector at St. Philip's. She had shown Ruth the American Express receipt, and Ruth's indignation had fueled Phyllis' own fury, and they had sat in the living room, drinking coffee and berating Leonard. Then the Pohls' frail son had tripped coming up the porch steps. Ruth had jumped up and run to the back door, and Phyllis had followed. Poor boy had turned blue. Bluer than his everyday normal blue. Phyllis thought he might die then and there. From birth the child had had a malformed heart, a rare and potentially fatal disorder; but with Ruth holding him, and Phyllis holding Ruth, Danny had finally caught his breath. The hour was pressing, but how could she leave Ruth in such straits? It was only on Ruth's insistence that Phyllis left for her appointment—with the damning charge receipt on the coffee table.

But now no one was home at the Pohls'. Phyllis drove back to Main, crossed Chodokee Creek, turned at her road and followed it past the large yellow barn and silo, then along Maple Ridge. On command, the garage door went up. The inside was empty; she pulled into the left berth, parked, lowered the garage door and went inside. Afternoon sunlight was shining through the high windows in the living room. She stopped at the bedroom door, caught up in the spectacle; and understanding, again, her charge to Guy Sroka, the young Atlanta architect she had hired. "Call it a house," she had told him secretly, "but build me a church." Feeling less vindictive than she had earlier in the day, Phyllis entered the master bedroom.

She took off her light gray pantsuit, hanging it in her closet, then slipped into a full-cut banker's gray skirt and a green turtleneck shirt. Sitting on the edge of her bed, she removed one of her buffed, repaired shoes from the grocery bag and put it on.

She smiled inwardly and lifted out the second shoe, feeling blessed that Dudley Wilbraham, at this juncture, had come into her life. She had an ally. As she finished tying the second shoe, she suddenly became conscious of sounds—was someone coming along the hallway from the garage? She looked up; through the open doorway Phyllis saw, thought she saw, a shadow on the floor.

"Hello?"

No reply. The shadow—there was no mistaking it now—became darker. Someone was right outside her door. "Leonard, is that you?"

Still no reply. "Who's *out* there?"

A man in a dark brown T-shirt and light brown trousers—a plain paper bag with holes cut for the eyes over his head—appeared in the doorway. He had strong arms and a muscular chest, and he was holding a gun.

Phyllis stood up, began backing away.

He came into the room. "Sorry to barge in on you like this, Mrs. Bradley."

It was almost said as if he meant it; he didn't seem nervous or deranged. She saw his eyes move through the holes.

"Who are you?"

"I can't really say that, can I? Open your husband's closet."

"Why?"

"Just do like I say."

She went unsteadily to Leonard's closet, bumping her dresser and rattling bottles, and opened the doors.

"OK, let's see. That pair of pants on the hook, take those—and those boots."

She lifted the pants from the hook and picked up the pair of ankle height boots.

"Wrap the pants around the boots."

"Tell me what you *want!*"

"Make a little bundle there, Mrs. Bradley. Good. Now out to the hall."

She went out into the hall.

"Downstairs to your husband's office."

Going down the steps, Phyllis told herself she mustn't panic; she had to keep control of herself—observe his mannerisms, note his height and weight, listen to his voice. In Leonard's office, he told her to put the pants and boots on the desk. "Now get me the key to the gun cases," he said.

"I—I don't know where it is."

"Come on now, Mrs. Bradley."

"What are you going to do?"

"Do like I say, Mrs. Bradley. Get me the key."

Maybe she should cooperate. She had heard it was always best to do exactly what a person holding a gun on you asked . . . She looked under the desk, saw the key dangling from a hook and removed it. Standing, she put it into his outstretched hand.

"Thank you," the man said. He was wearing thin leather gloves. His eyes, through the cup-sized holes, were dark brown; they didn't look like a madman's eyes. Maybe he wasn't going to hurt her. On the paper bag, above the eye holes, perhaps at the man's temple, she noticed a brownish red stain. He unlocked the right-hand case, jammed a pistol in his belt, closed the glass top and opened the ammunition drawer, pushing through several boxes and finally, from one, picking out several shells.

"Put back the key," he said.

She put it back.

"Now open the safe."

The safe was behind Leonard's swivel chair, in the wall, and she kneeled, having to steady her hand as she turned the dial. The door, small but heavy, swung open.

"Cash, whatever you have. Valuables."

Phyllis handed him a manila envelope containing money. He told her to step aside, then brushed through legal-sized envelopes, papers, deeds, messing everything up. By accident, she seemed to think, he came upon a long, velvet-covered box. He stood, pushing it into his rear pocket. "OK, grab the bundle," he said. "Back upstairs."

In the living room he directed her to the main door.

"W...where are you taking me?"

"I understand you like to walk, Mrs. Bradley."

"Who told you that?"

"A friend," he said.

And for one wild moment she wondered if that friend could possibly be Leonard...

She stumbled through the thick woods behind her house, the man always a step behind, urging her forward, almost giving her encouragement. They came to a low stone wall marking the property line, following it until they were opposite an old ramshackle barn. Parked behind the barn, in tall grass, was a blue car. He helped her over the wall. At the car he told her to drop the bundle she was carrying on the back seat. She did. He unlocked the trunk.

"All right—get in," he said.

Phyllis stared into the trunk. The grass came up to the shiny chrome bumper of the car.

"Come on now."

"No!"

"Mrs. Bradley, do like I say." He raised the gun just a little, so it was pointing at her chest.

"What are you going to do?"

"Just get in the trunk."

He assisted her inside, then took her arms, pulling them behind her back and tying her hands. He forced a twirled piece of cloth between her teeth, knotted it, and closed the trunk. She was surrounded by darkness.

The motor caught. She heard the rush of exhaust. Her head was crammed against the tire housing. The car moved, jounced along. A sharp object kept jabbing her thigh. Grass swept the underbody of the car, gasoline sloshed in the tank, tossed up pebbles began striking the fender wells, the tires hissed. The trunk mat had a rubbery, sickening smell. There was a red glow as the car slowed. Her fingers worked frantically to loosen her bonds, her tears ran into her mouth, then the tires were hissing again, flinging up pebbles.

"Help me!" She was sobbing; her thoughts screamed in her head. "Please help me, Leonard!"

Chapter 4

Leonard parked beside his wife's station wagon, passed between the two cars, lowered the garage door and went inside the house—and had an odd reaction. He couldn't tell, didn't seem to know, whether Phyllis was or wasn't home. Strange. He walked down the long hallway, going past the bedroom doorway and, just beyond it, the sliding front door. His eyes fell to the toe lock: "off." So she was out walking after all. In the kitchen he set his attaché case down and made for his bar.

Vodka and tonic in hand, he picked up the mail and walked into the living room, settling into the leather sofa. He had a quick taste of his drink, then sat quietly, thinking about his day— especially his visit just now with Chet. So it was starting. Two years of charges and counter-charges, court appearances, motions, delays, appeals. Legal fees. He didn't like any of it, but driving home just now from Willow he'd clearly seen the importance of his moving on. His marriage to Phyllis had lasted a good long time but now it was over. Nothing was left. Why should he stay with her? Or she with him? For appearance's sake? He had to get on with his life. Diane or no Diane. Tomorrow he'd check out the new townhouses on Plains Road, as Chet had suggested.

Leonard had another taste of his drink and picked up a letter from Town Supervisor Alfred Abbot—who was urging all Winwar residents to conserve water during the current drought. He also wanted to remind all townsfolk that September 30 was the deadline for obtaining new landfill stickers. Leonard put the letter aside and picked up the latest issue of *U.S. News and World Report.* As always, he went directly to the business pages, reading still another article on Ellis-International. On Monday the nation's largest manufacturers of farm machinery had filed for bankruptcy, and economists were now saying—

He stopped reading, laid the magazine down and looked about. He didn't know what it was but he might have thought someone was staring at him. Then, even while that feeling persisted, he took notice of the front door. It wasn't fully closed. A sliver of light—a quarter-inch wide—shone between the leading edge of the glass panel and the frame.

Leonard got up and walked over. Conceivably Phyllis might leave without locking up, if only going for a ten minute stroll, but she certainly wouldn't leave the house without sliding the front door fully shut. Leonard nudged the door all the way, then returned to the sofa; only he didn't sit back down, deciding instead to take his drink up to the pond.

First he'd change his clothes. In the master bedroom, he noticed a large-sized grocery bag on the floor. Next to God, his wife revered order. Leonard picked up the bag, folded it along its creases and laid it temporarily on the bed. He undid his tie, took off his business shoes, hung trousers and jacket on a hanger and reached for his khakis. They weren't on the hook where he had hung them last night. He had put them on after work, newly washed and ironed, and hadn't done anything but sit around the house. Sadie, their house cleaner, was a sweet woman, she did her job well—sometimes, he thought, *too* well.

No big deal. He pulled new trousers from his shelf and zipped them up, then pushed his feet into a pair of loafers. In the main part of the house he freshened his drink, picked up a newspaper and went outside, walking the length of the driveway and taking a secluded path starting at the woodpile, the overhanging branches of maples and hemlocks sifting the sun's rays.

The stroll, by itself, was relaxing; it brought Leonard back to the days when the whole family would take the path to the pond for a swim and a barbecue and Catherine and Tony would always run ahead, and he and Phyllis would carry the baskets filled with good things to cook and drink, then set the baskets on the table in the picnic house and settle back in the redwood chaises at the water's edge while the kids played. Good memories. But only that now. Barely that...

He reached the pond just as a trout jumped. Years ago he and his son Tony had stocked it with a dozen fingerlings, thinking to create their own "fish for fun" water, agreeing they would only use barbless flies. Today the spring-fed, acre-and-a-half pond teemed with natives and rainbows fourteen, sixteen inches long. But even with snipped hooks, he hadn't fished it for years.

He settled back in one of the old chaises, resting his drink on the cracked, paddlelike arm. The whole area was run down, untended. The yellow brick barbecue, built to withstand earthquakes, hadn't quite started to crumble, but everywhere around it, especially in the pit, weeds grew thickly. He could not remember the last time he had built a fire here and thrown on some steaks and boiled corn, water taken straight from the pond. He could not remember, but he missed the days, those wonderful days when Catherine and Tony were children and he and Phyllis would sit here at the pond and they were a family. An afternoon shadow was moving across the water. Leonard picked up his glass. In the pond he saw the reflection of a few clouds drifting by, and looking up he saw them in the sky.

In all, Leonard stayed at the pond for half an hour. Then feeling a hunger pang, he stood and returned to the house—wondering what he could cook up. As he was nearing the front door he was momentarily startled. By the edge of the turn-around, the thick bushes parted and scampering toward him across the crushed stone was a big black cat.

Leonard leaned down and scratched the tom's scarred ears, recalling the bitter cold night last winter he'd first seen it while carrying in logs: emaciated, dried blood on its neck, half-frozen. Phyllis was at one of her meetings, and he had taken the stray in and fed it tuna and hard-boiled egg, with a bowl of warm milk, then had fixed a place for it in the garage. Now it lived here; it lived here, but it only came back for food and rest.

He slid open the glass door, and the cat—it went by the name Black Cat—scooted in. Sensing that the house was still empty— some walk she was taking—Leonard nevertheless called out, "Hello—anyone home?"

He fixed a meal for the cat. In his bedroom, he again noted the grocery bag that had been on the floor—when, by rights, it should have been tucked neatly away in the kitchen drawer. He walked about, absently righting a bottle of skin moisturizer on his wife's dresser. The inside of her closet told him nothing, except to remind him how fastidious she was. Then he thought, Why am I getting worked up? She's on a longer walk than usual. Maybe she stopped by someone's house and isn't calling. Why *should* she call? We're not speaking...

He found a beef stew and some broccoli in the refrigerator; when he was waiting for the food to heat he made himself another vodka and tonic, again having the sensation, as he stood at the window looking across the driveway to the woods, of a quiet, so quiet a quiet as to make it almost ominous. He sat down to his meal, fully expecting to hear his wife any minute at the door. But no. He rinsed his dish and the pots, leaving them in the sink, then made himself a cup of coffee. Though Phyllis often walked on their property, usually her longer walks were on the network of back roads in the township. He would finish his coffee, hop in his car and go looking for her while there was still daylight.

He decided to use Phyllis' car, however, instead of his when five minutes later he went into the garage. One of her favorite walks was along Pioneer Trail, a badly gutted, unpaved road through local farmland, and he might "bottom out" in his Continental. Long ago, for convenience or emergency's sake, they had agreed to leave car keys above the visor. Leonard activated the garage door mechanism and backed out the station wagon. As he drove past his farm, he saw one of his hands hauling a buckboard, piled high with hay bales, to the barn. All tranquil, all in order . . .

Forty minutes later he returned, having seen no one on the back roads—let alone Phyllis. As his house came into view, he was hoping to see lights inside—and end this silliness. No lights. Estimating that he had thirty more minutes before darkness, he parked at the woodpile and walked quickly to the pond. From here, she could go in any number of directions, but it was always her starting point. Perhaps she had fallen and injured herself. Leonard moved into the woods, suddenly more than a little worried—and a little annoyed too. Playing this bizarre game of hare and hounds with an estranged wife wasn't something he'd exactly choose to do.

"Phyllis!"

He came out on the edge of a meadow, seeing eight or ten deer browsing, then went into the woods again, following an overgrown trail once used by loggers. Tony and Catherine had liked this particular walk because it emerged at another meadow, in the center of which stood an old twisted oak Catherine had named the "witch tree." Long ago lightning had blasted it, giving it a distinctly hunched appearance; and in the fall the poison ivy growing on the trunk and branches turned bright red and resembled a cape. He came to the end of the trail now; fifty yards away the disfigured tree, in the slow process of changing cloaks, stood eerily in the twilight.

"Phyllis!"

He moved on. The woods were getting dark, and he began circling back toward the house, stopping only to look at a pair of tattered pistol targets positioned against a steep shale bank. One last time he called his wife's name.

*   *   *

Back in the garage as he was getting out of her car he heard the telephone ringing inside; quickly he opened the house door and ran down the hall, picking up the receiver in the bedroom. "Yes—hello."

It was Ruth Pohl. She asked to speak with Phyllis.

"She . . . she's not here."

"Would you have her call me when she gets in?"

He paused. "Have *you* seen her?"

"Excuse me?"

"I—I'm not sure where she is, Ruth. I thought she was out walking. But now—it's getting awfully late."

"Maybe Tony or Debby came by."

"That's possible."

"She didn't leave you any note?"

"No. Nothing."

"Well, please let me know, Leonard."

He said he would, and a second later jabbed out a local number. His daughter-in-law Debby answered; in the background Buck, his son's springer spaniel, was barking. Leonard told Debby that Phyllis wasn't home—did she happen to know where she was?

"I haven't seen her. Is her car there?"

"Yes."

"Let me ask Tony," Debby said.

He heard his son's voice across the main room of the three-room cottage in Mink Hollow, an isolated, mountainous area of Winwar township. Debby came back and said Tony had no information. She asked Leonard to call when he had any news; again, he said he would.

He sat on the edge of the bed, his eyes going to the folded paper bag. Perhaps he shouldn't have touched it or, for that matter, closed the front door. Then he thought of something and could only wonder why he hadn't thought of it sooner. He walked through the kitchen to the cool, formal dining room, glanced about and continued into the west wing, first searching Phyllis' office and the closet in the room, then each of the two guest rooms that once were the children's rooms. After entering the north wing where the guest room, in fact, was located, he returned to the kitchen; standing at the bar, he stared directly across the living room to the stairs leading to his downstairs office. Oddly, his heartbeat picked up.

At the head of the steps he flipped on a light and started down, pausing on the landing to take in an overall view of the room. Nothing seemed out of place. He crossed to the metal furnace-room door, opened it and went in. Overhead, thick wooden buttresses supported the main floor; copper tubing and electrical cables, also overhead, ran in all directions. He looked behind the furnace, then scanned the shadowy crawlspace extending to the farthest corners of the house. The last thing he wanted to do was call the police. He had always considered himself a very private person; certainly, under the current circumstances in his life, he didn't want publicity now. Neither would Phyllis.

At his desk he made two calls, the first to the local taxi service, the second to the bus depot. Phyllis still had family in Charlottesville. Perhaps, on the spur, she had decided to get away from Winwar and go for a visit. But no taxi had come to Maple Ridge during the day, and the woman in the rinky-dink Trailways ticket office said she couldn't *recall* selling a ticket to Charlottesville but she'd check. What was his number? Leonard told her, hung up, swiveled in his chair and saw in a kind of double take that the door to his wall safe was ajar.

He opened it all the way and looked in. The contents, always in perfect order, resembled a rat's nest. He turned back to his desk and without hesitating dialed the local police, asking personally for the chief; the dispatcher said he'd just left for the day.

Leonard introduced himself, stated the problem. His wife hadn't come home from a walk, and someone had ransacked the family safe. At this point he couldn't say what—if anything—was missing...

His voice trailed off. The dispatcher said she'd try to raise the chief but an officer would be there shortly, regardless. Leonard put down the phone, still staring across the room. The padlock on the righthand display case was loose! Not only that, it was in a backward, or reverse, position. The lock hanging in the left hasp said YALE; its twin, nothing. Leonard stood, walked over to the case, and peered in.

"This is Sergeant O'Shea," Chief Flick was saying to Leonard, just inside the sliding front door.

"Sergeant."

O'Shea, a round faced, stocky officer about thirty-three, was carrying a black vinyl grip. "How'd do, sir."

Leonard spoke to the chief. "One of my display chests is also open, in addition to the safe. A gun's missing."

"Let's have a look."

The three men went downstairs. Unlike most police chiefs in the county, or state, Oscar Flick always wore his uniform. He had lived in Winwar for forty-one years; before that, as a kid growing up, in Wyoming. Town called Difficulty. His hat was a dark brown Stetson; its color matched the single stripe on the outside of his tan trouser-legs and the flap pockets of his tan shirt. He wore his sidearm low. For shoes, he had on western boots. No spurs.

Seated at his desk, Leonard explained how he had first noticed the open padlock. He had gone over and counted the individual handguns without lifting the glass top, coming up with twenty. He picked up the green ledger from his desk and handed it to the chief. "In the right case I'm *supposed* to have twenty-one—"

He stopped in mid-sentence, jumping for the phone the second it rang. It was his daughter, Catherine, calling from Santa Barbara; she had just heard from Tony. Leonard said he had no news on Phyllis's whereabouts, but someone had ransacked the safe and taken one of his collector's pistols.

"What does it mean?"

"I don't know."

"Do you think she's all right?"

"It's a mystery, Catherine. The police just got here."

"Will you call me back when they leave?"

Leonard said he would, put down the receiver and joined the two officers.

"Well, I'm not familiar with *all* these weapons, Len," the chief said. The ledger, open, was in the hands of Sgt. O'Shea. "But I know a .38 when I see one, and I don't see one."

"It's the one that's missing."

"I see you also keep records of rounds expended and rounds on hand."

"Yes."

Inside the ammo drawer, among many assorted boxes, were three boxes of .38 Super-Match wad-cutter bullets. Two were factory sealed. With the tip of a ballpoint pen, the chief counted the cartridges in the open box. "How many 'rounds on hand'?" he asked O'Shea.

"Says 'sixty-three.'"

"Fifty untouched. That means the open box *should* have thirteen bullets."

"It has seven."

Leonard broke in. "Then whoever took the gun—"

"—loaded it right up," said the chief.

Chief Flick's dark brown Stetson was hanging from the back of the kitchen chair. He was having coffee with Leonard while Sgt. O'Shea was still dusting for prints and generally checking around. "I don't know *what* to make of it, to be real honest with you."

He picked up his mug. Leonard had asked him if he wanted a drink, but he had reminded his old friend that he never drank on duty. In uniform was on duty, regardless of the hour. "Say it was a robbery—the cash and pearls," Chief Flick went on. "Then why the Smith & Wesson? OK, it's a classic handgun—a collector's piece, for sure. But what's it worth? $300? Why not one of those French or Italian beauties?"

"I don't know."

"You must have guns in those cases worth thousands."

"I do."

The chief slipped a spiral notebook and mechanical pencil from his shirt pocket. His tie, loosely knotted, was also dark brown. He was no longer burly, as Leonard remembered him as a kid; now he was distinctly beefy. But he still had the same quick eyes. To Leonard, they would always be a "blocker's eyes." For the three years Leonard had carried the ball at Winwar High, setting state records for scoring, a kid from Wyoming had run the interference. Behind each Bradley touchdown, it was said, was an Oscar Flick block.

"The pearl necklace, anything special about it—length, color? Registration number anywhere, anything like that?"

"It's been years since I've looked at it, seen it," Leonard said. "It's a beautiful string of pearls, belonged to Phyllis' grandmother. Oh, the clasp! It's a black semi-precious stone—I think onyx."

The chief made a little scribble. "The cash—small bills, large?"

"Mostly twenties. Some fifties."

"How were these bills stored, Len? In a box? An envelope?"

"Envelope."

"Any markings on it?"

"No."

"White?"

"Manila."

Leonard's elbow was on the table; he was rubbing his forehead. "Do you think it's possible the two things could be separate?" he asked the chief. "Phyllis missing on one hand, a robbery on the other?"

"I'd be guessing—it's too early to say. When was the last time you saw her?"

"This morning, before I went to work."

"What time did you leave the house?"

"About twenty minutes to eight."

"Did you talk to her during the day?"

"No."

"When did you get home from your office, Len?"

"About five-twenty. But I'd driven in from Willow. I'd spent an hour with Chet Evers."

"Haven't seen him recently. How is he?"

"Chet leads some life—does a little lawyering and a lot of fishing."

Chief Flick grinned. It wasn't a sparkling grin but it was full, warm. "Remember the day we borrowed old man Tomlinson's boat on Lake Dunmore? Now *that* was a day of fishing. We spied these two girls from Camp Mohonk wearing shorts, those *short* shorts, and carrying bamboo poles. They asked us where the big ones were. Quick as a wink you say, 'Get in, we'll show you—'"

"Chief, come here a minute."

It was O'Shea in the living room. Leonard followed Oscar out of the kitchen. The sergeant was kneeling on the carpet just inside the sliding door, holding a saucer-sized magnifying glass. "Take a look," he said, handing it up.

The chief dropped—not all at once—to one knee. He moved his index finger lightly over the carpet while using the glass. "What do you make of it, Jim?"

"It's not your everyday Cooper County dirt. Lot of ash mixed in."

"When's the last time you cleaned out your fireplace, Len?"

"Late last spring sometime. Unless Sadie did it recently."

Oscar Flick handed O'Shea the glass with instructions to get up every last speck. He and Leonard went back to the kitchen. "Who's Sadie?"

"Sadie Wojciechowski, our house cleaner."

"Where does she live?"

"Winwar Trailer Park."

They sat down at the table. "Now, Len, I want you to tell me everything you did today, from when you left your office until you called headquarters."

He did, in detail; then, interrupting for the first time, Oscar Flick asked if his visit with Chet was for old-time's sake.

Leonard hesitated, then heard himself say: "The I.R.S. has started hassling me about my farm again. Chet does my taxes. I needed some advice."

"Go ahead," said the chief.

Fifteen minutes later he laid his mechanical pencil down and finished his coffee, long cool. "Len, I want to touch all bases. When we have a missing person, how they were when last seen—

their mood, what clothes they were wearing and the like—is very important."

"Of course."

"How about Phyllis? How's she been lately?"

Leonard made a little offhand gesture. "She never really changes all that much, in her mood. She seemed fine—we talked about a project her Beautification and Improvement Committee is starting at the library. As for what she had on—she wasn't dressed yet. She was in a robe."

"When she takes these walks, does she wear a special outfit?"

"Skirts, usually quite long; sturdy shoes."

The chief made a few notes. "Has anything been bothering her recently? Like someone die in the family, her own health—"

"No."

"You two gettin' along okay?"

Leonard's coffee mug was empty but he picked it up. Then he set it down and scratched a knuckle, unable to answer, "No, chief, I've been seeing another woman and I've asked Phyllis for a divorce and we're not speaking." It was just too personal, and he didn't want to go into it, not yet, anyway, even if the man asking *was* the chief of police. He was also his friend, after all; he'd understand...

"We're getting along fine..."

Chief Flick tucked his notebook into his shirt pocket. "If it's any relief to you, Len, most missing people show up within twenty-four hours. Tired and hungry, a little scared. It's likely Phyllis just lost her way in the woods—happens around here all the time."

He stood up. "I'll talk to you in the morning. We don't hear anything by eight o'clock, we'll get a search going. Also, I want you to arrange for cash—a lot. I don't mean ten thousand dollars. I'm talking a million dollars, Len. A man of your means, that's what they'd ask for, and we have to have it ready. This will involve the FBI, I'll handle that. You just arrange for the money, let me know the bank or banks."

"Okay."

"Try not to worry, I know that's easy to say."

"Thanks, Oscar."

They walked out to the sliding door where Sgt. O'Shea was waiting, vinyl grip in hand. Oscar asked the stocky officer if he had the grocery bag from the bedroom; he said he did. Then both officers said good night and left the house.

It was late. He lay in bed, unable to sleep. He wanted a drink but he'd already drunk too much. The same question kept running through his mind. Why did he feel so anxious? He had visited Chet at his office, driven home, looked for Phyllis and finally called the police. What had he done? Nothing. Anyway, it was crazy . . . she was going to show up in the morning. Why should he even imagine something bad had happened to her? He stared at the continuous band of glass, near the ceiling. It looked like a ribbon of black crepe. He shut his eyes, rolled over and buried his face in the pillow.

Chapter 5

He sat at his desk in the police department wing of Village Hall, trying to do some paperwork. He hadn't slept well, the odd disappearance of his old friend's wife bouncing around in his mind through the night, while his own wife lay beside him like a filing cabinet. Then just before dawn Sylvia had begun snoring. As on so many previous occasions, Oscar Flick had watched the sun come up from a booth in Winwar's all-night Corner Restaurant.

By the round clock on his office wall it was now 9:35. He sipped coffee from a big white mug, then picked up a folder from the stack lying on his desk. Though other matters were considerably more weighty, calling more for his attention, he couldn't put it off any longer. The Civilian Police Review Board had to have his recommendations by next week.

The tab on the first folder bore the name *Albert G. Baxter.* Oscar opened it, fingered through the forms and documents inside. Smart kid, terrific scores on the state-wide tests, solid high school record. But at 5′ 7″ and 134 pounds—well, the chief liked his men just a little bigger.

He made some notes on a separate sheet of paper, then looked at the next folder. Originally the applicants had numbered thirty-three, everyone and their uncle putting in for the new opening in the department.

Zachary D. Ingersol.

Fourteen years' experience in the state police, willing to take a cut in pay to join the W.P.D. Wants the slower-paced routine of a community police officer. Oscar reached for his coffee, eyes continuing over Ingersol's record. This had to be the front runner. Officers Carlussi and Diehl both knew him, vouched for his character and professionalism. Possible drawback. Under Medical: "Ulcer condition for the past two years."

He checked over three more applications, pausing only to answer his phone—one call from the head of the security force of Winwar State informed him of a break-in and burglary at the college bookstore—then left his office to follow Sgt. O'Shea down a small corridor. At the end two steel doors faced each other— one marked *LAB*, the other *ARMORY*. The two officers entered the lab.

It was minimally equipped, had no windows; a bank of fluorescent lights illuminated the counter where the chief and O'Shea stood. "Three distinct elements, as I make them out," the sergeant said. "First—glass bits, like from broken bottles and jars."

The husky officer held a small steel probe like a dentist's pick. "Then here, oxidized material, your basic tin can. And the ash we talked about—cinders."

Oscar was nodding. "What do you think?"

"I was thinking dump site," O'Shea said. "Or maybe an old house fire."

"Sure—either."

Chief Flick glanced at the lab clock. He had told his officer in charge of the search that he'd meet him on the Bradley property at 10:00, and here it was already seventeen after. "This is real good work, Jim," he said.

"Thanks, Chief."

"See you later. I'm meeting Dave."

Back in his office, Oscar buckled a dark leather holster around his waist, though in actuality the pearl-handled revolver rode on his hip. He took a last sip of his coffee, finally at the temperature he liked, and left headquarters.

Lt. Dave Bock, tall, thin, dark-haired, with a neat black mustache, didn't have a hell of a lot to tell the chief when he arrived on Maple Ridge—so far all his six-man team had kicked up was dust. What he needed to comb the woods and back roads of Winwar was six times that number. Oscar said with unemployment high, beefing up the force with deputies posed no problem, but he wanted to hold off for a full twenty-four hours. As they continued talking an armored Morrissey truck lumbered up the driveway and parked beside the chief's cruiser. Two armed, gray-uniformed guards got out, unlocked the back of the vehicle and carried four bulging sacks up the path to the house.

The chief continued talking with his lieutenant, going over search strategy with him and making a few suggestions. Dave should take two of his men off the roadway and parking area and put them on the path leading to the Bradleys' pond.

"How about the pond itself?"

"Check the banks carefully, the shoreline; then start a dragging operation."

Oscar ambled up to the house, went in and found Leonard in his downstairs office counting out money—$210,000 without getting through the first sack. When he stopped for a breather, Oscar informed him that a specialist from the FBI would be here shortly to wire his Lincoln. Wherever he had to go—except to deliver ransom money—he should drive Phyllis' station wagon. Leonard nodded. He didn't look, to Oscar, like he'd slept any better than he had. They talked vaguely for a few minutes, then Leonard went back to counting. Outside again, Oscar noticed a young woman by the door of his car, peering in.

"See anything interesting in there, Audrey?" he asked, going up to her.

"Oh. Hi, Chief. Nah."

She didn't step aside as he made to open his door.

"You seem to be in my way," Oscar said.

She smiled up at him, at a mere five feet, *way* up, kind of flirting with him like she always did. "Give me a statement."

"No statements."

"Then how about some opinions."

She was wearing a light blue T-shirt, maroon cords and a pair of jogging shoes, still looking like the undergraduate journalism major at Winwar State he'd first known her as three years ago. What particularly irked the chief was that Audrey Ryder had her foot propped against his cruiser door—so she could rest her pad on her thigh. "The day I give you an opinion, Audrey, and let you blow it all to hell—"

"I'll settle for facts then."

"Get your foot off my car."

Her foot dropped, leaving a dusty squiggle on the tan finish.

"I don't trust you with facts either," he said.

"Right! You didn't like my front page story when your department won the Governor's Award!"

He calmed down slightly. "Look, we don't know very much. It's early, we're just starting our investigation."

"How much cash was delivered to Mr. Bradley?"

"Don't know."

"Are you convinced it's a kidnapping?"

"I'm not convinced of anything."

"What are your men looking for?"

"Clues, Audrey. What in hell do you think?"

"Clues to what?"

"To what happened, where Mrs. Bradley might be—to anything pertaining to the crime—"

"Then it *is* a crime, not just a missing person."

The chief felt like choking her. "Audrey, I've a lot of people to interview. Excuse me."

"Besides 'an undisclosed amount of cash and a string of heirloom pearls,' was anything else taken?"

The quote was his, available to the media at headquarters. Considering that most missing people showed up—he hadn't just *told* Leonard that—he'd held back on the .38. It was some-

thing the citizens of Winwar, not to mention certain county officials, didn't need to know right away.

"We're still searching, it's a big house," Oscar said to the reporter. "OK? Can I leave now, go about my duties?"

"Chief, would I keep you from your duties?" Audrey Ryder
said, flirting with him again.

Once, several years ago, Oscar and Adam Pohl had sat
together on a special School Board panel on teenage suicide
prevention, and afterward he had met Ruth Pohl. So had Sylvia.
On the ride home, with the seatbelt around her middle resembling a barrel hoop, Sylvia had said she felt sorry for the good
father whose wife "obviously worshipped at a different altar."
Oscar had replied that he didn't feel sorry for the good father
at all. Now, sitting with Ruth Pohl in the living room of her
house, he was realizing—all over again—why he'd said it.

"What time did Mrs. Bradley come to see you yesterday?" he
asked.

"It was about one, maybe a little after."

"Did she call, or just drop in?"

"She called."

Oscar picked up a cup; it felt tiny. He was used to hooking
his finger *through* the handle, not pinching it like he was holding
a damn butterfly. But apart from the elegant china, and the
attractive woman, everything else in the Pohl living room had a
down-at-the-heels look. The green-and-blue Oriental carpet was
threadbare; the floral wallpaper, loose in places; the fabric of
the loveseat and chair were thin. Oscar had heard that Father
Pohl drank up most of his pay. People liked to talk, but now he
thought maybe there was some truth to what they were saying.

"Was there a specific reason she came by, Mrs. Pohl?" he asked.
"By the way, this is excellent coffee. I'm glad you persuaded me."

"You persuade easily, Chief." She smiled.

He let it go. "How did she seem to you?"

"Serious. She had some things on her mind."

"What kind of things?"

"Personal. I really don't feel at liberty—"

"Are you and Mrs. Bradley good friends?"

Ruth, seated in the chair, crossed her legs. Oscar was on business, important business, but he didn't rightly see how a man, sitting with Mrs. Pohl, could keep his thoughts one-hundred percent focused, important business or no. She was thirty-five or so with shoulder-length blond hair, full lips and beautiful bluish green eyes. "Yes, we're very good friends," she said.

"What was she wearing? Do you recall?"

"She was in a pantsuit, what she always wears whenever she has an appointment." Ruth paused, then added, as if correcting herself, "Goes anywhere."

"After leaving you, *was* she going anywhere?"

She began fingering a button on her silk blouse. Not the top one. The next-to-top one. "I believe she was driving into Bancroft."

"For what purpose?"

"She—she was going to the mall."

The chief sipped his coffee and set the cup in the saucer, which had a wheat stalk design. "Mrs. Pohl," he said after a moment, "if it's of any concern to you, I also respect people's privacy. But we have a woman who's missing and it's my job to find her. I'm a policeman—I'm not here to gossip."

Her fingers, still on the button, became still. "She had an appointment with a lawyer."

"Did she say who?"

"Something *Wilbraham*—I forget."

Just then a small skinny boy came into the living room. He had soft blond hair, alert eyes and an intelligent face, but his shoulders were forward, pinched together like a slouching old man—and his lips and skin had a blue tint. The lips especially. The kid looked weak and ill.

"Danny," Ruth said, "come meet our chief of police."

The boy walked up, said hello in a straightforward friendly manner, then spoke privately to his mother. Ruth excused herself, stood up and went out with her son; in two minutes she was back. Oscar, ready to go, had his Stetson in his hands.

"A nice boy, Mrs. Pohl."

"Thank you."

"Is there any chance he'll ever—?"

"Lead a normal life?"

"I was going to say 'get better,' but yes."

"Only if we agree to surgery."

"Why don't you?"

"The odds he'd survive are fifty-fifty. My husband's afraid to take the chance."

"How about you?"

"I'd have had it done years ago."

Oscar stood up and Ruth walked him to the front door. It had an opaque glass panel and an old-fashioned mechanical ringer beneath the glass. The chief looked into Mrs. Pohl's eyes and thanked her for the coffee—and her help.

"If I can be of any further help, stop by again."

His fingers itched to fix the button on her blouse, half in, half out, of the hole. "I'll do that," he said.

From behind his polished wooden desk, Dudley Wilbraham inquired about what was on the chief's mind.

"Mrs. Leonard Bradley, of Winwar, is missing."

The tubby, smooth-skinned man scowled. "Missing?"

"No one's seen her since yesterday. I understand you had an appointment with her in the afternoon."

"We—we talked for almost an hour. Yes."

"About what?"

"Chief Flick, I'm not free to disclose—"

"How did she seem to you?"

The attorney reached for a pipe, from one of six in a gleaming apple wood rack. He loaded it in his over-deliberate fashion. Oscar had never seen a man talk, move—perhaps think—with such slow precision. A cloud of bluish smoke rose over Wilbraham's head. "She was on edge, highly agitated when she first came in. She left feeling more at ease, in my view."

"Why was she so agitated?"

"Chief Flick, you know I am bound professionally to keep such matters confidential."

Oscar got a whiff of the lawyer's cherry-flavored tobacco; it was enough to make a cowhand retch. "A substantial sum of cash and a string of expensive pearls are missing from the family safe, Mr. Wilbraham."

"Certainly the woman of the house may avail herself—"

"Also an old but a hundred percent functional .38 caliber revolver. From her husband's collection."

The lawyer puffed thoughtfully away.

"I need your help," said Oscar.

"I—there is only so much I can tell you, regardless. It would be a breach—"

"Tell me what you *can*."

The lawyer put down his pipe. He weighed, he considered, he reflected; then he picked up the pipe and put a new match to the bowl. "Mrs. Bradley came to see me," he said at long last, "because she was very upset by a... turn of events."

"Financial? Personal?"

"She is going through a serious crisis at home. What is generally called marital discord."

Oscar gave his chin a rough scrape with his forefinger. "When she left, did she say where she was going, what she might be doing?"

"Let me see. Yes. She said she'd be stopping—for her shoes."

"In the mall, to buy a pair?"

"No, no—I'm sorry. She'd had them repaired. Where, she didn't say."

"Thank you."

"Please keep me informed, chief."

Oscar's cruiser was at the curb in front of a No Parking sign in downtown Bancroft, the county seat, some thirteen miles from Winwar. He opened the door, slid behind the wheel and inserted the key. But he didn't start his engine; he sat staring through the windshield at the sign. *Marital discord*, he thought.

He almost broke a spring turning off Route 21 into Winwar Trailer Park. Oscar swore, slowed, and drove on, exercising more care now that he realized the park entrance resembled the surface of the moon. He didn't know the exact address but he knew the name, though he wouldn't have wanted to spell it. The park was such a crummy place that half the mailboxes didn't have names and half the trailers didn't have mailboxes. He stopped and asked a bony-hipped woman hanging up wash and smoking a cigarette if she knew anyone lived hereabouts named "Woj-cuff-ski."

"No."

The next person, a kid polishing a car with oversized rear tires and a jacked-up back end, was more helpful. He pointed. "See that truck?"

The chief looked over.

"That's their place."

A few moments later Oscar was parking in the big tractor's shadow. He got out and went up to the mobile home, though by how it rested on concrete blocks he didn't reckon it was ever going anywhere again. The blinds were tightly closed. His knock rattled the aluminum door. From inside came a snarl. It might've been a dog, except it spoke.

"Yeah?"

"Winwar police. Chief Flick."

"Whad'd'ya want?"

"I'd like to have a few words with Sadie Woj—"

"What about?"

"About one of the families she does housework for."

"She ain't in."

"When do you expect her back?"

"Dunno."

"Do you expect her back?"

"She lives here!"

"Well, much obliged to you. This your rig?"

"What about it?"

"I just like to know these things," said Oscar.

He went down the rickety steps; as he was opening the door to his cruiser a Chevy sedan, old but in mint condition, pulled up to the adjacent trailer. A strongly built man in his early thirties, with closely cut muskrat brown hair, got out.

"Dwayne!"

The man glanced over. "Hey, Chief!"

"I forgot you lived here."

"If you want to call it that, I live here."

The two men came together, shook hands, Oscar's eyes going to a round bandage, the size of a beer coaster, on the side of Dwayne's head. "What happened?"

"Building me a tree-stand. I'm on the ground, leaning over to pick up a board. Next thing I know, this loose length of two by four comes sailing down and clips me."

"It's dangerous out there, Dwayne."

"I felt like a fucking idiot."

Oscar grinned; there was no better deer hunter in the county. Probably the whole state. "Where they movin'?"

"Plutarch Pond, Brenner Heights—that whole area." He held out his hand, fingers spread. "Tracks—like that."

"I'm getting the fever just listening to you."

"I got some braces to nail up—if I don't kill myself doin' it. But when the season starts the stand's yours, chief. Park at the old mill, go east through the woods—"

"Maybe we can get out together."

"I'd like that."

Despite the ease and friendliness of chatting with Dwayne, Oscar couldn't help feeling a distinct awkwardness because of what had happened the previous spring. It had been a bitter pill for the hometown boy to swallow when the Civilian Police Review Board, because of a fatal auto incident that had occurred twelve years earlier, had turned Dwayne down for a spot in the department—this after he'd given up a career in the army and in spite of the chief's unequivocal support. And Oscar, who remembered the incident but had thought after all that time people would forget, still felt angry about what had happened. He'd rather have Dwayne McManus in uniform than all the candidates on his desk combined. He motioned with his head. "Know that couple?"

"See 'em come and go," Dwayne said.

"He's a real sweetheart. Anyway, I wanted to ask Sadie a few questions. One of the families she works for, the woman of the house is missing."

"What's it look like?"

"I'm gettin' worried, to be real honest."

Though he appeared to be facing the chief directly, Dwayne's eyes shifted to the Wojciechowski trailer. The chief saw it as a professional move. Small, nothing great, but he liked it. "He lookin'?"

"Sure is," said Dwayne.

"When's Sadie get home, as a rule? You know?"

"About four-thirty, five."

"She like her old man?"

"We haven't spoke ten words. Good morning. Like that. But she seems real nice."

Oscar put out his hand. Somehow—he didn't know how—he wanted to make it up to the returned veteran. "How's your little girl?" he asked.

"She's doing OK."

"Glad to hear it. Take care, Dwayne."

Dwayne smiled, nodded. "You too, chief, . . ."

Chapter 6

"Let's go to your study," Chet Evers said.

Leonard led the attorney across the living room, then down the stairs into his at-home office. He had called Chet at noon and it was now 4:05. A six-foot-four Morrissey guard, with a drooping yellow mustache and a small head, was sitting at Leonard's desk. He got leisurely to his feet. Leonard requested that he post himself upstairs until further notice. Like a sailor preparing to go topside, the guard squared his cap.

Chet walked over to the pistol-display chests, looked in, then turned, his eyes going to the safe, then to the fireproof door at the far end of the room. "That opens to the furnace, right?"

"Yes. Also crawlspace beneath the house."

"Is there any access to the crawlspace from outside?"

"There are four or five steel grills in the foundation for air flow. But you'd have to break them in with a sledge hammer—and they're very narrow."

The tall display chest in the corner, holding the rifles and fly rods, caught Chet's attention. Then he came back to Leonard. "Do you know if Phyllis ever opened your gun cases?"

"No. She never did, I'm pretty sure."

"Does she know where you keep the key?"

Leonard sat down wearily in his swivel chair. "She's seen me store pistols, take them out—I'd say she does."

Chet leaned against the edge of the desk, legs extended. "When you went to look for her in her station wagon, did anyone see you leave?"

"One of my farmhands."

"Are you positive he saw you?"

"No, but I assume he did—I saw him."

Just then the telephone rang and Leonard picked it up. It was Catherine calling from California, wanting to know if he had any word yet. Leonard said he didn't, but tomorrow the police were going to deputize thirty men and begin an extensive search. So far they had no clues. Chet Evers was with him at the moment going over some things.

"How are *you*, daddy?"

"Tired, I haven't been sleeping too well. Worried..."

"Are they still saying it's a kidnapping."

"It's one of the theories."

"Before this happened, was mom feeling okay?"

Leonard pushed against an eyebrow with his thumb. "I'd say so. Keeping busy. Her improvement committee is turning the old basement in the library into a community room."

They talked for a while longer. His daughter said she'd come east whenever he wanted. Leonard thanked her and put down the phone.

"That was Catherine."

"How is she?"

Leonard rocked back in his chair; the springs groaned. "Fine."

"What's the matter, Len?"

"Nothing. I mean, I have a wife who's missing—"

"No, something else," Chet said.

Leonard was staring at the landing.

"When you said, 'Keeping busy,' did you mean Phyllis?" Chet asked.

"Yes."

"What was the question?"

"She wanted to know how her mother had been feeling."

"Why didn't you tell her the truth?"

"I don't think, at this point, she has to know."

"I'd suggest your daughter has every right to know."

"Why? This time tomorrow Phyllis might be back."

"What did you tell the chief?"

"I told him..." His voice trailed off.

"You told him she was keeping herself busy with her committees, didn't you?"

"Well, damn it, I didn't want him thinking—" Again he stopped.

"What?"

"Just...thinking."

"That you had a girlfriend in New York and maybe were up to no good?"

"Why should I tell him about Diane, or anyone? It's nobody's goddamn business that Phyllis and I are getting a divorce—"

"You don't think the chief already knows you lied to him?"

"How could he? He didn't see Phyllis."

"But by now he's interviewed others who did see her," Chet said.

Leonard wanted a vodka and tonic with a lot of ice in the worst possible way. "Well, I couldn't tell him," Leonard said.

"'Couldn't?'"

"That's what I said. 'Couldn't!'"

Chet Evers looked at his old friend. "Is there anything you're not telling me, Len?"

"No! What are you thinking?"

"What are *you* thinking?"

"I'm thinking I want a lawyer who believes me and supports me and doesn't question me at every goddamn turn—"

"All I want you to do is tell me the truth," Chet said, "and I'll support you no matter what." He smiled and gave a nod toward the steps. "Show me those steel grates."

"Let's get a drink."

"First, let's look at the grates," said the lawyer.

The Rev. Adam Pohl sat in his church office working on his sermon for Sunday. Crowded in the dark green file cabinet

near his veneered mahogany desk were some 200 sermons, pre-
pared and given by him during his years at St. Philip's; but he
simply couldn't take one out and deliver it again. What he had
written, what he had felt at an earlier time, no longer applied.
He must either revise thoroughly or start fresh. The only con-
stant was the source, in this particular instance the first book of
Corinthians, Chapter 13, Verse 12.

"For now we see through a glass, darkly; but then face to face."

It was a sparsely furnished room with a pair of diamond-paned
casements, a thin-cushioned chair next to the desk and a three-
foot-high crucifix hanging on the plastered wall opposite the
windows. On his desk was a gold-framed photograph of his wife
and son. Adam pondered the line, referred to the sermon he
had given almost three years ago, read from an open Bible and
added three lines to his text for Sunday. Then he took a drag
on the cigarette he was smoking and leaned back in his chair.

His telephone rang. Mrs. Nass, an old widow who had been
coming to see him regularly for the past year, said she wasn't
feeling well and had better stay in. Adam asked if she would like
him to stop by but she said it wasn't necessary, she would see
him next week. He looked at his sermon. Feeling uninspired,
too preoccupied to work on it any longer today, he put his cigarette out after a long final drag. As he passed before the cross,
Adam Pohl blessed himself. He opened the dark brown door to
his office and went outside.

He shuffled along Mulberry Street, overweight and out of
condition—it was easier to scrape than lift one's feet. The two-
block walk to and from his house was all the exercise he ever
took. Mrs. Holland, another widow, was raking up a few leaves
on her lawn—she never let more than a few accumulate—and
when it would first start snowing on a winter day she was immediately out with a broom. Adam gave her a greeting and
noticed the tan-and-brown car at the curb ahead. That the police
were calling again didn't surprise him. Ruth was one of the last
people to have seen Phyllis. Naturally they were going to come
back for more visits. Phyllis' odd disappearance was an upsetting
business, and Adam was still hoping—and praying—that she
was all right. Even now, he asked the Lord for her safe return.

He noticed the police chief's insignia on the cruiser's door, then walked up the path. The sight of his house, so run-down, so in need of paint and repair, depressed Adam—as did the recollection of the letter, received last spring, that the Bishop was unable to honor the Winwar rector's request for funds necessary to maintain his residence. Bishop Beaman was afraid, Adam had heard through a reliable source, that Father Pohl might "drink up the allocation." Word of the refusal had got around; to many it meant that the priest's days at St. Philip's were numbered.

Adam crossed the porch, which had a small slope, and went in. Chief Flick and Ruth were sitting in the living room. A coffee service rested on the small table, and Adam might have thought his wife looked particularly alluring. He didn't dwell on it. He gave her a small kiss, shook hands and spoke briefly with the chief about Mrs. Bradley's disappearance and went upstairs.

In his bedroom he changed from collar and suit to open shirt and casual trousers, his heartbeat from climbing the steps slowly subsiding. Standing at the window, he looked out at the enclosed yard behind the house. Their son—from birth he had suffered from an especially complex case of Tetralogy of Fallot—was slouching at the table, working on his book, *Braxon, King of the Wondrous Beasts*, about a "good monster" in a world of fiends, werewolves, ghouls, demons and other unsavory creatures of the netherworld. Adam thought the book creative and positive. Braxon got himself into some tight fixes but always won his battles at the end. Ruth didn't see it so brightly, however, thinking the book a reflection of Danny's deep inner turmoil.

Adam heard her laughter drift up the stairs. From a pack lying on his dresser he removed a cigarette and lighted it. He inhaled, looked at his bloated face in the smoke-clouded mirror. *Through a glass, darkly.*

Once he had believed that the Lord would hear and grant his request. How sure he had felt after the birth of their child that Jesus would give him a sign about Danny. If not of sound limb, he was superbly intelligent and amazingly accepting of his condition. Did one take the gamble? Risk the life of so lovely and sensitive a child? Adam had known the Lord would tell him what to do. Ruth had screamed that expecting guidance from above was naive: not proof of one's faith but evidence of one's lack of it! Their son had an even chance of surviving open-heart surgery, but Danny was not the only crippled child here on earth—and the good Lord wasn't going to single out the boy's father and tell him what to do.

And now he believed she was right. And the pain of that knowledge, and of his own weakness, daily tore at him. He heard quiet conversation between Chief Flick and Ruth at the front door; when it ended he went downstairs and into the kitchen. His wife came in, carrying the coffee service, but they didn't speak. Father Pohl reached into the corner cupboard, took down a bottle of vodka, packed ice into a glass, and poured.

Tony Bradley turned off the county highway onto a one-lane dirt road that rose, winding, through the hills west of Winwar. A stream, virtually dry, followed the rising road. His truck, piled with logs, rumbled over a series of crude bridges. Approaching a steeply pitched hairpin turn, he blew the horn on his four-wheel-drive vehicle—a hand-painted sign at the curve gave drivers that instruction—then down-shifted. The brown-and-white springer spaniel beside him on the seat braced his front legs to keep from sliding. Tony, as he always did, grabbed the dog's collar.

After the hairpin turn the road ran straight for three hundred yards; then, on his left, he came to a small red house trimmed in white. It had a single chimney and sat very close to the road. Tony backed his truck into a shale driveway, parked beside a yellow VW with a dented fender and got out.

The drive sloped down, terminating at a large pile of logs, unstacked and unsplit. Just beyond this pile, a hundred and fifty cords of split, seasoned, neatly stacked firewood formed an L-shaped, six-foot-high barricade. Slightly beyond, on the open side, lay an apple orchard untended for decades. The house sat alone, surrounded by a mountain wilderness. Tony waited for his dog to jump clear, then swung the door shut. Buck, nose lowered, ran off toward the overgrown orchard, home to many a partridge and rabbit. Tony followed squares of stone across a narrow strip of brown grass to the house.

His wife was reading a story to their young daughter, who immediately got up from the sofa and asked him if he had seen any of his "woodland friends." He said he'd seen Gracie Gray Squirrel—she was so busy storing up nuts for the winter she'd hardly had time to say hello, but he'd had a good long talk with Billy Woodchuck.

"About what?"

"Forest news. Jenny Red Fox got married!" He forced a happy face, then looked at his wife. "Hi, Deb. Any word?"

"Chief Flick came by again. Nothing."

At one end of the single room was the kitchen; two small bedrooms opened off it. Tony grabbed a bar of soap at the old enamel sink and turned the tap. A few drops of tepid water came out, then nothing. Same with the cold. He swore under his breath and went to the refrigerator.

"Beer, Deb?"

"No, thanks."

He grabbed one for himself. A beef stew was simmering on the range; its aroma made his stomach churn. Returning to the main part of the house, he said: "I'll check the spring in the morning but I think we're dry."

"I know we are."

"We'll have to start bringing home water."

She made a face. She was wearing a blue shirt and a pair of dark gray slacks. Her hair, black, made a striking contrast with her fair skin and fell straight down her back. She had a lithe body and a beautiful, oval-shaped face; her eyes were a smoky brown. "That means no baths," she said. "Good times in Mink Hollow."

"We should be getting some rain soon."

"You said that last year."

He sat down beside her and took a long swallow, suddenly seeing how drawn and tired she looked. "What did the chief have to say?"

"I don't want to change the subject," she said.

"Honey, what can I do? I can't bring rain."

"You can get us a place in the village."

Tony blew out a breath. "My mother's missing, Debby—I'd like to know what the chief had to say."

She sighed; one day she might stop deferring to him. "He came by around two o'clock. No clues, no leads on where Phyllis is—nothing."

"Is that why he stopped by, to tell you that?"

"I thought so, for a while. Then he began talking about Leonard."

Tony took a second tug on his beer. "In what connection?"

"He seemed . . . concerned."

"His oldest friend's wife is missing, of course he's concerned."

"I mean with Leonard. He wanted to know if he was seeing anyone that I knew of."

"Why did he ask that?"

"He said he had a sales receipt with your father's signature on it, recently dated. From Cartier in New York. To the tune of $8,300."

"Maybe it was something for Phyllis."

"That's what I said. But where is it?"

Tony picked up his beer can. "How in hell did he get hold of the receipt?"

"He wouldn't say."

"So he's assuming my father has a girlfriend."

"That's what it points to. Phyllis saw a lawyer," Debby said.

"My mother saw a lawyer?"

"On the same day she disappeared."

"Why?"

"Marital discord, Oscar said. He spoke to the lawyer."

Tony was quiet again, his eyes focusing on the braided rug under his feet. Debby had made it when they had lived in the farmhouse on Plains Road. The scarlet center was a hunting shirt from his high school days; the two navy blue circles a coat she'd worn in college; the charcoal gray ring one of his first business suits when he had worked for his father.

"What do you think, Tony?"

"I don't know what to think."

"Leonard told Oscar Thursday night that he and Phyllis were getting along fine."

"What in hell was he supposed to say?"

There was a scratching at the door and Tony got up and opened it. Buck trotted in and went immediately to the kitchen area to examine his bowl. Amy was in the corner of the room, coloring in a book. "I agree," Debby said when Tony sat back down, "but now Oscar has to be *thinking*, wouldn't you say?"

"If he wants to think, let him think."

Buck came into the living room and dropped down at Tony's feet. "I'm really not arguing with you about this," Debby said. "But the chief's worried, and he's also at least a little suspicious—"

"If he wasn't suspicious he wouldn't be a cop."

"How about the missing gun?"

"Debby, *you're* thinking too much."

"But it's odd, isn't it?"

"Maybe the *police* think it's odd."

"Aren't they the ones who matter?"

The beer can buckled in his hand. "What *matters* here is the whereabouts of my mother. My father doesn't know the answer to those questions any more than you, me or Chief Oscar Flick."

She looked at her husband.

"What's that look supposed to mean?"

"I haven't heard you support your father in years."

"I'm trying to be fair."

"You're being very understanding, it seems to me."

"You think he's involved somehow with Phyllis' disappearance?"

"I didn't *say* that. I don't think it at all. But Chief Flick made me nervous. Why would an old friend who had nothing to hide lie to him? That's what he's asking himself."

"Why? Because people are entitled to privacy. My father has always held his cards close to his chest."

"Tony, I'm just trying to understand this myself."

"I know, it's frustrating—who the hell knows what's going on?" He stood up. "If you want to sit down with Amy, go ahead."

"I've waited all day to sit down with *you*."

"Well, I'm sorry about that," her husband said, and went out.

From the sofa, she heard the crashing of the logs. She winced, feeling a small sharp pain in her abdomen as each log landed on the unstacked pile behind the house. She stood up, wanting to keep busy; in the kitchen she stirred the stew and called to her daughter. *Thud.* The little girl came in. Help set the table, Amy. *Crash.*

The child was a chatterer, and Debby listened, joined in—but she wasn't there. She said yes and no; she was elsewhere—in the Plains Road house where she and Tony had lived when they were first married. Where they had had Amy, where she had felt happy, where they had shared dreams.

Thud. Dreams they had begun having—she often thought— the first day they met. She had driven up from Merion to watch her fiancé play in the final round of the Eastern Inter-Collegiates on the Yale course. She liked golf and played it occasionally. Her father played, and Bart, her fiancé, was the number-one man on the Penn team and sometimes would talk about turning pro; but no one in the foursome—no one she had ever seen play the game—swung a golf club like the player from Cornell. He was great looking too, not as tall as Bart but physically more attractive, stronger. It was a very close match. The Wake Forest player kept making miraculous recovery shots and was leading Bart by one stroke and the Cornell player by one stroke halfway through the back nine. Until Tony—by now she had learned his name— sank a long putt for an eagle. At which point Debby made the mistake of clapping.

Her fiancé looked over as if to kill her, and Tony looked over and gave her a big smile. Bart then began losing it, making bogeys on the last four holes, and the Wake Forest player, who had scrambled to draw even with Tony, had the misfortune of having his ball take a high terrible bounce on an approach shot to the seventeenth green. When they all drew closer, there, taking its good time crossing in front of the green, was a turtle. Source of the bad bounce. Tony Bradley won the tournament by a stroke. Debby thought she was in love with him as he walked off the course—

Thud.

Bart got drunk at the banquet and passed out in his car, and she and Tony began talking, then went outside and sat down on the bench on the first tee. He was a senior. When he graduated in three weeks he was going to take a month off and play in a few amateur tournaments before going to work for his father for the rest of the summer. In the fall he'd be starting Harvard Business School. He lived in a small town in upstate New York called Winwar; his father was CEO of a company that made power ground-care equipment; *his* father had started the company in the mid-20s with the first hydraulic lawn mower ever manufactured, which had revolutionized golf-course maintenance. When he finished grad school his plan was to work for Bradley, learn the business inside and out and when his father retired, take over.

Thud.

They walked down the fairway. She asked him more about Winwar. It was a pretty town with plenty of fishing and hunting if you liked fishing and hunting, and a state college. But he didn't imagine it was a very exciting place. Then they stopped walking and, in the dusk, looked at the flagstick on the first green seventy yards away. It looked like a skinny old woman wearing a drooping bonnet, she thought. She also thought he was going to kiss her. Maybe before the summer was over she would visit him in Winwar and see for herself, he said, and she said she would love to—

Crash.

He wanted to build his own course, he said, on a piece of property he'd had his eye on for years. Just three holes. A par 3, a par 4 and a par 5. It was beautiful land, twenty-seven acres in all, and had a great old farmhouse on it—and even as he talked about it that evening on the Yale course, she knew one day she'd live in that house with Tony Bradley.

Crash.

Debby walked to the back window so her daughter wouldn't

see her crying—thinking of that course now, visible from the kitchen of the farmhouse; seeing Tony on weekends working on it, moving ground, building tees and greens. The amount of work he was capable of was extraordinary; since he'd started at Bradley, annual sales topped $100 million for the first time— and it wasn't by coincidence. His father was the first to say Tony was infusing new life, new energy into the business. They had their first child, and Debby would often wake up in the morning thinking she had to be one of the happiest women in the world. And about then Tony began to change. He stopped work on the course, on the house, he stopped playing golf—he almost stopped talking. And one day he came home from the office and said he could no longer work for Bradley.

Thud.

"Tony, what are you talking about?"

"It's not what I want," he said. "I'm tired of working for my father—I can't do it any longer."

"Tony! He respects you, he knows how important you are to the company's future. You *are* Bradley's future."

They were sitting on the back terrace. All three flags of the course, spaced at the points of a right triangle, were fluttering. He was wearing a handsome gray suit. She had no idea that she would never see him in a suit again. He didn't speak.

"Talk to me, Tony."

"My father's still under his father's shadow, still looking up to him—his loyalty to his father is so strong it's costing the company! The Bradley culture, I've had it with the Bradley culture! I'm not happy working for Leonard Bradley. I'm not myself at Bradley. I want to be myself—"

Crash.

She didn't argue with him. What he said, she understood. He had the background, the credentials, the experience. He wouldn't have trouble landing a new job, maybe even a better job. Who wouldn't want an executive like Tony Bradley? She was nervous but she wasn't afraid.

"What would you like to do?"

"Something on my own...More and more people, with the rising price of oil, are wanting cord wood," he said.

Thud.

She was at the little side window now, looking out at the man whose graceful fairway wood had traveled 225 yards to the green almost ten years ago. To set up the eagle putt. Even now, in her mind, Debby heard herself clapping and saw him glance over; his smile so quick and genuine was still in her heart. He was lifting a knotty pine log over his head, about to throw it. In the twilight she saw his teeth, clenched. She did not like to think of these past four years as a waste. There was nothing wrong with cutting and splitting firewood. And why was a big house with central heating better than a small one with an iron stove? Was a golf course on your property better than a wilderness outside your door?

But for how long could she do it? Did she want to have their new baby in Mink Hollow, with its icy roads and five-foot drifts and late summer droughts? How many logs? Oh Jesus, Tony, she thought. How many logs will you have to throw?

Crash. Thud. Crash.

The chief was trying to catch up on his paperwork. He had managed, just under the wire, to get off his recommendations for the job opening in the department, running with Zach Ingersol, and now he was going over his officers' semi-annual fitness reports; and seeing where Dave Bock, usually so thorough in preparing them, hadn't given the job enough attention.

Oscar wasn't upset. Dave's comments were superficial, no doubt. But at this point he'd rather have his second-in-charge concentrate his energies on locating Mrs. Bradley—

His phone rang. He glanced at the big clock on his wall. 6:25. Sylvia usually gave him until seven. "Chief Flick," he said, picking up.

"Bill Woolever here. How's everything, Chief?"

"Moving along, Mr. Woolever," he told the D.A., positioning a sheet of paper and picking up a pencil.

"What can you tell me?"

There was no way he'd take the district attorney's bait. "About what?"

"What I've been reading about, hearing about. There's a high-visibility person missing in your township."

"Oh. Right."

"Any *developments?*"

"She's still missing, we've put out an all-state—"

"What do you think?"

"Too soon to say anything."

"It's too early to arrest anyone, isn't that what you mean?"

"If and when we find Mrs. Bradley, I'll be able to answer your question."

"You'd also like to find a missing revolver, am I correct?"

"We're looking for one."

"I hope to hell you are, because the man who *owns* it is the husband of your missing woman—and he happens to have a girlfriend in New York!"

The chief's pencil came to a slow stop. "What's your source for that, Mr. Woolever?"

"It's reliable."

"I'm sure."

"Chief, why are you fighting me on this? I would think you'd be looking for a suspect—"

"I'm looking for a woman. *You're* looking for a suspect."

"And with cause good reason. You have a rifled safe and a stolen gun—"

"You're not calling me about a burglary," said Oscar.

"Only as it's part of a larger picture."

"You don't know that it is."

"I know you're not sounding like a police chief."

"Let me tell you something—"

"No, let me tell *you* something," said the District Attorney of Cooper County. "You're too close to this. You can't see your badge for your friendship with Leonard Bradley—"

"My friendship with Len Bradley has nothing to do with it."

"It better goddamn not," said William Woolever, and hung up.

Oscar slammed down the receiver. For a long time he sat at his desk, staring straight out, his lips tight and a grayness in his face. Then he looked down, his eyes going to his notes, scribblings really—a series of X's and O's. Whether there were eleven of each he didn't know, but the different characters were roughly facing each other across an imaginary line.

Oscar studied the diagram, reminded by it of their best gainer, their bread-and-butter play. "52 slant-right." Bradley carrying, Flick leading the interference. The papers had called them the Tom Harmon–Forrest Evashevski of high-school football. . . .

Could it be I'm still doing it? Oscar thought. Still knockin' 'em down for Len? He curled up the sheet of paper—

His phone rang. It was 7:13. Chief Flick stood, grabbed his Stetson and uniform jacket and went out to his car.

He didn't go home. Instead he drove up to Maple Ridge and parked in front of the big cedar-and-glass house next to a gray sedan with the bold imprint, *Morrissey Armored Car,* on the door. Oscar followed the broad path to the house. It was a chilly evening, and as he stood at the glass door, before knocking, he saw Leonard at the hearth putting a log on the fire. Oscar tapped and Leonard turned quickly, by his expression, anxiously waiting for news.

"Hello, Oscar," Leonard said, coming up and sliding the door open.

"I thought I'd see how you were doing."

"Well, everything considered . . ."

"Got a minute?"

"Sure. I know you won't take a drink, so I won't ask. Coffee?"

"Nothing. Thanks." The chief closed the door.

"Let me just freshen up what I've got here," Leonard said as Oscar walked in. The chief didn't sit. He waited for Leonard in front of the fire. "Gettin' a little nippy out," Leonard said from his bar.

"That time."

He walked in with a brimming vodka and tonic; to Oscar's eye he appeared unsteady, and the chief thought he was hitting the sauce pretty hard. "Sit down, Oscar."

"I'll stand for a while."

"What's happening?" Leonard asked, settling into the leather sofa.

"Len, I'll lay it right out. What I've picked up in the past couple of days doesn't fit with what *you* told me, and I'm not feeling good about it."

Leonard didn't reply immediately; then he said, "I'm not feeling good about it either."

"Why did you do it?"

"I'm really sorry."

"I didn't ask if you were sorry."

"But I am. I want you to know—"

"Fine—tell it to Bill Woolever."

"Why him?"

"Because he just called me."

"Woolever just called you?"

"He sure did."

"What did he say?"

"Wait a minute, Len. I'm no expert on parliamentary procedure, but I think we've got a question on the floor."

Leonard sat back, his head against the smooth brown leather. His chest expanded. "I lied to you, Oscar. It was wrong, it was a mistake. But maybe you can understand."

"I'm not making any promises."

Leonard rolled forward, grabbed his glass and drank. "What I did—I've been thinking about it. In one sense I just didn't want to tell you. I was seeing another woman, Phyllis and I were on the rocks—it was *personal* stuff. But then, you were here in an official capacity—you had a right to know. Oscar, what I did reminded me of something we both knew as kids—how a gray squirrel will always spook, even when it's way the hell up in a tree, safe. It's like they know better but they still make a break for it. I don't know, Oscar. I began thinking of who I was seeing in New York, I began thinking of all the stuff that looked bad—like the detective's report, my missing .38. And the thing was—Oscar, *listen* to me—if Phyllis was to come back in a couple of hours or the next day even, as I had

every reason to think and like you yourself were saying, well,
I would've been spared talking about all that. I took a chance—
I made a break for the next pine, and now they're all taking
shots at me."

The chief spoke after a long beat. "Why should I believe you
this time?"

"If you don't believe me, that means you think I'm involved—
with this whole business?"

"Maybe."

"Is that what you think?"

The chief didn't answer.

"Oscar, is it? Tell me, damn it."

Oscar looked at his old sidekick. Elusive Len. Oscar Flick was
an excellent blocker, they said, but in an open field when you
went to grab Len Bradley, most all you ever got was air. "I don't
want to be suspicious of you—"

"But are you?"

"You lied to me, Len! I'm not happy with the way things are
adding up."

"I can't *believe* I'm hearing this."

"You'd better. We're not kids hunting gray squirrels, Len."

A log settled; sparks shot against the screen. "Oscar, listen to
me—"

"No, just tell me if you know where Phyllis is—"

"I *don't* know."

"Did you kill her?"

Leonard's head rolled forward. He pressed against his eyebrows. "You've known me forty years. What are you making me
do this for?"

"Don't give me that forty-years bullshit. I'm the same guy, Len.
I'm doing my job like you do yours. *OK?* So answer me. Did you
kill her?"

"*No.* No, chief, I didn't kill her."

"Are you behind her disappearance in any way? Like arranging
for it, contracting for it—?"

"No. Jesus fucking Christ. *No!*"

Both men were silent. Leonard's head was clasped in his hands.
On his ring finger a gold band flickered. The chief kept looking

at it. "Will you do something for me, Len?" he said at last, his tone softer.

"Anything. You know that."

Oscar Flick walked to the leather chair close to the sofa. He unsnapped his badge and put it on the brass coffee table and sat down. "Pour me a double bourbon on the rocks," he said.

Chapter 7

Chuck Wojciechowski pulled his Freightliner into the space next to his mobile home in Winwar Trailer Park. His car was setting where he'd left it four days ago, but Sadie's yellow Pontiac wasn't. To hell with this shit. A man come back from a haul, he wanted his woman inside, waitin' for him.

He killed the ignition on his grumbling diesel and eased himself to the ground, stiff and aching from the last five hours of non-stop driving. He had a quid in his mouth and spit out the whole works; then he stretched, cut one, and hobbled up to the trailer door. He hadn't shaved or showered in three days, and had a case of ball stink that would drive off a skunk.

The door was locked, something she never done if she was just going to the store—she was out somewheres and she wasn't doing no cleaning at ten minutes after six! Chuck yanked out his keys. In the kitchen he made himself a rum and Coke, guzzled half of it, brung up gas loud, ripped another one, then walked into the living room. Standing at the plate window, he looked through the blinds at his neighbor's trailer. McManus. Dwayne McManus. Come home with a lot of medals last spring, cop's job in his pocket, then they turn around and give it to some quim.

Chuck had laughed real good over it. Big-deal ex-army asshole losing out to a quim! He'd laughed real good over it.

In the bedroom he checked Sadie's weekly work schedule laying next to the telephone. Today, between 1 and 4, she was at the Abernathy house. "Vac & dust, laund, do bathrms, chg sheets kids rms." Bitch, running around—he din't like it. Yesterday when he called he'd said he'd probably roll in around ten, then the fuck-up in Charleston with the Ettinger Co. The dock workers had went out just three hours before he arrived, so he was out $850. Like he could run his rig on love! But at least, dead-heading it, he'd get home early. Chuck finished his drink. And where was the bitch?

He opened the night-stand drawer, thinking to look at some gash in his new *Penthouse*, maybe even take a few strokes over it, like for a warm-up. He pushed aside the phone book, finding the August issue, the September. Here it was. October. He'd meant to bring it on his trip, Snatch-of-the-Month was one of the best he'd ever saw. They had her in one pose where she was on her knees with long white stockings on—he was flipping the pages—her jugs hangin' low and fingers curled back between her legs.

Yeah, here she was, still at it. Bitch still friggin' herself off.

He had a mind to take out his johnson when a car drove up and stopped, he dropped the magazine. Through the blinds he saw her touch her hair, straighten the collar of her shirt. She was fixin' herself up, nervous. Chuck went into the kitchen and threw together a new drink—just waitin' by the door. Then she come in.

"You're back early," she said.

"Where you been?"

"What're you talking about?"

"You knock off at four today."

"So, you ain't supposta be home till ten!"

"That don't mean you can prance all around the town!"

"I don't hafta come right home, either!"

She went to walk by him, he grabbed her arm. "Where'd you go?"

"I went to the mall."

"Watcha buy?"

"I just looked."

"Bullshit!"

Suddenly his nose started twitching, working like a dog's. "What's that?"

"What?"

"That smell!"

"That's the sulfur."

"I know the sulfur!"

He continued sniffing. "You been seeing someone!"

"You're crazy, Chuck."

"I know jizz when I smell it." He pushed her shoulder. "You been out fuckin' someone!"

"I ain't been fucking nobody. That's Clorox. What'd'ya think I work with, 'Charlie'?"

He stopped. He went back to the counter and picked up his drink, slurping it. "Let me see 'em," he said.

"I have to go to the bathroom—"

"Let me *see* 'em!"

She unbuttoned her shirt and unsnapped her bra; it was a front snap and her breasts fell out. "Yeah, them's good, them's real good tits, Sadie."

Dwayne McManus got up from his chair in the bedroom of his mobile home, where he'd been reading *Police Gazette,* and went to his bureau. A bottle of whiskey sat on top of it next to a hair brush, his wallet and two shot glasses. One glass was empty, the other held toothpicks. The room was cramped but orderly. It contained a narrow bed, an easy chair and a low, crowded bookshelf beneath a small window. Dwayne poured himself a shot and recapped the bottle.

To one side of the mirror his Army Honorable Discharge was fastened to the wall; next to it was a color photograph of him in full-dress uniform, staff sergeant in the military police, Hawaiian palms and all. On the other side of the bureau a dozen sharpshooter awards, fourteen service ribbons and five army medals, including two Bronze Stars and a Purple Heart, decorated a varnished square of pine.

Dwayne swallowed off the whiskey, slid a couple of toothpicks in the ticket slot in his wallet and slipped it into his back pocket. In the kitchenette he fixed himself a baloney and cheese with plenty of mustard, poured a glass of milk and carried the sandwich and milk to the small formica table. He ate facing the living room. On the wall over the sofa was his buck; officials still called it the all-time finest white-tail ever killed in the state. His picture was in all the papers, High-School Junior Wins State's "Big Buck" Contest. He had wounded it with a passing shot through brush at eighty yards. Then for seven hours, never stopping once, he'd tracked the deer. At first the blood spoor was thin, but then it started getting heavier, and then, way back in the deepest part of the Shaggs, just as dusk was coming on, he saw what looked like, on the edge of Kelly Lake, a turned-over rowboat tied to a big spiky shrub, and he went up, half-dead himself but overcome with a sense of pride and conquest, and when he was just twelve feet away, the buck raised up fast, his massive rack low and blood in his eyes, and charged, used whatever strength he had left to make a final lunge at this man who had inflicted such huge pain on him and had tracked him all day, but the man fell to one side and pulled the trigger on his ought–6, sending a 180-grain soft-point slug crashing through the great animal's chest.

Dwayne finished his sandwich and carried the plate and glass to the sink, running water over them; the water smelled when it came out—he would never get used to it. Goddamn sulfur. He rinsed his hands and face, used a dish towel, folded it neatly back through the oven handle, and went out to his car.

He drove south for a mile, running a check on his CB, then curved into the mountains on Rte. 33–44. Just past a road sign warning motorists of crossing deer he branched off and traveled on a narrow dirt road for another mile, parking at the old lumber mill on the edge of Plutarch Pond. He opened his trunk, took out a length of two-by-four and some tools and pushed into the woods. After last night's shower the mosquitoes came at him extra heavy but they didn't bother him; didn't like his blood. Never had. It was the only way he'd ever been able to explain it.

He circled a swampy area filled with a thousand dead trees, like a crowd of skeletons all standing around bored at a party, then passed where he'd knocked off the rotten rung two weeks ago to the stand he'd built before going in the army when he was a kid. Soon he was at the new stand. It was in a big ash that commanded an excellent view of the area. To his left, a hundred and fifty feet away, turkey buzzards were circling about, while others perched, along with crows, in the branches of the trees.

Dwayne's eyes came back to the big ash. First he cut the two-by-four into four sections; then he climbed the eight rungs to the platform and nailed the cut sections between the platform and trunk as buttresses. He dropped the tools to the ground, clambered onto the perch and sat for a while, testing it, getting used to the height. The buzzards kept circling. A putrid odor hung in the air. It reminded him of 'Nam. The cut on his head began itching and he pushed at it through the bandage. He spit out the toothpick he was chewing on and twisted about on the platform; directly beneath where the buzzards were circling, something that resembled a human body lay on the ground, but with the buzzards and crows perched on it, tearing at it, one couldn't say for sure. It might have been the carcass of an animal.

They stood at the base of the big ash, by the tools and bits of cut lumber, looking up. "Not right now," the chief said to Sgt. O'Shea, "but I want pictures. Exactly what Dwayne saw from the stand, how it looked to him."

He fanned at the insects buzzing about his head. "OK, let's go take a look."

The three continued through the woods. Dwayne, leading, held a branch for the two officers. Then they were at the scene, standing just outside the crumbled foundation to an 8' × 10' burned-down hut, staring at a human corpse dressed—once dressed—in a full skirt and long-sleeved shirt. The body lay face down, left hand thrown out, the right one tucked underneath. A couple of buzzards and crows, perched in nearby trees, fluttered away. "I always wanted to be a car mechanic," O'Shea said.

"Well, don't turn your badge in yet," said the chief.

"Oh, boy—oh, Jesus," the police sergeant moaned, covering his nose and mouth, feeling sick. He turned away, taking deep breaths.

The chief noticed the shoes; the soles and heels looked new, and on the heels were protective nylon caps. He moved around to get a different view, closely observing the left hand, then the position of the legs and torso; he was making an awful face. "What do you think?" he asked Dwayne.

"I'm thinkin' a lot of things. Poor damn woman, is what I'm thinkin'."

"Think she was raped?"

"Possibility. Her underwear's off."

"Then the way she's laying," said the chief.

"Plus you got to consider—you got to consider—all that larva around her parts," Dwayne said.

O'Shea, back, spoke through a folded handkerchief. "He's right, chief. Flies love a fresh-fucked vagina."

"Now I'm gettin' sick," said Oscar.

His radio crackled on his belt: "Signal 2 to Signal 1."

"Good, it's Dave." The chief spit, without much spit coming out, and grabbed the radio. "Ten-four, Signal 2. Over."

"Just arrived—I'm out on Plutarch Pond Road."

"How is it out there?"

"They keep coming—Audrey Ryder's bitching because we won't let her in. Over."

"She sets one foot across that line, I want her arrested!"

"Loud and clear, Signal 1."

"I'm coming back out," said the chief.

O'Shea was securing the area with a spool of lightweight orange rope. Oscar returned his radio to its case. "When you're finished with that, Jim, take plenty of pictures. After that, start looking around."

The chief forced a last look at the body, then gave his head a solemn shake. "Come on," he said to Dwayne.

From the moment Chief Flick emerged from the woods, questions began flying. He told the dozen reporters from the local papers, radio and TV stations that a body, apparently female, in an advanced state of decay and animal molestation, had been found in the woods. Did the chief think it was Mrs. Bradley? He couldn't be sure at this point, but he thought it probably was. What evidence was there to make him think so? Her shoes appeared to match the pair she was reportedly wearing last Thursday.

"Are there any signs of violence or struggle at the scene?"

"Hard to say."

"What position is she in?"

"Face down."

"Who found her?"

"A Winwar resident. He was building a tree stand and spotted the body."

"What's his name?"

"Dwayne McManus."

"Any leads as to who killed her?"

"We're working on it."

"Do you—?"

Oscar held up his hand, cutting off the next question. "That's it for now." He started walking toward his waiting officers.

But one of the reporters tailed him, actually taking a tug at his sleeve. "Chief, how about a picture of you and McManus?"

"Forget it, Audrey."

"What gives? Come on."

He stopped, glaring down at the young woman. "You fed Woolever a lot of crap, is what gives! You've got him thinking biggest murder trial of his career, and we don't even have a suspect—"

"If Mrs. Pohl gave *me* crap, she gave *you* crap."

"I'm in charge of the investigation," Oscar said, angry and

showing it. "I don't need any reporter making a sweetheart deal with a local politician—"

"So Woolever's pushing you—b.f.d. If there's nothing there, there's nothing there. You shouldn't drive around with 'Chief' on your car when you're doing interviews."

"Audrey, do me a favor. Buy a one-way ticket to Spokane."

She smiled her most disarming smile. "How about it?"

"How about *what?*"

"That picture of you and McManus."

"No way. Now beat it."

But she wouldn't let him go. "Wasn't he your choice to fill a spot in the department last spring?"

"So?"

"Give him a little recognition. Local boy, returned Vietnam hero. That was a raw deal he got and you know it."

Oscar looked over at the W.P.D. search-and-recovery unit standing at the edge of the woods—with Dwayne, who'd be leading them in. What the hell. "OK, one shot," he told the reporter.

He was drafting a statement—no love letter—to the regional director of OSHA, saying exactly what he thought of the agency's recent decision—

"Excuse me, Mr. Bradley."

Leonard looked up. "Yes, Eleanor?"

"Chief Flick of the Winwar Police Department is here to see you."

"Send him in."

Oscar appeared with another officer, a blond woman about thirty. She stayed in the doorway, and Oscar walked toward Leonard. His western boots, always polished, were caked with mud. Leonard stood up, sensing something was wrong. The chief kept coming toward him, not stopping. His hands rose, going behind Leonard's shoulders—

"I'm sorry, Len," Oscar said softly. "We found Phyllis—in the woods near Plutarch Pond . . ."

"Found her?"

"Her body. She was killed probably the same day she didn't come home."

Leonard was silent, thinking terrible thoughts, thoughts that would send a man to hell. Then his shoulders heaved and he turned away, walked to the window, staring out for several moments, the awful thoughts still there—but diminishing. "What happened?" he asked finally.

"She was shot in the back of the head and—and from appearances . . . raped."

"Oh, God!" Leonard brought his hands to his face.

"I'm very, very sorry, Len."

"Raped?"

"It looks that way. It's up to the medical examiner to actually say it."

He was beginning to feel nauseous, weak. He sat down, his arms heavy on his desk. "Why would anyone—?"

"We're trying to establish that."

Leonard groaned, pushed against his forehead.

"While I'm thinking of it, Len, did Phyllis wear a wedding band?"

"She's never had it off."

"She wasn't wearing one when we found her."

"I—I don't know what to say . . ."

"We found a handgun in the bushes, approximately fifteen feet from the body," the chief said.

"That's a hell of a lead, isn't it?"

"I suppose," Oscar said flatly.

"What would a gun be doing near her body unless it was used to—?"

"It's your missing .38, Len."

Leonard felt a sudden pressure on his skull, as if he were under thirty feet of water. "Are you sure?"

"It's a classic Smith & Wesson, bearing the serial number 799."

"Then the person who stole it killed Phyllis . . ."

"Bill Woolever's thinking the same thing."

"Meaning . . . ?"

"He's saying that person is you."

"What? Come on, Oscar. I told you I didn't do it, you know

damn well I didn't. My God . . . Besides, it doesn't make any *sense*. Would someone who killed his wife leave his own easily identifiable weapon at the scene? Is that what you'd do?"

"No."

"So, tell Woolever! You're the chief of police, for God's sake."

Oscar Flick inhaled deeply, then blew out a loud breath. The plains, gullies, draws of Wyoming were etched in his face. "Yeah, Len, but *he's* the district attorney."

Chapter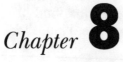

"I'll say it one more time," Lt. Dave Bock was saying. "There's evidence in these woods. The killer didn't vanish into thin air."

The tall officer pulled at the collar of his foul-weather jacket; a cold 7 a.m. drizzle was falling. Some thirty-four men, divided into groups of four and five, stood around the crumbled stone foundation; inside, spray-painted on the cindery ground, was a rough outline of the body. "Deputies are under the command of the Winwar police officer assigned," Bock went on. "Any questions?"

There were none. The search units began fanning out in different directions, patrolman Burt Diehl's unit to the northeast. In it were three deputies: an out-of-work car salesman named Fred Lutz; a bartender at Stubby's Bar & Grill, Rupert Kocsis; and Dwayne McManus. The four men began a slow, careful search of the ground, bark of trees, underbrush as they moved away from the murder site. Almost immediately Lutz began to complain. First it was the rain, then the goddamn mosquitoes; then he had to take a crap.

"Well, go ahead," said Patrolman Diehl, whose cheeks were so hollow they looked gouged out.

"Just do the rest of us a favor and bury it," Dwayne said.

Lutz, no small man, shot McManus a look, then stumbled away through the brush. The bartender Rupert Kocsis wiped water from his brownish red beard. "You sure his name is Lutz—not Klutz?"

"He'll probably be the one that finds something," said Patrolman Diehl.

But he didn't, none of them did; and a long five hours later Diehl's team and the other units converged on Plutarch Pond Road near the old lumber mill. Set up in the back of a tan-and-brown police van were two fifty-cup coffee urns and three cardboard boxes filled with sandwiches. Reporters were everywhere, asking questions, taking pictures.

Several reporters approached Dwayne as the one who had found Mrs. Bradley's body; he answered all their questions the same way: "Nothing new to add. Ask the chief." Then the out-of-work car salesman, Fred Lutz, sauntered up with a copy of the Bancroft *Times Herald*.

"I guess if I had my picture taken with the chief," he said sarcastically, flicking the paper with his fingers, "I'd act like a big shot too."

"What's your problem?" said Dwayne.

"Just stay off my case, dog breath. Next time—"

It was like turning a sack of potatoes. Dwayne spun the man around, wrenched his arm behind his back and forced his head to the drip-edge of the van. " 'Next time?' You want *next time?* How's this for next time—"

"Ease off, McManus!" Lt. Buck yelled, looking over with the chief.

He shoved Lutz away, and fifteen minutes later the search teams were in the woods again—Burt Diehl's reduced to three.

"I was just thinking," Dwayne said. All morning he'd held back, played the W.P.D.'s game; now he felt free, ready, to play his.

"What's that?" said Officer Diehl.

They were in a rocky, thickly wooded area, getting wetter and colder as the afternoon progressed. "Yesterday the chief says, 'Secure Brenner Heights,' remember?"

"We don't want a lot of curious people—"

"That's just it," Dwayne said. "It's an easy way to come in."

They were standing by the trunk of a massive white pine toppled over in a storm; the network of roots, clogged with dirt and stones, extended eight feet over their heads. "This is rough country," Dwayne said. "Nobody walked no woman through here. Just a hunch, maybe they come in via Brenner Heights."

"How far's that?"

"From where we're at now, six hundred yards—more east than we're heading." He pointed. "Across that rise."

Soon after crossing the rise they came on an old wood trail. One way led to Brenner Creek, Dwayne said. The other way took you to the old foundation. They began walking toward the creek. "This is a whole lot easier going," Kocsis said.

"That's for sure," said Officer Diehl.

"You think Bradley done it?" Kocsis said.

"It don't look good for him—that's my personal opinion," said Diehl.

"Last night in Stubby's, everyone's talking New York girlfriend."

"Plus, look at whose gun it is."

"I can't buy that," said Dwayne coming in.

"Why not?" Diehl asked.

"If you commit a crime you cover your tracks." He was warming to it now. "Bradley's a smart man. Not likely he'd chuck his gun into the bushes like a Dixie cup."

"Maybe he panicked," said Diehl."

"I say he done it," said Kocsis.

They were drawing near the creek, silent now, looking hard for evidence. When they reached the water Dwayne jumped across and searched the far bank. Every few steps he glanced over to see how Diehl and Kocsis were doing. Then he saw the patrolman suddenly halt, stare at the ground.

"Look at this," Diehl said.

"What is it?" said Kocsis, coming closer.

"Shoe prints!"

Dwayne crossed the creek, going over to where the two were standing.

"'Course, they could be anybody's," Diehl said.

"I'd call it in, Burt," Dwayne said.

The officer yanked at his hip radio. "Search 6 to Signal 2."

"Go ahead, Search 6." Lieutenant Bock's voice.

"We have shoe prints—one a man's—another smaller. Over."

"Give location."

"Wait, Signal 2."

Diehl looked at McManus, who gave him directions; the Winwar patrolman repeated them over his radio. "Drive to the parking lot for Brenner Heights, then follow the creek 200 yards."

"Ten-four, Search 6."

The officer stowed his radio and from a back pocket took a section of Day-Glo ribbon and wrapped it around a stone next to the prints. "Okay, let's keep at it. Dwayne, stay on this side."

The three men spread out, working the bank, the brush. Through the deep woods came the sound of a siren. Then the bartender stopped and stared, just like Diehl had done. "Hey, Dwayne," he said.

"Yeah?"

"Take a look!"

Dwayne walked over. Kocsis pointed at a bramble. "Does that look like pulled threads or something?"

"Sure does."

"Burt!" Kocsis yelled. "We got something else!"

The officer came up quickly; his eyes opened wide when he saw the tan tuft of material. "If I've ever seen cloth fibers, we're lookin' at 'em."

Kocsis, grinning, draped a big wet arm around his fellow deputy's shoulder. "Hey, McManus, are we the best search unit that ever fucking searched?"

"You guys are doing great."

Diehl attached another section of fluorescent ribbon. The siren was getting closer. Still on his knees, the officer looked up. "Who said maybe they come in via Brenner Heights, answer me that!"

"Yeah, answer us that," said Kocsis.

Chapter

"That was Catherine," Tony Bradley said, walking back into the living room in his father's house. "She's flying in tomorrow afternoon."

Adam Pohl and Leonard were seated on the big leather sofa, drinking. In the fireplace a small blaze flickered, but did little to dispel the gloom pervading the big house. "Would you like me to meet her at the airport?" asked the clergyman.

Tony sat down in one of the easy chairs near the hearth. "Thanks, Adam. I'll do it."

They were quiet for a minute. "When was the last time Catherine was here, Leonard?" Adam asked.

Leonard was frowning as if he were standing on the edge of a canyon with thoughts of jumping. "I can't remember."

"It was Thanksgiving, four years ago," Tony said. "I remember she showed up with a keyboard player. Black. Funny guy. Mom had a fit."

"Is she seeing anyone now?" Adam asked.

"Catherine will be 'seeing someone' for the rest of her life," Tony said.

"For some people it takes a long time," Adam said, picking up his cocktail; his hand trembled noticeably as he brought the long-stemmed glass to his lips.

"I'm going to look around a little," Tony said.

He crossed the room and went downstairs to his father's office, firmly believing that the police had missed something in their search—what, he didn't know. He stood in front of the right-hand gun case gripping the fine oak frame. His mother was dead. Maybe she wasn't the kind of woman who would take a little boy in her arms or tell him stories, but she was always there, cared about him, and he supposed he had learned from Phyllis values like patience and a sense of perspective. She would never let him brag. Pride goes before a fall, Tony. He had thought of that when he had won the Eastern Intercollegiates, when he had graduated first in his class at Harvard Business. Pride goes before a fall. Be grateful, even for small things. It had stayed with him all his life, that philosophy of never to expect. He was much more his mother than Catherine was—she'd resented and fought Phyllis all her life. He had learned from her, had inherited a viewpoint from her that made it okay to chop trees and sell wood for a living because it was God's honest work. And now she was dead. He stood at the display case. She's dead. Somebody killed her. Somebody took her by force from this house and then to the lower Shagg Mountains and raped and murdered her. Oh God . . .

He turned and looked about the room, at the furnace door, at the tall case holding his father's rods, rifles and shotguns, at the desk, at the safe behind the desk, at the landing and the door on the landing. I'm going to find out who did it, Tony thought. If it's the last thing on earth I do, I'll find out who killed my mother. He went up the steps to the main floor, said good night to Adam and his father—he tended to think of them at that moment as the blind leading the blind—and walked out to his truck.

The fire was dying out. Adam Pohl could hear his friend's thoughts—raging, wild, incongruous—as he sat beside him in the sofa. "Leonard," he said, slurring his words, "*say* something. Doesn't matter what. Talk...tell me what you're feeling."

"I'm fine."

"You're not fine. You're under huge strain. You're suffering and you're holding it all in!"

Leonard was silent.

"Do you want me to leave?"

"No."

"I'll fix us something to eat."

"Make a dividend."

"We just had a dividend."

"Make another. Make us another dividend, Adam."

With difficulty—the sofa was soft and deep—Father Pohl heaved himself up and went, none too steadily, to Leonard's bar. The bottle of fine imported gin was all but empty; he emptied it completely into the crystal pitcher; then, as he had done so often through the years, he reached beneath the stainless-steel sink and took out a new bottle. He opened it, poured freely, added a few drops of dry vermouth and plenty of ice and reflected on his role as a priest, as a tender of the flock. To bring succor to those in need. By getting them drunk. He picked up the slender glass stirrer, stirred, then poured and returned to the living room.

"Thank you, Adam."

One of the logs, burning in the fireplace, sputtered; for a second the flame was green. They sat, drinking, and outside it grew dark. The telephone rang, and Rev. Pohl struggled up and managed to reach it by the fourth ring. It was the local undertaker. The question of an open or closed casket still had to be decided on, and Mr. Lapham wondered if the family had arrived at a consensus. He could assure the good Father that the late Mrs. Bradley looked very peaceful, after his careful attention to her physiognomy, and he would recommend—

"The consensus is a closed casket," Adam said.

Going back to the living room, he saw Leonard leaning forward in the sofa, hands made into fists and pressing against the sides of his head—as if to crush it. Adam placed a new log on the fire. Leonard picked up his martini and took a sip, staring over the top of the glass.

"Let me tell you what I'm thinking, what I know about the death of loved ones," Adam said, seated again. "It takes a terrible toll. When the loved one dies a horrible death it's that much more debilitating to the survivors. But we can't punish ourselves. You might *feel* blame, Leonard, but you're *not* to blame..."

No response from his old friend, who seemed in a strange, faraway place. The clergyman lit a cigarette. "Guilt leads one down twisted roads, Leonard. Years ago I dreamt I was building a cross. When I'd finished, soldiers came and nailed me up. When their work was done, suddenly *I* was standing there with the soldiers looking up at the person they'd really crucified. It was my son, Danny."

Leonard was staring at the fire. Adam had a swallow of his martini. "I was thinking as I was driving up here today," he said, "of the first time Ruth and I ever came to your house. We all had a cook-out at the pond. Then we all did some fishing, remember? You had a fly without a hook—without the barb—and we took turns casting it. It was the best time I'd had in years. Remember that, Leonard?"

No reply. Adam decided he'd finish his drink and go home, while he could still drive. Right now he'd just let his friend sit and grieve. He leaned back in the sofa. Blood pulsed in his throat. Sometimes he didn't think he had long to live.

The phone rang and Leonard got to his feet and went, hands slightly out for balance, to answer it. He sat down at the low counter and put the phone to his ear and spoke into the mouthpiece. He said, "Hello," and a woman at the other end said, "Hello, Leonard?"

"Yes?"

"This is Diane."

"Diane..."

"Is it a bad time?"

"No, it's okay."

"I heard the news—it was on TV. God, I'm so sorry..."

"Thank you."

"How are you?"

"Not so good."

"Leonard, what can I do?"

"I don't know, nothing anyone can do."

"Do they have any idea...I mean, who did it? Why?"

He didn't answer right away. "They found my gun, the missing .38 revolver I told you 'bout."

"Near the body—I know."

"District attorney's saying *I'm* a suspect."

"Leonard, that's ridiculous. I'll be a witness for you. Anything!"

He was silent, out of words.

"I miss you," she said.

"Me too." And meant it. And felt guilty, meaning it.

"I have to go now. Good night, Diane..."

He put down the phone and stumbled back into the living room. The priest was still there. Ruth had telephoned and told him to spend the night, he was in no condition to drive.

"That was Diane."

Adam nodded.

"It's been on TV in New York. I'm famous. Infamous! I didn't do it, Adam—"

"Of course you didn't do it!"

"I loved her for years. She was devoted to me, Adam. Yes, things had cooled, gone sour, but, my God, I wouldn't *kill* her!"

"Leonard, let me get you to bed, you need sleep."

"Make us div'dend."

"No. Putting you bed. Get up."

Leonard stood and Adam helped him —or he helped Adam— into the master bedroom. They sat down on the bed and Adam made sure his friend's belt was loosened, his shoes were off and his shirt buttons undone. Leonard lay down and Adam covered him with the comforter.

"Don't think anymore tonight, just close your eyes."

"Stay, Adam."

"I will. Have to."

Adam sat on the side of the bed until Leonard was asleep,

then went back to the living room and stood at the hearth. His mind was swirling. He thought of Ruth. *His* wife. Probably out somewhere; she had said she might get a sitter. He couldn't blame her, was the last one to judge her. He remembered the first time he had ever seen her, in the lobby of the theater at Indiana State, where he was the assistant chaplain. Intermission at a drama department presentation of *Death of a Salesman*; she was standing alone in the main doorway getting a breath of air—such a beautiful young woman, probably a college senior. He had gone over and they had talked and she was an English major and lived off campus and as the lights flickered she said she wrote poetry, maybe he would like to see some of her poems.

She had shown him her poems and taught him things young midwestern clergymen never learned in theology school. Late that same year they were married, and two years later they had a child. With a blue face and a malformed heart. Then it had started. What to do? Opinions on top of opinions. Only alcohol brought him peace, made his indecision bearable.

He thought of Leonard, the C.E.O., the man in the estate on the ridge overlooking the village, his strong and successful friend, Leonard Bradley. Now bleeding on the thorns of life; now needing him.

Adam turned at the hearth, saw the crystal pitcher and stirrer on Leonard's bar, the new bottle of gin—and wondered if he could quit. Oh, Lord, help me! his thoughts cried out. That *I* may help.

Chapter 10

Sadie Wojciechowski twisted the paper napkin in her hands, her eyes red from crying. "How could anyone have done something so awful to her?"

"That's what we're trying to find out," said the chief.

The inside of the mobile home was so clean and tidy Oscar knew he couldn't be smelling rotten eggs, but it sure smelled like rotten eggs. "When she'd have these talks with you, like you were saying, what were they about?"

"Marriage, men, things like that."

"Did she tell you personal things about herself?"

"Oh, sure. She thought her husband was having an affair. Poor woman, she was always so nice to me, chief. She gave me so many things—that blender came from the Bradley house, and a nice waffle iron, only Chuck don't like waffles—and all kinds of fine clothes. Sweaters and robes. And I've taken baths there and a couple of times when I wasn't feeling good she made me lay down, and paid me too."

"In your opinion, Mrs. Woj—"

"Sadie. Is the smell bothering you, chief? Everyone in the Park has sulfur water. You get used to it after a while."

Oscar smiled. Sadie's teeth were crooked and her skin wasn't that good but she had a lot of natural appeal and a fine figure. Plus she seemed honest, which for him counted most right now. "What was Mrs. Bradley's marriage like—say in the past six months?"

"I never thought it was very good, she was upset when we'd talk."

"Over what?"

"About what maybe her husband was up to. I told you. She used to ask me questions about Chuck—"

"Why would she want to know about Chuck?"

"Funny...her a married smart woman and all, but it was like she didn't know much about men. She'd ask me if he messed around on the road. She didn't use those words but that's what she meant."

"What did you tell her?"

"I told her I couldn't care less. I hoped he'd *die* on the damn road."

"Why do you stay with him, Sadie?"

"I ain't gonna, just for a while longer."

"Then what?"

"Plans."

"Just plans."

She smiled. "Real nice plans."

"Good for you."

Oscar got back on track. "So you knew Mr. Bradley was having an affair, or at least Mrs. Bradley thought so?"

"Oh, yes. I remember when she was thinking of hiring a detective, she wanted to know what I thought—should she do it?"

"What did you say?"

"I said sure. Like it was, she wasn't sure what was going on and it wasn't good to live like that."

"Why do you suppose she talked to you this way, Sadie?"

She pressed the napkin under her eyes, again suddenly crying. "I don't know, it just sort of clicked for us. In a funny way Mrs. Bradley looked up to me."

"How do you mean?"

"I knew things she didn't."

The chief nodded, glanced at his notebook. "One last question.

When you do house cleaning for the Bradleys, do you ever clean out the fireplace—you know, shovel out the ashes?"

"It's something Mr. Bradley does."

"Have you ever done it, since you've worked there?"

"No, never."

Oscar put his notebook inside his shirt pocket. "Thanks, Sadie. I hope everything works out for you."

"Oh, it's gonna work out fine. You bet."

Listening to Dudley Wilbraham was like watching the Winwar reservoir go down during a dry spell, but at least *now* the lawyer was cooperating; with his client savagely murdered, he was obliged to give Oscar all the help he could. He handed the chief a photocopy of detective Zicca's report, then launched into a ponderous dialogue about his interview with Mrs. Bradley, flipping through pages of notes in a leather-jacketed book as he spoke—although he really didn't speak so much as sort and choose.

"He came back from New York on his last business trip and she threw up to him his affair with this Wirth woman," Dudley Wilbraham said. "Mr. Bradley said, after some discussion, that he would be seeking a divorce."

"What did she say to that?"

"She was deeply hurt. She said she would never grant him one."

"Why did she go to the trouble of having her husband tailed, if that was the way she felt?"

The lawyer flipped a page in his handsome notebook. "I have an entry here," he said, deciding to use his glasses, sliding them off his polished head, "that speaks to your question. It is my own: 'Mrs. Bradley felt powerless in the face of an all-consuming curiosity, and so she hired a private investigator to follow her husband, fearing where that investigation would lead but having to find out—in much the way King Oedipus questioned his wife fearing where *his* investigation would lead.'"

Oscar frowned. "Run that by me again, counsellor."

"She was driven, irrationally, to learn the identity of the woman her husband was seeing. I honestly believe she thought he would mend his ways, once she confronted him. As it developed, he opted, instead, for divorce. Grievously wounded, she told him, and I quote again: 'Over my dead body.' A commonplace, to be sure, but taken in the context of Mr. Bradley's gun found near her body and a lady friend in New York, very interesting, I think."

The attorney reached for a light brown pipe; the bowl looked like an egg with the top sliced off. "Under those circumstances, it leads one down a certain road of suspision, wouldn't you say, chief?"

He was sitting back, legs stretched out beneath his desk, trying to sort out the evidence so far, when his phone rang. "Chief Flick."

"We got something here," Lt. Bock said.

Oscar went out, skirted communications central and walked down the hallway to the lab door, pushing it open. In the small brightly lighted room Jim O'Shea and Dave Bock were standing at the slate counter in work clothes, sleeves of both their chambray shirts rolled up.

On the counter lay a pair of still damp plaster casts, one larger than the other, each on a square of plywood. "She was definitely there, came down along the creek," Bock said.

He handed a woman's brown brogue to Oscar, who examined the sole and heelplate, then the moulage—the comparison immediate and obvious. He glanced at the larger print. "Question is, who made this one?"

"That's next," said O'Shea.

"Listen, Jim," the chief said after a moment, "put the man's cast on the floor, could you? Real easy."

Sgt. O'Shea picked up the square of plywood and knelt down with it, setting it gently down on the lab floor. Oscar rolled up his trouser cuff to see better, then carefully placed his foot over the moulage.

The styles were different, Oscar's western boot as against a flat-heeled shoe. But someone with a foot comparable in size to his had made the print.

How many times, through the years, had they worn the other's fishing waders, gym sneakers, cleats? He tried to dismiss the thought, couldn't . . .

The chief drew his foot away, and O'Shea returned the moulage to the counter. "This is an outstanding job," Oscar said.

He left the lab, and a few minutes later was saying good night to Ursula Bauer at Communications Central and walking out to the parking lot behind Village Hall. It was a cool, damp evening, smelling more of spring than fall. On the hill, lights in the college windows shone warmly. He stood with his hand on his car door looking up at the glowing buildings and thinking how mostly all he'd done with his life was put on his uniform. He had the reputation for being a police officer's police officer. Governors had written him personal letters congratulating him on his department's best-in-state awards. But sometimes Oscar thought he put his uniform on every day to keep from thinking what he really was—just a dump 'poke from Wyoming.

"You seem lost, chief."

He looked over, seeing in the shadows a woman looking at him through the rolled-down window of a dark sedan.

The light from the parking lot lamp fell on her face and hair. He tried to understand why someone so attractive would be parked behind headquarters at night. "Got a few things on my mind," he said, going over.

"Would you like to forget them for a while?"

"I wish I could—"

"Maybe I can help."

He was standing by her door, looking down; she was wearing a white, pleated skirt pulled up slightly above her knees, and a red blouse undone a couple of buttons. "That's right kind of you."

"Well," she said.

"Mrs. Pohl—"

"Ruth," she said.

"You'd better go," he said.

"I thought you liked me."

"That's why you'd better go."

She laughed. "I don't follow your reasoning, chief."

"Sure you do."

"In the living room of my house you had me undressed."

"It seemed safe."

"Is that what you are? A safe man?"

He hesitated. "You sure you want to do this?"

"Very."

"Where?"

She dangled some keys in her open window. "These are to an old farmhouse in Craigville."

"Is it yours?"

"I do part-time selling for Brenda Klein, remember? It's mine to show."

"Then let's have a look at it."

Ruth drove slowly away and Oscar went back to his cruiser. In the misty, darkening air the raucous sounds of Canadian geese, heading south, reached his ear—like a pack of dogs barking in the sky.

"I have not brought him in for questioning, I don't plan to until we get the readings on the .38 slug—and then I'm not sure I will!"

He was yelling into his phone, the veins in his neck pressing against his tan uniform collar. Outside his office window rain fell from a great silvery vault, drops bouncing off the macadam like dimes.

"You don't give me much choice but to undertake my own investigation," said the district attorney.

"That's your prerogative. I'm sure you'd come up with something."

"I'd come up with a suspect, is what I'd come up with!"

Oscar leaned back; his old swivel chair squeaked. "Mr. Woolever, you really don't know what's going on—that's the whole problem here. A lot of people in Winwar are talking, but you really don't know what the hell is going on. We're working around the clock on this case—my men are dead on their feet. So don't make it seem like we're derelict—"

"Okay, what *is* going on?"

"We're waiting on a ballistics report from the state lab in the capital. When that comes in—"

"Do you think it's going to tell you something you don't already know?" the D.A. asked quickly.

"Probably not."

"Why are you waiting on it then?"

"Because it could. There are procedures—which I'd like to think you recognize."

"I recognize procrastination in your department, chief."

"And I'm telling you, stop pushing on me for an arrest."

Oscar hung up, began to shuffle around the reports, papers, forms crowding his desk. They made no pattern he liked. He left headquarters and drove to the Corner Restaurant in the village, sitting alone in a booth. The waitress, Rita, served him a grilled cheese, bacon and tomato sandwich. She told him he looked like he'd just lost his best friend. He told her she was about right. Her hair was either platinum or gray; for the past five years he'd wondered about it. Sometimes he would think platinum, sometimes gray. Today he was thinking gray.

Oscar paid, put on his raincoat and went out, deciding to take a drive into the mountains. His office wasn't a good place for thinking. He put on his wipers. If there was any evidence left in the woods, this rain would kill it. He headed west on Main Street, stopping at the last traffic light where Route 21 cut across. On his radio, Communications Central was calling Car 17— "disturbance inside Stubby's Bar & Grill."

A few days ago that would have been major stuff in Winwar.

When he got to the mountains fog threw pearly arms around his cruiser. He turned on his low-mounted lamps, continued cautiously and finally pulled into the shale parking area at Brenner Heights. As kids he and Len would bike here two or three times a week in summer; it was torture—a continuous uphill pump for forty-five minutes. But jumping in was so great, so terrific a reward, you immediately knew you'd do it again tomorrow. Oscar pulled up his collar, tugged at his Stetson and stepped out.

The state police barricade was still in place, and as he crossed it he thought how years ago, when local police departments only had two or three men, the troopers would immediately come in and take over a case, especially if it involved a major crime. No questions asked. The very reason for the formation of the state police, in fact, was to serve rural areas like Cooper County. Hands in his pockets, Oscar moved along the down-sloping path through a small stand of dripping hemlocks, thinking someone had walked Phyllis Bradley here, through these trees, past the swimming hole. Who? Someone who knew the area. No stranger to Brenner Heights.

Oscar stood on the rocks overlooking the creek, the deep pool. Raindrops pocked the surface like noiseless barrages of #9 shot. On the other side the rocks were wider, better for sunning on, and higher, better for jumping from. Water dripped from the brim of his hat. Except for the creek sounds, the woods were silent, and a heavy mist rose from the pool.

Oscar bowed his head. He could feel the rain, the dampness, through his coat, jacket, shirt. It didn't matter; he hadn't had a cold for twenty years and maybe it was time he caught one, a good case of double pneumonia. That was one way around it.

A single crow, wet, miserable-looking, appeared through the fog and landed on the high branch of a scraggy pine that arched over the pool. The bird let out three distressful caws, waited for a response that never came and vanished in the murky air. Oscar kept looking up. He saw a boy, a kid from Wyoming, standing on the last branch, waiting only to catch his breath. The pool was plenty deep, it just didn't give you a very big area to land in. No one else in Winwar would climb so high. But then they hadn't grown up in Difficulty, with wolves and blizzards and grizzlies and tornadoes and rattlesnakes. He was used to danger; long ago he had conquered fear.

But he was afraid of something. What? If he had to arrest his own father who lived in a wheelchair in Orlando, he'd do it, damn it. Or his daughter, God bless her, with her five kids in

Devil's Lake and no husband. *And* he'd arrest Len Bradley. This afternoon. This very goddamn minute!

If he had to.

When, he asked himself, do you have to?

Oscar shivered, gave his head an agonizing shake and trudged back to his car.

When he entered headquarters fifteen minutes later several officers were standing about the hallways and looked at him with expressions ranging from curiosity to amusement. Art Carlussi quipped something to the effect he hoped the chief had bedded down his pony. Oscar went into his office. The jokes never bothered him; it was OK to let your men kid you to your face—it kept down the gibes behind your back. He hung up his soaked hat and coat and took off his wet uniform jacket, then went back out. It was one thing to have a little fun when Chief Flick walked in; no one kidded him now. As he was standing at the coffee machine the door to Lt. Bock's office opened. Looking pale and harried, the officer in charge of the Bradley investigation came up to the chief; he'd just heard from the state lab.

"Come on in," said Oscar.

Bock waited until they were behind the closed door before speaking. "It's a positive match-up—the slug and Bradley's .38."

"Now we know what we knew."

"Everything's pointing in one direction, Chief."

The officers sat down. Dave had never had any meat on him, but to Oscar it actually appeared like he'd lost weight in the past couple of weeks. "I think we should definitely question him," the police lieutenant said.

"I already have."

"I mean here."

"I know what you mean, Dave." Oscar sipped his coffee. "But something still tells me he's not our man."

"We got a barnful of evidence, Chief. The weapon, motive..."

"Suppose we read Bradley his rights—then what?"

"We'd have the D.A. off our backs."

"Why are you sweating the D.A.?"

"We've broke our backs on this case—I don't want no goddamn pol taking it away from us."

Oscar looked through his window at the rain. "Me neither. I
just think we're barking up the wrong tree."

"Name me the right tree."

"I can't."

Dave Bock rubbed a bony hand over his leathery face. "With
the evidence we've got, I'm with the D.A. I say we at least bring
him in."

"Dave, would you rape your wife—if you were going to kill
her?"

"Come on, chief."

"I'm asking you a question. Imagine it!"

"That's hard to imagine."

"Try!"

"I don't . . . I suppose not."

"That's what I'm talking about," the chief said. "It just doesn't
fit."

"Neither does stealing the pearls and cash, then."

"Same difference."

"Or throwing away the .38 in the bushes."

"Same."

"Unless—" Lieutenant Bock spread his thin hands, then
brought them together, "—unless he took the pearls and money
to make it seem like *someone else* did it. Do you know what I'm
saying? Someone, say, who had a burglary going and Mrs. Bradley walked in, surprising him."

"How about the rape?" the chief said.

"Like you just asked—would *I* do it? No. But . . . if doing it
would protect me from a murder rap, misleading everyone, then
yes, I'd do it—"

"Fuck."

"What's the matter?"

"Nothing." Chief Flick made a series of X's and O's on a sheet
of paper, this time intentionally.

"I'm sure Judge LaValle would say we had 'reasonable cause'
to ask for a search warrant," the lieutenant said.

"What's that imprint on the moulage?" Oscar asked.

"Du-Flex."

"Use it on the affidavit. Be exact about what you're looking for. We're also looking for a pair of tan or khaki trousers. Go with O'Shea. If LaValle delivers the warrant today, execute it first thing tomorrow. And if we find what we're looking for, we'll bring Bradley in."

Lieutenant Bock stood and went out. Oscar stayed at his desk, seeing himself stopping by his friend's house later tonight, advising him to do a little "pre-search" of his own. Because the W.P.D. would be dropping by in the morning.

One of the lower drawers to the chief's steel desk was partly open and he slammed it shut with the side of his western boot. What kind of a cop was he, for even thinking it?

Chapter 11

The District Attorney of Cooper County was holding Leonard Bradley's upland hunting boot in one hand and comparing its sole with the moulage lying on the slate counter in the W.P.D. lab. And the longer he compared, the more times his eyes went back and forth between the cast and the boot's sole, the bigger his smile became. "Chief," he said, "this is some kind of work!"

Oscar didn't smile in gratitude.

William Woolever was a man in his mid-forties with dark, carefully trimmed hair that had several waves in it, or maybe ripples. He had an aquiline nose and extraordinarily blue eyes, and he was wearing a finely tailored gray suit, blue silk tie and Italian shoes.

"We also had these listed on our warrant, Mr. Woolever," said Sgt. O'Shea.

As if he was taking a cake from the oven, the Winwar officer gingerly slid a pair of khaki trousers from a plastic zip-lock bag. "First, right here—blood." He pointed to the left cuff. "Next, look at the knees. Ground-in soil particles. Then the fibers we found on our search mission? They're a perfect visual match with the material."

"Excellent. Just excellent!"

"And get a load of this," said O'Shea. "I'm going to ask you to hold your breath, Mr. Woolever. We don't want you blowing this little jewel away. Down here, in the cranny of the fly."

The district attorney leaned forward, head lowered, his lips pressed shut. Then, glancing up: "I'm not sure I see anything, sergeant."

"Look again."

"That tiny curlicue of hair?"

"*Pubic* hair, Mr. Woolever."

The D.A. stood erect. "What about it? If these are Bradley's pants, then it's his . . ."

"We're betting it's his wife's."

A smile spread slowly over the D.A.'s salon-tanned face, and kept spreading. "Goddamn, you boys are something else!"

"It's falling into place," said Dave Bock.

"When's this stuff going to the state lab?"

"As soon as you leave, sir."

The District Attorney of Cooper County gave a good-natured laugh and shook each officer's hand. "I mean, we *have* this guy," he said, walking out with the chief.

For a moment, lying in bed, Leonard had the notion that Phyllis was coming back at last—she was knocking on the door because she'd lost her key—then he came full-awake. The red numerals on the clock-radio showed 5:03. He turned on his reading light, put on a robe and slippers, walked out to the hall and flipped on the entrance lights. Standing outside the glass door in an old pair of bluejeans, a lined denim jacket and his western boots, was Oscar Flick. Leonard let him in.

"Sorry to come calling so early, Len."

"No problem. Coffee?"

"Love some."

Leonard went into the kitchen, casting a more than occasional glance at his beefy-shouldered old friend facing the dark hearth. As he spooned out the coffee, his hand was shaking. Whether from too many drinks last night or Oscar's predawn appearance now, he didn't know. He stood at the counter, waiting for the water to run through the machine. The coffee poured, he walked past his bar to the living room, stopping to top off his mug with a shot of cognac.

"Thanks, Len."

Leonard sat in the soft leather sofa. The chief, sipping his coffee, seemed to ponder the dead ashes. "Len," he said finally, without turning, "I want you to get yourself a good lawyer. Maybe that's Chet, maybe it isn't. I want you to get the best lawyer in the state."

"What are you saying?"

"I have to arrest you."

"Arrest me?"

"We have enough evidence to—"

"I don't believe you're saying this to me, Oscar!"

The chief was holding the mug in both hands. "I've waited— I've put this off, put it off—and I can't any longer. The blood on your trousers is Phyllis' type, the ground-in soil on the knees came from the scene of the crime, we have shoe-prints from Brenner Heights that match your upland boots."

Oscar stopped, went on: "I haven't slept for two days, Len, hashing this over, and an hour ago I told myself I had no choice—even resigning wasn't an alternative. I'd be out of a job and they'd still come for you."

Leonard's head fell, then jerked upward. "Oscar, look at me— *look at me,* for God's sake? Did I rape Phyllis? Did I rape her and blow her brains out?"

He remembered what his lieutenant had said about raping his wife. If doing it would mislead the authorities, then he'd do it—

"Oscar answer me! In your heart you know it isn't so!"

"There's a time you stop listening to your heart, Len."

"Then in your *guts.*"

"I *hope* you didn't do it, Len. That's all I can say . . . Except like I just said, you need a good lawyer."

Leonard pressed against his eyes, so hard he began seeing red swirls, then looked up at his oldest living friend. "Oscar, remember those days? When you'd make daylight for me. Make it for me this last time . . ."

The chief took a sip of coffee, set his mug down, the sound reverberating in Leonard's head like the last rap of a gavel. "A police uniform isn't a football jersey, Len. Recently I've been a little mixed up on that—I'm not now. I'll be here at two this afternoon."

Oscar strode across the floor. At the door he stopped and turned around and looked at his friend sitting in the sofa holding his head. "Good luck, Len. *That* comes from the heart."

He went out, sliding the door shut. Headlights threw eerie patterns on the wall. They flickered, glided along, vanished. A moment later an attractive woman in her early thirties came in, barefooted, wearing a light-blue robe, wanting to know what was going on. She had short, light brown hair, brown eyes and a slender body. The starting of a car's engine, she said, had awakened her.

He did not answer. He was staring down, fingers pressed against his forehead.

"What is it, daddy?"

He still didn't speak.

"*Tell* me."

"They're saying—I did it—"

"*Did* it?"

"Your mother . . . they're saying it was me. That was the chief."

He put his arms around his daughter to comfort her—but also to hold on. "They're going to arrest me, Catherine."

"Oh, God! No . . . *no.*"

Dwayne McManus pulled his blue Chevy into the dusty parking space outside his trailer. Three bags of groceries rested on the back seat. Getting out, he opened the rear door and grabbed the two heaviest; his daughter took the third bag. They went up the steps—loose planks on cinder blocks.

Inside at the kitchen sink Dwayne washed his hands. The water, as usual, smelled terrible. "What do you want tonight, Julie? We got chicken, turkey—how about sliced roast beef with gravy and mashed potatoes?"

She didn't answer. She was already sitting on the floor watching

TV. The school counselor, Mrs. Gross, said she was getting better but he couldn't see any change. "Acquired Autistic Behavior Syndrome" was what she called it. But she really didn't know what the fuck it was or what the fuck to do about it. No one did. Dwayne lit off the gas oven and slid in the two frozen dinners and stored the other items, then went into his room and poured himself a hit.

His room, as always, was picked up. He liked a neat place. Even before Wanda had started doing drugs she had never kept a clean house. Most of the time when they were stationed at Bragg and Leavenworth, the bed wouldn't be made or the dishes washed when he came home. She was too pretty to yell at—at first—so he would make the bed and do the dishes, hoping she'd get the idea. He picked up the shot glass. But there was one thing that got him right from the start. She would wrap her tampons in toilet paper and drop them in the wastebasket instead of the commode, which didn't bother him by itself—except this dog they had, a fidgety fox terrier type named Fritz, would get into the basket at night, then upchuck right when they were having breakfast. One time he kicked the dog, catching it good. Wanda went berserk. Yell, scream at him? Okay, maybe he shouldn't have kicked the stupid animal, but she carried on like it was a baby for God's sake! Which was when he'd begun thinking she was losing it.

He downed the shot, poured another and took it to the window. It was getting dark. The huge diesel blocked out the front third of the adjacent trailer. Through the blinds in the living room window a bluish light filtered. At the far end of the Woj home a snowmobile lay under a black cover; the way it sat there, low and black, Dwayne always thought it was going to spring. He sipped the whiskey. Suddenly a light went on in the small window just to the right of the front door, and the next moment a woman appeared in the window. She looked out, saw Dwayne and made a T with her two index fingers; then she held up three fingers. *Tomorrow. Three o'clock.*

Dwayne smiled, gave a little nod. He hoped she would do what she sometimes did, and he hoped she wouldn't—because it drove him crazy when she did it. Then he saw she was going to. He brought the whiskey to his lips, to kind of quiet himself down. She unbuttoned her blouse and unsnapped her bra. She had the kind of breasts that didn't just fall out when she let them go, they tumbled out. She wiggled and shook her shoulders. He sipped his whiskey. It was a show—goddamn, it was a show! Then, suddenly, Sadie turned out the lights.

The telephone rang and he walked into the kitchen area to pick it up.

"Hello."

"Dwayne?"

"Yeah."

"This is Sgt. O'Shea of the Winwar Police. Chief Flick tried getting you earlier. He wants you to come by headquarters tomorrow morning."

He pulled out the stool at the cramped little counter. "What's it about?"

"He didn't say."

"Any special time."

"Early."

Dwayne rubbed some sweat from his neck. "I'll be there."

He hung up. On TV a blonde with long legs and a flowing white dress was running through a soft, sunny field. Then came the bottom line: she had on a Stay-Free Maxi-Pad.

Dwayne went to his room and poured out a third shot, taking it down and looking at himself in the dresser mirror. Something in his reflection brought him back to a remote village in Quang Tri and the thirteen-year-old, the prettiest girl he'd ever seen. She was moving her lips, looking at him with huge dark eyes. Then Lieutenant Barkam gave the order and they opened up, and afterward they dug a big goddamn hole in the damp earth and dumped in the bodies, fifty-five altogether, men, women and children. And six or seven dogs.

When Dwayne arrived at headquarters the next morning at 8:35, Patrolman Williams was standing at Communications Central talking with one of the dispatchers; the officer, neatly attired in tan and brown, greeted him in a friendly way and asked if he could help him. Dwayne said why he was there, and Williams ducked into the chief's office. A few moments later he came back out. "Okay," he said.

"Thanks, Luke."

He went in, and Oscar, at his desk, said good morning and told him to have a seat. "Coffee?"

"No, thanks. I'm easing off."

"I've been easing off now for twenty-five years."

Oscar picked up his mug. "I tried calling you yesterday afternoon."

"Jim told me."

"Got some developments here."

"What's up?"

"Dwayne, listen—I know you have a lot of pride, but I want you to hear me out."

"Sure," he said, his nerves settling a little.

"Ted Marzocca called me yesterday afternoon," the chief said. "He's chairman of the Review Board, as you know. He said he'd got my recommendations for the new opening in the department."

"It don't much interest me what Ted Marzocca says."

"I hear you, just listen to me. I said to him, Any problem? He said, No problem. Maybe an oversight. I asked him what he meant. He said he didn't have an application for Dwayne McManus. I said to him, He didn't apply. He said, Get his application to the board before twelve noon tomorrow."

Oscar sipped his coffee and set the mug down on an envelope with half a dozen brown rings on it, each resembling a total eclipse of the sun. "I said to him, what are you saying? Is this some kind of joke? Because after last spring, it's a lousy joke. He said he'd seen our picture in the *Times-Herald* and it got him thinking—how long could he hold onto bad feelings, keep a man from a job he'd always wanted? You stayed in the community, you went about your business after the defeat last spring. He said he'd gained a lot of respect for you and wanted to forget the whole business."

"Marzocca's an asshole."

The chief sat back. "Regardless, it's a new day."

Dwayne glanced down at his palm, rubbed it with his thumb. The lines were like routes, roads he knew so well suddenly unfamiliar, detours to nowhere. He rolled his hands together and looked up at the chief. "It's a new day," he said. "What about it?"

"The job's yours, Dwayne."

"I've heard that before."

"Never from Marzocca."

"So now he barks, I jump?"

"I know how you feel," said the chief.

"Twice. *Twice* I've had a position promised me on the W.P.D. And now again. Well, it's too late, chief." In more ways than one, he thought.

"I was hoping you'd let bygones be bygones."

"A man wants to serve," Dwayne said. "He has the qualifications, he loves the work and the chief of police wants him on the force—and *they* keep shooting him down. Why should he let bygones be bygones?"

"Dwayne, I still think you want to serve. Because once it's in a man's blood it's always in his blood. I know."

Oscar leaned forward and spoke quietly. "I had a job for you when you were a kid. Graduate, Dwayne, you got your badge. We all know what happened..."

Sweat shone on Dwayne McManus's face and neck.

"You're a natural," the chief said. "Most cops aren't. When you found the body of Mrs. Bradley, okay—there it was. It could've been anyone who found her, you say. But the fact is, *you* found her. That isn't all luck. You didn't find the footprints and fibers, but Diehl told me about your hunch. Half of police work is playing a hunch—being in the right place at the right time."

The chief paused. "This is your work, it's always been, Dwayne, since your high school days when you used to stop by afternoons and man the radios or ride with the guys or just shoot the shit with us about deer hunting. One time we nabbed a guy scattering shotgun pellets over old Mrs. Whitridge's roof because you told us how to go in—we were going to drive straight up her road, remember? He was an unlicensed hunter from New Jersey and

Judge LaValle fined him $500. All right, at eighteen you had a real tough break, but it's hard to raise a daughter and have her die on the highway. It's understandable how the Marzoccas felt, and the rest of the community too—whether Lucy gave you the blow job in Captain Black's parking lot or on the way home. I always believed you, you know that. I always believed your side of the story that *she* was driving."

Oscar finished what was left of his coffee. "You went in the army, Marzocca made good his threat twelve years later—Dwayne McManus would *never* be a cop in this town. Me, hell, I'd forgotten all about it—a lot of jack rabbits cross the range in twelve years. When the Review Board backed Marzocca and chose Mary Teevan it *hurt* me, personally—I damn near resigned. But that's all behind us now. This is a new beginning. People forget. I want you on the force, Dwayne. I'm asking you—once again I'm asking you—to put on the tan and brown."

The chief opened his desk drawer and withdrew an official application, already filled out, and placed a pen beside it. "What do you say?"

He did not know how he could say yes, he did not want to say no. Oscar Flick slid the application across his blotter. "Damn it, *sign* it!"

More relieved than the chief could know, Dwayne took the pen and signed.

Standing just inside the sliding glass door, Oscar read Leonard his rights; then Sgt. O'Shea put handcuffs on him. Watching and listening were Leonard's son and daughter and his lawyer, Chet Evers.

Leonard and Chet, followed by the two officers, walked out to the parked W.P.D. cruiser. "What do they think he's going to do," Catherine said to her brother, "attack the judge?"

"It's called going by the book."

"By the *medieval* book."

The police vehicle moved slowly away from the house. "Can you stay for a minute?" Catherine asked.

They went into the kitchen. While Catherine made coffee

Tony spent a minute at both windows, looking first in the direction of the farm and pastureland, then south over the parking area to the woods. Sitting at the round table, she asked him how Debby was, and he said she was all right; if and when their spring came back, she'd be better. "I'm praying for a good steady rain."

"Why don't you just move?"

"Can't afford to."

"Tony, come on!"

"You asked me, Catherine. I told you."

They sipped their coffee, not talking. They had never had much of anything to say to each other. He had always been such a perfect son, she such an imperfect daughter. Years had gone by since their high school and college days, but resentment was a tough deposit; it got in your bloodstream and wouldn't go away.

"What's going to happen?" she asked.

"He's in real trouble. I don't know. I suppose . . . he could go to jail."

"For *what?*"

"For what the evidence says—"

"The evidence is bogus!"

"*We* know that. Can Chet convince a jury?"

Catherine rubbed her fingers lightly over her forehead. "It's all so awful . . . do you think they'll find out who did it?"

"They better. We know he didn't, so that means there's someone out there who killed her . . ."

"But if the police say it's dad, they've stopped looking!"

"*I* haven't."

He sipped his coffee; she remembered his hands as very fine. Now he had a laborer's hands, rough, callused. "I have to make deliveries," he said.

"You sound like a country doctor."

"I am, Dr. Wood."

She leaned across and kissed his face through his whiskers. "Give my love to Debby."

"Tomorrow night have dinner with us."

"I'd like that."

He walked out to his truck. Through the kitchen window she watched him open the passenger door and saw Buck jump down for a quick run. Tony crossed the turn-around area to the edge of the encroaching brush, leaned down as if he had found something. But it was only a long stick that he used in the weeds and bushes, poking around with it.

And she thought—the boy. First the girl, then—thank God—the boy! To carry on in the great Bradley tradition of winning tournaments and running companies. While she—while the daughter drifted on, no one much caring if she finished her education or even got one, because she wasn't "the boy." She had never felt important; Tony was the important one.

He whistled and Buck came out of the woods and he tossed away the stick. Whether it was because he was now just a country boy, or because their mother was dead, or because they were simply no longer kids, Catherine didn't know. But suddenly she realized she was no longer envious or resentful of her brother. Right now she felt a love for her brother she had never felt before . . .

Chapter 12

It was one of those October thunder storms that run through just like a deer will come down off a ridge with a couple of dogs chasing it, stones flying every whichway, just fucking hell-bent. Dwayne's reading lamp flickered. He glanced up at the low ceiling of his room, set aside an article in *Popular Mechanics* on the latest in electronic security systems, got out of his easy chair and went to the window.

Hail stones were ricocheting off the aluminum awning over the door to the Woj trailer. Then the lights dimmed in Dwayne's own trailer, went out altogether for a second, and came on again.

He poured himself a little whiskey at his dresser and returned to his chair, picking up the local paper. Even looking at the headlines for the third time, they jumped out at him: BRADLEY INDICTED; D.A. CALLS EVIDENCE "OVERWHELMING." Then the sub-head: *Bail Set At $1,000,000*.

Dwayne skimmed the article by Audrey Ryder, going slow over the last paragraph: "The body of Mrs. Bradley was spotted September 30 by Vietnam veteran Dwayne McManus, a resident of Winwar and well-known area hunter, while he was testing a tree stand he had just built in the lower Shagg Mountains near Plutarch Pond."

He let the paper drop and sat quietly, just sipping the whiskey. The buck was way the hell down the ridge now. He glanced at his watch and finished the article, then went to the window again, hoping to see Sadie walk by, or better, have her duck into the bathroom for a little show 'n' tell. Husband of hers hadn't had a haul in a week! Dwayne was climbing the walls, but worse by far was knowing Chuck was banging her every night. Then, even as he stood there, the door opened and Wojciechowski stepped out, wearing a ratty thigh-length coat, walked to his car, got in and moved down Deerpath. Dwayne stayed at the window, waiting for the bathroom light to go on—and his telephone rang.

She wanted to talk for a minute; maybe Chuck was getting a haul to California! Or she just wanted to hear his voice. Dwayne was smiling when he picked up the receiver just before the third ring. "Hey, baby—what's the good word?"

"Dwayne?"

"Yes?"

"Chief Flick speaking."

He squeezed the back of his neck, hard. "Chief . . . sorry about that."

"No apologies necessary." Oscar gave a good-natured laugh.

Dwayne reached for the stool. It made him weak to think he could've said "Sadie." Almost had! "I was expecting someone else," he said.

"No problem, happy for you. Listen, come by tomorrow and sign some papers, then head over to Celli Brothers in Bancroft. They'll be wanting your measurements."

He didn't say anything for a full second; here his life's dream was suddenly a reality and he felt miserable. But he made his voice sound excited. "I got it?"

"Unanimous. Good salary too, because of your military experience."

"Great."

"I've looked forward to this day for a long time, I mean that, Dwayne."

"I appreciate that."

"See you tomorrow."

"Thanks, chief—for everything."

"Good night, Officer McManus."

Dwayne hung up slowly. Julie was watching television. They would be able to move now, get a better place. He walked back into his room and went over to the window. He stood there, breathing deeply, relieved he hadn't compromised himself by saying Sadie's name. Then his phone rang again and he went back to the kitchenette.

"Hello."

"Honey—hi! How are you?"

"I got the job."

"You got it! Dwayne! When did you hear?"

"Just now."

"I'm so happy for you. And guess what, he's leaving day after tomorrow."

"Great."

"Oh, honey, I love you!"

"I love you too, Sadie."

"I'm so proud of you—damn, he's back!"

She hung up. Dwayne walked into his bedroom and stood by the window; the runt was going up the steps to the trailer with a couple of 6's.

I'm a cop, he thought. It don't make sense.

Chapter  13

They were in Leonard's downstairs office. Chet Evers was holding a seven foot split-bamboo rod by its cork grip. "This is a sweetheart," the lawyer said, waggling it, appraising the action.

"It was my dad's. Picked it up from James Payne himself."

"That's like going to Picasso to buy a Picasso!"

Leonard smiled, almost.

"Was your father a good fisherman, Len?"

"He could work water like no one I ever saw. I'd be up and down the stream, he'd be on the same stretch all morning."

Chet pulled the two sections apart and slid them into a cloth sack. "You know what I still think about? Those three days we spent on the Beaverkill as kids—Well, *I* was a kid. We had that old wall tent of yours. Heavy double-O canvas, bastard weighed a ton."

He slid the cloth sack into a polished aluminum tube. "And you get the idea on the second day we're going to test the stocked waters of one of the most famous fly-fishing clubs in America eight miles upstream. We parked the car down the road and hiked up—and suddenly everything's posted. 'Private Water—

No Trespassing! Beaverkill Trout Club.' You say, 'Let's go in here.' I'm saying to myself my father's going to kill me if we get caught. We steal in. Christ, what water! I can just smell those big goddamn rainbows, and then we both stop dead in our tracks. Some guy, some fat-assed Wall Street broker, has his waders down and he's banging this redhead on the bank!"

"Hadn't even taken his creel off..."

"Well, first things first—we hire a private investigator," the attorney said, having stowed Leonard's rods and secured the glass door. "Because there's someone out there who's sure as hell framing you."

"I agree."

"How about Frank Zicca? The detective who tailed you in New York."

"He did a good job for Phyllis."

"I'll give him a call."

Chet walked out to the center of the room. Leonard was sitting at his desk. "But we have to proceed as if Zicca's going to come up empty. We're not going to assume anything. I take that back. We're going to *assume* you'll be standing trial."

"Chet, don't say that. Let's see what he uncovers."

"Suppose it's nothing."

"We take it from there, we'll still have plenty of time."

"Len, this case could be in court by then."

"In three or four months?"

"In five or six months, yes. Cooper County doesn't have a crowded docket. Plus Woolever's pushing. Elections coming up, nothing like a conviction in a big murder trial."

"I think I'll get myself a drink," Leonard said, feeling pale.

"We'll have one together, in a while. Let's practice—"

"*Practice?*"

"Rehearse."

"For what?"

"What do you think for what? Okay, you're on. I've just called you to the witness stand."

"Wait a minute."

"No! You're on."

Chet stood in front of the desk. "Mr. Bradley, I'd like to go back to the day, or rather to the hour and the minute, when you first learned your wife was dead. Where were you?"

"You want me to answer that?"

"That's the idea, Len."

"This takes *practice?*"

"Answer the question!"

Leonard gave a deep sigh. His hands were like two people trying to get comfortable in bed. "I was in my company office, working at my desk. It was mid-afternoon."

"Go ahead. What happened then?"

"My secretary knocked and said the chief of the Winwar police was here to see me. Chief Flick walked in, a woman officer stayed by the door. He told me they'd found the . . . the body."

"What was your immediate reaction?"

"My what?"

"Your immediate emotional response when he told you."

"Well, you can imagine . . . I thought I'd die from the shock, I was devastated . . ."

Chet nodded but didn't speak.

"Well?" Leonard said. "Now what?"

"I'm not exactly sure."

"Ask me another question."

"I will, but I don't think you answered the one I just gave you."

"What are you talking about?"

"I asked you for your *immediate* reaction."

"And I *told* you! It was devastating, I . . ."

"I'm sure you felt that—still do. But I said *immediate.*"

"We're banging heads here—what the hell am I giving you?"

"You're giving me stock replies, if you want to know the truth."

Leonard flared. "My wife was shot in the head and raped and I'm giving you stock replies!"

"I think so. Yes."

"That's goddamn insulting, Chet!"

"Why are you getting so defensive?"

"Because you're making a judgment on me—and you have no right to—"

"The jury has no right to make a judgment on you either, I suppose."

"Let them make one—let them see a man who was crushed by what happened! Is that bad? Would it be better if they saw someone who didn't care, who *wasn't* crushed?"

"If that was how he truthfully felt, yes."

"I don't get it, Chet. A man should never put himself in a bad light—"

"You're saying the truth is a bad light? Your honest feelings about Phyllis' death—"

"I *gave* you my honest feelings..."

Leonard stared at the lawyer. The lawyer at Leonard. He wouldn't push it, not now. The man was, understandably, too shaken. Too scared. But later, if all else failed...

Tony Bradley, searching the woods behind the house on Maple Ridge, came to the low stone wall marking the northern property line. He walked along, eyes on the ground, on the wall. Poking with a stick. Kicking up crinkly leaves, dead branches. It was a cold day—the bright colors had come and gone in Cooper County. And now the hunters were here, and every so often a shot would echo, reverberate through the crisp, clean air. He followed the wall, always searching; then he stopped and looked up. At the barn.

The old Vandermark barn. Years ago when he had played here with pals the walls were crumbling and the roof had leaked. Now the roof was gone; the main beam, like the backbone of some great quadrupedal skeleton, had caved in. Tony could only wonder that the barn was still standing.

He climbed over the stone wall, whistled to bring his dog closer and walked through the tall grass. They had had good times here. In a different way, so had older kids and grown-ups who had used the area behind the barn for parking, even in broad daylight, and sometimes when he and his friends were inside the barn swinging on a big rope or playing in the loft a car would come bobbing down the grass-crowded road and they would gather around the loft window and watch.

He looked up at the collapsed window in the peak, remembering how Joe Longo, who now owned and operated the Mobil station in town, had thought of charging a fee for new kids. Who wouldn't pay a dollar to see "The Greatest Show on Earth?" It was a swell idea, everyone said—they'd all be rich! Tony wasn't so sure. They might get kids to fork over a buck, but how were they going to guarantee a show? If no couples showed up they'd have to refund the money. Longo called him a square like his old man, and Tony threw a punch at him.

He moved on, noticing pressed-down grass in parallel strips; even now the area was still being used for parking. Some things never changed. Then he got another idea. He looked back at the stone wall, then out toward Freer Road, which ran past the town landfill and intersected with Rte. 21. He glanced back and forth again, thinking it was at least a possibility, *something*. He followed the tire depressions around to the front of the dilapidated structure, then continued up the grassy roadway—some two hundred steps—to Freer Road. Here he stopped. The biggest question, of course, was how the killer had got inside the house; but another important question was how he had transported Phyllis to the lower Shaggs. Whoever had abducted his mother sure hadn't walked her there. And it was unlikely that her killer had just driven up to the house at four in the afternoon. With the always present farm hands about, that wouldn't be too smart.

Standing on the side of Freer Road, one of the many unpaved thoroughfares in the township, he looked back toward the stone wall. His father's house was a third of a mile in, slightly off to the right, or east. The killer could have walked Phyllis through the woods to his car, which he'd left behind the old barn. Just then a pickup truck came along loaded with trash barrels and junk. It passed, leaving a cloud of dust, and Tony walked down the grassy incline, whistled to Buck and headed back through the woods.

Smoke was coming from the chimney of the big house when he arrived but he didn't go in. His truck was piled high with green logs. He had to drive to Mink Hollow, unload them, load on seasoned wood and make a delivery to an old couple up the line in Jonesville Flats. Tony glanced at the falling sun; the temperature was dropping. He gave Buck a boost, circled the hood and climbed up to the cab. Getting back to his routine might help relieve the awful feeling. Except he knew it wouldn't.

Whenever the phone rang, Debby only answered it because she hoped it might be Tony calling from the village telling her to bring Amy and meet him for lunch, or a pizza, or a movie. It never was, it was always somebody wanting wood.

She scribbled down the message. Two cords. Chas. Bucey, Chodokee Forks. "Seasoned," the man said.

"*All* our wood is seasoned," Debby said. "What length?"

"Don't rightly know."

"For stove or fireplace?"

"Stove—brand new. Sears had a special—"

"You'll have it day after tomorrow."

"How much?"

"Sixty dollars a cord."

"I called someone else, they wanted seventy-five," the man said, sharing the information happily.

"My husband likes staying busy."

"Well, he's got my business."

"Thank you." She hung up. It was the fourth order of the afternoon, and he was already swamped, mostly because he was spending at least two hours each day looking for clues in his mother's murder. She wasn't blaming him, it was just knocking hell out of his schedule and their time together.

She returned to her work table located against the back wall, beneath the window. Was a time, not so long ago, it afforded her a lovely view of the fields and forest behind the house. Now, except for the old orchard, you could only see the fortress of cord wood—Tony called it inventory—he had constructed, log by log.

She picked up the stone she was working on, an old-fashioned pot-bellied stove—that was what she'd recognized *in* the stone after finding it on one of her walks with Amy. Now she was painting the stove already there: "bringing it out," as she liked to think. On her table, along with dozens of small paint jars and brushes, were twenty or thirty additional stones, half unpainted; the other half were coffee pots and sleeping dogs and crank-type telephones and country school houses. Several stores in Winwar carried them; the small stones went for thirty-five dollars, the larger ones for fifty.

It was time to see what Amy was up to—to bring her in and start thinking about dinner. Debby crossed to the door and went out. It was a beautiful fall afternoon, sunny, brisk, still exceedingly dry. Her daughter was in the small yard with three or four of her dolls playing school. Next year Amy would be going to kindergarten, and Debby didn't know if the child's ability to entertain herself—by *necessity* her ability—would help or hinder her in an actual classroom.

The little girl looked up as her mother walked across the parched ground; then Debby suddenly stopped. A hundred feet behind her daughter, standing on the edge of the creek, was a huge black bear.

Debby ran to her daughter, snatched her up and carried her inside the house. The child was frightened and wanted to know what the matter was. Her mother said nothing.

"Will you get my dolls?"

"Later."

She went to the front window and looked out. The bear was gone—but how far away? Would it come back? She sat down, still feeling the terrible start in her chest; then, low in her abdomen, she had a sharp, jabbing pain.

"Ohhh!"

"Mommy, are you okay?"

It came again but then subsided. "I'm all right, angel. I didn't mean to frighten you."

She heard the sound of Tony's truck coming up the road. It pulled past the house; then there was a shifting of gears and the noise of the engine in reverse. A door slammed; in her mind, she saw Buck jumping down. Then she waited...

Thud. Her eyes closed.

Crash. Thud. Crash.

　　　　It was just growing dark as he sounded his horn going into the hairpin turn. He down-shifted. Buck braced his feet and instinctively he reached for his collar. Then he was through the turn and on the rising straightaway leading to his house.

He had popped in quickly an hour and twenty minutes ago, saying to his wife don't wait—he had to make a delivery to Jonesville Flats. She had stood at the range, hardly turning as he'd spoken. Now, as he drew near the house, he saw that her car was gone; a single light shone in the living room.

He parked and went in. On the table was a folded sheet of paper. He read a few lines, sat down, and started over.

Dear Tony,

I understand you trying to find out who killed your mother. It's natural. Someone has to make the police see the false trail they're on! I wish you luck, and of course success.

But I can't go on living with you now in Mink Hollow. In the beginning it was romantic—our own "little house in the mountain" —but four years...the dangerous winter driving, the isolation, the drought. And today, just before you drove up, I saw a bear. And Amy was outside! I was a nervous wreck and still feel jumpy. I just can't live this way any longer, taking those messages for you—more your secretary than your wife I've gone to my parents' with Amy, and I intend to stay there at least until I have the new baby. Please don't come after me. You often told me how much you loved Thoreau, but as you know, *he* left the pond because he had other lives to live.

What lies ahead of us, I don't know. I love you, Tony. But I can't go on living here like this. If, or when, you ever throw your last log, let me know.

　　　　　　　　　　　　　　　　　　　　　　　　Love,
　　　　　　　　　　　　　　　　　　　　　　　　Debby

Tony dropped the letter. He looked about the room, over at Amy's corner, then stood and went out, leaving the door open, and crossed the road to the dusty weeds on the edge of the creek. Then he yelled, shouting into the dark woods, his cries rumbling around in the hills of Mink Hollow like thunder.

Chapter 14

Chodokee Creek came out of the mountains nine miles north of Winwar in the hamlet of Woodland; the first bridge crossed at this point—red-painted steel with a plank floor. Dwayne McManus clattered over in his blue Chevy and followed a one-lane road on the other side that curved and rose through thick woods. Then, where a big hemlock leaned across the road, he turned off, taking a hidden driveway about sixty feet to a small log cabin, deeply shadowed. The roof was new but he still had work to do on the sills. Dwayne got out of his car and carried a couple of grocery bags to the front door, inserted a key in the heavy padlock and went in.

A dank, musty odor hung in the air but he'd take it any day to the rotten-egg smell in his trailer. He put the food and beer in the wooden-sided icebox, tossed in a bag of ice and snagged one of the brews. It was a single good-sized room with a platform bed against one wall, a closet, a narrow loft above the closet, a sturdy table and chairs and two stoves, one for heating, one for cooking. Several kerosene lamps stood about—on the counter, the table, on a stand by the bed.

He pushed aside a steel bolt to the back door and stepped out to a small deck he had completely rebuilt early this past summer.

It was sunnier here than in the front because he'd cut down dozens of trees on the steep bank. What his daughter liked most was the path he'd made leading down to the creek. Used to be a job and a half for her getting down and she'd hardly ever do it, but now that he'd built natural stone steps it was a lot easier, and she'd make little dams in the water or go wading or just sit on the rocks and watch the current.

He sat down in a canvas chair, resting his beer on the pressure-treated deck boards. A red squirrel started complaining, and he looked over, spying it in the branches of a stunted hemlock. There was nothing among all God's creatures so bitchy as a red squirrel. They got in your roof and kept you awake at night playing tag among the rafters.

Dwayne put his feet up on the railing and took a slug of beer. He'd cleared some of the land; otherwise the place was just how it was thirty years ago when his mother and father had bought the cabin and 3.3 acres it sat on for "taxes owed"—$625. As a hideaway. His parents had never wanted much, had never asked for anything really; and this was like heaven for them, just being together—no electricity, no neighbors, no nothing—only the cabin and the headwaters of Chodokee Creek below.

Dutch. Emma and Dutch, thought Dwayne.

He wasn't in the church because he wasn't born yet, but he'd heard tell many times about the midnight service when his father appeared in the church vestibule in his full-dress army uniform. The war was still on; for the past year he'd served under Patton in North Africa. Then, as people told it, Dutch walked down the aisle with a cane, limping, and every heart in the congregation stopped. Many of the worshippers wept, it touched them so to see one of their boys walk down the aisle a wounded veteran, ribbons on his chest, home for Christmas.

Later, here at the camp, that man would spend hours with his son teaching him what he called the "lore of Cooper County," though for years Dwayne thought he was saying "law." Then Dwayne came home from school one day, thinking they would all be heading up to the camp when his father finished work, and two or three cars were in the driveway—and he learned from his Uncle Ned that Dutch had had an accident at the Bradley plant—his left hand was mauled bad, two fingers cut clear off.

And nothing after that—Dwayne thought about it now as he brought his bottle of beer to his mouth—nothing after that was ever the same. Complications set in—infection, blood poisoning, pneumonia—and it was a year and a half before his father was up and around. Workmen's compensation kept the family going during his convalescence. But it was the lawsuit against Bradley that would take care of them in the years ahead, they had every right to believe. Everyone knew about the violations and hazards on the floor, and old-man Bradley hired a staff of lawyers to fight the claim, and Dwayne remembered when his father put out his maimed hand and took the check—for peanuts—and tore it up in the company lawyer's face. Dutch had gone civil service after that, and for the rest of Dwayne's boyhood he would see his father on the village sidewalks, lugging a heavy leather bag on his shoulder, growing old and weary before his eyes.

He was starting on a new beer when he heard a car pull into the drive and a few moments later the cabin door opened.

"Hi, honey!"

"I'm out here."

She walked through the room and came out on the deck wearing jeans and a yellow T-shirt. Sometimes she would wear a bra and sometimes she wouldn't. A bra gave her tits class. But when she wasn't wearing one, like now, you didn't even think of class— all you thought of was her tits. He stood up, kissed her easy, and noticed her face, the bruises.

"Someday I'm gonna kill that sonofabitch," he said.

"Just give us a better kiss."

He did, his hands still on her back but moving a little forward, just to the sides of her breasts. You never wanted to go too fast with a woman, even one you were seeing regular.

"No way was I gonna give him 'one for the road,' " she said.

"Where's he going?"

"Georgia. The south. I don't pay no attention."

He kissed her again, longer than the one before even. Then she did what he 'specially liked—she reached down and gave his cock a good hard squeeze.

His hands moved all the way around and she made a little motion with her head toward the door.

They went inside. She sat down on the bed and took off her shoes and jeans. She had violet panties on. Dwayne kicked off his shoes and pulled off his T-shirt, then helped her off with hers. Her nipples were shaped like those miniature marshmallows, and he leaned down, kissing one, kind of biting the other. It never seemed to hurt her. She always started to move around when he did it, squirm and moan. Her feet were still over the side of the bed, she was kind of sitting back with her hands behind her for support. He slid off the bed, kneeling on the floor between her knees and pulling her in, eating her through her panties. His tongue made her wet but she was getting wet on her own too, and he reached up and drew her panties down.

"Here," he said.

"What?"

He was holding his bottle of beer. "Pour it down."

"Pour what down?"

"The beer. Between your legs."

"Dwayne!"

"Just do it—easy."

She poured the beer through her thighs and cried out a little and he licked it as it trickled down. "That's good, that's nice, keep pouring."

She poured a little faster. The beer was beginning to run down his neck.

"Dwayne . . ."

"Keep doing it."

"Dwayne!"

"That's nice, keep pourin'!"

She said his name again and all at once beer flooded his head and face. She was yelling and carrying-on and he was eating her and drowning. Then she lurched violently, clamping his head with her beer-drenched thighs. Finally she relaxed a little and he could breathe again.

"Baby, guess what?"

"What, honey?" she said, her voice low.

He was soaked, grinning. "It's Miller time!"

"What's the matter, honey?"

They were sitting on the deck, each with a beer. The whole side of the cliff was in shadows but the creek, moving shallow and slow, was still catching the sun.

"Nothing," he said. "I've got a lot on my mind."

"Do you love me?"

He twisted in the chair, facing her. "Of course. What do you think, I don't love you?"

"I just asked."

She put her hand on his forearm. "Do you think we could have a baby? I mean, when we get married."

"You bet. A couple of them."

She smiled. "I never wanted kids with Chuck."

"Who would?" How she was rubbing his arm felt nice.

"Our first year, I got caught," Sadie said. "I never told him, I just had it took care of."

"And you ain't been caught since?"

"After the first time I went on the pill."

Dwayne picked up his beer and took a swig. "How'd you meet Chuck? What did you ever see in him?"

"It was in a place in Port Charlotte—where me and my girlfriend used to go after I left home. This guy comes up and asks me to dance. He was short but he had a look—I can't explain it. He was a sharp dresser then—my girlfriend thought he looked like Jimmy Cagney. We danced and he bought me a drink and we danced some more. Then this other guy comes up and starts talking to me and he's twice Chuck's size almost, and Chuck don't like it. He tells him to back off. And the big guy, who I really could of liked, thought about it and backed off."

"Then what happened?"

"We started going out."

"Was he working?"

"No, he was looking around. He'd just got out of the marines."

"Chuck was in the marines?"

"Yeah."

"What was his rate?"

"His rate?"

"What was he in the marines?"

"I don't know. He don't ever talk about it."

"What he was?"

"The marines."

"Then how do you know he was in?"

"He has one of those security boxes, and this one time he went on the road and left it open. I saw his discharge—it said Medical Discharge. Then another paper said he'd been to a naval hospital."

"What for?"

"Something mental, I don't remember. Observation."

They were quiet for a while. Below, where the water trickled past the big stones, patches of foam glistened. Sadie reached out and held his hand. "Why don't we get a place together, honey?"

"We will. We're gettin' married, ain't we? We just can't right now."

"I could get a separation and one of them protection orders—"

"That's not it."

"Are you worried Chuck would make trouble—?"

He gave a laugh. "I'd *like* for Chuck to make trouble."

"Then what is it? When you were working at Agway you weren't making enough, you said. Now you're a policeman and making good money and got benefits besides."

"I can't explain it," he said.

"Would it look bad—I mean because you're a police officer and I'm married?"

"That's got nothing to do with it. Lawyers and doctors can do shit like that, cops can't?"

"It's just so awful for me," she said. "If I only knew when we could really start being together, I could stand it better."

He leaned across, put his arms around her. "I love you, baby— just hold on."

"For how long?"

"Until after Bradley's trial."

"What does that have to do with *us?*"

He suddenly felt warm. "It's complicated. Just remember what I've always said—you know me to say hello to. That's *it*. It's not likely the police will be asking you any more questions, but if that private investigator comes around again, remember—"

"I would never say nothin', Dwayne."

"Good. We're neighbors. Hello. Good morning. Nice day."

"I'm glad we're neighbors," Sadie said.

He kissed her. "Want another beer?"

She didn't answer right away. "Where'd you ever learn that?"

"What?"

"That Miller Time business."

"I never learned it. It just came to me. Why?"

"It gave me a headache."

"Sorry."

"No, it was unbelievable!"

He laughed, then left and came back with a new beer. They sat without talking for a few minutes. Then Sadie said, "Remember how I'd always tell you about Mrs. Bradley and how she thought her husband was seeing someone?"

"You told me a little about it, I guess."

"I told you everything, Dwayne."

"What about it?" he said.

"I don't know, it's just odd—that what happened, *happened*. Do you know what I mean?"

"Not really."

"I can't explain it. Like I lived it before I seen it."

"That's why they're still knocking on your door," he said, "asking questions."

"I can't believe he did it, though," she said.

"I wouldn't weep no tears," Dwayne said. "Maybe you clean their house but you don't really know the family."

"You can't say nothin' against Mrs. Bradley!"

"I don't mean her—"

"Mr. Bradley always treats me nice too."

"It's an act," he said, feeling the old anger come back. "The old man treated people nice too, but when push come to shove he stepped all over them. I was just thinking about it, Sadie.

They offered my dad a big thousand dollars when by every right he should've got one hundred thousand! The machinery was dangerous and the modifications to improve it was never done. Because it would've cost money. They said my father was drunk. Don't talk to me about the Bradleys. Leonard Bradley, today, ain't no different. Believe me. He's just a younger version of his father—and that Tony Bradley don't fool no one selling firewood."

"That stuff with your father happened so long ago, honey."

"Tell Dutch that. The money he never saw sent Tony Bradley to Cornell and Harvard. Maybe I could've went to Cornell or Harvard. But I went to 'Nam and fought for my country and saw a lot of men die. I never kicked about it and never will, because I had a job to do, but it was a nightmare. I did some things in 'Nam I'm not proud of but more I am proud of, and when I come back to serve my community, they threw the same shit up to my face they did when I left as a kid—the same lousy shit!"

"It wasn't the Bradleys that kept you off the force—"

"But it always goes back to them," Dwayne said, "because that's where it really started. Do you know what it's like when you're a kid to see your father with a couple of his fingers missing and all you see is a stump? It's like they cut off more than his fingers. That's not good for a boy to see, Sadie—and it's hard for a man to forget."

"But you *got* to forget, honey. You're a police officer now, people look up to *you*."

He didn't say anything. He *was* an officer now, but last spring when he'd got turned down he'd thought that was it for the only job he'd ever wanted—well, if they didn't want him on the force he'd show them something the town wouldn't soon forget. Especially Mr. Leonard Bradley. It was a knife scratch on ice anyway, that's all it was, the difference between a cop and a criminal—and if you could be good at one you could be goddamn good at the other. Dwayne stared out at the woods behind the cabin. A red squirrel, probably the same one, was bitching again in the hemlock.

PART TWO

Chapter **15**

"How long have you been with the Winwar police?"

"Eleven years."

"And now you're second-in-command."

"Yes, sir."

"How many officers constitute your department?"

"We went up to twenty-one last fall."

The district attorney slid a thumb casually beneath his belt. "Is it common practice, Lt. Bock, for a police force of twenty-one officers—there are smaller departments in the state but surely Winwar isn't large—to conduct the investigation into a crime of the magnitude of Mrs. Bradley's murder?"

"I wouldn't say it's common practice. Most small-town forces would turn this kind of case over to outside agencies. Usually the state police."

"In this regard, what makes the W.P.D. different?"

In the tan-and-brown uniform of the department, perfectly tailored to his tall, lean body, Lt. Bock looked every inch a competent, confident, officer of the law. "It's just the way we are," he said. "Like some people are energetic and have a lot of pride and others are lazy and content to lay around. But if you want a specific reason—it's Chief Flick. He's made the W.P.D. what it is, it's taken time and a tremendous amount of effort on his part—he's the kind of chief that doesn't like depending on anyone, except himself and his officers. We're all well trained in our jobs, we have three officers in school right now. We won the Governor's Award last year, for the third time. Only four departments in the state have ever won it *twice*."

"How would you describe the W.P.D. lab?"

"Basic—but a whole lot better than most small forces have. We've built it up through the years. The Winwar Town Board's always been generous in providing us funds."

"Getting down to specifics, lieutenant. Did your lab make any tests with regard to the evidence now before this court?"

"Yes, sir, we did. We made an initial comparison of the soil found on the sole of the defendant's boot with the soil at the scene of the murder. Then we compared both these samples with the bits of soil found on the carpet in Mr. Bradley's house on the day his wife was first reported missing."

"Why do you say initial comparison?"

"Because the state lab made the final one. Our tests were visual, using a microscope—they made a chemical analysis."

"In your opinion, Lt. Bock, which is a better test for ascertaining similarity in soil samples?"

"They're both important, you need both. You could take soil from a murder site and someone's front hall, say, and determine their chemical make-ups to be the same. But it wouldn't prove that much if soil of similar chemical make-up existed *elsewhere* in the area. Do you see what I'm saying? So you also look for physical characteristics, which the eye sees."

"And what did 'the eye' see in the soil: at the murder site in the woods near Plutarch Pond; in the front foyer in Bradley's home; and clinging to the sole of his boot?"

"Identical characteristics."

"Did *your* eye see these 'identical characteristics?'"

"Yes, sir."

William Woolever walked over to his table and picked up a heavy-gauge glass dish divided into three parts and sealed with a transparent plastic cover. The D.A. brought the dish to the center of the floor. "I would like to introduce Exhibit A into evidence."

Judge Cruikshank nodded; the D.A. then held the plate for the witness to examine. "What do you see here, Officer Bock?"

"I see soil, bits of dirt—three separate samples."

"Can you identify these samples?"

"Yes, I can. It's the soil we just spoke of, taken from the murder site, Bradley's foyer carpet and his upland hunting boot."

"How did you determine these samples to be identical?"

"The color is the same, a chalky kind of light brown. The texture of all three samples is gritty, sandlike. And in each sample we have identical foreign materials—bits of broken glass, oxidized metal and particles of ash."

"One last question about the soil, lieutenant. Why is the amount labeled Scene of Crime considerably more abundant than the amounts labeled Upland Boot and Bradley Foyer Carpet?"

"The boot and carpet amounts are what we actually discovered on Bradley's boot and carpet, not all that much—on the carpet, very little. From the murder location, on the other hand, we filled a jar."

William Woolever, as if showing off a valuable possession, carried the dish to the jury box, holding it for each man and woman to see. Then he deposited it on the table adjacent to the table holding the state's remarkable display. "Before I ask your professional opinion, Lt. Bock, as to what the similarity of the three soil samples show or indicate, I'd like to talk about a second piece of evidence directly related to Exhibit A."

Woolever went closer to the witness. "What procedures does an investigating team take when a body is found in the middle of nowhere—say in the mountains? How do they differ from the steps taken if a body is found in a house or a room in a house?"

"Generally speaking," Lt. Bock said, "the less confining the space, the greater the difficulty in coming up with clues. You know, it's easier finding a needle in a tuft of grass than a haystack."

"Could you explain how you went about your investigation of Mrs. Bradley? I mean, once her body was discovered."

"The body was the focal point, we worked outward in concentric circles—the first circle extended out to 500 feet, the second 1,000 feet, and the third as far as we wanted to go. Then we made up teams of three or four deputies with a Winwar officer in charge—and we gave each team a section, you might say a pie-shaped area, to search. I was in contact with each officer in charge via two-way radio."

"Was anything discovered in the first circle?"

"Yes, sir—a Smith and Wesson revolver, but this was before we formed the teams. Our evidence handler, Sgt. O'Shea, found the weapon shortly after arriving on the scene."

"Was the gun identified?"

"Yes. It matched the make and description of the revolver missing from Mr. Bradley's collection—an Army/Navy .38 special from the last century. Later that same day we matched its serial number to the number in Bradley's log."

"Isn't the serial number everything? How could you say identification was made *before* matching numbers?"

"Because Chief Flick had jotted down the number when he'd visited Bradley the evening his wife, and the revolver, were reported missing. He checked his notebook and the number matched the numbers on the weapon Sgt. O'Shea had just uncovered."

"What did you conclude from these matching numbers?"

"Nothing more than we could, that the revolver belonged to Mr. Bradley."

"What do you mean, 'than we could'?"

"Mr. Woolever, when you find a corpse in a remote area and laying fifteen feet away is a handgun, even the most conservative agent is going to let their mind run a little. Some things just fit. But you can't *say* it's the murder weapon just because it's found close by."

"Was proof established that the .38 special found near Mrs. Bradley's body *was* the murder weapon?"

"I didn't take the slug from her head, I didn't run the ballistics on it, but I read the Medical Examiner's report and studied the tests performed by the state lab. To answer your question, proof was established—yes."

"Is this the weapon?"

The district attorney went to his table and picked up a chromed handgun with a checkered walnut grip. He walked over to the witness and let him examine it. "Yes," said the officer.

Woolever returned to his table and picked up a long green ledger, asking Lt. Bock to identify it, then carried it to the jury box and handed it to the foreman, Ron Zack, the assistant manager of Bancroft Home Heating, pointing out the specific entry. "Lt. Bock, please read the number from the gun," Woolever said.

"7-9-9."

"Yes, sir—it corresponds," said the foreman.

"Thank you, Mr. Zack."

Woolever turned to the judge. "At this point, Your Honor, I would like to introduce as evidence Exhibit B, the murder weapon, and Exhibit C, Mr. Bradley's personal log, which establishes his ownership of said weapon."

The D.A. placed the gun and log on the table next to the glass dish. "Now then, Officer Bock, was anything else discovered in the so-called first circle?"

"No, sir."

"In the 'second circle'?"

"No, sir."

"In the 'third'?"

"Yes, sir. Search Team 6, led by Officer Burt Diehl, found shoe imprints and some cloth fibers."

"Simultaneously?"

"No. Officer Diehl saw the shoe prints and radioed in. One of his deputies found a tuft of tan material snagged on a bush a few minutes later while Sgt. O'Shea and I were en route. There's a small parking area for the Brenner Heights swimming hole. Sgt. O'Shea pulled in, parked—then we went past the swimming hole and followed the creek, and that's where we met Officer Diehl, Kocsis and the other deputy in Search 6, Dwayne McManus."

"Then what happened?"

"First Diehl showed us the prints, then the tuft of material."

"What did you do then?"

"O'Shea photographed the prints."

"Which way were they pointing, Lt. Bock—*toward* the old burned-down foundation, where the body was found, or *away* from it?"

"Toward it, roughly speaking."

"Why roughly speaking?"

"The prints weren't pointing straight at the foundation, they were following the creek—but if you were going to walk from the swimming hole to the foundation it's how you'd go."

"Why wouldn't you go straight, as the crow flies?"

"You'd be going over a lot of rough terrain, there'd be no point to it. Farther along the creek an old trail comes in—it leads to the hut."

"Were any other shoe prints found in the area beside the two already mentioned?" Woolever asked.

"One other—I came across it myself."

"What direction was *it* pointing?"

"Roughly toward the swimming-hole parking lot."

"Was it similar to either of the first two?"

"It was identical to the largest of those two."

"So you found a large and a small print pointing *away* from the parking area, and just one large print pointing *toward* it."

"Yes, sir."

"What did Sergeant O'Shea do after he took photographs of the shoe prints?"

"He made moulages of them—plaster casts."

"Is that difficult?"

"It's a touchy business, very tricky—yes, sir. Especially because when you make the cast you destroy the print. It's why you take all the photographs first, in case the moulage doesn't turn out."

Woolever was standing close to the witness, talking with him as if having a personal conversation. "And how did Sergeant O'Shea's casts turn out?"

"Perfect."

"Your Honor," the D.A. said to the judge, "I'd like to introduce Exhibits D, E and F into evidence: the plaster casts made of the shoe prints discovered in the vicinity of Brenner Heights, Winwar Township; and Exhibit G, the corresponding photographs of these prints."

Judge Cruikshank gave a nod, and Woolever went to the table and picked up one of the larger casts, which he showed to the witness, then to the jurors. The cast was identified with the words: "Bradley's Boot—Heading North." The D.A. then picked up a second moulage labeled: "Bradley's Boot—Heading South." Lt. Bock, when questioned, said the two prints were made by one and the same article of footwear; the measurements, the sole design, even distinct markings on the sole, were identical.

Woolever put the moulages down and asked the police officer if he would make a sketch of Brenner Heights and the surrounding area, putting in points of interest such as the swimming hole, the parking area, the creek, the loggers' trail, the foundation of the old hut and Plutarch Pond Road—and of course points of the compass.

The policeman stood and crossed to the chalkboard positioned near the jury box. Carefully, Bock made the drawing. Pleased with himself, he returned to the witness stand.

Woolever looked at the sketch. "Then 'heading north' means walking away from the parking area into the woods, and 'heading south' back toward the parking lot."

"Yes, sir."

"So both a large and small foot print were discovered going into the woods, heading north; but heading south you found only a single large print."

"That's correct."

The district attorney walked to his table, spoke momentarily to his angular-faced assistant, Rhonda Fisch, then picked up the last plaster cast. "Is this imprint familiar to you?" he asked Lt. Bock.

"Yes, sir, it is."

"How so?"

"It was made from a print near the one we just looked at."

"We've examined *two* prints so far, lieutenant—one heading north, one heading south. Which do you mean?"

"The one heading north—going into the woods."

"And how near is *near*, as you just said."

"Exactly five feet."

"Who made this smaller print, Lt. Bock?"

"Mrs. Bradley."

"What do you base this on?"

"The shoe she was wearing on her right foot when we examined the body matched the print in the woods."

"Of which this is the cast?" The D.A. held up the moulage.

"Yes, sir."

With his other hand Woolever picked up a sturdy brown brogue for the witness, judge and jury to see, introducing it as evidence. "Lt. Bock, is this the shoe, or one of the shoes, Mrs. Bradley had on when her body was found?"

"Yes, it is."

"How can you be certain the shoe and this cast are the same?"

"They fit together, to start with."

The D.A., as if he had never done it before, positioned the shoe in the plaster cast. Bock said, "You'll notice there isn't any play between shoe and cast. By itself this wouldn't constitute proof, because a woman's size 7 is common. Still, it's the first thing you check—size. What you need is a distinct mark, one you couldn't likely call coincidence."

"Does such a mark exist here?"

"Yes, sir. On the heel is a new nylon plate, to cut wear. Mrs. Bradley had just picked up her shoes at Luigi's Repair Shop in Winwar. The nylon plate stands out clearly in the cast."

Woolever showed the jury both the shoe and the moulage, then carefully set them down and moved to the evidence table and picked up a man's ankle-height boot. "Is this item of footwear familiar to you, Officer Bock?"

"It's the upland boot belonging to Leonard Bradley."

"How do you know it belongs to Mr. Bradley?"

"It was taken from his closet in his house—on a search warrant."

"That means—unless you violated the warrant—you went to his house *looking* for a shoe or boot. Is that correct?"

"Yes, sir."

"Why would you want to enter Mr. Bradley's house to look

for a shoe? I'm sure the judge who issued the warrant asked that question."

"Things were adding up, Mr. Woolever. We had the murder weapon—it belonged to Mr. Bradley. We had a detective's report that Mr. Bradley was keeping company with a woman, Diane Wirth by name, in New York City. Then we had those shoe prints and that tuft of tan material. Judge LaValle considered this sufficient cause and issued the warrant, and Sgt. O'Shea and I carried it out the next morning."

"Did you find what you were looking for?"

"We did."

Woolever picked up one of the large plaster casts, and now holding cast and boot approached the witness. "Are you positive that this article of footwear made this imprint?"

"I'm one hundred percent positive. The size, like I already said, is the same—that's the first thing. Second, take a look at the lug formation—it's an exact match. Third, if you look close you can see the word Du Flex on the instep of the cast. It appears on the boot proper. And last, a certain mark—something like a fishhook—appears on the cast and also on the sole."

As the officer spoke, the D.A.'s eyes went back and forth between sole and moulage; then he carried the boot and cast to the jurors for their inspection and finally put them beside the other articles already entered as evidence. Next he picked up the glass dish. "Lt. Bock, we've established that these three soil samples are one and the same. The soil at the murder site, on the hunting boot and on Bradley's carpet. Please identify the boot you brushed the soil from."

"Behind you on the table—the one we just looked at."

The district attorney paused. He'd played the hand. Now all that remained for him was to rake in the pot. "Lt. Bock," he said, "you also found a pair of trousers in Mr. Bradley's house when you exercised your warrant. However—largely because the lab tests on this garment were performed by a different agency— I'm putting off entering the trousers as evidence at this time."

He came close to the witness. "But from your testimony and from the evidence discussed *so far*, I'd like to ask you a final question. Lieutenant, just from the shoe and boot prints—as we've examined them in this court—would you say certain *identifiable* people had walked in the woods in the vicinity of Brenner Heights?"

"Yes. Mr. Bradley and his wife."

"Is there any doubt in your mind about this?"

"No. None."

"How would you describe that walk? Where did it start?"

"We can only guess where it started, probably in the parking area for the swimming hole. But it followed Brenner Heights Creek and ended up at the burned-down hut."

"From this evidence—the soil, the prints, the weapon—could you tell us what you believe happened on the afternoon of September 23?"

"Mr. and Mrs. Bradley drove to Brenner Heights. There's no way of determining if he had her hostage or if they were merely taking a drive and a stroll, like a couple might do on a fall day. They walked past the swimming hole, along the creek, branched off at the old loggers' trail and followed it to the site of the burned-down hut. He then raped and murdered her."

"Or vice versa."

"Or vice versa."

"Thank you, Lt. Bock."

The district attorney turned to the bench. "I have no further questions, Your Honor."

Judge Cruikshank scribbled some notes on a pad of paper, then, as if pitying the defense lawyer his job, he gave Chet a long, slow look. "Mr. Evers, you may cross-examine."

Chet stood up and walked toward the witness. "Lt. Bock," he said, stopping ten feet away, "you have expressed yourself very well—the soil particles, the .38 Army/Navy revolver, the prints and plaster casts and corresponding boot and shoe . . . it all adds up, doesn't it?"

"Yes, sir."

"As to what?"

"As to what I just said."

"What did you just say?"

"Are you asking me to repeat what I just told the district attorney?"

"Yes. Please repeat it."

The officer folded his arms across his chest. "I said that Leonard Bradley was in Brenner Heights with his wife. They walked to the old foundation where Mr. Bradley raped and killed Mrs. Bradley."

Chet moved to the evidence tables and studied the display, like a man trying to decide on a wallet or a watch for his father-in-law. "This upland hunting boot," he said, hefting it, "as we all know was taken from Mr. Bradley's closet by the Winwar police. Lt. Bock"—Chet set the boot back down—"in your opinion is Exhibit H, the boot, an important piece of evidence?"

"Yes. Very."

"Why?"

"Because it places Mr. Bradley in the area of Brenner Heights and more precisely at the scene of the crime."

"Where he raped and murdered his wife. Or vice versa."

"Take your pick, Mr. Evers."

There was a smile from the D.A.'s table. In the back of the room, media artists were sketching away. The jurors looked on as if wondering what the defendant's lawyer was up to.

Chet Evers said, "Lt. Bock, what was your reaction when you determined that the larger prints in the woods were made by Leonard Bradley's hunting boot?"

"I figured we were getting somewhere."

"Would it be fair to say you were excited?"

"Yes."

"Why were you excited?"

"Counselor, you seem to going around in circles," interrupted the judge. "Kindly endeavor to move *forward* with your argument."

Chet acknowledged the comment. "Lieutenant, you told this court no doubt existed in your mind that Leonard Bradley and his wife walked together along Brenner Heights Creek. Is that correct?"

"Yes, sir."

"Their walk led them to the old foundation, is that correct?"

"Yes."

"Are you willing to go on record, Lt. Bock, as to say what happened next?"

"I already have."

"Please say it again."

Lt. Bock inhaled and gave his head a small shake of incredulity. "Mr. Bradley raped and shot, or shot and raped, his wife."

Chet half-faced the witness, half-faced the evidence table. "Then the man who wore that hunting boot in the woods on September 23 murdered Mrs. Bradley."

"Yes."

"Would you point to that man and name him."

"Leonard Bradley." The officer extended his arm. "Right there."

William Woolever looked dumbfounded but, for all that, delighted. "If the court will bear with me, I'd like to conduct a small experiment at this time," Chet said. "It involves the defendant. During the course of the experiment I'll ask Mr. Bradley a single yes-no question."

"Is it germane? Because I've already had enough of what appears to be an *un*germane line of questioning," the judge put in.

"Yes, sir."

"Well, then—go ahead."

Chet returned to his table and from a cardboard box lying on the floor beneath it slid out a plastic pan like the ones used to contain cat litter. This pan, however, contained a dark soil. He carried the pan to the jury box, displaying it, then set it on the floor in front of the witness. "Mr. Bradley, would you please step forward here?"

Leonard stood and came out from behind the table. Chet instructed him to place his foot in the pan, which he did. "Please be seated, Mr. Bradley." Then to Lt. Bock, "Now, what do we have here?"

"A foot print."

"Who made it?"

"Mr. Bradley."

"Notice the distinct nature of the sole," Chet said. "It has a minute ripple to it, a little like lands and grooves."

The police officer was looking down but remained silent.

"Do you see what I'm referring to, officer?"

"Yes."

"Could you make a moulage of this print?"

"Probably."

"Why just probably?"

"The soil is very loose—it might crumble—but in all likelihood we could make a moulage."

"Then what would you have?"

"We'd have a cast, a moulage."

"What would your next step be—say this was crucial evidence."

"To try and find the shoe."

"And if you found the shoe?"

"We'd know who made the print."

"And if that knowledge was *germane* to your case, you'd have a first-class piece of evidence, wouldn't you?"

"Yes, we would."

With the edge of an envelope taken from his inner jacket pocket, Chet leaned down and smoothed out the imprint in the soil. He went back to the table and moved his chair from behind to a place in front of it. Leonard did the same. Chet then took off his left shoe and placed it on the floor. Leonard took off his left shoe and handed it to his attorney, who inquired if, in fact, it was the defendant's.

"Yes," Leonard answered.

Chet put on Leonard's shoe and tied the lace. "Not a bad fit," he said, standing up. "A little snug, maybe."

He went up to the kitty-litter pan and placed his left foot inside. "Now, Lt. Bock," he said, "again, what do we have?"

"A foot print."

"Correct. And if you were to make a successful cast of it, what would you have then?"

"A cast of the sole."

"And if you had an idea where this shoe was—say in *whose closet*—what would you then know, if the cast and the sole matched?"

The district attorney was on his feet. "Your Honor, I object! Mr. Evers is leading the witness down a spurious road. Facts are facts. His suppositions—his game playing—have no bearing on the actual events!"

Chet stood with his head bowed. If the judge sustained, he could kiss his defense goodbye. He just kept staring down, waiting.

"Objection overruled. Continue, counselor."

His eyes didn't rise to the bench, even for a moment; they went straight to the face of Dave Bock. "If you saw this print in the woods, lieutenant—this print here"—Chet pointed down with his finger—"and you made a cast of it and then successfully matched the cast to the shoe, what would you then know?"

The lieutenant did not answer. He was looking directly at Chet but did not say a word. "Let me help, officer," Chet said. "Would you know who made the print?"

The witness remained silent.

"Well, *would you?*"

"You'd have an idea," the police officer said.

"You would, that's true. But would it be right or wrong? In this particular instance." Chet again pointed at the soil.

"This isn't the instance that concerns us," Bock said. "We're talking about a print found on Brenner Heights, not one fabricated in a courtroom—"

"I like your choice of words: fabricated. Thank you. Then answer me this . . . did the man who owns this shoe—" Chet lifted his left foot, pulling up his trouser leg—"did the man who owns *this* shoe make *that* print?" He jabbed at the box of soil.

"It has no bearing—"

"Did the man who owns this shoe make that print?"

The D.A. was on his feet. "Your Honor, defense is bullying the witness, trying to make him answer a question which isn't a question but a trick—"

"Overruled," Judge Cruikshank said gruffly. "I do not consider the witness a damsel in distress. Lt. Bock, you've been asked a direct question. Answer it. Counselor, repeat the question."

"Did the man who owns this shoe make that print?"

"No."

"Who was it made by?"

"Someone else."

"And is it possible, Lt. Bock, that these prints"—he crossed quickly to the exhibit table and pointed at the two larger moulages—"that these prints discovered on Brenner Heights on the afternoon of October first were similarly made by someone else? Someone who borrowed Mr. Bradley's hunting boots, as I've just borrowed one of his street shoes?"

"The circumstances—"

"No circumstances. Is it possible?"

The officer's left eye twitched. He didn't answer.

"Yes or no?"

"It's possible. Yes."

Chet gave a quiet nod. "Thank you, Lt. Bock. No further questions."

Chapter 16

Sadie buttoned the lightweight wool coat that Mrs. Bradley had given her the previous year, opened the front door to
the big house she had just cleaned in the township and walked
down the flagstone path toward her car. A tennis court, which
she had never seen Mr. or Mrs. Marzocca anywhere near, was
to one side of the house. A bird was perched on the net. Dwayne
could of told her what kind but to her it just looked cold and
lost. Spring seemed awful slow in coming this year. Sadie got in
her car. The battery was low and the engine turned over weak,
but finally it caught and she drove off.

Instead of going down Main Street when she reached the village, she turned left at the Winwar Hotel. It was a quieter street,
bypassing traffic; at the stop sign where it ended she touched
her brake, then moved onto the highway. From here the trailer
park was only a mile away. But she hadn't went a hundred yards
when she spotted revolving red lights in her rear-view mirror.

Sadie pulled over. She didn't need a ticket, couldn't *afford* one,
but the cop had her dead. Then she recognized who it was. At
her window he said, "License and registration, please."

"Don't have 'em."

"You just run the stop, I'm gonna have to bring you in."

"Sounds good. You're kinda cute, officer."

"You're pretty cute yourself, miss."

She had a laugh. She loved him so much it made her weak and warm all over how he was leaning inside a little like he was. A milk tanker rumbled by. Then at once she was sad, depressed again, thinking who was back waiting for her. "This don't seem right," she said. "I should be heading up to Woodland!"

"I know."

"It was such a perfect five days for us, honey."

"It won't be much longer now," he said.

"I heard another week."

"For the trial, then you got the jury."

"When it's all over I'm never gonna let you go!"

He was just kind of looking at her, staring. He was doing that more and more lately, she seemed to think. Staring kind of funny. "You okay, Dwayne?"

He smiled, focusing better. "I drove by the house today."

"How'd it look?" she asked excitedly.

He had put a binder on it two weeks before. "Real pretty, sitting there on the hill."

"It's the prettiest house in the whole world!"

"It's gonna be ours. Listen, I gotta go."

"Just tell me one thing," she said. "You know, like you do."

"Okay. The Dutch doors it's got? It's a nice summer day and I come home and you're standing behind the bottom half, shakin' your boobs at me."

She laughed. "I love you, honey."

"I love you too, Sadie."

She touched his hand on the door, where the window was rolled down. "I'll see you."

"Hold on, we're almost there," he said.

She noticed his daughter come to the window as she pulled up behind the Freightliner. Sadie got out and waved, not that she expected Julie to wave back. She was a pretty girl but Sadie had never once seen her smile. Dwayne said she would maybe say a dozen words to him all week—mostly yes and no—

and put the blame on Julie's mother. Drugs, alcohol. Then she'd tried getting Julie into kid porn to support her habit. It killed Sadie just thinking of it. She went up her steps.

Chuck was watching a rerun of a M*A*S*H episode and swigging on a beer when she walked in, a large bag of chips by his chair. Sadie dropped her purse on a kitchen stool. She went into the living room. He had on a pair of crusty brown pants and a western shirt with plaid shoulders—the same clothes, she seemed to think, he'd had on when he'd left. She sat down on the convertible sofa with the nubby greenish brown fabric. Maybe he had shaved once in five days. Instead of an even growth, however, his whiskers were splotchy. His face looked like a cow flop.

"Well, ain't you gonna say nothin'?" he said without looking over.

"Hello."

"How's ever'thing?"

"I'm not feeling good. Mrs. Marzocca had me laying down—"

"So lay down again."

"My stomach's really actin' up."

"I got somethin' else actin' up."

"You're a mess," she said.

He finished his beer and wiped his mangy stubble with the back of his hand. "Sadie, I'll say it once—I ain't in the mood to take no shit!"

"Well, less'n you clean up I ain't gonna—"

Not aiming, just blindly, Chuck threw the empty. It missed the TV by six inches and broke against the back door of the trailer. "*Never* tell me you 'ain't gonna'! Now git in there!"

She went into the bedroom. At the window, looking out at Rt. 21, she thought of how her mother had run off with a wheel-alignment specialist and how she'd grown up with her father who bagged groceries at the local Quik Chek and carried them out for people. Then how he'd come home after working all day and sit in his chair in the shade by the fruit trees he'd planted special for her mom and never move, his toes all bruised because people were always stepping on them in the parking lot. He'd take the quarter they'd sometimes give him and hobble back inside the store—

"Why ain't you undressed?"

She turned and looked at the man she'd met, and married, after leaving home. Maybe—it never crossed her mind before—because he was so opposite to her meek-mannered father. But she didn't know, she'd never really know why she'd done it.

Sadie took off her shirt, her fingers unfastening the front catch to her bra. Then she took off the rest of her clothes. She went to the bed, but before she reached it Chuck moved toward her and spun her around, dropping to his knees, and began eating her out.

"Lay down!"

She lay down on the bed. He tore off his stiff sweaty clothes. "You like this, Sadie?" he said. "You want this?"

She didn't look. She saw it anyway—thin, bent, like a death-curve in a road; like a pit viper without eyes.

"You been waiting for this?"

He pushed forward, and in a quick stab was in. She turned her head to the side, then moved her hips in the circular motion that always got him off quick. He sucked on her nipples and she kept on grinding and soon he let out a short squeal, like a pig nipped by the barnyard dog.

Sadie lay there; he always pulled out right after. Then he would light a cigarette and swill a beer. But he didn't pull out. He raised up a little and looked at her. "Bitch, you brung me off too fast."

"That ain't my fault—"

He began pawing her breasts. "Move on it, Sadie!"

She was breathing heavy, lying still, hating it. *Him.*

"You know how to fuck, so fuck!"

Suddenly she twisted left, then right, her hands going to Chuck's shoulders and pushing out, shoving him away; simultaneously she pulled back her pelvis, freeing herself. "*You* fuck. You want to come again, stick it up your exhaust pipe."

He lunged for her. She grabbed the telephone from the night table, using the receiver as a club. Chuck took a glancing hit on the arm, then hit her on the side of the face, knocking her to the floor. Her mind was spinning, everything was blurred. She seemed to think he was crawling on top of her and spreading her legs; her head was angled against the baseboard and she was afraid her neck would break. She vaguely heard him tell her she was a good cunt, this time he was gonna get off good. Then, blessedly, she blacked out.

She smoothed the spread on Leonard Bradley's king-sized bed, then carried the wrinkled shirts and other soiled articles in his closet to the laundry alcove at the end of the hall and stuffed them in the washing machine. From the hamper she removed additional soiled clothes, put them in the machine and turned it on. Back in the master bedroom she vacuumed the thick beige carpet, dusted the furniture and straightened out the top of Mr. Bradley's dresser. In the mirror she saw her puffed, bruised face. Then, as Catherine Bradley had instructed, she went to the late Mrs. Bradley's closet and started carrying out all her things, loading up sturdy cartons in the garage. When she finished she emptied the washing machine, started the dryer and made herself a ham and tomato sandwich in the kitchen. It was 12:05. As she was putting away the utensils, she heard a car drive up.

She went to the window, thinking it might be the replacement for the police officer parked in the driveway—the next shift. But it wasn't a tan and brown cruiser that turned at the woodpile; it was a pick-up truck with big tires. It stopped next to her car, and Mr. Bradley's son got out and a dog jumped out too. As Mr. Bradley's son began walking toward the house, Sadie left the kitchen and in the living room unlocked the door and slid it open. She couldn't rightly pinpoint the expression in his eyes. She could only think it was the look of someone who'd recently had too many bad dreams.

"Thanks, Sadie."

"Hello, Mr. Bradley."

He was staring at her bruised face. "You all right?"

"I'm okay now. Would you like a sandwich?"

"Sure."

Tony took off his checkered overshirt, hung it on the back of a chair at the kitchen table while Sadie busied herself at the counter. When she brought the sandwich over he surprised her by saying she should sit down and keep him company.

"I've already had my break, Mr. Bradley."

"I won't tell." She smiled and sat down. "Where do you live, Sadie?"

"In Winwar Trailer Park. Or I did. Where do you live, Mr. Bradley?"

"Mink Hollow. Call me Tony."

Sadie brushed a crumb from the table and held it in her hand. She had something she had to say; it was burning in her chest. "I know it's very personal to you, Mr. Bradley—but I wouldn't feel right unless I told you. No matter what the papers say and all that evidence, I don't believe your father done it."

"I appreciate that, Sadie."

"I told the chief when he spoke to me last fall, your mother was the kindest woman who ever lived. It's what I told the detective too who came around." Her eyes filled. "I'm still not over it."

Tony nodded, looking at her close. "Who do you suppose might have killed her, Sadie? Did she ever mention names to you—names you didn't recognize?"

"No. I've thought about it, too. A whole lot, who could of done it."

"Why don't you think it was my father?"

"He's just too nice a man. My . . . boyfriend gets mad at me."

"How come?"

"He says I'm not looking at the facts."

"Your boyfriend sounds like the district attorney."

She gave him a little smile. As a rule she didn't like men with beards, but Tony Bradley was an awfully attractive man. She'd heard—she couldn't remember where—that his wife had left him. Maybe Catherine Bradley had said it. "What do *you* think happened?" she asked.

"I know as much today as I did last fall. I don't know."

Tony finished the first half of his sandwich. He was staring at her again, her face. "Those are pretty bad bruises, Sadie."

"My husband's a low-life, but we're finished. I left him."

"I thought maybe it was your boyfriend."

"Who hit me?"

"You said he gets mad at you."

"But he doesn't hit me!"

"I'm glad to hear it," Tony said.

As she was twisting the key in her trunk, the heavy wooden door to the cabin swung open and Dwayne talked toward her; then he just stood there, looking at her. She'd seen him upset before but never like this—so upset he didn't talk. He wrapped his arms around her, then finally she could cry. It felt so good just to let go. You would wait and wait to make love to only one man. The same was true for crying. You just couldn't do it with anyone. Dwayne carried the shopping bags inside. He had a fire going and the cabin was warm, so warm he cracked the back door a couple of inches so cool air could come in.

Sadie sat on the edge of the bed, taking off her shoes. He asked her if she'd like a beer.

"Do you have any tea?"

"Just coffee."

"Would you make me a cup, honey?"

"Sure."

She swung her feet up. He put water on. She told him everything. He stood at the little kerosene stove, listening. "... Finally he passed out," Sadie said. "I didn't want to take no suitcase and get him all suspicious right off, so I threw some stuff in a couple of bags—"

"Why didn't you leave right then?"

"You were working."

"You know where I keep the spare key."

"It was dark, I decided to wait."

He took hold of the handle and poured the boiling water. "I won't be able to stay here with you," he said.

"That's OK, I'm not worried."

Dwayne brought her the coffee. "That's easy to say. How about when I leave?"

"The trial's ending, ain't it? How long—?"

"Sadie, you got to understand something. That doesn't mean we can start going out—like right away the next day!"

"When, then?"

He sat beside her on the edge of the bed. "A lot will depend on how the verdict comes in—guilty, not guilty."

"Why is that?"

"I *told* you, you're never going to understand everything that goes on. When you're involved with a cop, that's the way it is."

She sipped her coffee. "Which verdict is better for us?"

"What do you mean?"

"For us going out together in public."

A truck was coming up the road. Dwayne waited for the sound to pass. "Guilty." He didn't want to tell her that, but now maybe she'd let it drop.

"But if he's cleared that ends the case, you can't try a person twice—"

"They'd be looking around for someone else... I'd be awfully busy... We'd have to keep going like we are."

"*Why?*"

"It just wouldn't look good—"

"What wouldn't?"

"You work for the Bradleys. I found the body—do you see what I'm saying?"

"No!"

"Well, I'm just telling you. Police are funny."

"*You're* the police, Dwayne."

"I wouldn't want it known I was seeing the Bradleys' housekeeper."

She set her cup on the small table by the bed, then swung her feet up and settled back against a pillow. "I just hate how this hangs over our heads, month after month after month!"

"Anyway, there's no way Bradley will walk," he said.

"I want us to start living."

"We will, believe me—soon."

"I love you, Dwayne. I don't think a woman could love a man more."

"I'm leaving you a gun," he said.

"A gun?"

"Just to have. It can't hurt."

"You don't have to go yet, do you?"

"No."

"Do you want a little rub?"

"You're the one who needs the rub!"

"That's okay. I'm better now. Lay down next to me, honey."

He kicked off his shoes. She put her fingers in his hair, just gentle, then rubbed his shoulders, chest, arms. "Dwayne?"

"Yes?"

"I won't bug you anymore."

"Don't worry about it."

"Just relax, honey."

"I am."

She heard him, but he was frowning; something was sure bothering him. What? Wasn't he doing what he always said he wanted? Didn't they have each other? Sadie tried to smooth out the wrinkles in his forehead. They had everything, didn't they?

It was quarter to seven when he drove up to his trailer. The Freightliner was parked in front of the Wojciechowski mobile home. Dwayne walked up his rickety steps, keeping his eyes straight. His daughter was watching TV.

His uniform, ready for tomorrow's shift, hung on the outside of his closet door. After dinner he'd polish his shoes and clean his revolver. He'd taken practice today, his hand had shook, he hadn't scored that good. He washed up, turned out the bathroom light and looked across the dingy yard. The pressure was so heavy, so unrelenting, he sometimes just wanted to leave, head for Alaska, anywhere. But he couldn't. He wasn't a man to run. Besides, it was going to work out. When they convicted Bradley he could start breathing again, start making a real life with Sadie.

Chuck came out of his trailer and stood in his doorway, staring down the road.

* * *

Since he had taken the pledge driving home from Leonard's that morning seven months ago, Adam Pohl had lost forty-one pounds; that, in itself, made physical chores—such as tying his shoes, raking the yard, or climbing the stairs in his house, as he now was doing—much less difficult for him. He felt better than he had in years, and he looked good too; everyone in his congregation was coming up and telling him. But they didn't know the tightrope he walked. And today, as he knocked lightly on his son's door, that tightrope had never been thinner, his balance on it more precarious. How easily—with his son scheduled for open-heart surgery in the morning—could he sit down with a bottle!

The boy was reading and Adam sat beside him on the bed. It was a biography. Adam asked him where he was in it, and Danny said he was at the part where Benjamin Franklin was experimenting with a new type of eyeglass, called the bifocal.

"One pair serving two purposes. It was a marvelous invention," Adam said.

"I'd like to invent something."

"If you want to, you will, Danny."

"How do you start?"

"With an idea. Ideas start everything. You also look around and see what's needed. If it's not needed, it probably won't catch on."

"Did you ever invent anything?"

Adam smiled at his son who was lying with two pillows behind his back, his chest thin, his breathing so shallow. He couldn't bear to think he might never see him again, here in this bed; but he didn't dwell on it. He had to think positively. "When I was your age we used to have a mulch pile for the garbage," he said. "It was my job to carry it out. The pile was about seventy-five yards from the back door of the house. So I rigged up this set of ropes and supports. You know what a chair lift looks like, for skiers. That was the idea. The garbage pail rode out on a big hook."

"Did it work?"

"I made the mistake of testing it with real garbage. What a mess!"

The boy laughed. "I want you to get some sleep now," his father said. "It's getting late."

Danny folded over a corner of the page and closed his book. Adam put it on his desk, then removed one of the pillows and helped the boy get comfortable. He kissed his cheek and turned off the light.

"Good night, Danny."

"Good night, dad."

At the door Adam looked back for a moment, then went downstairs. Ruth was in the den watching television, and he sat down beside her.

"How is he?" she asked.

"He's fine—it's like any other night."

"Do you think he understands? I mean, the seriousness of it?"

"We've talked about it enough. He seems to."

"That it's a life or death situation?"

"Ruth, please. He's OK."

She clicked off the set with a remote switch. "We don't have to go ahead with it."

"We don't have to but we've decided to."

"We didn't carve our decision in stone, Adam!"

He inhaled deeply. About a week ago she had started having second thoughts, looking at the operation as *he* always had—just too risky to undertake. Because he was holding on by a thread, her new position was making Adam extremely uneasy. "But it's a decision that took a long time coming," he said, "and I think at this point—"

"What if he dies?"

"We lose a beautiful son. God gains one."

"That doesn't work for me, I'm sorry!" Ruth cried out, taking her hand from his and joining it with her other, squeezing her fingers. "I don't want to lose Danny—to God or anyone!"

"Ruth, I wish you wouldn't do this," Adam said. "It's hard enough—"

"It's my child's life. I have to say what I'm feeling!"

"You've always felt we should—"

"I've had a change of heart. Is that all right?"

He leaned forward, shaking his head, emitting a low moan. Then he said, "What do you want to do?"

"We have to talk," she said.

"All right."

"Make us a drink, will you?"

"I'll make *you* one."

"For goodness' sake, one drink isn't going to kill you, Adam!"

She knew the consequences of his taking a drink, and he was surprised to hear her urging him to have one. "I don't think you understand," he said.

"Then make me one."

He walked into the kitchen and opened the corner cupboard and took down a liter of vodka, three-quarters full; exactly how he'd left it when he'd poured his last drink. He set a glass beside the bottle. From the freezer he grabbed ice cubes and dropped them into the glass. She needed a drink. His temples were pulsing, sweat was forming on his neck and chest. *She* needed a drink! As he picked up the bottle, his hand trembled. Adam poured, filling her glass; then on impulse he reached for a second glass and filled it also—and knew it was over; he saw himself calling Dr. Donaldson in the morning. They couldn't do it, he would tell the surgeon; they would pay him what they owed him, but they couldn't go through with the operation. He carried the drinks into the den and sat beside the wife.

"Thank you," she said.

Perhaps this was the way it was meant to be, Adam thought— a man's weakness, not his strength, prevailed; and it was his weakness, he told himself now, that would save his son's life. Here was the signal from God he had waited for all this time. Don't put Danny under the knife, the Lord was saying. If you want to see him again, keep him home in the morning. Drink, Adam Pohl, and spare your only son.

They both drank, then Ruth sipped quickly again. She stared at her glass. "This is water!"

Adam was scowling. "I don't understand."

"Did you take water from the tap?"

"No."

"Well, this is water!"

"It came from the bottle, Ruth."

"Vodka does not turn to water! What's going on here?" she demanded.

"I don't know."

"Well, I'd like a drink."

"There's nothing else."

"Take me out for one. We have to talk, Adam."

"We don't have to at all," he said firmly.

"Are you going to buy me a drink?"

"No."

She glared at him. "If anything happens to Danny—"

But she didn't go on. Ruth got up, grabbed her keys in the kitchen and let the back door slam. The next moment a car engine started and she drove off, too fast. He remained in the den for a few minutes, staring at the pair of ice-filled glasses; then he stood and went upstairs, pausing at Danny's door before going in and crossing to the bed.

Father Pohl stood in the shadows looking down at his sleeping son, then, closing his eyes, began softly to recite the Lord's Prayer. But when he came to the line "—thy will be done," he stopped. His eyes opened, and looking at Danny he repeated the line slowly, and went on . . .

Chapter 17

Who was the better actor, Chet Evers would've been hard pressed to say. Probably Woolever. Dr. Ernst Schmellner's forte was more in the fine art of bullshit. But because, Chet thought, acting and bullshitting overlapped, the two made an excellent team.

"Then," the D.A. was saying, restating what the witness had just offered in a long, convoluted statement, "sex and violence are closely linked, related."

"Most assuredly. Soft music, moonlight, see-through garments are erotic stimulants, to be sure—but not the only ones, Mr. Woolever. Every man, to varying degrees, feels sexual excitation by the bizarre, the unusual, the wild. A beautiful woman in chains, a lady dressed in black leather carrying a whip—there is something in the male, whether he admits to it or not, that is aroused by such manifestations, symbols if you will, of sexual violence. These symbols pull a libidinous trigger deep within his unconscious. Freud was distinctly aware of this. There is also a well-known link between sex and death—which answers, in part, the question of why rape and murder often go hand in hand. Recently I interviewed a man arrested in the death of a thirteen-year-old girl. He told me he'd been in love with her for over a year. Finally he lured her to his apartment-house roof where he forced himself upon her. Then what did he do? He pushed her off the roof. It is well known in the animal kingdom that certain species, most frequently the males, will fight to the death to win their mate; and the salmon, that most noble of fish, braves treacherous miles to fertilize the female's eggs, only to swim a short distance away afterward and die. Sex and death—and sex and killing—are historically, biologically and psychically bonded."

Woolever rubbed his smooth palms together, as if he had just applied a scented emollient. "Considering all of this, Dr. Schmellner, do you believe a man in his fifties, healthy in all regards, could have sex with his wife knowing he'd momentarily be firing a bullet into her brain?"

"Most assuredly."

The psychologist smiled a knowing smile. "I dare say, in fact, that a husband who had otherwise lost sexual interest in his mate would find himself, under these circumstances, sexually aroused to a degree unprecedented in their relationship!"

"Thank you, Dr. Schmellner," said the district attorney.

"You are the chief psychologist at Bancroft General Hospital," Chet Evers said, starting his cross-examination.

"Chief psychiatrist."

"Forgive me—I know there's a distinction there somewhere. If you'd be so kind—"

"A psychiatrist is also a doctor of medicine. His training is more extensive."

"Of course." Chet scanned the pool, looking for the perfect spot to place that first, all-important cast. "Are you married, Dr. Schmellner?"

"No."

"Were you ever?"

"Yes."

"How long ago?"

"Two years."

"Before that marriage, were you previously married?"

"Yes."

"And before *that* marriage?"

"I had a very short marriage just after medical school."

"How long were your longer marriages?"

"Four and seven years."

"In today's society," Chet said, "the way things are going, three marriages by early mid-life isn't extraordinary, is it?"

"No man or woman is ever proud of a divorce, Mr. Evers. Sometimes they're necessary."

"I didn't mean to imply they were done on whim."

Chet stared at the witness. "Was there any pattern, if I might ask, to your divorces—as to the reasons they occurred?"

"Objection! Is defense counsel writing a book, Your Honor?"

"Sustained," said Judge Cruikshank. "Counselor, such probing infringes upon the witness's rights—rephrase."

"Dr. Schmellner, who filed for these divorces—who brought the action?"

"Your Honor, I persist in my objection!" Woolever called out.

"Overruled. I see it as a question of fact. Witness will answer."

"My wives."

"Your wives. All your wives chose to divorce you," Chet said. "I won't ask why—I'd be accused of writing a book. Dr. Schmellner, what professional position did you hold before coming to Bancroft General?"

"I was director at the state mental hospital in Nashville."

"And before that?"

"I was director of counseling at the University of Maryland."

"And prior to that?"

"I had my own practice in Baltimore for nine years."

"Anything clsc?"

"Not of any significance."

"Then the year you spent at the Esalen Institute in Big Sur, California, wasn't...of any significance?"

Dr. Schmellner crossed his legs, revealing a black sock; a garter, concealed, tugged at it, like a hook snagged on a submerged log. "It was a year I took off from my private practice."

"What did you do at the Esalen Institute, doctor?"

"I was on the staff—I conducted psychotherapeutic workshops."

"Did you like working at the institute?"

"Yes...it's a dramatic, exciting place."

"Why didn't you stay on?"

"I just mentioned, it was a year I took off from my private practice—"

"So Esalen had nothing to say about it."

Ernst Schmellner made no comment. A tiny bit of spittle was beginning to form, or collect, between his lips.

"Isn't it true you were asked to leave the staff of the institute?"

"It was a mutual decision."

"What does that mean?"

"It was as much my decision as theirs."

"From their viewpoint, why were you asked to leave?"

"You'll have to ask them."

"Certainly it wasn't over how best to cultivate the carrots. I understand they have a superb vegetable garden at the institute."

It wasn't a question, and the psychiatrist didn't choose to make it one. Chet tied on a new fly. "I believe you called yourself, at that juncture, a bioenergeticist. Is that correct?"

"Yes."

"Weren't you, in fact, billed as the 'energy-man' at the institute?"

"In my workshops we tried to tap the great amount of stored-up energy in our bodies—"

"Until certain individuals, paying customers, began complaining about the highly sexual nature of your techniques—to the point where a few came right out and called your methods sado-masochistic. Isn't that correct?"

The district attorney was on his feet. "Your Honor, I object! That is pure unmitigated slander!"

"There's an easy test, isn't there, counselor?" Cruikshank spoke directly to the witness. "Dr. Schmellner, is defense counsel's last statement true or false?"

"The charge was made, but it was unfounded—there are always those in every group who are disgruntled."

"Thank you. Mr. Evers, continue."

"Then whoever made the charge was just taking shots at you, so to speak," Chet said.

"They didn't know what they were talking about."

"So what you were doing wasn't *really* s/m—it just seemed like s/m to certain individuals."

The witness made no comment.

"Do you have an overview, as it were, on sexual preference, Dr. Schmellner?"

"Whatever consenting adults do is their right."

"You reserve that right for yourself, of course."

The therapist set his jaw. He had crinkly brown hair. As he spoke the spittle between his lips coalesced, then parted; coalesced, then parted. "I consider myself an adult with an adult's—"

"Do you practice sadomasochism?"

"I refuse to answer—"

"On what grounds?"

"That my private life is nobody's business—certainly not yours."

"I disagree. Let me explain. Someone with sadomasochistic leanings might well find imminent murder sexually stimulating— but *not* your average husband of thirty-three years! Such as the defendant. So again, do you practice sadomasochism?"

"And again, that's *my business!*"

"Then tell us, do you have any others?"

Blood rushed to the psychiatrist's face, and Chet walked away.

The D.A. was ready to kill. "You may step down, Dr. Schmellner," said the judge.

She was wearing a tweed suit, tan blouse and brown leather heels. Leonard didn't remember that her hair was so short. She had probably had it cut; he liked it longer but she still looked beautiful. Her hands were folded in her lap and she was focusing her blue green eyes on the district attorney, who was standing directly before her, smiling his best, his warmest smile. He had just asked her where she lived and what she did for a living.

"I live in New York, I'm a painter of children's portraits."

"What is your marital status, Ms. Wirth?"

"Divorced."

"Do you have children?"

"A daughter, twelve."

"Besides your fees as a portrait painter, do you have any sources of income? Stocks and bonds, generous parents, alimony?"

"My ex-husband sends child support—not regularly. If and when it comes, it's two hundred a month."

"When was the last time you received this support?"

"Last summer."

"How about health insurance, life insurance?"

"No, none."

The D.A. stepped back, as if to allow the jurors a better view of the witness. "Ms. Wirth," he said after a moment, "do you know an individual named Leonard A. Bradley?"

"Yes."

"In what capacity?"

"We were friends."

"Is that a modern-day euphemism for lovers?"

"I've never thought of Leonard as my lover—"

"But he was. Wasn't he?"

"No."

"Well, when he visited you did you make love?"

"Yes."

"Then why wasn't he your lover?"

"I don't like that term. The connotation."

The district attorney smiled. "Are you and Mr. Bradley still friends?"

"I like to think so."

"Do you still see each other?"

"No, we haven't seen each other since last fall."

"How did you meet?"

"At a cocktail party in Manhattan."

"Did you know he was married?"

"He wore a wedding band."

"When did you see each other a second time?"

"He called me from his office a few days later, saying he was coming back to the city the following week—could we have dinner."

"And you accepted the invitation."

"Yes."

"Did it bother you that he was married?"

"It crossed my mind. It didn't bother me."

"Would you have liked it more if he *wasn't* married?"

"No."

"Why is that?"

"It kept our relationship simpler."

"Simpler?"

"Because Leonard was married, it helped define our relationship. Prevented it from getting too complicated."

"Where he might start sending you expensive jewelry, that kind of thing," the district attorney offered.

"One can send a gift and still keep a relationship simple," Diane said.

"If the gift is, say, a blouse. But what if the gift is an emerald and diamond necklace?"

"It's a gold necklace, Mr. Woolever, with a few diamonds and emeralds—"

"So you have other necklaces more costly, Ms. Wirth—with diamonds and emeralds all the way around."

"I didn't say that."

"Do you have *any* jewelry more valuable than the necklace Mr. Bradley gave you?"

"I'm not sure. I haven't had it all appraised."

Woolever smiled. "By the way, was there a special occasion for the gift? Your birthday, perhaps?"

"We had known each other for six months."

The district attorney walked to his evidence table and picked up an oblong box, opened it and told the judge he was introducing as Exhibit J the costly necklace Mr. Bradley had presented to Ms. Wirth the previous September. He brought the box over, asked her if it were the necklace in question, then took it out of its box and showed it to the jurors. When he had finished displaying the jewelry he returned it to its box and laid the box on the exhibit table.

"Do you know what Mr. Bradley paid for this necklace?" he asked Diane Wirth from a distance.

"No, I don't."

"$8,300. Plus a goodly sales tax. I have the American Express sales slip, your honor—Exhibit K."

Woolever drew it from an envelope and showed it to the jurors, then placed the slip and envelope beside the oblong box. "I wouldn't want to make an $8,300 necklace something it isn't, Ms. Wirth. You're absolutely right, it's more gold than precious stones—but it's still quite special, I'd say."

He came back slowly toward the witness. "Not something one casually gives somebody after just knowing them for a few months."

"I never suggested it was."

"Then you placed some importance on your relationship with Mr. Bradley," Woolever said.

"A great deal of importance."

"When he would come to New York, what sort of things would you do?"

"We'd go to movies, concerts, have dinner. A couple of times we went to the ball park."

"Shea? The Stadium?"

"Leonard liked the Yankees, so we went to the Stadium."

"How about the theater?"

"We went once."

"What did you see?"

"An off-Broadway production of *The Iceman Cometh.*"

"The last time you saw each other, do you remember where you went for dinner?"

"Four Seasons."

The District Attorney of Cooper County nodded and smiled. "What a nice time, all in all, you had with Mr. Bradley. Are you *sure* you didn't want to marry him?"

"Yes . . ."

"Why?"

"I was married once—unhappily—and I didn't want to risk it again."

"You were content, then, just to be a wealthy man's mistress—"

"Objection! The term is biased and doesn't at all state the relationship!" said Chet.

"Sustained."

"From what you knew of Mr. Bradley in the six months you were friends," the D.A. went on, "do you think *he* wanted to marry *you?*"

"We never discussed it. He was married."

"But the day after giving you a beautiful necklace he asked his wife for a divorce! Why, if he didn't want to marry you?"

"Perhaps to have more freedom."

"Oh, he said that to you?"

"I knew it to be true."

"Once he had this freedom, what was he going to do with it?"

"I don't know."

"I believe you do know! Come, Ms. Wirth, was he going to start hanging out at the college bars in Winwar, do you suppose?"

She did not reply.

"What was he going to do with his new freedom, Ms. Wirth?"

"I don't know."

"Then I'll tell you—"

"Objection. To say what Mr. Bradley would do—"

"Sustained."

William Woolever cupped his hand and pointed his fingers at his chest. "Myself," he said, "if it were me, and I suddenly had a whole lot of new freedom, and there was a woman in the picture as attractive as you—I'd spend it knocking on her door, pursuing her. But that's only me, or most any other male. No, Mr. Bradley's not the aggressive sort, he doesn't run companies, he doesn't make decisions affecting the lives of a thousand people...he'd spend *his* new freedom sitting in a chaise in his backyard watching the gray squirrels. Is that it, Ms. Wirth?"

No reply.

The district attorney linked his fingers, twisted his hands so the palms were facing down and gave a small push. "Ms. Wirth," he said, "do you know an individual named Barry Abrams?"

"Yes."

"Would you tell the court who he is?"

"He's...an ex-boyfriend of mine."

"Time out." Woolever made a T with his hands. "I see we're facing a semantic problem here. Mr. Abrams was a boyfriend.

Mr. Bradley simply a friend. Can you help us out as to the distinction?"

"Barry is three years younger than me, Leonard is twelve years older—that's probably why I said it—"

"So older men can never be boyfriends. Just younger ones."

"I don't see what the point of this is," Diane said.

"Would Barry Abrams ever call you at your apartment when Leonard was there?"

"There were times he did."

"Was he ever at your apartment when Mr. Bradley would call you?"

"Rarely...but there were times."

"Would that cause Mr. Bradley any concern?"

"Mr. Bradley and I had no commitment. He was a married man, sometimes we wouldn't see each other for three or four weeks. He never dictated—never attempted to dictate—what I should do, whom I should see."

"Because he knew you would have left him!"

"I was never *with* him in that sense—"

"Stopped seeing him then."

"If he had attempted to lay down the law, perhaps. But Leonard never did that. He's not that sort of person—"

"Deep down, Ms. Wirth, how do you think he was feeling, knowing Barry Abrams might drop by your apartment an hour after he left?"

"That never happened."

"When Mr. Bradley would visit you in New York, would he ever spend the night with you?"

"No."

"Was it his decision that he should leave or yours?"

"His."

"Based on?"

"His wife would often call his hotel room at eleven o'clock, he liked being there when she called."

"*Liked* being there?"

"Well, wanted to be there."

"And he never varied from this practice?"

"No, he would always leave my apartment at 10:40 sharp."

"Solely to answer the phone if his wife called."

"Yes, I believe so."

"How did he feel about this situation?"

"It frustrated him, I think. But that's only natural—"

"'Frustrated him'." Woolever cut off her attempt to recoup. "Tell me, do you still see Mr. Abrams?"

"No."

"You loved him, didn't you?"

"Yes..."

"It must have driven poor Mr. Bradley crazy, knowing you still loved your old boyfriend."

"When I knew Leonard, I didn't love Barry the way I *had* loved him."

"But you still loved him."

"Barry was, and is, a very special person."

"Still dear to you at the time you were seeing Mr. Bradley."

"Yes..."

"Did you convey those sentiments to Mr. Bradley?"

"He knew how I felt."

"How did that make him feel?"

"He wasn't pleased."

At the defense table Chet Evers ran the fingers of his left hand across his chin, then scratched the side of his face.

"How about jealous? Was he jealous? Threatened?"

"Not overly."

"To a degree?"

"Perhaps."

"Feeling threatened and jealous are strong emotions," the D.A. said. "Add these emotions to the *frustration* Mr. Bradley was already feeling, it's a wonder he didn't run amok on the streets. Or worse."

"Objection!"

"Sustained."

"Mr. Bradley wanted you all to himself, didn't he?" said Woolever.

"He was willing to go along with the way things were."

"For how long?" said the district attorney. "No man, in love with a woman, wants to share her forever! Leonard Bradley was being pushed to the limit, both at home and in New York, he felt compelled to act—"

"Your Honor, the assumptions being made here are incredible!" said Chet.

"There is some basis for the assumptions, however," said the judge. "The witness has testified that Mr. Bradley was frustrated, jealous—"

"To a degree," said Chet. "Mr. Woolever is implying the defendant was an emotional basket case!"

"I'm overruling your objection, Mr. Evers. Mr. Woolever—"

"No more questions," said the district attorney, giving Chet a grateful smile. "Your witness."

Defense counsel stood, furious with himself for having played into Woolever's hand, for saying exactly what Woolever wanted the jurors to hear. It was a bad—he hoped not a fatal—slip.

"Hello, Ms. Wirth," Chet said.

"Hello, Mr. Evers."

"As an artist—when you do your portraits of children, what medium do you prefer?"

"I work in oils."

"Are you always busy?"

"I have slow periods. Right now I have a waiting list."

"What would you call the biggest headache in your work?"

"Headache?"

"Well, no job is all fun."

"Handling the parents."

"Do they ever want you to make Tommy's ears a little smaller than they really are or Sally's eyes a little bigger?"

"Yes, they do."

"What do you do in these instances?"

"I ask the parents if they want *their* child or a child that *resembles* their child."

"How do the majority of parents answer?"

"The majority want their child."

"That's encouraging." Chet smiled. "What did your husband do, Ms. Wirth?"

"He's a composer."

"Modern stuff, classical?"

"Very modern."

"Do you like his work?"

"No. But then, I don't understand it."

"Does anyone?"

"He's won several international awards."

"What was he like to live with?"

"Not pleasant."

"In what way?"

"He was arrogant, superior. Everything was beneath him—writing checks, doing laundry, taking care of the baby."

"That can wear," Chet said.

"It wore."

"Was Barry Abrams arrogant when he lived with you?"

"Heavens, no. He was a gentle man, wonderful with my daughter. But he wasn't going anywhere. *We* weren't going anywhere."

"Wasn't he writing a novel?"

"Yes, it took place on the New York subways. The first year we lived together he finished chapter one; the second year, chapter two."

Chet nodded. Let the jury see, learn about Diane Wirth, understand her liaison with Len in sympathetic terms, not the sort Woolever had tried to paint. "Then Leonard Bradley came into your life."

"Yes."

"What was it like, Ms. Wirth? Your relationship with Mr. Bradley."

"In some ways it was perfect. I liked that he was older—by comparison Barry seemed so very young. He was energetic, also kind to Kate, caring. And very generous."

"And the less-than-perfect?"

"The time would just go too fast . . ."

"How about that he would always go back to his hotel?"

"Yes. I would have liked waking up with him."

"Anything else?"

"We had different backgrounds. My friends, by and large, were writers, artists." She smiled. "The first time I mentioned the Guggenheim, Leonard drew a blank. Jackson Pollock could have played second base for the Mets—"

"If you had so little in common why did you continue seeing him?"

"I *liked* him. I knew those things to be superficial differences. Besides, a lot of arty people are phony—Leonard isn't."

"Ms. Wirth, you testified earlier that it didn't bother you that Len Bradley was married, that it helped to define your relationship. Was there ever a time, or moments of time, when you wished he wasn't married?"

"Yes—very often when we were making love."

"Did you ever tell him that?"

"No." And then, very suddenly, Diane Wirth began to cry.

Chet moved back a little, a step or two, and the courtroom was silent as she gathered herself.

"Ms. Wirth, I have a few more questions for you. When you first heard that Mrs. Bradley's body was found—that she had been murdered—did you ever think that *maybe* her husband—your friend, Leonard Bradley—was involved?"

"For a moment, maybe it crossed my mind. The sensationalism in the press, all that lurid speculation..."

"How long did you feel that way?"

"A day, maybe, but even then it was never a strong feeling. It was never that I really *believed* he had done such a thing. And then I saw how absurd it all was. There was no way Leonard could have done these things to his wife. Leonard is not an insecure man. Maybe he didn't like the way things were, but he could live with them." She looked up, as though remembering. "There was something he once told me."

"What was that?"

"He was telling me about Winwar," she said, "maybe on our third or fourth date, saying how everyone hunted. I didn't say anything but I thought he was going to tell me how much he loved hunting—and it was going to be, it was going to put a barricade, of sorts, between us. I've never liked hunting, and I'm not fond of hunters. I could accept that he wasn't the most urbane man I'd ever met; in a way it was refreshing. But hunting—anyway, do you know what he said?"

"No, please tell me."

"He said he didn't hunt anymore. He used to get the fever in September, he said. But he didn't hunt anymore. He wasn't sure why. Then he said maybe it was because he was older now, and life was more important to him, *all* life."

She was looking straight at Leonard for the first time since she had taken the stand, and tears were in her eyes again. Then she came back to the lawyer. "I liked that he said that, and I believed him. And I believe him now. Leonard Bradley did not kill his wife!"

Chapter 18

Diane Wirth had been a biased witness, certainly, but she at least had helped offset some of the D.A.'s destructive, negative spin that he'd put on her relationship with Leonard, as the motive for Len's alleged murderous action. It wasn't enough, though, and Chet knew it.

He was sitting in Leonard's downstairs office. In his hands was a 93-page report, which he was reading over for the third or fourth time since Frank Zicca had originally delivered it to him six weeks earlier. In the beginning of his investigation the ex-chief of police in Buffalo had kept Chet informed on a regular basis. "No clues, Mr. Evers." If Frank Zicca had told him that once, he'd told him fifty times. "Nothing so far." "No leads, Mr. Evers."

Zicca had interviewed everyone with any connection to the crime—as the length and thoroughness of his report indicated—but everyone's story held. Leonard had written the investigator a handsome check as a retainer so Zicca wasn't going to come down on the side of the police even if he were an old cop. But his conclusion—Chet was reading it now with a feeling of despair—might have been written by Lieutenant Dave Bock: all the early evidence uncovered by the W.P.D. was probably the reason nothing else had ever turned up. There was nothing else *to* turn up.

Chet shuffled the report across the desk, then reached for a green-covered notebook, feeling an entry brewing. Since law school, he had filled nineteen such books; he knew the number exactly, because *this* notebook was An Attorney's Diary–20.

Chet opened to his last entry of six days ago, put the day's date three lines beneath it, thought for a few moments and wrote: "It is easier to defend a guilty person than an innocent one. In defending the guilty you have countless paths open to you—as many as the lawyer's mind or imagination can conceive; in defending the innocent, you have only *one* path—at that, a damn narrow one!"

Like many of his entries, as soon as he'd made it he wanted to edit it (some he wanted to cross out entirely); but at the outset—twenty notebooks ago—he had promised himself he wouldn't. An entry was what it was. An idea spontaneously expressed. You couldn't take back a cast. You made some bad ones, where the fly dragged across the water, scarring it, and instead of raising one trout you scattered five; so you tried again, and every now and then cast, fly and current all came together, working perfectly, and a fish rose. His "Attorney's Diary" was a life-long notebook of casts.

Chet stood and walked about the room, stopping as he so often did at the tall case holding Leonard's rods. The season had already started and he hadn't wet a line yet. Not that a dry fly "produced" many fish in the chilly waters of mid-April; it wasn't until *Iron Fraudator*—the artificial, intending to represent it, was the world-famed Quill Gordon—emerged in the final days of the month that a floating fly would make a trout look. Still, he missed the stream; sometimes in the early part of the season he would tie on a bucktail, which represented a minnow—but it was always with the feeling of doing something a little shady.

He turned; headlights were coming up the long, rising driveway. Chet crossed to the window and looked out. A few minutes later a car went back down. Midnight changing of the guard, W.P.D. From the start he hadn't liked the idea of 24-hour surveillance but hadn't lodged any official objection. This way, Len, standing trial for murder, could have breakfast in his own kitchen and sleep in his own bed. Also on the plus side, Flick's men kept the media—and the plain old curious—from swarming all over Maple Ridge.

Chet yawned. He went to the sofa, sat down wearily and reached to untie a shoe. On the stairway wall came a knock and he looked up. Leonard's daughter was on the landing in robe and slippers.

"Oh, hi," Chet said.

"I saw your lights on. Am I interrupting anything?"

"No. I was just thinking of turning in."

"Oh. Well, I don't want to keep you—"

"No, please. I'd rather talk."

"Would you like some coffee?" Catherine asked, continuing on down.

"No, thanks. I'm wired as it is."

"How about a drink?"

"That sounds better."

"Out," she said.

"At a bar?"

"Where do you go for a drink?"

"I walk to the liquor cabinet."

"I was thinking of Captain Black's."

"*Captain Black's?*"

"For old times' sake."

He liked Catherine but had been so busy, so preoccupied with the trial, that he hadn't thought of her in any kind of intimate way. Besides, the phone rang for her so often—someone from San Francisco—that he had come to think of her as spoken for. At New Year's she had flown to the Coast for two weeks; then in February again. Chet didn't know anything about the guy except what Leonard had given out. Namely, that he was a forty-year-old manufacturer of computer chips who still "followed the waves." But whoever he was or whatever he did, he was just another man in Catherine's life, Leonard had said, whom he would never meet—and she would never marry.

"What do you say, counselor?"

"Okay. Sure."

"Great. Give me three minutes," said Catherine.

It was seven miles from Winwar to Jonesville Flats, and they parked on the empty street outside the gin mill and went in; at the bar three men slouched toward oblivion. Catherine and Chet chose one of six formica-topped tables, all empty, to sit down at. The bartender, a man in his mid-sixties with a flat nose, came over; on his head a merchant seaman's cap rode jauntily. "Catherine Bradley," he said.

"Hello, captain."

"Long time no. You get more beautiful every time I see you."

She smiled. "Thank you. This is my friend, Chet Evers."

"Happy to meet you, Chet. Any friend of Catherine's is a friend of mine."

Amazingly, the captain seemed unaware that Chet Evers was the defense counsel in the big trial in Winwar. Or maybe he was just being discreet, Catherine decided.

She ordered a brandy, Chet a bourbon and water. When the drinks arrived there was no difference between glasses; both were really for short beers. Captain Black told them to give a holler if they wanted anything and returned to his bar. Or, as it seemed when he stood behind it, the bridge of his ship.

"Cheers," Chet said.

"Cheers. It looks smaller to me," Catherine said.

"To me, it looks just the same."

"When's the last time you were here?"

"I was here once in my life. With your father, driving home from a day's fishing. I couldn't have been sixteen. We had a couple of Schlitzes. I remember how serious Leonard was when he said, 'Chet, this is the beer that made Milwaukee famous.'"

She laughed.

"I drank Schlitz for years because of your dad."

The door opened and a fat woman about fifty-five wearing a quilted blue shirt-jac trundled in and hoisted herself onto a barstool; once perched, it looked as if she were sitting directly on the legs.

"What else do you remember about those days?" Catherine asked.

"Leonard's girlfriend. June somebody"

"Brkich."

"That's it," said Chet. "I remember thinking she was the sexiest thing alive."

"She's famous in the family," Catherine said.

"Oh?"

"After Leonard married Phyllis he saw June on the street one day and got the bright idea she'd make a great receptionist, so he convinced his father to hire her. She was the first receptionist the company ever had. All the visiting businessmen loved her, she really perked up the front office. Then Phyllis walked in one day—she might drop by once every six months—and saw *this woman* sitting at a desk in the main lobby. Two days later June Brkich was history."

"Did Phyllis know who she was?"

"She found out easy enough."

"Didn't she trust Leonard?"

"She trusted him," Catherine said, "but there was still the connection. My mother believed in total fidelity. Total every-thing.... Do you know what she called this place?"

"A den of iniquity."

"Close. 'A slough of dissolution'."

"Shades of *Pilgrim's Progress*."

"She loved that book," Catherine said. "She could quote whole sections. She used to remind me every Sunday that the chart Christian used on his great journey was his Bible. Then she would always say, 'Isn't that wonderful, Catherine? To make the Bible your chart through life!'"

Chet took a sip of his bourbon. "How would you answer?"

"Yes—until I was fifteen."

"Then you started hanging out in this slough of dissolution."

"I was a bad girl."

He smiled, felt himself beginning to unwind. At the start of the day he wouldn't have said—given a hundred guesses—he'd be ending it in Captain Black's with the defendant's daughter. "Was this always a hangout for kids from Winwar High?"

"For my generation, it was," Catherine said. "Then a girl was killed going back home one night—that pretty much ended it."

"Not Lucy Marzocca?"

"Yes, driving with Dwayne McManus."

"Leonard and I were talking about it just last week," Chet said, "in reference to McManus. He was going to be Woolever's lead-off witness."

"I thought it was a good move, letting him step down," Catherine said.

"Hometown boy, taking the stand in a policeman's uniform—it could've backfired on me. Besides, I had no argument with him."

One of the men at the bar, not yet forty but looking old, crossed to a jukebox and made some selections. "Lucy Marzocca was *Tony's* girlfriend, you know," Catherine said.

"She was going with McManus when she was killed, I thought."

"She was seeing Dwayne behind Tony's back."

"Leonard didn't mention that. He told me briefly about the investigation."

"It was pretty sordid," Catherine said.

"How so?"

"He always claimed Lucy was driving. The catch was, during the autopsy traces of semen were found in her mouth."

"That would seem proof *he* was driving."

"Everyone thought the same thing," Catherine said. "Ted Marzocca blew a gasket when Dwayne was cleared."

"Why was he cleared if everyone knew he was lying?"

"No one could disprove his story—that he and Lucy had fooled around in the parking lot behind Captain Black's, and *then* started back for Winwar."

"Since when do high-school boys let girls do the driving—that's what I would've asked."

"It wasn't Dwayne's car, it was Mrs. Marzocca's Cadillac—Lucy had taken it without permission."

A popular country tune was playing on the jukebox. "What did you think?" Chet asked.

"It was all so terribly sad, whether he was telling the truth or not. I never really decided."

"Did you know McManus?"

"Not well, he was a couple of years behind me—well, Tony's class. He always reminded me of a young Marlon Brando."

At the bar, Captain Black yanked down the middle of three beer spigots, all shaped like belaying pins, and filled a customer's glass. "You never went to Winwar High, did you?" Catherine said.

"No."

"Why not?"

"My parents sent me away."

"Didn't they like you?"

"I've thought about that," he said with a smile. "They thought I'd get a better education someplace else."

"Did you?"

"It doesn't matter where you go."

"Where *did* you go?"

"Andover."

"I'll be damned, I'm out with a preppy!"

"Ex."

"Once a preppy, always a preppy."

"Untrue."

"Some of my best friends are preppies."

"I'll allow you to rescind that statement, Catherine."

She laughed. "I used to have a terrible crush on Captain Black."

"Old salt that he is."

"How about another drink?"

"Sure."

In the dim light of the tavern Chet's hair had a silvery shine. "...verdict came in Not Guilty and Mrs. Ellis was a free woman. From that point on, my career took off. Clients were pounding at my door. Wealthy clients. The richest people in New York and Long Island. All of which was fine, except I never got home before eleven o'clock at night. We didn't have any kids, and Abby started a career in psychotherapy—studying, traveling here and there, conferences. I was making a big salary by then, bonuses on top of bonuses for winning, so wherever she wanted to go off she went. One summer London, a month at the Esalen Institute, two weeks—"

"Esalen. So, *that's* how you knew about Ernst Schmellner!"

"He led one of Abby's groups."

"Was she one of the ones who complained?"

"She complained because he was a phony."

"Go on," Catherine said.

A bowl of peanuts was on the table, and Chet popped a few into his mouth. "We were both very busy," he said. "Abby's mentor/therapist had begun giving her referrals. Clients—never call them patients—would come to our apartment while I was downtown. She was an excellent therapist—especially with women. And she didn't charge an outrageous fee. At thirty dollars an hour she was making a hundred and twenty, a hundred and fifty dollars a day—and was happy, proud of herself. She was doing what she wanted to do and making money at it."

Chet's voice was becoming quieter. "But nothing gold can stay. I was wrapped up in my own career. I didn't know she was having an affair. She was, with her mentor. I wasn't doing a very good job watching the store but it hurt me, it hurt bad when I found out. I remember looking at myself in the mirror the next morning and seeing the first gray. And a lot of it, not just a strand here and there! Abby said she wanted out. She and Sheldon were going to set up their own clinic and in the summer they would conduct workshops on the island of Corfu! She was riding that high wave, I could see it in her eyes. She didn't need me any more. She had a favorite expression, they all did in those days— Risk Taking. Whole workshops were built around risk taking."

Chet picked up his bourbon in the short beer glass. "She decided she wanted to leave the routine life she had with me and strike out in a brand-new direction. Then, less than a month later, her affair ended; and overnight her life went to hell. She no longer believed in herself. All those wonderful clients—the referrals—were only hers because of Sheldon. I told her that wasn't true! I was willing to start over with her. Who needed Sheldon? She listened, but it was deep—it wasn't just the breakup, though I heard later he'd led her on, he was seeing a couple of other women at the same time. A real creep! It was a terrible month. I was working on a big case, trumping up a story about a prowler to save the skin of some Long Island heiress who'd shot her husband in cold blood; then rushing home to help Abby, as best I could. Something was gnawing at her, some demon—I don't know to this day. Then on the day the case ended—with an acquittal—another win, another huge bonus—I came home and she wasn't there. Just a note saying she'd gone to Connecticut to catch up on some rest. We had a little place near the New York line. When I got there Abby was dead. She'd taken my shotgun—my favorite grouse gun—and blown her heart out."

Catherine groaned.

"Something went out of me then," he went on slowly. "I lost interest in the game of law, the bullshit and the pretense—the outright lies. Mostly the lies. I'd lied to save Mrs. Reinhardt's life and lost my wife's while doing it."

"... Last year it brought me in fifty-three thousand," she was saying halfway through their third drink.

"Tony too?"

"They're identical funds."

"Everyone should have such a grandfather," Chet said.

"Maybe, but I never much liked him."

"Why not?"

"The man had steel for a heart. Leonard likes to tell the story of the company during the Depression. Businesses were going under left and right but Winwar Iron Works—that was what it was called then—stayed afloat. Why? Because his father kept laying people off. Do you know how many people made up the company in 1929?"

"Forty?"

"Two and a half. My grandfather, an assistant and a part-time secretary."

"He knew what he had to do."

"I suppose," Catherine said. "And he did set me up for life. He just never let a soul warm up to him."

"How did Leonard and Phyllis feel about the trusts?"

"My mother dreaded the day when I'd turn twenty-one and could start drawing the interest. Then I'd *really* be a doomed woman!"

"Weren't you already, in her opinion?"

"Parents are always hopeful, I guess. I'll never forget the fights we used to have about how much breast a nice girl could show."

The door opened and a chill breeze preceded an old timer into the establishment. He had on a khaki cap with a long bill, the kind worn by marlin fishermen. Captain Black promptly yanked at a belaying pin.

"What about Tony?" Chet said. "How did he get along with your mother?"

"She loved him. They both did. He graduated with a 3.85 average at Cornell, I screwed up at Ithaca College. The administration didn't want me back. It was a classic letter... Your daughter seems to think the primary purpose of college is to pursue a career in sociability."

Chet had to laugh.

"Then there's the company," she said. "Bradley will always be run by a Bradley! I can still hear my grandfather saying that. Leonard was right there to step into his father' shoes, then when the time came take up the reins of leadership. However, *his* first child was a girl. No good. His father told him to try again and get it right this time. Fortunately the man child came along."

"Who now splits and sells firewood."

"It's so weird. He has to have three hundred thousand in interest alone! He refuses to touch it. I really think my brother's one of the great weirdos of all time."

"Because he hasn't touched the interest on his trust fund?"

"For not seeing the handwriting on the wall about his marriage. Now Debby's about to have a baby and where the hell is he? He's still in Mink Hollow."

The fat woman shuffled to the door and went out. Captain Black swabbed down his bar, turned out the Bud and Miller signs—the ship's running lights—in the windows. "To coin a phrase, people do what they have to do. You know that," Chet said.

"Okay, but after a while—what's he looking for?"

"What's the sound of one hand clapping?"

"It's nothing. He's looking for nothing?"

"Is that the sound of one hand clapping?"

She tried it. "What do you hear?"

"I hear something. Tony's looking for something. He doesn't know what it is but for him it's something."

Chet slid his glass diagonally on the smooth formica surface, as if it were a board, his glass a bishop. But he seemed unhappy with the move. He shook his head, eyes lowered.

"What is it?" Catherine asked.

"What I suspect your brother's looking for, I'm losing."

"I don't understand."

He looked up. "I'm starting to think it's wrong, a mistake to have Leonard speak the truth, the whole unvarnished truth, on the stand. It could lose for us. Catherine, I have to keep him out of jail—that's primary, that's *everything.*"

"What else would you do?"

"What I've done in the past. What I do so well. I have a brilliant story I've worked up."

"Are you committed to it?"

"No. I'm struggling!"

"What does Leonard say?"

"I haven't said anything to him. He's just getting used to the idea of opening up in our practice sessions—that's the irony."

"Why would it be a mistake just to have him tell the truth?"

"Are people—the jury—ready for it? Will it work? Will it make Leonard appear an honest man—or Count Dracula?"

"You're the expert, Chet, but I'd go for the truth."

"I'm afraid he'll go to jail."

"Is it *that* bad?"

"Yes and no. But for sure, lies are so much prettier to hear. I can't let Leonard go to jail..."

Captain Black announced last call. "Will you make me one small promise?" Catherine asked.

"Sure."

"Will you sleep on it?"

"Of course."

"With me?"

He looked into her eyes, not saying anything. He didn't need to.

Captain Black sauntered up with the tab. "Like old times, Catherine," he said.

Chapter **19**

He din't do anything the next day except grub around the kitchen, drink brew, watch TV, look at skin and generally make a mess out of the trailer. She cleaned up other people's places, when she come back she could clean up this one. Only where in hell was she? Yesterday she din't come home and here it was almost seven. She thought last time was bad . . . A car pulled up and he looked through the blinds. It was the new big-deal police officer—getting in late hisself. Doing a little overtime, eh, McManus? Chuck snapped a beer. Where was the bitch?

Next day she still din't call or show up, and now he was really going to give it to her when she come through the door. *After* he fucked her. He slid his tongue over Viki LaRosa's wide-open guinea twat, then flipped the magazine across the living room floor and picked up another issue. This one had the story of "Georgia, the Cat Girl." He opened it, looked at the pictures, read a few lines here and there. She liked "indulging her animal instinct." That sounded good to him. His favorite shot showed her in the branches of a tree wearing a leopard garter belt and black heels, tight ass curved up and blond snatch right there waitin' to get stuck.

Chuck took a few pulls at his johnson, then zipped up his fly. He searched the refrigerator. He din't believe he'd run out of beer! With his hand and forearm, he sickled through the middle shelf, cutting down all the sundry crap it contained, and found the last can. He flipped through the earlier copies of the magazine, watched television, fell asleep and woke up an hour later. Still not back, he would kill the bitch. He went through some more T & A, then stumbled into his bedroom. His wallet was on the dresser. He picked it up, swore at the few measly bills it contained, dragged a comb through his stringy brown hair, dense as weed cover over a septic tank, then looked out the window. They kept saying heavy rains, he should get in a few things—some pickles, a pack of franks and plenty of chips and brew. Bitch always done the buying, he was really going to kill her when she got home. After he fucked her.

He looked at Dwayne McManus' trailer. Then it come to him, all at once—shithead was working overtime again.

The next morning at 7:39—through the blockade of empties he glimpsed the numbers on the clock radio—he watched McManus leave his trailer, in uniform. That gave him the eight to four shift. About two he'd circle behind Village Hall and look for his car; then at 4:30 he'd do it again. There was more than one guy round these parts that could play dick. She hadn't taken no suitcase with her but he was sure some of her stuff was missing. It din't seem likely she'd went to Florida to see her kin, because common sense would say if she'd made the trip she'd've packed her bags—what difference would it make if he knew, he wasn't going to drive no 1,693 miles to bring the bitch back. Then if McManus' car wasn't behind Village Hall after his shift he'd have something to go on—at least he'd know McManus wasn't working overtime.

Chuck went into the kitchen. There wasn't an inch of counter space open, there wasn't a clean dish, pot or glass—a man couldn't even make hisself a cup of coffee. He'd go out for breakfast, then cruise around a little and maybe catch her car—

he should of thought of that sooner. Except seeing her car wouldn't really mean that much. If he pushed into somebody's house and shoved her around he'd be looking at time. Besides, he din't give a shit where she spent her days.

His head pounded and he thought he might have a brew before going out. He reached inside the refrigerator. As he pulled the tab the phone rang and he grabbed the receiver. It was the shipping department at Bradley, wanting him at the docks in an hour for a haul to Kansas City. Chuck took a backhand swipe at the counter. He din't want to go, with Sadie gone—suddenly that she'd maybe split made him feel off in the head. The woman in shipping said, "Mr. Wojciechowski?" All the shit was laying on the floor. He said he'd be there and hung up.

He swilled down the beer, scraped some old minestrone from a pot—dried on like tile glue—put in water, dropped in three eggs and turned on the range. He ate them off the counter with the last slice of bread, then shaved and took a quick shower. In the bedroom he dragged out some fresh clothes, thinking he wouldn't be able to check for McManus' car at 4:30. Well, when he come back. He grabbed his jacket and went out.

He fired up his rig, he usually liked the rumble it made—now the rumble din't sound good, it sounded like shit. Maybe she was hanging out with the cop, maybe she wasn't—one thing for sure, bitch wasn't coming home. It would eat at his guts for the next five days thinking about it. He stomped the accelerator to level out the diesel, then the door to McManus' trailer opened and the girl come out, carrying her books.

Chuck watched her walk across her yard to the road. She was a quiet little girl. He din't think he'd ever actually saw her smile. She had on a blue coat. Chuck dug at the side of his chin with the nails of his left hand, then cut his engine and rolled down the window. "'Morning, Julie," he said.

She looked up. She never spoke, he din't expect her to now. He give her a wave and she walked on. Before moving out, he let her get to the corner, then he kicked over his diesel a second time and bumped down Deerpath past the seven or eight kids waiting where Park Lane come in. Chuck waved again and smiled. "Have a nice day in school, Julie."

He moved on, hooked a left on the highway. When he come back, he might try loosening the girl up a little. He bet she knew somethin'.

Chapter 20

"Do you swear to tell the truth, the whole truth, and nothing but the truth, so help you God?" intoned the parrot-faced court clerk.

Leonard's hand was on the Bible. "I do."

"Be seated."

He sat down, and Chet Evers approached the witness box. "State your name, please, and your profession."

"Leonard A. Bradley Jr. I'm chairman and chief executive officer of the Bradley Corporation."

"Where do you live, Mr. Bradley?"

"In Winwar."

"How long have you lived there?"

"All my life."

"What's the connection between your name and the Bradley Corporation, in Winwar?"

"My father founded the company the year I was born."

"When did you take over the top managerial position?"

"Twelve years ago. He was in poor health and died three years later."

"Is there a difference between the company then—and now?"

"Yes. it's larger now, we've tripled our sales, and seven years ago we went public."

"What percentage of the company do you personally own today, Mr. Bradley?"

"Twenty-one percent."

"When your wife was alive, was this shared equally?"

"The stock was in both our names—yes."

"Roughly speaking, how much is this stock worth, as of now?"

"About forty-seven million dollars."

"What is your annual salary, Mr. Bradley?"

"Two hundred and eighty thousand, not including bonuses."

"Are there always bonuses?"

"We haven't had any now for two years."

"Why is that?"

"The recession is hurting us. Bonuses depend on profits."

So far, so good, thought Chet. But it was the easy part, the trek to the floe. Now came the first step out. He felt tentative, unsure of the outcome, but he would proceed. He did not discount last night, the influence of Catherine. If it weren't for her—for the truth about each other that had passed between them—he might now be starting on an all-too-familiar journey of fabrications, clever scenarios . . . lies.

"Mr. Bradley, did you carry insurance on your late wife's life?"

"Yes."

"At the time you took out this policy, what was its value and who was the beneficiary?"

"Two million dollars. I was."

"Let me give you a statistic," said Chet. "Only nine percent of American wives have *any* life insurance; on average, these policies have a value of $3750—their main purpose, to defray funeral expenses. But your wife had *two million* dollars' worth of insurance. Isn't this, by any standard, a huge amount?"

"I'd say so, yes."

"Why so big?" Chet asked.

"My agent presented it to me—we were upgrading my portfolio. Two million didn't cost significantly more than the million dollar policy Phyllis already had—so I took it."

"Was this before or after you had met Diane Wirth?"

Leonard hesitated, then: "After, by maybe a month."

"So you were having an affair, and shortly after the affair began you increased the value of your wife's life insurance policy. Is that correct?"

Leonard folded his arms across his chest. "Yes."

"What were your thoughts about doing this?"

"My thoughts?"

"About upping your wife's insurance by a million dollars while you were seeing another woman."

"It was business. There was no connection in my mind between the two."

Chet gave Leonard a long, hard look. As though *he* were the D.A. "No connection. Are you positive of that?"

"Yes."

"I'll ask you again, Mr. Bradley. When you took out the new policy on your wife's life, what were your thoughts—?"

"Counselor, obviously the witness has said what he wants to say!" Judge Cruikshank put in, fairly mystified by the defense counsel's grilling of his own client.

"Your Honor—"

"Proceed with your examination."

Chet gave a small nod and looked at Leonard. In a voice hardly above a whisper, he said, "Don't back out now, Len."

"Mr. Evers, speak up!" ordered Cruikshank.

The jurors exchanged confused glances. "Repeat your last question, counselor. What did you say to the witness?"

"I reminded Mr. Bradley he was under oath."

"For what reason?"

"I don't believe he's telling the truth, Your Honor."

The judge smashed down his gavel. To Chet: "What are you saying?"

"I don't believe the defendant is speaking the whole truth."

Cruikshank muttered something under his breath; his eyes were leveled squarely on Chet. "If you know the defendant to be perjuring himself, you have an obligation to tell this court!"

"Isn't that what I'm doing?"

"Mr. Bradley, are you telling the truth?" Judge Cruikshank asked, glaring at Leonard.

"I am, yes."

Cruikshank asked the court stenographer to read back Mr. Evers' last question before the disruption, and Mr. Bradley's reply. The reply that began, "It was business."

After a moment the woman with the tightly set, caramel colored hair read from her tape. "Question: 'About upping your wife's insurance by a million dollars while you were seeing another woman.'"

"Answer: 'It was business; there was no connection in my mind, between the two.'"

"Mr. Evers," the judge said, "the defendant has said he answered truthfully. I do not find, or see, anything in his answer that would have the appearance of a falsehood. So continue your examination."

"I have no further questions."

"Excuse me," the judge said.

"I have finished my examination of Mr. Bradley, Your Honor."

Chet looked at the district attorney. "Your witness."

He started toward his table, and Woolever, nonplused, stood up slowly.

The expression on Leonard's face was that of a man stranded on a raft, without provisions, in the middle of the ocean. "Mr. Evers!"

Chet turned. "Yes?"

"That's not all I was thinking."

Chet came back a step. "What else *were* you thinking then?"

Judge Cruikshank half rose from his chair. "Counselor, you informed the bench you had no further questions."

"Perhaps I spoke too soon, your honor."

"I would say you spoke recklessly!"

"I would like to resume."

"Mr. Evers, I'm about to hold you in contempt for these shenanigans."

"I can assure the court engaging in shenanigans was not, and is not, my intention in this trial."

"You're on notice. *Resume.*"

Chet took a moment; he looked at Leonard. "Mr. Bradley, how are you, sir?" Knowing damn well how Leonard was. Really miserable, and scared.

"Fine."

"Good. Now, that wasn't *all* you were thinking. In reference to—?"

"The new insurance policy for my wife . . ." Leonard was twisting in his chair, obviously nervous and uneasy.

"Yes. Can you elaborate?"

"It seemed . . . hypocritical to me."

"Why was that?"

"Because it appeared generous of me, when in fact . . . the opposite was more like it."

"What was the opposite?"

"I had little feeling left for my wife at that time. When I signed the policy I even . . . I had a flash wish she'd die."

There was a low murmuring in the courtroom. "To narrow this down farther," Chet said, "was this because of Ms. Wirth, or because you'd stand to get two million dollars?"

"They were linked, I thought of the two together."

"Were you in love with Diane Wirth at this time?"

"Yes."

"If your wife were to die, going back to that flash wish, what would you have done with the two million dollars?"

"I'd have refurbished Ms. Wirth's apartment in New York and built a new house."

"A new house? For her?"

"For the two of us—here in Cooper County. If she'd marry me and move out."

"Did you really think, at that point, she might?"

"The whole thing was a fantasy, Mr. Evers. But it seemed real."

"Yes . . . well, in your fantasy, if your wife were to die, you could approach Diane with the proposal."

"Yes . . ."

"Mr. Bradley, you're not—by any stretch of the imagination—a poor man. Wouldn't you have been willing, or able, to build a beautiful house and refurbish Ms. Wirth's apartment *without* your wife's policy?"

"Yes . . . but it would be nicer to do it with John Hancock's money."

A few people in the courtroom laughed, not unsympathetically. Who knew, though, what the jurors were thinking. "Did you ever mention this fantasy to Diane?"

"No."

Chet nodded, took a deep breath. No turning back now. But he was becoming concerned about Leonard's condition . . . he was beginning to look sickish, which was hardly surprising. "Tell us about your relationship with your wife, Mr. Bradley."

"For the last seven, eight years it was . . . formal."

"As opposed to informal?"

"As opposed to intimate."

"Was your relationship with your wife *ever* intimate?"

"Yes, it was. For twenty years—"

"Then what happened?"

"What happens?" He shook his head. "The spark died . . ."

"After the spark died, did you still have sex with her?"

"Occasionally."

"Were you faithful to your wife?"

"I began seeing other women about ten years ago."

"Who were these other women?"

"Business women, women traveling by themselves. We'd start talking. Maybe we'd go to bed and maybe we wouldn't."

"So these affairs always took place on your business trips?"

"Yes."

"How often?"

"Three, maybe four times a year."

"Did you ever make plans, in advance, to meet a woman? Say someone you'd already met or knew?"

"No."

"Did any of these women ever make contact with you?"

"No. I told them from the start there would be no future in it."

"Because you were married?"

"Yes."

"Then you *felt* married, even after the spark had died."

"Yes. Very much so."

"Did Phyllis suspect you were seeing other women?"

"I can't say, I don't honestly know. She'd frequently call me when I was traveling, ostensibly to say good night."

"Were you ever *not* in your room when she called?"

"Never."

"Would you ever leave *after* she phoned you?"

"No."

"Why not?"

"It sounds foolish, I suppose, but I thought she might call back."

"So if you wanted to go somewhere at 11:30, say, to buy a paper, you wouldn't do it."

"When I got to my room, I stayed."

"Did it bother you, Mr. Bradley, that you were, as the saying goes, carrying on behind your wife's back?"

"Some."

"In what way, some?"

"I'd feel guilty, I'm a conventional man..."

Chet noticed a trembling in Leonard's left arm, his lips were losing color. "Then you met Diane Wirth. What was different?"

He didn't answer immediately, fighting himself. "I was swept away by her."

"These other women—I'm sure they were attractive, intelligent. Yet *they* never swept you away. Why?"

"It just never happened. With Diane it happened. I fell in love with her, I suppose."

"Why do you say 'suppose'?"

"Because it wasn't a two-way street. I didn't want to make a fool of myself, I didn't want to get hurt—so I kept the brakes on as best I could."

"How did you feel about your wife during this period, as opposed to the pre-Diane period?"

"She became a...a burden to me. The reality of it—"

"*Became* one."

"Before Diane, my life was the way it was. I accepted it."

"After you met Diane, what was the most prevalent feeling you had about your marriage?"

"It was something to endure."

"Then, in actuality, your marriage meant little to you during your affair with Diane."

"Just that it existed."

"But you would still be in your room by eleven p.m."

"It's hard to break old habits."

"Did you want to break *that* old habit?"

"I did. But I also wasn't sure of my relationship with Diane."

"Yet when your wife had you followed and threw the detective's report up to you, you asked for a divorce."

Leonard was holding both elbows with opposite hands. "I had to, then—whatever my relationship with Diane was. I was tired of cheating, hated it. It wasn't good for me or Phyllis. I had to admit to both of us that our marriage was over."

"How did she take it?"

"She seemed devastated, and very angry. I had never seen her so angry. I suppose it was naive of me, wishful thinking, but now that she knew about Diane, I thought she might go along. I had forgotten, or chose to forget, the side of Phyllis that could not accept divorce, that believed vows were forever."

"What were the last words she said to you, when you asked for a divorce?"

"As she was leaving, she said, 'Over my dead body.'"

"Meaning what, do you think?"

"That she'd fight a divorce every inch of the way."

"How did that make you feel?"

"It depressed me. I didn't look forward to a drawn-out, acrimonious divorce."

Chet stepped slightly away. "Did you call your lawyer?"

"Yes. We made an appointment."

"Would you state the name and address of his lawyer, Mr. Bradley?"

"Chester Evers of Willow—yourself."

"Do you recall the time and date of this visit?"

"September 23—at three p.m."

"How long did you talk with me?"

"A little over an hour."

Chet walked to his table, picked up a spiral notebook with maroon cover and flipped it open. "I have you arriving at 3:03 and leaving at 4:11," he said, "on that date." He looked at the judge. "I would like to introduce this book, of my official appointments, as defense Exhibit A, your honor."

"Very well."

Chet placed the book on the table; somehow it looked lonely compared to the state's legion of exhibits. Leonard summarized their talk in Chet's office. "What was your frame of mind when you left?" the lawyer asked.

"I was glad to get things started, but I was also feeling bad. The guilt kept at me. Whatever else, my wife was a faithful woman with strong principles. What was I doing?"

"Do you remember your last words to me?"

"'Get started.'"

"So that was your wish, everything else aside."

"Yes."

Chet introduced as Exhibit B his "Clients' Log," which contained notes and comments on cases as they progressed. He read a few lines from his meeting with Leonard Bradley, concluding with: "Counseled client on debilitating aspect of guilt and suggested he go about getting his own place."

He positioned the log beside the appointment book. "Mr. Bradley," he said, "how many times have you made the trip between Winwar and Willow—say in the past three years?"

"Fifteen times."

"Then you have a good idea of how long the drive takes."

"Yes."

"Did you stop anywhere on your drive home, after you left my office?"

"No."

"Then, by my calculation, you arrived in Winwar about 4:45."

"Yes."

"As you pulled into your garage, what did you see?"

"My wife's car."

"Did that make you think she was home?"

"Yes—but maybe not in. Phyllis was an avid walker. Frequently when I'd come home she'd be out walking."

"What happened when you went inside?"

Leonard told how he had looked at the mail and made himself a drink, then noticed that the sliding front door was open a crack—totally unlike his wife. But he attributed the lapse to her preoccupation—or perhaps the cleaning girl had inadvertently left the door open. He closed it and went into his bedroom to change his clothes. There on the floor was a brown paper bag, which also struck him as odd. But what annoyed him was that his khaki trousers, which he'd only worn for a little while the day before, weren't in his closet where he himself had hung them. He took down another pair, made himself a second drink and walked up to the pond to read the paper. When he got back Phyllis wasn't in, so he decided to go look for her along the quiet township roads where she sometimes walked.

"Did you really think you might find her?" Chet asked.

"I don't remember thinking if I would or wouldn't. I didn't know what else to do."

"Why didn't you call the police?"

"I was beginning to feel worried, but not that worried."

"Were there any other reasons why you didn't summon help at that particular moment?"

Leonard's jaw looked set, almost as if to keep his teeth from chattering. "I also . . . I didn't want the publicity. Winwar is a small town. It's the town I grew up in. If Leonard Bradley's wife is missing, everyone knows it, they start talking . . ."

"What's talk? A timely call—how did you know?—might have saved her life!" Again he was the defense sounding like the prosecution. All part of his risky plan.

"I kept hoping she'd call, or come back momentarily."

"Mr. Bradley, it's a few years ago. Your daughter doesn't come home after school and no one knows where she is. What do you do?"

"A fifty-year-old woman isn't the same as a fifteen-year-old girl."

"Rape is rape and murder is murder," Chet came back. "Fear and horror don't diminish with age."

"But older, more mature women can usually take better care of themselves—"

"Case in point, your late wife." Chet came closer to his client. "Now, Mr. Bradley, tell this court why you didn't call the police when you came back from the pond to a still empty house."

"I didn't want the publicity—"

"You're a private man, I understand. Why else?"

"Because it looked"—Leonard paused, swallowed—"suspicious."

"As to *what*?"

"As to *me*. I was having an affair, my wife was digging in her heels against a divorce, I had a two-million-dollar policy on her life—"

Enough. "So you went searching for her," the lawyer said. "Whose car did you take?"

"Hers. Its suspension is better suited for back roads—"

"Are the back roads of Winwar *that* bad?"

"A few are unpaved, where Phyllis liked to walk. It probably didn't make any difference, though."

"What happened?"

Leonard then described the ride. He didn't see his wife or, for that matter, anyone—except for a hired hand as he drove past his barn. When he got home he didn't go in right away but took a walk through the woods and fields on the property, periodically calling out her name until it got dark. Inside again, he realized he had never searched the house. Was it possible that in a state of despondency she had killed herself?

"Mr. Bradley, what were your thoughts at this time? While you were searching the house."

"It quickly seemed pointless to be looking for her."

"Why?"

"Phyllis wasn't the suicidal type."

"Were you having any other thoughts or notions?"

Pause. "It crossed my mind . . ."

"Go ahead," said Chet.

"...that my problems would be over if I were to find her."

"Hanging from a basement rafter, say."

Leonard tried to answer, couldn't.

"What would her death mean to you, have meant to you, at that time?"

"No divorce...no legal battling at huge financial and emotional expense." Leonard inhaled shallowly. "Plus...plus I'd be able to start seeing Diane more often, without having to lie about it."

"How did your search conclude, Mr. Bradley?"

"The last place I looked was the furnace room, just off my downstairs office. Coming out, I sat at my desk, trying to collect myself, and saw my safe door was ajar. I looked in, it was a complete mess. Then I knew without question something was definitely wrong. And at that point I called the police. While I was talking to them I noticed the padlock on my gun case was open."

"Did you mention that also?"

"No. The police would be arriving shortly."

"What did you do next?"

Leonard said he examined his collection of pistols, determining, by checking each weapon against his log, that one was missing—his .38 Smith & Wesson. Of all his pistols, it was among the most functional, hardly the pistol someone would take—to sell.

"Why did you have it in your collection?"

"It's a classic Army/Navy revolver manufactured just before the turn of the century. It's an exceptionally handsome piece."

"Is this the gun?" Chet went to the evidence table, picked up the .38 and showed it to Leonard.

"Yes."

"Are you willing to say, Mr. Bradley, that this revolver is the weapon that killed your wife?"

"It's established—yes."

Leonard then related what happened after Chief Flick and Sgt. O'Shea came to his house. He and the chief inventoried the ammunition and determined that six .38 cartridges were gone.

Then, while he and Chief Flick were talking in the kitchen, Officer O'Shea discovered some soil particles on the carpet near the front door.

"Is there any doubt in your mind, Mr. Bradley, that these particles—as introduced by the state—came from the murder site and match the soil found on the soles of your boots and the knees of your trousers?"

"There's no doubt."

Chet Evers walked away from the witness, his eyes scanning the faces of the men and women in the jury box. Then he turned and said, "What did you and Chief Flick talk about in the kitchen?"

"The possibilities of what might have happened."

"What did he think?"

"Money was missing from the safe, about $1,700 in cash—also a string of my wife's pearls."

"He didn't *know* that. You had to tell him—is that correct?"

"I told him what the safe contained. When we went through it the cash and pearls weren't there."

"How did it look to him?"

"Possible robbery. Maybe Phyllis was lost somewhere in the woods, he said. Then he considered the possibility of robbery-kidnapping combined. There was really no way for him to know exactly."

"Did he want to know anything about your wife's mental state—how she'd been feeling, how you and she were getting along?"

"Yes."

"Well?"

"I said she'd been working hard at her committee jobs, she seemed fine."

"Anything else?"

"We were getting along okay."

"You said that?" Chet asked the question with disbelief, reflecting what he knew the jurors were thinking.

"Yes."

"What about the detective's report? What about Diane Wirth, whom you were in love with and wanted to see more frequently, more openly? How about your asking Phyllis for a divorce—and her biting reply, 'Over my dead body!' What about all *that*, Mr. Bradley? Had it slipped your mind?"

"No."

"How long have you known Oscar Flick?"

"Over forty years."

"Besides coming to your house in a professional capacity, didn't he also come as your old friend, to ease your mind a little?"

"I think so. Yes."

"And you told this friend and this officer of the law that your wife was keeping busy with *committee work?*"

"Yes."

"Mr. Bradley, what were you thinking of?"

He stared back at Chet. His lips were almost blue.

"An answer, please," Chet said. "What did you think you'd gain by covering up what was really going on in your home?"

Leonard didn't answer.

"I'm waiting," Chet said. As he knew the jury was.

"It wasn't his or anyone's business that I'd just seen my lawyer—"

"*No.* The *truth*, Mr. Bradley."

"I was also—I was afraid Chief Flick might think I knew more than I was saying."

"How could that be? You were in Willow, you came back and had a drink at your pond, then went looking for your wife by car and by foot. And when you saw the rifled safe you called the police. Why were you afraid? That was your complete day."

No answer.

"Something was worrying you, Mr. Bradley. What was it?"

"I didn't want Chief Flick to get the wrong idea."

"You've said that. What wrong idea could he get?"

"That I was involved—"

"Well, *were* you?"

"I felt involved," Leonard said.

"Because of your affair with Diane Wirth?"

"That, yes."

"How else?"

"I had a terrible feeling Phyllis was dead."

"Then why were you telling the chief lies? Couldn't you see he was going to have some heavy-duty questions for you when he learned you were carrying on in New York—and some *super* heavy-duty questions if or when they found your wife's body?"

"I knew the feeling was irrational. *Rationally*, I had every right to believe she was all right, just lost somewhere, the way the chief had theorized."

"Which would effectively end the investigation."

"Yes."

"But then you'd have Phyllis to contend with, the divorce."

"Yes."

By now the judge saw Leonard's condition, as did the District Attorney of Cooper County and most of the people in the courtroom. Still Chet Evers went on. "Which did you hope for," he said. "It had to be one or the other. You couldn't hope for both. Which was it? That your wife would be found dead, with that scenario—the questions, the suspicion, the terrible guilt you'd feel. Or that she'd come back, let's say from a relaxing week in St. Thomas, with that scenario—the bitterly contested divorce, the huge costs, the acrimony?"

Leonard's shoulders convulsed.

"I've asked you a question, Mr. Bradley."

But he didn't, or couldn't, answer it.

Chet Evers blew out a breath of air, then turned to the judge. "Your Honor," he said, "I would like to continue my examination of the witness tomorrow morning. At the moment he appears unable to go on."

Judge Cruikshank observed Leonard, then to Chet, "I concur, counselor." He thought but did not say, You're taking some big chances with your client's skin, counselor.

The grizzly old hod carrier struck once with his gavel. "This court is adjourned until ten a.m. tomorrow."

Chapter 21

A camera panned the facade of the Cooper County Courthouse, drifted down the broad stone steps and finally focused on the defense lawyer. A blue-jacketed woman about thirty-five, holding a microphone, was standing in front of him on the sidewalk. Q: "Mr. Evers, will you be staying with your truth defense tomorrow?" A: "Mr. Bradley will continue telling the truth, if that's what you mean." Q: "Do you think it's working to your advantage?" A: "Yes." He hoped. Q: "What made you decide on a truth defense in the first place?" A: "What should I have decided on, an *un*truthful one?"

Next the camera caught Woolever leaving the building. Q: "Mr. Woolever, how does it look to you for conviction?" A: "Excellent." Q: "What's your opinion of Mr. Evers's truth defense." A: "I hope he keeps on with it." Q: "Why is that, sir?" A: "He's letting his client dig his own grave."

The reporter then said to the viewers that Leonard Bradley would be taking the stand again in the morning, with cross-examination by the district attorney beginning in the afternoon or Thursday...

Rain drove against the tall window in the living room; it had been pouring since early afternoon. Chet stood and switched off the set.

"See you guys later," he said to Catherine and Tony. He crossed the room to the stairs and went down to Leonard's office.

"I should be going," Tony said.

"Why?"

"I'm worried about the Mink Hollow Creek."

"That's a good reason to stay!"

"I'd like to be there if it runs over."

"Tony, isn't that a little crazy?"

"There are a few things I'd want to save."

"Like your life, I hope."

"Don't worry about me, Catherine. I'm not going to get washed away."

He crossed the room with his dog and put on his heavy coat. "Please be careful," Catherine said.

Tony and Buck ran out and the phone rang. She took it at the low ceramic counter. It was Adam Pohl. He wouldn't keep her, he said, he just wanted to let them know Danny had made it through the operation, his vital signs were holding. It looked hopeful.

"I'm so happy for you and Ruth," Catherine said. "Leonard will be delighted. This is the best news."

"I know . . . how'd it go today?"

She told him, without elaborating. How it had started, how it had ended; she had thought he was dying.

"The poor man," Adam said.

"Dr. Jacobs was here earlier—"

A knocking at the door. She told Adam, excused herself. Her brother was standing there, water running down his face.

"My battery's dead. I'll get a jump from the station wagon."

She looked at him, exasperated. "Just let me say good night to Adam and I'll drive it out for you. His son made it through the operation."

"That's great," Tony said. He went back out. Catherine spoke briefly with Adam, put down the receiver and walked the length of the hallway to the garage, getting in and starting the station wagon; the wide door rose at the touch of a button. She put the

shift in reverse, turned on wipers and headlights and maneu-
vered the car so that it was nose-to-nose with her brother's truck.
She yanked at the hood-release handle and Tony did the rest.
In a moment he was disconnecting the cables and lowering the
hood to both vehicles. He knocked at her window and she gave
the handle a half-turn; even then the rain came in.

"Thanks," he said.

"What'll you do in the morning?"

"I live on a hill, remember?" They were both shouting.

"Call when you get home!"

"Okay!"

He waited for Catherine to pull the wagon back into the
garage—his foot heavy on the pedal to keep the engine revving.
Then the braced, cedar-paneled door started coming down. As
he eased forward in 4-wheel drive, Tony noticed a blur—a small
dark form—scoot in front of his truck. Just before the door
touched, it slipped beneath and was in.

Black Cat. Home from the wars.

Tony turned at the woodpile, following the driveway along
the ridge, past his father's farm. He crossed the bridge spanning
Chodokee Creek. The water was brown, swirling. Main Street
was deserted but the bars seemed to be doing well. The lights
in Stubby's looked warm, inviting. He felt like stopping in but
kept going. Soon the village was behind him; the land was rising.
He down-shifted, flipped wipers to high speed. Then he was at
the hairpin turn; his lights illuminated the sign he had painted
when they had first moved here from the farm house. But he
didn't sound his horn. Who was there to warn?

Skidding, wheels churning, Tony steered through the bend.

She set the dish of cat food on the floor with a side bowl
of milk and went into her father's room. He was in bed with a
flannel robe over his pajamas, watching television.

"Adam called," she said, going over. "The operation was
successful."

"Danny made it through!"

"Dr. Donaldson is optimistic."

"That's wonderful, I have to call him. They agonized over that for years—for as long as I've known them." Leonard reached for the clicker and turned off the TV.

"It was a flip of the coin, you know, if he'd survive surgery."

"It's a decision I wouldn't have wanted to make," Catherine said.

"Goddamn, good news." A smile, the first in months, came to his lips. "Stay with me for a while, Catherine. Tony still here?"

She sat down on the bed. "His battery went dead. I just gave him a jump start."

"In this weather? Is he crazy? Why didn't he spend the night?"

"He had to get home in case the Mink Hollow stream overflowed."

"Just like his grandmother. She was always afraid their pipes were going to freeze. I can still hear her saying to my dad, 'Leonard, I'm worried about our pipes, we have to get home.'"

He looked better than he had but still very pale, and he still felt cold. The medication Dr. Jacobs had him on appeared to be working; the downside, in Leonard's opinion, was that alcohol was ruled out.

He held his daughter's hand. "I'm sorry about today, Catherine."

She was surprised. "For what?"

"Saying those things about your mother, our marriage—"

"Dad, what did you say? You talked honestly about yourself and mom—you were terrific—"

"Chet would've left me there, swinging in the breeze."

"What did he actually say to you?"

"'Don't back out, Len.' At the last minute I couldn't do it, not go all the way, decided not to really. A big part of me still thinks it was a mistake."

"Why?"

"My God, right now these jurors must hate me," Leonard said. "Would you vote for someone who said those things?"

"This isn't an election, it's a trial."

"There's still a vote . . ."

She was silent for a moment. As they had at times during the day, her thoughts went back to last night, to the pleasure, the ease and sweetness of sleeping with Chet. "Did your father ever lie that you know of?" she asked.

"He was an honest man. He *lived* the Bradley culture—he didn't just give lip service to it. People knew where they stood with him."

"Did you?"

"I crossed him twice when I first started working for the company. He fired me both times."

"Your father fired you?"

"He rehired me but he hit me for a week's pay each time."

"You say that proudly," Catherine said.

"I'm proud of my father," Leonard said. "I'll be the first and last to say I still look up to him. 'Are you glass or are you steel?' That was what he used to say to me."

"What you did today, your father would've never dared do."

"Bull! Never explain, never apologize. What I did today was beneath him."

Catherine gave her head a harsh shake. "I'm really surprised Diane Wirth had anything to do with you, you know that!"

"What have you done in your life to judge me?" he said, feeling hurt, not understanding his daughter. "Except spend your fifty thousand a year on partying and good times—"

If he had said that to her on her last visit she would've left his room in tears; not now. "I haven't done very much, you're right," she said. "But I'm through acting out, playing the bad little girl whose parents only looked at their son. I'm not the same girl, dad, the same woman. A lot of it has to do with mom, her death— and this trial. What we're *all* going through. Seeing you today, hearing you tell the truth like that . . . I never knew you and mom had a good physical relationship, even liked each other . . . I always thought she was frigid—"

"No, no. Phyllis enjoyed sex," he said.

"That blows me away. It changes so much for me, how I see her . . . it changes me. But *you're* still trying to decide if you're glass or steel. Because your father said it thirty-five years ago—"

"It's worth knowing—"

"You lost Tony as your top executive—you lost the last Bradley male—because of that glass and steel crap."

"Tony couldn't take the pressure of the job."

"He's glass, right? Tony is glass!"

She stood up. She hadn't come in to fight with her father, there was enough emotion and tension in their lives already. "I'm sorry, you ought to rest. Would you like something?"

He looked up at her. At his suddenly grown-up daughter. "Catherine, I'm just in a terrible way here."

She leaned down and squeezed his shoulders, kissing him. "Oh, dad. Dad! Be yourself. You're a beautiful man, goddamn it. *Be yourself.*"

He was awakened by the sound of the creek raging out of the mountain. He got out of bed and went to turn on his light: no light. He reached into the top drawer of his dresser, grabbed a flashlight and lighted the kerosene lamp in the kitchen. Then he dragged on a pair of trousers, a sweatshirt and a long yellow slicker and opened the front door. Buck went out first.

Tony crossed the road and stared at the creek, as it rushed wildly, a frothy, chocolate brown, along its downward path. At least it wasn't spilling over. The rain had let up and the sky looked to be clearing. Maybe it wouldn't. Inside again, he sat down at the table in the kitchen, thinking to check the creek in another hour. Because the roar was so steady, it came to seem like silence. Buck lay at his feet, and he thought briefly of leaving Maple Ridge in his truck, thinking to tell his sister once he got home that Black Cat had slipped in, in case she had already gone inside the house; but he'd forgotten to mention it and now the animal was in the garage, cold and hungry . . . Tony shook his head, took off his boots. Mindful of the swollen stream but figuring he was in no real danger, he went back to his bedroom.

He awoke to a bright clear day. Getting up, he immediately looked through the front window. Muddy water from the creek was splashing on the road, the extent of the flooding.

He made breakfast, deciding he'd drive to the Ford dealership and pick up a new battery when he finished. His phone rang.

He hurried over and picked up, thinking it could be Debby or Debby's mother—the baby was just about due. A man's voice asked if this was the "wood place."

"I have wood but I'm out of the business. If you want any you have to come for it yourself—half-price."

"How kin I find yeh?"

Tony gave directions and the man hung up. He finished eating, then tested one of the lamps in the living room—power still down. He let Buck out and crossed to the rear window. Three days ago a young couple had driven up in an old hearse, in which they appeared also to live, and had loaded in as many logs as they could; then they had got themselves stuck and Tony had had to press his 4x4 into service, snapping a towing line in the process—all for twenty-five dollars.

Buck, nose to the ground, came into view near the pile of loose, unseasoned logs. Even as Tony watched, the dog's stubby tail started going excitedly, and the next moment a rabbit squirted away toward the old orchard, Buck in close pursuit.

Tony suddenly frowned, seeming to recall the odd turnings of his brain after he'd come in from observing the creek earlier this morning. The truth was, he *had* told Catherine over the phone, once he'd got home, that Black Cat had ducked in beneath the garage door. He'd just worried, in his sleepy daze, that he hadn't.

He went into the kitchen, stopped—once again the image of Black Cat slipping inside the garage crossed his mind. This time it wouldn't leave . . .

An hour later he was walking down the long hall in the house on Maple Ridge; he opened the door and went inside the garage. Tools and a disassembled Bradley chainsaw lay on the work bench. Where the bench ended was a steel sink; behind it, a roll of paper towels. Tony moved to a spot between the two automobiles and, stopping, looked at the bottom of the wide, sturdily braced garage door.

He moved closer to it, then turned and faced the interior of the garage. Station wagon on left, sedan on right. He let his mind run. If someone had entered the house via the garage, like Black Cat, this wasn't what he had seen. His father had left for his office in the morning. That would have made the *Lincoln* side of the garage empty.

So do it, he thought.

He slid behind the wheel of his father's automobile, reached above the visor for the keys, raised the door with a button push and backed out; once out, he cut the ignition, put the transmission in "park" and walked back to the garage, standing in the empty space. Assuming that the killer had entered the garage when Leonard had left for work, where had he stood while waiting for Phyllis to come out of the house and get in her car? More to the point, how had he entered the garage without Leonard's noticing him? Hadn't *he*, last night in a driving rain, noticed a small black animal scoot in?

He looked at his mother's car—wondering, suddenly, why he was assuming that the killer had ducked in as *Leonard* had left. Certainly he would have taken Phyllis to the woods a lot sooner, in that case, and she had had, and had kept, an afternoon appointment with her lawyer. Her killer had waited for her to come back to the house, OK. But *not* since early morning...

Tony stepped outside. The sky was a hard blue and a brisk northwesterly wind made the still-leafless maples on the property rattle. He looked at the open garage. If he wanted to get inside, unnoticed, what would *he* do?

As he stood there, Catherine came into the garage from the house and said they were leaving—Leonard wasn't feeling much better but he wanted to get it over with. Did Tony want to come with them? He said he'd meet them at the courthouse later. She said all right. Two minutes later the door to the house opened and Chet, Catherine and his father came out. Leonard looking dead-tired. He gave them a quick wave as they got in the lawyer's car and drove off.

For the next two hours Tony walked about, inside the garage and out, thinking, talking to himself, finally deducing that his mother's killer had made one of two possible moves:

sneaking inside the garage as she left for her appointment, or slipping inside when she returned from it later in the day.

The second—slipping in when she returned—struck him as more plausible. Less risky. The killer could easily have concealed himself behind the trash barrels on the house side—as opposed to the driveway side—of the garage. Then, as Phyllis drove in, he could have circled about and surprised her as she stepped out of her car. Tony tried it, to see how it felt. But, even as he crouched behind the plastic barrels, he realized that anyone in the house could easily see him from the laundry-alcove window. Not that anyone was inside with both Leonard and Phyllis gone. But how was the killer to know? And how could the killer be sure Phyllis was already out of her car? Very often a driver—he was thinking of women but it also applied to men—lowered the garage door *before* getting out, as a kind of security precaution.

Tony glanced at his watch. Maybe—just maybe—the man had gotten in as his mother had left for her lawyer's appointment, *not* when she had returned. And from the *far* side of the garage.

That too posed dangers, because as he stood at the far corner, Tony recognized that someone coming up the drive would see him immediately. On the other hand, he could spot or hear a car long before it came into view. And easily slip into the woods. Tony made the tight circle around the corner into the garage. Great—as long as his mother hadn't looked over her right shoulder while backing out. Well, he would assume she had glanced over her left shoulder. With any kind of luck, and good timing, a person could slip in unnoticed and have space to conceal himself in the corner as the door came down. Maybe he was getting somewhere . . . He tried the move again, this time ducking deeper into the corner, closer to a bunch of garden tools—no way would anyone know he was there.

He went outside, pulling up the collar of his jacket, then had an idea . . . He went to the driver's side of the station wagon and unclipped the remote control panel from the visor. Again outside, he lowered the garage door and took a position just around the corner. When he felt ready, he pushed the up button and the door rose. He waited, in his imagination, for Phyllis' car to back out. As it passed the sill he slipped inside and hid in the corner, then touched the down button—the way his mother had from her station wagon. The door started down and he felt safe—he'd done it! Now all he . . . the killer . . . had to do was wait for her to come back—the side window, opening to the ridge, would notify him in advance. The next instant an object—it seemed like something was falling from a shelf—caught his eye. He glanced up, then lurched back to keep a black metal box, attached to the edge of the descending door, from striking his head. A second later the door was fully closed.

He stood, legs apart, in an unlikely embrace with a shovel. The box—the electrical door-control mechanism—could've given him a wicked gash. Glad nobody was around to see him playing detective and almost getting himself killed while at it, he spotted on the cement floor behind the blade of the shovel a common wooden toothpick. He kneeled, curious, to examine it.

Who in the family used a toothpick?

No one . . .

Chapter 22

"Your wife's body was found, Mr. Bradley, in the woods to the southeast of Plutarch Pond—are you familiar with this area?" Chet asked.

"Yes."

"In what connection?"

"As a boy I used to swim at Brenner Heights. The creek circles that whole region. And I've hunted there—in years past."

"Anything else?"

"When the Plutarch Lumber Mill was operating it was an outing for my family. We'd drive up there occasionally."

"Then your wife was also familiar with the area."

"Not well, but she knew it."

"Was she familiar with the swimming hole at Brenner Heights?"

"When we were first married we'd go there now and then."

"Did you and your wife ever walk along the banks of Brenner Heights Creek?"

"Yes. Phyllis was fond of wild flowers. There isn't a better spot in the county for lady slippers."

Chet pushed on. "Mr. Bradley, your wife's body—to narrow down further the location—was discovered in the foundation of a small burned-down hut or cabin in these woods. Do you know this spot—specifically, this foundation?"

"Yes."

"Again, in what connection?"

"As kids we'd sometimes spend the night there—in the cabin. That was before it burned down."

"Was it private property?"

"It belonged to a trapper at the turn of the century—that's the story. It's what we believed."

"If you had to go to this spot today, how would you go?"

"I'd drive to Brenner Heights and follow the creek past the swimming hole. A trail hits the creek about 175 yards along, it leads to the hut."

"To the hut?"

"The foundation," said Leonard.

Chet stole a glance at the large round clock on the wall. It was important that he end by mid-afternoon—not later than 2:30—so Cruikshank wouldn't be so likely to grant Woolever an adjournment: time for the D.A. to think, marshal his arguments. "Mr. Bradley, exactly one week went by between the disappearance of your wife and the discovery of her body. What kind of week was it for you?"

"It was...difficult."

"Can you name how? Specifically?"

"My wife was missing."

"Of course. What else?"

"Business problems."

"Anything else?"

"...Not being able to see Diane Wirth in Atlantic City, the way we'd planned. I was to speak at a convention and we'd made arrangements..."

"Did this—not being able to see Ms. Wirth—upset you more or less than the fact that your wife was missing?" Again, the sort of set-up question a defense counsel wouldn't normally ask.

Leonard didn't answer right away. Chet waited, wondering if Leonard might have decided, during the night, to—

"More." Tone flat, tight.

The defense lawyer nodded. "Any other matter, Mr. Bradley, that especially weighed on you that week?"

"I'd lied to the chief, like I said yesterday. That worried me."

"Can you explain further?"

"I didn't want him to discover I had a girlfriend in New York, that my marriage was on the rocks."

"How could that best be prevented, as you saw it?"

"By having Phyllis call or by having her show up at the house. Then the chief would go about his routine business..."

Chet paused. "Which brings us back to where we left off yesterday. Are you up to continuing, Mr. Bradley?"

Leonard paused, slightly longer than his lawyer had. "Yes."

"Very well. During the week you've just described, did you think your overall ends would be better served if your wife showed up unharmed, as you just said. Or as a second option, if she were discovered in some remote wooded area—dead?"

The lapels to Leonard's blue pinstripe suit rose and fell. "I thought of both... I couldn't decide."

"But if she came back—or surfaced unharmed, say in Virginia—the police wouldn't have any reason to question you, would they? As you just said."

"No, they wouldn't."

"Then why wasn't that preferable?".

"Because... because, if she were found dead somewhere it would be... I'd be free right away to start a new life..."

Good. "From the perspective of seven months, can you *now* say which was the stronger desire on your part?"

Leonard stared at Chet.

"Do you understand the question, Mr. Bradley?"

"Yes."

"Can you answer it?" Come on, Len. The truth.

"That she was dead... was the stronger desire..."

"But then you'd have to face police interrogation. You might even find yourself arrested—"

"That frightened me," Leonard said. "I was very worried how it might look, but when I made myself think rationally—I knew I hadn't done anything."

"Except lie."

"Yes."

Chet Evers drew in a long breath. "Mr. Bradley, I have three more questions for you. First, when you arrived home from my office in Willow and your wife wasn't in the house, what did you think?"

"I thought she was on one of her walks."

"Second, did it cross your mind that afternoon—as you were driving home from my office or later—to do her any harm?"

"*No.*"

"And finally. Did you walk your wife into the woods once you got home, rape her in the burned-out foundation of the trapper's shack, then fire a bullet into her head?"

"*No, I did not!*"

Chet Evers stepped a few feet back; he was nodding, eyes focused on Leonard. "Last night, as I was doing a little reading before turning out the lights, I came across an essay by Francis Bacon, the Seventeenth Century English essayist. I'm not sure why. Maybe I was looking for some help from the wisest about a subject close to our hearts these days. Mr. Bradley, I would like to quote you an opening line of one of Bacon's essays."

Chet pulled a slip of paper from his pocket. "As a side note," he said, "I read in the introduction that this particular essay, 'Of Truth,' was always the *first* in any Francis Bacon collection. While he was alive and to this day. The quote is simply—and here Chet lowered his eyes and read—"'What is truth? asked jesting Pilate, and would not stay for an answer.'"

Chet's eyes smiled. "*You* stayed for the answer, Mr. Bradley."

The defense lawyer then turned and looked at the jurors. "I want the people of New York to know, Leonard Bradley stayed for the answer."

Judge Cruikshank made a few notations, glancing up once in the process; then, taking off his glasses and finding the district attorney, he said, "The prosecution may begin its cross-examination."

"Your Honor, considering the hour," the D.A. said, "the state would like to ask for a recess until tomorrow morning."

"What's wrong with the hour?"

"It's getting on."

"Not for me. Please begin."

The district attorney stood, left his corner and his seconds and made several small passes before the witness. He was perfectly attired in a brown suit, tan shirt and yellow polkadot tie. Finally he stopped and, looking straight into Leonard's face, asked him if it was true that he raised cattle on his property in Winwar.

"Yes."

"How long have you done this?"

"Ten years."

"What is the main purpose of this venture?"

"It's mostly a tax shelter."

"But you run it as a business."

"Yes."

"Why would you stay in a business that has never made any money for you?"

"I said it was mostly a tax shelter."

"But you didn't say that to the I.R.S. when they investigated Maple Ridge Farm four years ago. You called it a business."

"It *is* a business. Its purpose—"

"You attempted to justify your huge writeoffs, isn't that true?"

"I went too far in this instance."

"After the fact, Mr. Bradley. Honesty is easy *after the fact*. But at the time you fought the government at considerable personal expense, vigorously defending your so-called business practices."

"I felt justified, most of my write-offs were perfectly legal—"

"In other words, you were just a *little* fraudulent."

William Woolever studied the witness, as if to pinpoint a second vulnerable spot. "Could you tell us for a second time, Mr. Bradley, what your salary is at the Bradley Corporation?"

"Two hundred and eighty thousand dollars."

"And this figure could be increased, as you testified, depending on bonuses."

"Yes."

"Of up to how much?"

"A hundred percent."

"But you've received no bonuses at all for two years."

"That's right."

"Mr. Bradley, how badly is the recession hurting your company? Can you give us any figures?"

"Our work force is down to its lowest level in several years."

"How about corporate stock?"

"Off."

"A lot, a little?"

"Nine points since the start of the years, about fifteen dollars all told since the recession hit."

"How does that affect you personally?"

"Mr. Woolever, I believe I'm repeating myself."

"I'm not bored—if you're worried."

Leonard was silent.

"You own 240,000 shares of Bradley stock. Is that correct?"

"Yes."

He went to his table and picked up a copy of the Wall Street *Journal*, reading the date as April 14 last. He entered it as evidence, then opened to the stock market page. "*Bradley Corp.*— here we are. *22.* Down from your high of 30—off $8.25." From his pocket Woolever withdrew a wafer-thin calculator and worked a few buttons. "Off $8.25 per share or . . . $1,980,000, your personal loss as of that date, a year ago."

He looked up. "Then five days later, on April 19, you sweetened the policy on your wife's life to an even two million dollars. What you were losing on Bradley shares, you'd stand to gain as your wife's beneficiary. If—heaven forbid!—she were to die—"

"Objection!" Chet was on his feet.

"Sustained." The judge stared at Woolever. "Kindly restrict yourself to a more focused questioning of the witness." Then, to the court stenographer: "Strike the state's last comment from the record."

The D.A. moved closer to Leonard, eager to tangle. "How long after you started dating Ms. Wirth was it before the name Barry Abrams came up?"

"It came up the day we met."

"In what connection?"

"I asked her if she was involved with anyone."

"What did she say?"

"She said she was trying to break off with a man she'd been seeing for two and a half years."

"Trying to break off."

"That's what she said."

"Did you ever learn more about this man?"

"His name would come up from time to time."

"What about their relationship? Did that ever come up?"

"Occasionally. She described it as romantic but it had never really gone anywhere."

"One can't base a relationship, in other words, on dim lights, soft music and physical intimacy."

"She never said that."

"Isn't that what she meant?"

"I never asked her."

"But you thought about it, especially when you were away from her. Didn't you, Mr. Bradley?"

"She told me she was no longer interested in Barry Abrams."

"Maybe not to live with. But to still see once in awhile, while you were back home! Truthfully now—because you are a *truthful* man, Mr. Bradley—were you threatened by Barry Abrams?'"

"Not in the beginning."

"How about later on?"

"Some."

"What happened that made you feel *threatened—some?*"

"I began to see that Diane was still involved with Abrams on an emotional level."

"How does one 'see' that?"

Leonard's hands moved in his lap, as if he were washing them, slowly. "She told me."

"Did you feel something was still going on between her and Mr. Abrams?"

"I began to think something might be."

"How did that make you feel?"

Leonard rubbed the knuckle on his right index finger. "I was worried."

"How worried were you, Mr. Bradley?"

"Enough to wake up thinking about it."

"It?"

"That she was . . . intimate with him when I wasn't there."

"In other words," said Woolever, "you were jealous."

"I became jealous—yes."

"How many times in your life, Mr. Bradley, would you say you've been jealous?"

"A couple of times, years ago."

"How would you describe the feeling?"

"It . . . nags at you."

Woolever turned away. From his seat at the defense table, Chet saw the D.A. glance toward the jury box, half-expecting Woolever to give a little wave to his female fans. "You're an executive, a man who makes things happen," the D.A. said, facing Leonard from a formal distance. "How were you planning to exorcise this feeling that, as you say, 'nags at you'?"

"I didn't know. Maybe I wouldn't be able to."

"How about by divorcing your wife?"

"That only came up when Phyllis brought up the detective's report to me. But yes, that would give me freedom to do more . . ."

"Divorces in New York aren't accomplished by snapping the fingers, especially if contested—you understood that."

"Just starting the proceeding—obtaining a separation agreement—would've allowed me to spend more time with Diane."

"Did you really think your wife was going to stand idly by while you were scooting back and forth to New York? And aren't you forgetting? If you were going to get a divorce from your wife, it was going to be *over her dead body.*"

"That's a common expression."

"Not when it's said and *comes to pass.*"

"Objection!"

"Sustained."

The D.A. walked in front of the exhibit table and thoughtfully fingered the cuff of the defendant's khaki trousers.

"When you were in New York on business, the last time you saw Ms. Wirth, how and when did you leave the city?"

"I left on an Eastern flight out of LaGuardia at 3:52 P.M."

"And landed—"

"Here in Bancroft an hour later."

"What did you do then?"

"I drove to my house in Winwar."

"When did the topic of a divorce come up?"

"Shortly after I got home, after Phyllis told me about the detective's report."

"When did you first telephone Diane after getting back to Winwar?"

"Two days later, from my office."

"What did you say to her?"

"I told her Phyllis was missing, that if she didn't show up we'd have to cancel our date in Atlantic City."

"Did you ever call Diane from your home?"

"Never . . . when Phyllis was alive."

"Weren't there times when you could have easily enough, when she was out walking?"

"Yes, but she always went over the bills."

At the defense table, Chet Evers flattened his eyebrows with thumb and forefinger.

"Then all that week your wife was missing," the D.A. asked pointedly, "why does New York Telephone have three calls from your home number to Diane Wirth?"

Leonard wet his lips. "I began thinking something was seriously wrong when Phyllis didn't come back. And because she already knew of the affair, it no longer made a difference."

"Then you would've called Diane from your house in any case, even if your wife was there?"

"Probably not—to spare her feelings."

"But if or when she came back, you wouldn't mind if she saw the bill."

"I had a feeling she wouldn't be going over it right away."

"I guess she wouldn't, Mr. Bradley. *Right away.*"

Like a boy passing through the sporting goods department of

a store, loving one item more than the next, Woolever again walked past the table holding the state's evidence. "You telephoned Diane Wirth on the afternoon your wife's body was found," he said. "Who answered the phone?"

"A man."

"What did you say to him?"

"Nothing. I asked for Diane."

"Did you know who it was?"

"I assumed it was Abrams."

"What did he say?"

"He said she was taking a shower."

"A man, a former boyfriend of the woman you were in love with—and with whom she still had an emotional involvement—was in her apartment at 3:30 in the afternoon and she's *taking a shower*. How did that make you feel?"

"Not good."

"Why?"

"For the reason you just said."

"Did you trust Diane Wirth, Mr. Bradley?"

"I didn't believe she'd start up with someone new, but with Abrams, I wasn't sure."

"With Barry Abrams, an electrician working for New York Transit, you never knew. With Barry Abrams, some bearded writer pecking away at a novel in a couple of rented rooms on Macdougal Street, *you never knew*. That must have, to put it mildly, irked you, Mr. Bradley. A man who hires and fires executives asking six-figure salaries. Who took over a family business with 54 million dollars in annual sales, went public with it and increases sales to 230 million dollars in a few years. To have some subway employee give you competition. And you weren't sure . . . maybe Barry Abrams was even, as they say, beating your time! So before you left New York you gave Ms. Wirth a small token of your esteem from Cartier, made plans to meet her in Atlantic City—and when you got home your wife greeted you with what was really very *good* news. Because now that she knew, the door to divorce was open. Perfect, you thought. Until she tossed a nasty wrench into the works by saying, and meaning, 'Over my dead body!'"

The district attorney slipped his hands into the side pockets of his dark brown suit. "So...if you openly went to New York to visit Diane, your wife would make your life *miserable*. When it came to settlement and alimony time, she would hit you where it really hurt. But you couldn't sit in Winwar. Your affair with Diane had reached a crisis. You weren't sure of her affections, and lurking in the shadows—while Diane showered—was the old boyfriend, the subway employee."

Woolever came closer to the defendant. "You could not sit passively in Winwar—that was against your constitutional makeup. And if you filed for a divorce, it was going to take years and cost you millions of dollars by the time it came through. So you devised a plan that would enable you to see Diane, take away the strain and burden of cheating, and make a few dollars for you in the bargain! *That plan was murdering your wife*—"

"That's a *lie*—"

"The evidence says *you're* lying, Mr. Bradley—evidence that no 'kitty-pan gimmickry' can discredit. It's all right here."

Woolever took three steps to the table. "The boot prints on Brenner Heights: *your* boots. The .38 slug taken from your wife's brain, *your* .38. The tuft of fabric found in the woods, from *your* khaki trousers. The blood on the cuff, your late wife's blood type. The strand of pubic hair in the fly, hers. The soil ground into the knees is the soil at the site of the murder. The soil discovered on the doorway carpet of your house matches the soil on your boots. And you ask us to believe your answer to Mr. Evers's final question to you, because you *supposedly* told the truth up to that point? Leonard Bradley, our very own George Washington, cannot tell a lie! Is that what you expect us to believe? On the afternoon of September 23 you were consumed by jealousy and ravaged by guilt. You wanted your wife gone, dead. Only *then* would your romantic and financial troubles be over. One day at a funeral—and you'd be free."

The D.A. turned and waved his hand at the evidence. "It's all here. A so-called truth defense is good stuff for the media. It's catchy, it has the ring that makes people watch and read. What lies there on that table is good for the people of the State of New York, because it proves beyond a reasonable doubt—"

"What lies on that table was *planted*," Leonard broke in, no longer able to contain himself.

"By *you*. Planted by *you*, Mr. Bradley."

Woolever came one slow step closer. "When you came back from your lawyer's on the afternoon of September 23, your wife was just starting on one of her walks. You talked her into taking a drive with you to the old swimming hole on Brenner Heights—"

"That's not true!" Leonard shouted.

"Mr. Bradley, I'm not just telling you what you did. I'm telling what the *evidence says* you did. In court, evidence counts. First, *you* robbed your own safe of jewels and cash, messing up the contents as an extra ruse to throw off the police. Then, in the woods, you raped your wife in a bestial fashion—something, of course, that no husband, especially conservative proper Leonard Bradley of St. Philip's Episcopal Church in Winwar, could *ever* do. This was your intended second false trail—"

"Your Honor," Chet said, standing at his table, "I strenuously object! My opponent is stating as fact what is only *at best* supposition! By doing so he is prompting the jury—"

Woolever turned toward Chet. "Mrs. Bradley's pubic hair in the fly of these trousers—*supposition?* The soil particles ground into the knees—*supposition?* With that kind of *supposition*, who needs facts?"

Judge Cruikshank beat with his gavel. "Mr. Woolever, you are cross-examining the defendant—*not* his attorney!"

"My apologies, Your Honor."

"Now, counselor," the judge said, turning to Chet, "if the prosecution had a few bits of soil on that table but nothing else, I'd sustain your objection. One can't make a skeleton from a finger joint. But the state has more than a finger joint to support its contentions. Physical evidence is mute, to be sure; at the same time it speaks. Mr. Woolever hears it say one thing. You hear it say something else. That is exactly why we are here. To decide between you. As to your statement that the district attorney is prompting the jury, I never knew a trial lawyer who didn't, Mr. Evers—yourself included—every chance he got." The judge paused, then said, "So let's get on with it. Mr. Woolever, proceed with the cross-examination. Of the *witness*."

At every turn Leonard denied what the D.A. said the evidence showed, and the D.A. kept right on, denial after denial. "You threw your gun in the bushes, *not* to get rid of it but to have it found! You tossed your collector's .38 revolver fifteen feet from your wife's body for the same reason you raped her. Because no one would believe—"

"I did *not* rape my wife." Leonard grabbed at the arms of the witness chair, as if to propel himself at the D.A. "Don't you tell me what I did—"

"I'm not, Mr. Bradley. I'm just reminding you."

"You can't remind someone of something they didn't do!"

"The evidence says you're lying, Mr. Bradley."

"The evidence is *bogus*. I came back from Willow and went looking for my wife. That was my only involvement with her on the day she was killed—"

"Was *killed?*" asked the D.A. "Interesting you should say that."

"We know now she was killed."

"But you're relating what you did on *that day*."

"On that day I thought missing, now I think killed."

"I hear what you say, Mr. Bradley. I'm more interested in what you *said*."

The district attorney smiled, giving it a little time to sink in. "To return. Where were we? Oh, yes. I was saying that *no one* who had just expended a bullet into someone's head, using his own gun, would then toss the weapon aside as if disposing of a gum wrapper. Unless he were interested in serving time."

Woolever raised a finger. "Still, you tossed the gun away. *Strategically* tossed it into some nearby bushes—to make it seem as if someone were trying to frame you—"

"Someone *is* trying to frame me!"

"'Someone we are not now, or yet, aware of. I'm sorry, Mr. Bradley—any framing around here is of *your* doing. Take your khaki trousers . . . these *are* your khaki trousers, you've agreed."

Woolever picked up the pair of pants from the evidence table. "Why didn't you dispose of them—throw them in a garbage bag, put them under a big stone—instead of simply stuffing them in the laundry hamper?"

"I didn't *stuff* them anywhere."

"'Someone we are not now, or yet, aware of' did it. Is that correct?"

"Yes!"

The D.A. shook his head. "You put them in the hamper, Mr. Bradley, for the same reason you tossed away your .38—precisely so they *would be discovered*, so you would appear the victim of a frame-up."

"I never *saw* the pants. I came home from the office and they weren't in my closet—"

"Do you know why they weren't in your closet, Mr. Bradley?"

"Now I do, then I didn't."

"Going back to then. You were upset, you said, that your trousers weren't where you'd hung them."

"Momentarily irritated—"

"Then why didn't you walk down the hall to your laundry alcove and retrieve them?"

"Mr. Woolever, I own more than a single pair of pants."

"No. The *reason* was, you wouldn't have found them."

"I would have. The police found them!"

"Later. You wouldn't have found them, Mr. Bradley, because you had them on!"

"I did *not* have them on!"

"And wearing them, you talked your wife into taking a little drive with you for old time's sake, to talk things over—smart move, by the way, using *her* car. The forensic specialists would have their hands tied determining if she was, or wasn't, with you. You parked in the lot at Brenner Heights. Then, as the shoe prints clearly show, you walked with your wife along the creek, then on the logger's trail. Lo and behold, you stumbled upon the old trapper's shack—or what there was left of it. Your wife kneeled to examine an artifact. Then you had to act quickly. Shoot and rape, or rape and shoot—"

"Objection!" Chet was livid. "My opponent is deliberately trying to inflame the minds of the jurors—."

"Sustained—tone it down, Mr. Woolever."

"Well," the D.A. said to Leonard, "*whichever* the sequence, you tossed your classic handgun away, returned hastily to your wife's car and drove home to Maple Ridge. Now, what to do with your pants with those telltale blood stains and soiled knees. What to do with them, indeed! They were just what you wanted. You stashed this veritable gold mine of evidence in the family hamper—all to make it seem as if someone else had done it, someone who it would be assumed was trying to make it look as though *you* had done it. Too bad you left those shoe prints and snagged your trousers on a briar bush . . ."

The district attorney went to the evidence table and picked up the collector's .38 lying beside five stubby cartridges and one empty shell. He held the pistol lightly, giving the impression it was fragile. Then, looking over at Leonard, he said, "I'm glad you 'stayed for the answer,' Mr. Bradley. So are all the good, law-abiding citizens of Cooper County."

William Woolever laid the revolver back down, not as something that might break—but as the hard steel it was. The sound, ominous and final, echoed in the courtroom.

Chapter **23**

Chuck Wojciechowski finished a beer and tossed the can on the bedroom floor of his trailer, landing it on a pile of other empties, dirty clothes and skin mags. He wanted another but should probably wait, he decided. Kids was funny. You had to be real careful how you come on, you couldn't be buzzed—they would draw back. Yesterday when he'd pulled in from K.C. the girl had said hello, but getting anything out of her was like pulling teeth. It was like she had some kind of problem, but what did he want from her? Ten lousy words.

Bitch run out on him but she was still around. He'd called the Abernathy house—she'd done her cleaning yesterday, woman said. He looked in the mirror and rubbed his chin. He'd shaved an hour ago and put on some foo-foo and he had on a clean shirt and a clean pair of pants. He din't know if the McManus kid was gonna talk but kids din't like talking to nobody who looked like a bum.

One while I wait, he thought. He snapped a can and walked to the end of the trailer and stood at the back window, drinking and waiting for the bus. Finally it came up, stopping at the end of Deerpath. Kids started getting out. When he saw the girl he took a last swallow, rinsed out his mouth with some minty crap

Sadie used and grabbed a small white box from the refrigerator. He then put on his leather wind-breaker and went out.

The girl was just coming past the end of his trailer, kind of angling toward hers, and he called out her name. She stopped and Chuck gave her a quick smile. "Guess what I got for you, Julie?"

She din't guess. "Eclairs," Chuck said. "I said to myself when I seen 'em in the store, I bet Julie loves eclairs."

Nothin'. She was just getting tits and he bet she had nice soft fuzz on her pussy. "Well, I'm havin' one," he said. "Hey, whad'd'ya say we have a little party in my truck—you and me? You ever talk on a C.B.? We'll call you Eclair. Breaker two–niner, this is Eclair."

Chuck grinned. Julie just looked at him.

"Ain't afraid, are you?"

She gave her head a little shake.

"Then come on. Know what my handle is?"

She gave her head another shake.

"'Jar Head.' For when I was in the Marines." They were at his rig. Chuck set the box on the fender and took both her elbows. "Up we go, Eclair."

Chapter  24

Tony Bradley let his dog jump clear of the truck, then walked across the dark yard to his house in Mink Hollow. A hint of spring was in the air and a few early stars were out. Inside, the house was cold and damp. Without taking off his coat he kneeled in front of the stove and grabbed old newspaper from a high lopsided stack, crumpling individual pages and tossing them in. As he reached for the last sheet to roll up, the whole stack toppled. Well, it was time to haul the newspapers away. Maybe next week. He struck a match, added sticks of kindling, put on a couple of small oak logs and closed the cast-iron door.

In the kitchen he emptied a can of sauerkraut into a pan, added two franks and turned the burner on low, then pulled a beer from the refrigerator and went back to the living area, angling the sofa toward the stove and sitting down.

What to do? Just thirty minutes ago Chet had stood with him in the corner of the garage gripping a glass of bourbon and had said, "You're right, it's a toothpick." Tony had then demonstrated how, as he viewed it, the killer had got inside the house.

"Interesting," the lawyer had said quietly.

"That's it—just interesting?"

"What else—what did you have in mind?"

"Tomorrow, introducing the toothpick as evidence."

Chet was weary, his nerves were humming. "It isn't evidence."

"Okay, then it's a clue."

His father's lawyer brought the glass—it looked like straight stuff—to his lips. "You can't introduce a clue. Look, I can't talk anymore."

"For Christ's sake, Chet. I'm trying to show you how—"

"I'm sorry, Tony."

Chet returned to the living room of the big house and Tony, steaming, walked out to his truck. But now he was only angry at himself. The toothpick proved nothing, he saw that clearly—except, of course, that he was a goddamn amateur.

There was a scratching at the door and he opened it, letting Buck in, then went back to the fire, mulling over his efforts since last fall at uncovering his mother's murderer. What did he *have*? He had a *toothpick*. Plus a notion—getting fuzzier as he thought about it—of how the killer had got inside the house. Plus another notion, fuzzier still, about the old ramshackle Vandermark barn as the place where the killer had parked his car.

Tony took off his denim jacket and threw it aside, then sat thinking—as he'd done for months now—trying to get some handle on his mother's death by deductive power, while seeming to know—to recognize for the first time—that he had failed. The trial was almost over and it was a toss up, talk was, how the jury would decide. His father might go free, he might spend the rest of his life in jail. But whatever the verdict, there was still a killer out there—someone who, as Tony saw it, had parked at the old barn, walked through the woods, ducked inside the garage, led his mother back to the barn and driven her to Brenner Heights, where he had raped and shot her. Then, at the house again, had stuffed the khakis in the hamper and returned Leonard's boots to his closet. Tony pressed against his skull. He saw it all but what could he do? What could he do to *prove* it, to prove even a shred of it? Buck came up and pushed his muzzle under his master's arm, sensing his misery.

Back in the living room he thought to add a log to the fire. As he was grabbing one, his eye was drawn to a picture on the front page of the newspaper now exposed, since the lopsided stack had toppled. Tony fed the log in, clamped shut the door and picked up the paper.

He vividly remembered the day last fall that he had read the lead story and had thought—as he was thinking now—how strange it was that the person who had figured so powerfully in his life when they were boys would again figure importantly in when they were men. True, in the first instance there had been an investigation about Dwayne's culpability in the death of Lucy Marzocca. In the second, as the Audrey Ryder picture and story testified, he was something of a local hero for finding Phyllis Bradley's body. It was odd, though. Both instances had to do with the death of women Tony had loved. My girlfriend, he thought, and my mother.

He let the paper fall, making nothing more of it. People's lives touched and rubbed in small towns, and touched and rubbed and touched again.

The room was warming now and Tony unlaced his boots and sipped coffee. This was always the hardest time for him, the nighttime hours, the loneliness, the longing for Debby. He sat and thought, remembering . . .

The day they had met on the Yale course, their wedding, their first weekend as a married couple visiting her parents. He was helping Dr. Brownell barbecue on the patio, then after dinner he and Debby went for a drive in her father's new Olds 98; she suggested they stop for a drink in a little wayside place she knew. She gave him directions. *And when he parked in front of the tavern she slid close and kissed him and said she had a gift for him and he asked, "What is it?" "You'll have to wait." Inside they sit at the bar, and who comes over to serve them but Captain Black. They hadn't driven five miles and here they were in Jonesville Flats. Tony looks around and recognizes kids from Winwar High, glances at Debby, except the girl beside him isn't Debby. It's Lucy Marzocca. She smiles, her eyes dark and shining in the dim light. "Can you guess?" she asks. "Guess?" "What your gift is." "No." "Then I'll tell you. It's an ebony box." "An ebony box?" "Yes." They finish their drinks and go out, he looking up and down a dark deserted street. Only it isn't Dr. Brownell's car any more, it's his mother's station wagon. They drive to Winwar and he raises the garage door to his parents' house by pushing the remote button on the visor. They're inside the garage, a full moon is centered in the window that overlooks the ridge. They crawl into the back and Lucy says, "Take your gift, Tony." She slips off her panties and there it is, waiting for him, glossy in the moonlight against her pale skin. He feels torn, wanting her but holding back. He is married to Debby, he loves Debby. He looks into Lucy's eyes, he has to tell her things are different now—and suddenly it is Debby, after all. And the garage is her parents' garage and the car her father's and they're back in Merion. He draws his beautiful bride closer, and the lights suddenly flash on. They jump up. The garage door is fully open. And standing on the sill in a tan-and-brown policeman's uniform, a round white bandage on his head, staring in, is Dwayne McManus—*

Tony's body jerked as he came abruptly awake. He squeezed the back of his neck with both hands, then stumbled into the kitchen, turned on the cold water tap and splashed his face. He stood there, water dripping from his beard, staring at the tarnished drain.

Outside, a fox barked.

The next morning he drove to Maple Ridge and parked in the big turn-around area. He had to run through the "killer's moves" again. He got out of his truck and began walking toward the house. Catherine and Chet were having breakfast and he sat down with them and had coffee. Leonard was still in his room. Tony asked the lawyer what the day's agenda was.

"Closing arguments."

He looked at his sister. "I called Debby last night."

"How is she? Isn't it any day now?"

"Actually the due date's tomorrow but she thinks she's going to be late."

"Are you going to go?"

"I'm planning on it."

"When are you leaving?"

"Maybe tomorrow."

"You should go today!"

"We'll see." He stood up. "Good luck, Chet."

"Thanks, Tony."

"Excuse me," Tony said leaving.
"Where are you going?" his sister asked.
"Out to the garage."
At the table, watching him go, Catherine sat shaking her head.

He removed the keys from his father's car and backed it out of the garage. With the automatic device in his hand, he then lowered the door, taking a position around the corner. His shoulders were flat against the outside wall. He was in plain view of the road, but how many cars, realistically, came up to the house? Then his head sank. Here he was, making the same moves, having the same thoughts as yesterday. He seemed to see himself next week, in six months, next year, his shoulders flat against the outside wall, thinking the killer, standing here, would be in plain view, but how many cars, realistically, came up to the house?

Maybe he should just get in his truck and go. Chet was a good lawyer, he knew what he was doing—his father had a chance at acquittal. Hanging around like this, hugging shovels and spying toothpicks wasn't helping his father's cause. And the trial was virtually over. "Closing arguments..." He looked up. A car was coming along the road, already past the barn, just starting on the straightaway following the ridge.

He saw how much time he would have to go across the road and disappear into the woods. Plenty of it. He could be a hundred yards in by now. The car kept coming, a rusting, yellow Pontiac. It turned at the garden, turned again at the woodpile and came to a stop beside Chet's old Volvo. Sadie Wojciechowski got out and walked up to the house.

Ten minutes later his father, sister and Chet left for court. And he was no longer standing against the side of the garage. He was sitting against it, looking out at the barn and silo and at the rough, rocky countryside beyond. He didn't know, something kept him here, kept him from simply cleaning up and getting in his truck and driving to Merion. In his hand was the remote device from his father's car. He stood up and without thinking—without thinking any more about what he should be doing—he touched the button and the door started to go up. He was doing it again, making the moves. Visualizing his mother's car backing out, he sidestepped around the corner and hid in the recess, near the tools. Then he pressed the button. He watched for the black electrical box fastened to the door as the door started down, remembering the close call he'd had yesterday. Today it wasn't a problem. The box slid by harmlessly; with the door fully closed it was exactly level with his knees.

Now what? Do it again.

He did. And then again. Each time trying to puzzle it out, literally to connect and fit pieces, trying to give his mind greater freedom . . . When he had played golf he had practiced not just to perfect his shots but because in the process of practicing, concepts and ideas about the whole game tended to come to him. One time he had tried explaining it to his father but he wasn't sure Leonard had understood. One practiced to groove the swing, his father believed. The idea in golf was to repeat, time after time, the stroke. They were so different, even during those years when they were very close, the best of friends . . .

One more time. He repeated the move, suddenly having the notion of enlisting the police officer's help—having him *actually back out* Phyllis's car in an effort to reconstruct the scene more faithfully. But looking over toward the W.P.D. cruiser he saw that the officer on duty—was Dwayne McManus. His dream of last night came back to him in a rush, and for a moment, several moments in fact, he felt emotionally drained. Then he recognized his idea as amateurish, once again. As if Dwayne, in the first place, would do it. The W.P.D. had its case, had worked hard to develop its case. And the cop out front wasn't going to participate in the defendant's son's attempt at upsetting it.

All right. Once more. Again he pressed himself against the outside wall, twisting deftly inside as, in his mind, his mother backed out her car. Before pushing the button to start the door down, he eyed the black box—an electrical wire trailed from it like a thin smooth vine. Then a new thought . . . All along, he had avoided the box. But suppose the killer hadn't—the way *he* almost hadn't that first time.

Tony looked up, thinking to make a closer inspection of the

box, then had a better idea. He quickly crossed the garage floor, went inside the house and took the stairs down to his father's— temporarily Chet's—office, where in the oak desk he found the magnifying glass Leonard used for his gun collection. He walked back to the garage. Remembering his thought of a few minutes ago about the W.P.D., Tony decided he didn't want Dwayne— it could've been any of the chief's men out there—actually observing what he was now about, and he lowered the door.

Which made looking more difficult but he liked the feeling of privacy. Flat on his back, Tony wriggled close to the door and lifted the glass. His eyes—the blood behind them—began pounding. In the crimp, where the side and bottom part of the metal box met, was a powdery, reddish brown substance. Stuck to this substance were two or three strands of dark-brown hair.

Chapter **25**

"But just suppose," Chet Evers was saying to the jurors, halfway through his closing argument, "Mr. Bradley *had* worn those khaki trousers the afternoon of September 23—and wearing those trousers *had* murdered and raped his wife. Then, having done this brutal act, he drove home and, cool as you will, deposited those trousers in the dirty-clothes hamper—to make the police think no man in his right mind would do anything so careless; and thus, the killer *had* to be someone else, someone who wanted to frame Mr. Bradley."

Chet paused. "Ladies and gentlemen, would *you* have that kind of presence of mind, under similar circumstances? And furthermore, would you really believe it would *work*? Such a complete scenario depending on so much iffy deduction by the police?"

He moved a little closer to the jurors. "And we're supposed to believe that Mr. Bradley deposited the shoes and pants he was wearing after raping and murdering his wife—so the district attorney claims—in his own closet and laundry hamper? Is that remotely likely? Put yourself in the position of a man who had committed a violent crime against someone living under the same roof, would *you* toss the articles of clothing you'd worn into the family clothes bin, dirt stains, blood stains and all, hoping by this action to somehow mislead the police? No, you or I would take those boots, put them in a strong bag filled with stones and drop them in the nearest river! As for the pants, set them on fire and scatter the ashes to the wind..."

Defense counsel paused. Then in a lower tone: "Ladies and gentlemen of the jury, some actions fly in the face of known psychological behavior. It is perfectly true that we all are individuals and act differently, but not to the extent that Mr. Bradley is said to have acted. There are certain pervasive responses. When people get hungry they eat; with chopsticks, fingers or sterling silver, the food gets in their mouths. It's a basic need— just like self-preservation is a basic need. After committing a crime, *evidence is destroyed*—how it is destroyed is up to the individual, but it is destroyed. You know the story about the English marm who clobbered her husband over the head with a frozen leg of lamb—boom! Two bobbies from the local constabulary came out to investigate the death. A bereft, kindly old lady met them at the door. She happened to be cooking up a little dinner, to boost her failing spirits, and invited the officers to partake."

It brought a laugh in the courtroom. Chet continued, his face serious. "Why is it that when someone speaks the truth, people listen? Why do we always know the sound of truth? The American writer, Herman Melville, called truth the 'shock of recognition'—when it's spoken, everyone sits up, recognizes it. Whether the person talking is a school child or the President of the United States, your heart tells you if he's telling the truth. When it became apparent that Mr. Bradley would be standing trial for allegedly killing his wife, I looked and looked for physical evidence supporting his innocence. Nary a shred of that existed! From the time he left my office in Willow, only one person saw him, a hired hand, but as that individual testified, he really couldn't see the driver of the station wagon because of the sun's reflection. Ladies and gentlemen, the defense *had nothing*. No witness to Mr. Bradley's movements. No alibi to establish his whereabouts for some two and a half hours. And every day the district attorney was adding to his cache. Shoe prints, cloth fibers, soil particles, a .38 revolver, a matching slug, hunting boots, a strand of pubic hair, blood samples—I mean, Mr. Woolever has nothing to worry about. If he loses the fall election, he has enough merchandise on that table to open a flea market."

Some laughter. Chet was grateful for it but reminded himself it was a momentary thing. A break in the tension of the trial. "The question facing the defense, long before the trial began, was how to fight the raft of state's evidence that had the *appearance* of truth but was, in fact, false: contrived, bogus, planted, factitious, artificial—call it what you will, you'll be right. How would the defense proceed? Frankly, I didn't know. I asked the defendant what his first feelings were when he learned his wife was dead—and he answered: Grief-stricken, emotionally shattered, deeply sorrowful. I sensed the response to be less than a hundred percent truthful and told him so. The shock of recognition wasn't there. Mr. Bradley was angry. He called me presumptuous for making such a judgment. Then he told me something else I'd like to share with you now. He said even if what he'd just told me *wasn't* the truth, he'd be damned if he'd ever tell *the* truth—what those first feelings *really* were when he learned of his wife's death—to a jury! What kind of fool, in effect, did I take him for?"

Chet stood at the jury box railing, the smile on his lips, faint; the nodding of his head, fainter. "Instead of an ally, Mr. Bradley looked on the truth as an enemy. I quoted him Scriptures, where it is written in John, 'Ye shall know the truth, and the truth shall make you free'; and in Ephesians, 'Put away falsehood, and speak every man the truth with his neighbor'. But Mr. Bradley held out. Only after many hours did he finally consent to speak *only* the truth when he testified. Then what did he do? He started backing off from that—and I walked away. That was no rehearsed act, ladies and gentlemen. Mr. Bradley was still so frightened of the truth that I had to *coerce* him to speak it by leaving him, as it were, for the district attorney. But as each of you witnessed, Mr. Bradley called me back. Do you remember? And from *then* on he told the whole truth."

Chet Evers put his hands loosely on the railing. "I have heard it said that *thinking* about adultery is the same as committing it. I do not see how that is true. It is a human condition to fantasize;

who knows but it saves many a marriage—and prevents many a murder. Ladies and gentlemen, wishing your spouse would die is *not* a punishable offense. Call Leonard Bradley guilty of adultery, of lying to his wife—call him anything you want, but recognize the difference between a personal moral judgment and the law. And remember that *this is a court of law.* We do not stand before St. Peter today —God help us all when we do. We stand before the laws of the state. America, as you know, is a land of laws, not of men.

"I am not of the Catholic faith. However, I understand confession. Leonard Bradley has made a perfect confession. Which is to say, he has told the truth. About himself, his relationships, his life. Judge him as you will, but say and know he has told the truth! And as you deliberate, remember the line from *John.* With God's help and following your own deepest consciences, I know you will find the defendant *not guilty*—and set him free."

A measured pause. Then: "Thank you, ladies and gentlemen."

He turned to the judge. "As you recall, your honor, I said on the first day of this trial that I did not have a case—I only had the truth. Nevertheless, because it is impossible to rest the truth, I now rest my case."

"My adversary has attempted to play with your emotions, I'm afraid," William Woolever was saying. His closing argument had preceded Chet's. Now he was taking advantage of the prosecution's right to speak again. "He's brought in Scriptures, thrown around philosophical and literary terms—anything to divert your minds. From what? I will tell you 'from what'."

The D.A.'s hand shot down, index finger extended. "From the *facts* of this case."

He pointed to the crowded exhibit table. "*There* is the sum and substance of *New York* v. *Bradley.* In black and white. Mr. Evers has *talked* about the truth—I have *shown* it to you. I have not had to hide behind the fancy smokescreens of Poe, Melville, Francis Bacon and St. John. The only so-called shock of recognition the state knows is that facts talk—and words are cheap. You were warned, Beware the House of Woolever—it would crack and fall after the defense got through with it. Well, I don't see any fissures. I see a structure built with the solid brick of physical evidence. I'll tell you which house will fall—the straw house of the defense. Why should you, or anyone, believe a man who *says* he is telling the truth when his biography is written in the watery ink of lying and deceit? Words do not erase one's record, and Mr. Bradley's record of telling the truth is dismal. Turning a new leaf, as he was here 'coerced' to do, is in the same category as a New Year's resolution. Both pave the road to hell."

The district attorney of Cooper County looked over his shoulder at the exhibit tables, laden with footwear and soil samples and clothing and guns and moulages. "That evidence tells you, ladies and gentlemen, that the defendant is guilty of an unspeakably brutal crime. Statute alone protects him from death row, but in your hearts you know it is where he belongs."

Chapter 26

Tony Bradley led the two police officers, his father's lawyer and his sister down the long hall past the laundry alcove. Entering the garage, he flipped on the lights and walked in front of the station wagon, then between the wagon and his father's car to the wide, heavily braced door. Here he turned and faced Chief Flick, Sgt. O'Shea, Chet and Catherine. At least Catherine looked interested. Chet seemed preoccupied. All arguments were over, Judge Cruikshank had instructed the jurors, and the waiting had begun.

Tony explained how he had come to see, or understand, how the *real* killer had gained entrance to the house. As his mother was backing out her station wagon on the day she was kidnapped and murdered, he said, her assailant had slipped around the corner from the outside. Tony gestured with his hand to indicate the killer's move.

"Wouldn't your mother have seen this man ducking in?" asked O'Shea, setting down the black vinyl case he toted everywhere.

"If you're looking over your left shoulder, you can't see what's happening over your right," Tony said.

"Did your mother favor her left shoulder when backing out? Do you know that for a fact?"

"No, I don't."

"Go ahead, Tony," said the chief.

Tony went to the station wagon, unclipped the remote-control device and depressed the button. The door went up. The group went out and Tony showed where he—and the killer—had stood. "I pretended to hear the motor start," he said, "pretended to see the rear bumper of the car break the plane. Then I circled around inside like this—and stood—just like this—perfectly concealed from outside, as you can see. I pushed the button to lower the door"—he did it now, all were again inside—"and this electrical box right here"—it had started coming down—"almost hit me on the head. I was lucky. It's my belief the killer wasn't."

"How do you know?"

"After doing the move a dozen times or more, it occurred to me to examine the box. My dad keeps a magnifying glass in his office downstairs. What I saw . . . well, see for yourself."

"Let's have a look," the chief said.

Tony raised the door and the stocky police sergeant, Jim O'Shea, positioned himself beneath the box, holding up his own glass, rectangular in shape; after a few moments he pulled it away and looked with his naked eye. Next he examined the glass itself, gave it a shot of breath and a rub on the round part of his shoulder, and extended it again. "I'm not seeing a thing," he said.

"It's there," said Tony.

"What am I looking for?"

"You'll see. Keep looking."

O'Shea examined the electrical box for another few seconds. "Sorry," he said, and handed the magnifying glass to Tony. "Here—tell me if I'm wrong."

Tony inspected the box. The crimp was perfectly clean—no foreign matter whatsoever was lodged in it. He lowered the glass—dumbfounded, stricken. "I saw it," he shouted at the sergeant. "Hair, strands of human hair. Dried blood—"

"You're sure it was blood," O'Shea said.

"It sure as hell looked like blood. And it was definitely hair."

"Was anyone here beside you?" the chief asked.

"Sadie . . . but she was scrubbing the kitchen floor."

"Was that door open or shut while you were out here?" Oscar pointed at the door leading to the inside of the house.

"Shut."

"How about outside on the grounds? Anybody see you?"

Tony shook his head. "Not that I noticed. It was quiet."

"Who was on this morning, do you know, Jim?" asked the chief.

"I think McManus."

"It was McManus," Tony said.

"Check his sheet when you get back to headquarters. Go talk with Diehl right now," the chief said.

O'Shea walked across the parking area toward the parked cruiser.

Oscar scraped his jaw. "Chet, when did Tony tell you about this?"

"After court today."

"Did he say what it was?"

"Hair and dried blood."

"Do you think I'm making this up?" Tony asked.

"People sometimes see what they want to see."

"Chief, I saw hair and dried blood—!"

"How about the toothpick?" Catherine said.

Tony grabbed the shovel, pointed.

Oscar looked down. "What about it?"

"Whoever stood here dropped it . . ."

A moment passed. "Okay. Thank you."

"That's it?"

"What do you want me to do, Tony?"

"Dismantle the box, take it to a lab. Examine the toothpick. What do I want from you? I want you to understand that my father did not kill my mother!"

"Excuse me," said the chief.

He walked over to O'Shea and Diehl, spoke with them at the parked cruiser, then got in his own car and left the ridge. Standing outside the garage, Tony kicked hard at the crushed stones in the driveway.

* * *

He was sitting in front of a small fire in his house, then, slowly, stood up, walked to one window and stared out toward the old orchard, then moved to the second window and looked out at his depleted supply of logs. He crossed the living room, standing in front of each of the two windows in front of the house. The creek, though still running fast, had subsided greatly. On the trees in Mink Hollow the first buds were starting to appear. Higher up the mountains were still brown; way higher, white.

When he finished his circle of windows Tony returned to the sofa, leaned forward, hands pressing against his face. He stood again, this time going into his bedroom and looking out that window. He couldn't see the village but he could see the Cho-dokee Valley with a late afternoon sun shining on it. He turned away, sat down on the bed, pushed fingers back through his hair. On his nightstand lay some snapshots he'd taken of Debby six, seven years ago and he looked through them—for as many times that day as he had gone from window to window in the house. Here she was in a bikini, here in a see-through gown. His eyes went to the dark shadow...and he was recalling his recent dream. What had it all meant, if anything? Why "ebony box," over and over? It wasn't an expression he would use, had *ever* used. And why the bandage on Dwayne's head? As he sat there, glad at least to have some focus, it occurred to Tony to take another look at the newspaper photograph.

He went into the living room, flipped through some old issues of the *Times-Herald*, wondering if the one he was looking for was now ashes in his stove....But then he found it. He sat down, this time carefully studying the picture. And saw on the side of Dwayne's head a round white spot. A bandage?

The paper slipped from his hand. Now what? White bandage, ebony box. What had his dream said? Ebony box, white bandage. What were the associations? Ebony box. Debby's ebony box. Lucy Marzocca's ebony box. Isn't an ebony box a *black* box? Debby's black box, Lucy's black box. Black box, white bandage...

Black box, white bandage. Sonofabitch, was he zeroing in or wasn't he? Black box, bandage. Bandage, box. Black box, ebony box, shadow, box, bandage, box, bandage...

What *was* it? Black box, white bandage, ebony box, bandage
...black box, bandage...injury, bandage, black box, injury,
metal box, electrical box...bandage, injury, box, injury, bandage, electrical box...garage door, electrical box, hair, blood...
killer, box, bandage, dream...bandage, blood, killer, bandage,
newspaper, picture, dream...

Tony grabbed the paper off the floor, and stared.

Chapter 27

He pushed open the cabin door and put down a grocery bag on the wood counter. Sadie was under his old army blanket on the bed. "It's cold in here, baby."

She didn't speak.

"What's the matter?"

She was still quiet, just curled up tight; her eyes were shut but she wasn't sleeping.

"I'll get the fire going," Dwayne said.

He went out the back door and picked up three logs from the small stack on the deck; inside again, he put two logs in the stove with some loose twigs. The coals were dimming but the fire would take up again quick. He walked over and sat next to her, putting his hand on the blanket and making a little circle where her hip made it rise. "Come on, tell me," he said; even though he knew what it was, he wanted her to get it out.

"I'm goin' to Florida, Dwayne." She moved a little so she now lay on her back.

"Florida!"

"I got people there."

"What's the deal?"

"I'm in your way here."

"That's not true."

"It is true!"

"Bullshit, Sadie!"

"Dwayne, listen to me," she said, half sitting up. "Today that look you had, it scared me half to death when you come to the door. Then how you said, 'You never seen me! You never let me in!' Like if I made a mistake, then what? It's been making me crazy!"

He didn't like keeping her in the dark but if he wanted to get through this mess, he had to. "Okay, just relax," he said.

"Why would you say that to me? Don't the chief know everything you're doing?"

"Of course he does."

"Then why did you say that, honey?"

He was holding her wrist gently and slid his hand up along her arm, his thumb and middle finger like an expandable bracelet. "Cops do a lot of things they can't talk about and this is one of them, but because you're so up-tight, I'll tell you. I'm on special assignment for the department. No one's supposed to know—and I mean *no one*."

"Doin' what?"

"I shouldn't be tellin' you this," Dwayne said. "It looks now like there's some chance Bradley didn't do it—and I'm working on a new lead."

"I told you he didn't do it!"

"Anyway, I had to work fast after Tony Bradley left, I didn't have time to talk to you, baby."

"Well if this is what police work does to someone, I don't know, Dwayne. I don't like what it's doing to you!"

"It's the trial."

"Ain't trials police work? You're always gonna have trials!"

"Not like this one."

"Then it's best I go to Florida till it's over."

He didn't know but she wasn't right. Because the hard truth was, she was the weak link—she was the one who might slip up and say, "Yes, I let Dwayne inside Bradley's house. I don't know what he did but I know he went in the garage." That's all it would take.

"Well, I know living out of paper bags can't be that great for you," he said.

"Honey, I could live out of my pocketbook, if I just felt we was really together. But I see things happening. Do you still love me?"

"I put down a binder on a house, didn't I?"

"You ain't seeing someone else?"

"Sadie, come on!"

"I want it to happen for us, Dwayne. It ain't happening!"

"Do you want me to quit the force? I'll quit the force," he said.

"I couldn't live with myself if you done that."

"Well, what's it you do want, just tell me."

"That feeling back between us."

"These just ain't normal times. Better times are coming for us, baby."

"Are they? I ain't sure, no more!" She began crying.

Christ almighty, thought Dwayne. "Sadie, I got something for you," he said. "I was gonna wait till we got settled in our house before giving it to you, but the hell with it."

"You got something, for me?"

"I sure do."

"What is it?"

"Close your eyes."

"Are you just teasing?"

"I'm not teasing you. Close your eyes."

He crossed to the closet, opening the single door. Inside a few of Sadie's dresses were hanging, also a robe and a coat. But most of the stuff was his. He reached in the rubberized game pouch of a canvas hunting jacket; deep inside was a long, narrow box that he took out. "Okay," he said, sitting beside her again.

She opened her eyes and he put the box, covered in blue velvet, in her hand.

"I didn't get a chance to wrap it," he said.

"Dwayne—"

"Go on, open it."

She lifted the top and gasped. Her mouth stayed open and her eyes were wide, staring—like she couldn't believe what she was seeing.

"Well?"

"I've never seen anything so beautiful!"

"I don't know how good they are but they looked nice. I picked them up at an estate sale."

"I've always wanted a string of pearls!" She had them out of the box now, holding them up. "Oh, Dwayne! Honey, they're gorgeous!"

"Let me put them on you," he said.

"Dwayne, these had to cost a fortune!"

"I got a real good buy. Lean forward a little."

She leaned forward. The clasp was set in a small black stone, and it had an intricate catch for security. "There," he said, finally getting it.

When he pulled back, Sadie was sitting straight, running her fingers over the pearls like she was reading Braille—a love letter.

"They look real pretty on you," Dwayne said.

She gave him a big kiss. "Thank you, honey."

"I just don't think you should wear them around, you know— like for everyday when you do your cleaning."

"You think I'm crazy?"

"Well, you might want to show them off."

"Can I bring them to Florida?"

"You still going?"

"Maybe not. What do you think?"

"Let's talk about it later," he said.

Sadie slipped off her shirt and bra. The pearls glistened against her breasts.

He figured maybe in the store they'd know, he never did get much out of the girl—and he din't have his whole life to work at it. A couple of times he thought about sliding his hand down inside her jeans while they were sitting in his cab eating eclairs and talking on the C.B. but he caught hisself, it wasn't what he was after. So he hung in just being nice to her, making hisself promise not to make no stupid moves though she was a lonely girl with a round little ass and tits just coming on who probably would of loved it.

It was called Woodland General Store, the kind of place that sold everything from ammo to cold cuts, from live bait to grass seed. Julie had said "on a creek," which was something, but Chodokee Creek run a long way and he couldn't find out if she meant above Winwar or below—or maybe some other creek. Young unfucked pussy had him running all over the county. Maybe he should of just gave her a quick look at his johnson. Young like that, they were hot and curiouser than shit—she might even have went down on it. Chuck got out of his car. He had on blue trousers and his leather windbreaker.

An old woman who must of once had super knockers because they were big now though dragging bad was filling the cigarette slots behind the counter. "Can I help you?" she said.

"Six pack of Bud."

The woman went to the cooler and got the beer and came back. She had a funny way of walking. She took a lot of steps but didn't cover no ground, like she was walking against a treadmill. She asked him if there was anything else.

"Cigarettes—Winston."

"Pack or box?"

He shot her a grin. "Box."

She put the cigs beside the brew. She had small stubby thumbs that looked like crawfish and her glasses had a black band that run around her head. He guessed she was early seventies. Even sagging, he wouldn't of minded grabbing her jugs. He didn't know much about old women, but he bet they still took it if the opportunity come up—took it and loved it.

"Anything else?"

"Chap Stick."

"Regular or cherry?"

"Cherry."

He shot her a second grin and slapped down a bill. "How was it for bear last year?"

"Back up in, they done real good. Four, I know of."

"Say, I'm looking for an old army buddy of mine lives around these parts. Good hunter. He always told me to look him up, name's Dwayne McManus."

"Oh, sure." The woman handed him change. "I went to school with his father, Dutch McManus."

"I know he lives on the creek somewheres," Chuck said.

"He's got a camp on the crik—he *lives* in Winwar."

"Where's this camp?"

The woman circled around and stood by the glass-paneled door. "See that bridge there? Cross t'other side, turn right, go along for three miles or so. You can't see the cabin but if you look careful you'll see the drive—it's at the top of a long rise where a big hemlock leans across."

"Thanks a lot," Chuck said.

"Tell him you spoke to Dorothy Shultis."

He said he would and went out, putting the purchases on the seat and driving to the bridge. He checked his mileage and twisted open a Bud. The road dipped, rose and turned. Chuck kept swigging nonstop, tossing the empty out the window when he finished and lighting a cigarette. Then he opened a new beer. So the girl had gave him a good lead after all.

He drove on, going real slow as he neared three miles. Then ahead, coming to the top of a long upslope like the old gash said, he saw a big tree leaning across the road—maybe it was a hemlock. Who knew a hemlock? Then he noticed the drive like she also said. It curved down and you couldn't see nothing, but the smoke wasn't from no Girl Scouts roasting wieners. Chuck went on by for a ways and stopped, pulling off to the side or what side to the road there was. Maybe two feet, then a ditch.

He finished his beer, got out, closing his door quiet, then opened the trunk and took out a 16-gauge pump, pressing down on the trunk lid till it caught. He started walking back. When he got near the cabin he cut off the road and walked in the woods. The land slanted pretty sharp and his feet slipped once on wet leaves but he caught hisself before going down. Then he saw the cabin through the trees, and the yellow Pontiac in front and next to it a blue Chevy. Chuck's right hand was tight on the pump grip. His nose began itching and he raised the gun, barrel pointing up, and brushed his nose with his sleeve.

He stood still for a couple of seconds, wondering if the door was locked; then he noticed a small deck in back and steps leading up. His nose itched again, so bad he wanted to reach up and tear it off like a scab. He moved closer to the cabin, no windows were on the side. Then he was at the bottom step looking up. If the steps creaked McManus would come to the door, and he'd blow his head off. Maybe then he wouldn't kill Sadie. She was a pretty good cunt. He would have to see. If McManus was fucking her, he'd kill them both. Maybe the judge would go easy on him with his history and all. Sometimes things come back to help you, like how he'd rubbed shit all over his chest, face and arms one time in Guam. He loved shit, he told them. He wanted to eat a shit sandwich. But he din't care. They could give him a full twenty, he din't give a fuck if it helped him or not.

Chuck Wojciechowski grabbed the pump grip and started up the steps. The finger on his left hand, inside the trigger guard, looked like the letter J.

They were fooling around, just going slow; then it was time and he glided in. Right off, she began talking. He liked it. Some women he'd had affairs with never said a word, they were all concentration. Not Sadie.

"That feels so nice," she said.

"It sure does, baby."

"I love you."

"I love you too."

"Dwayne?"

"What, baby?"

"Never stop fucking me, okay?"

"Okay."

"Tell me about our house."

"It's our first night, we're drinking champagne."

"Where are we?"

"First downstairs by the fireplace, then in our room with the slanted roof."

"I hope it's raining. Oh, honey. Never stop fuckin' me!"

"I won't stop, never."

"Ain't we lucky?"

"We're real lucky."

"I don't want to go to Florida."

"Then don't go."

"Never stop—honey!"

He held her close, and even as he held her, feeling her heart loud against his chest, and his own too, he heard a noise outside on the deck. He lifted up his shoulders, his head. "Sadie—"

"What, honey?"

He heard it again. "Someone's out there."

He rolled over, pulling away from her, and yanked open the drawer to the little table, grabbing his .45 just as the door crashed in. Sadie sat up—then came a deafening blast—it was like a lightning bolt had struck the cabin. Dwayne threw himself off the bed; a second blast came, an unholy column of shot tore over his shoulder. On the floor he raised the automatic. Chuck yanked at the pump grip, then frantically again. His eyes dropped to the mechanism and Dwayne fired and seemed to see Wojcie-chowski's nose vanish, like a knot reamed out by a high-speed bit. His runt neighbor reeled back, struck the icebox, and fell.

Dwayne stayed on the floor, panting. The ringing in his ears and the smoke in the room brought him back—he might have thought he was on the jungle floor after an ambush—and now all was quiet and he was telling himself he'd lived through it. The powder was thick and he coughed and got to his feet, looking at the bed. She lay with her mouth open and her eyes half open, a huge wound in her chest. The bed looked like the floor of a slaughter house. Behind the bed, blood and bits of skin and organs splattered the wall.

Sadie!

He looked away. Chuck lay in a contorted heap, his face black except for a hole dead in the center, blood oozing out. Opposite, the skull didn't really exist.

Dwayne set his gun on the counter and pulled on his under-wear and trousers, then poured some whiskey in a glass. He had to think, had to stay cool. He was a veteran, he'd seen heavy action. He was a police officer. The door was open and the air coming in was thinning the smoke. He drank the whiskey slow, thinking.

It wasn't common but it had happened, two people shooting each other dead. As for hitting someone in the face with a .45, if they were experienced with the gun it could happen; someone inexperienced with it like Sadie would be lucky to hit the wall. But it wasn't impossible. Her estranged husband broke down the door and the two fired simultaneously. As to what she was doing in the cabin, Dwayne had taken mercy on her—her husband was always beating on her, getting drunk and abusing her. So Dwayne, as a neighborly gesture, gave her the loan of his cabin. Nothing was going on between them. She had appealed to him as a friend and a police officer—

Then how come Sadie had just had sex? How come Wojciechowski had fired a shot nowhere near her side of the bed?

He looked at Woj's body crammed in the doorway, ugly as a possum squashed on the road. Still gripping the pump handle. Southpaw. *Fuckin' shell, go in!* must have been his last thought. Chuck could just as easy be standing where he was now, and *he* could be dead on the floor. Dwayne sipped the whiskey.

Maybe the thing to do was own up. He and Sadie were having an affair and planning to get married, and her crazy husband had surprised them and—and this was the tragic result. He had fired in self-defense after Wojciechowski had missed him once and was trying to pump in another round.

He would be questioned, but self-defense was self-defense, whether you were in bed with another man's wife or your own. It was an unfortunate involvement and he could lose his job—it would all depend on the Review Board's judgment. Still, he wasn't sure he wanted the job anyway, now, and in any case keeping or losing it was secondary to the other, all-important issue . . .

Dwayne put on his socks and shoes, buttoned his shirt and fastened on his shoulder holster with his off-duty .38, then slipped into his denim jacket. He had another sip of whiskey. Now it was just him, alone—and OK, he was sleeping with Sadie. These things happened. She was married to a scumbag and

they'd started keeping company late last year. That was key. *Late*
last year. He remembered telling the chief that day in the trailer
park he and Sadie hadn't spoken ten words. Who was there now
to disprove that? Suddenly he didn't see his relationship with
her as so potentially compromising, like he always used to, when
he knew if it ever came out he was seeing the Bradleys' house
cleaner, Oscar would drop by and ask him a few questions. He
could've stonewalled it most likely but the chief was quick—he
was a good interviewer... there was no telling what he might
pick up in Dwayne's answers.

But now it wasn't so bad, as he saw it. He would drive down
to the general store and call the chief. He would say, "Chief, we
got two people dead in my cabin in Woodland." He would say,
"Chief, you know Wojciechowski. I've been seeing his wife since
Christmas. Crazy sonofabitch came storming in, barrel blazing.
Third round jammed, or I'd be dead." That was what he'd say.
"Third round jammed or I'd be dead."

Dwayne finished the whiskey. He went to the front door,
turned to look at Sadie—but couldn't. Didn't want to really. He
had to think ahead, this was already behind him. He clenched
and unclenched his fist a couple of times, just to psych himself
a little, and walked out to his car.

Chapter 28

Chief Oscar Flick looked over the report he was preparing for the Review Board requesting discretionary pay increases—otherwise called merit raises—for selected members of the department. He was recommending the maximum for Dave Bock and Jim O'Shea for their "outstanding, highly professional work on the Leonard A. Bradley murder case—$600."

Oscar glanced at his next candidate for recognition, Dwayne McManus, whose "enthusiastic response to duty and loyalty to the force has—the chief changed "has" to "have"—"have already had a positive and cohesive effect on his fellow officers in the W.P.D.—$400."

He flipped through the other officers' jackets: $300 each to Burt Diehl and Art Carlussi for, respectively, "leading a successful search in the lower Shagg Mountains for evidence in the Phyllis Bradley murder" and "investigating and solving a series of burglaries at Winwar State College."

Which used up the Police Incentive Fund until next year, pleasure of the Town Board. Thank you, and amen.

Oscar's phone rang. Maybe this was it—the jury was coming in. Whenever his phone rang now, it was his first thought. But no. The dispatcher was telling him that Officer Williams had just had an accident with a hog on Rte. 207, east of the village, belonging to Mr. A. Doufekias. Williams was shaken up but didn't appear seriously hurt. His cruiser was demolished.

"Ursula, are you putting me on?"

"Chief, I'm not. Officer Moscatello's on his way out to investigate."

Oscar hung up, sat for a few moments shaking his head. Then he heard a knock on his door. Mary Teevan came in and said Tony Bradley wanted to see him. The chief put up his hands. "No! Tell him I'm busy, anything."

The blond officer went out. A few seconds later Oscar heard some talking, no idle chit-chat, in the hallway. His door opened abruptly and Tony pushed in with Officer Teevan trying to restrain him.

"Tony!"

"I have to talk to you!"

"You're resisting an officer of the law—"

"I know who killed my mother!"

Teevan was still trying to control him and then Officers Bock and Diehl came rushing in—and did. "You *have* to listen to me, chief," Tony said. "I know who murdered her."

Oscar's exasperation was at its limit; still, he dug a little deeper. Maybe Tony Bradley was losing it but he wasn't here to practice wrestling with members of the department. "Okay, let him go," he said to Lieutenant Bock.

The police officers left—Teevan mumbling something that didn't sound like meet me later for a drink —and Oscar stared at the man with the thick black beard, in rough jeans and flannel shirt, remembering when Tony Bradley had worn handsome suits and had probably pulled down at least eighty-five thou working for his dad. "I want you to know you're crowding me, Tony, really crowding me. Now—you got something to say, say it!"

Tony reached inside his shirt—and momentarily the chief started. But it was only an old newspaper that Tony pulled out. "Do you recognize this picture?" he said, handing the paper to Oscar.

The chief looked at it. "Yeah..."

"Look at Dwayne's head."

"Okay."

"*Look* at it."

"Tony, you're going to have to cool it," Oscar said, lifting his hand, forefinger pointed. "Now sit down."

"Tell me what you see on Dwayne's head."

Oscar looked at the picture again. "That bandage?"

"Why is it there?"

"I don't know—" But then he remembered. "It was an injury he got building a tree stand—"

"That was what he said."

"It's what happened. I saw the stand."

"It's an injury he got ducking inside my parents' garage."

The chief leaned back in his chair. "Tony, I know the strain you're under but I'm going to tell you now—you're way out of line."

"Sadie Wojciechowski let Dwayne in the house when I left earlier. They're having an affair."

"How do you know they're having an affair?"

"She's having an affair with someone. She told me. McManus is her neighbor—"

"*Someone*, okay. But just because they're neighbors—"

"Chief, I know I'm right. It all ties in. He saw me looking around, making those moves by the garage door—he was parked out front, remember? And he got nervous. Because he was afraid there might be telltale evidence on the electrical box that clipped him last fall—maybe he hadn't bothered wiping it down. He was right, he hadn't. The blood and hair were his—"

"False accusation is a serious offense, Tony."

"Oscar, for Christ's sake—open your mind! Dwayne McManus killed my mother. He walked her through the woods to his car that he'd already parked by the old Vandermark barn —"

"Why? Tell me goddamn why!"

"Think how burned he must've felt when he came home from the army and the Review Board turned him down—"

"I didn't know your mother was on the board!" the chief came back.

"Was Dwayne going to do something really stupid, like kill Ted Marzocca?"

"So he chose your mother. Give me a break, Tony!"

"When you stop to think about it, she's the one he *would* kill. The way he staged it, he'd be sending a Bradley to jail for life!"

"Am I missing something?"

"What happened to Dutch McManus? Remember the accident? If I were Dwayne, I'd want to send the CEO of the Bradley Corporation away..."

The chief sat quietly. He was more a student of common sense than of psychology, but he knew about "obsession," and he knew he was looking at an obsessed person. Almost in a gentle tone he said, "Someone has to tell you. You need a little help, Tony."

"You need help. You've got a goddamn killer in your department! Dwayne staged, produced and directed the whole murder, making it seem as if my father—"

"Tony, I haven't got all day. You've said what you've got to say, now if you don't mind—"

His phone jangled and he picked up quickly, glad for the interruption. "Chief Flick."

"Dwayne McManus speaking, chief."

Oscar gave his head a quick, hard shake. "Yeah," he said after a moment.

"I'm up in Woodland—in the general store. This isn't easy to say, chief..."

"Go ahead."

"Chuck Wojciechowski busted into my cabin ten minutes ago with a shotgun—killed his wife. Fired at me, missed. Third round jammed on him. I killed him in self-defense..."

Oscar gave himself a long second. "Jesus Christ, Dwayne!"

"I've been having an affair with Sadie, I didn't think he knew—"

"You told me you and her were just—"

"I know, we were. We started seeing each other around Christmas, things happened fast. We were planning on getting married."

The chief's head sagged, then he said, "Give me directions to your cabin. You cross the bridge, then what?"

"Bear right, exactly 3.4 miles, left side of Woodland Road."

"Second thought—wait for me at the store."

Oscar hung up, looked at the man sitting by his desk. The best way to end a conversation was by walking away from it, which the chief did. He went out into the hall and over to communications central. "Raise O'Shea," he told Ursula Bauer at the dispatcher's desk. "Tell him to get up to McManus' cabin in Woodland—two people are dead, a couple from Winwar named Wojciechowski."

"How do you spell that, Chief?"

"W-o-j—I don't know. Cross the bridge at the general store, tell him—turn right. Cabin's 3.4 miles on the left."

He turned from the counter and shouted for his second-in-command. Lt. Bock came out into the hall. "Yes, Chief."

"Dwayne McManus just called from Woodland," Oscar said quietly. "He's been having an affair with a married woman. Couple named Wojciechowski, live in the trailer park. Husband just now busted into Dwayne's cabin in Woodland, killed his wife. Dwayne shot and killed the husband—"

"What are we looking at?"

"Self-defense, but I don't like it."

"Do you want me to go up?"

"O'Shea's on his way. Keep it goin' here. Where's Diehl?"

"I just saw him a minute ago."

"Find him. Send him in."

Oscar went back into his office and grabbed his Stetson, belted on his holster, a tight, uncomfortable feeling in his stomach. He glanced at the statement he'd written supporting his rookie officer for a merit raise. Maybe he, the chief, was the one who was losing it, not Tony Bradley. Then he thought, no, the man's an eccentric, a hermit. It's pure coincidence...

"That guy ever find you, Dwayne? Kind of short, said he was a friend of yours from the army."

"Yeah, he stopped by."

"Anything else? I got a special this week on baloney."

"Thanks, Dorothy. Just the gum."

Dwayne unwrapped a stick and went outside to wait. He walked back and forth in front of the Woodland store, then decided to sit down on the wooden steps, he didn't want to give the impression he was nervous. The steps were worn; where knots were, they weren't so worn. The knots had a darker color. One was loose, you could knock it out with a screwdriver. Or a .45 slug. There was a taste in his mouth that wouldn't go away and he unwrapped a second stick of gum—

Suddenly Dwayne jumped up, like maybe a copperhead was at his feet. What had he gone and done! He went to his car, got in, twisted key—backed and turned easy and crossed the bridge slow, but on Woodland he gunned it. Gray squirrel scurried across, bump wasn't much—a little thud. Rammed car up long climb to leaning hemlock, then eased off and turned in, braking sharp at bottom of drive.

He got out and stopped for a second outside the door, telling himself he could do this, could handle it—no problem. He was alone, he had time—it was just a scare sitting on the steps when it hit him. He spit out his gum and took a toothpick from his wallet and put it between his lips and went in, crossed to the bed, standing so as not to step in the blood on the floor, and reached out, his hands passing over her torn-open chest and then going down and to the back of her neck and finding the clasp; it was bloody and hair was tangled in it and he looked down, his hands light, his fingers working at the clasp clogged with blood and gooey hair. The toothpick just twitched between his lips a little, not registering much tremor. His fingers were getting sticky but he couldn't wipe them on his pants—he didn't want blood on his clothes. Fingers it didn't matter, he could rinse his hands, and the pearls, and he worked at the catch in low-low, just going at one mph—and then he had it. He turned to go to the sink with the necklace dangling from his hand—and standing in the front door with a 30–30 leveled on him was Tony Bradley.

"Don't move."

"Put it down, Tony."

"Like hell."

"Drop it!"

"When the police get here you're going to tell them everything, the truth. Or I'm going to blow you away."

"When the police get here, you're dead. Now drop it!"

"You're going to tell them, Dwayne. Exactly what you did—how you got inside the house, the little accident you had with the garage door, how you took the gun and the pearls—"

From down along the narrow road a siren was wailing. "It's thoughtful of you to be holding them, by the way. Her pearls."

Dwayne said nothing; he began edging toward the back door.

"You're going to tell how you drove my mother to the Shaggs in your car and right where you'd be able to find her later, how you raped and killed her. Don't move!"

"Who's movin'?"

But he kept inching toward the door. The police car was at the bottom of the last rise. Rifles at the hip weren't your most accurate weapon, and he had a chance—

"Stop right there, Dwayne—"

He made a break for it—heard the sharp crack of the 30–30—felt a sting in his shoulder—his foot slipped on Wojciechowski's blood—fell on top of the body—made to get up and out to the deck—Tony tackled him and brought him back down, grabbing for the pearls. They fought, struggling on the hideous corpse. Dwayne managed to wrench free his snub-nosed .38, jammed it against Bradley and fired. Tony groaned, fell back. Dwayne got up, saw part of the pearl necklace under Bradley's hip where he lay. He stepped over Wojciechowski to snatch it up, and at that moment Sgt. O'Shea came running through the front doorway. The stocky officer looked quickly about, his sensibilities bombarded by the dead and the dying, by the blood, the murder—the total chaos—in Dwayne McManus' cabin.

For a second the two W.P.D. officers stared at each other. O'Shea's eyes fell to the red-tinted pearls in Dwayne's hand. "What's going on, Dwayne?"

"He fired first, Jim—"

"That don't really answer the question! Stow your gun."

O'Shea dropped to his knees, checked Tony Bradley's eyes, pulse, chest. He saw the pearls, also red-tinted, a broken string. He looked up quickly, confused, and Dwayne considered shooting him and taking the other half of the necklace. "What the hell happened?" demanded the sergeant.

Dwayne felt a dull ache starting to spread through his shoulder and reached up with his hand, fingers easy on the place.

"McManus, talk to me for Christ's sake!"

A new siren, echoing eerily, reached the cabin.

"You'd better sit down," said O'Shea.

What he did was back over Wojciechowski and go down the deck steps. Then he took the stone steps, the ones he'd made for Julie, down to the creek, fast.

"McManus—"

The water came crashing out of the big hills. He reached up and touched his shoulder again. O'Shea was shouting to him from the cabin to stop.

He ran. For the first time in his life, he ran.

The place was crawling with law enforcement personnel. Inside the cabin were the county medical examiner, two representatives from the sheriff's department and a state trooper. W.P.D. officers were moving about the property, and Jim O'Shea was searching McManus' car. Just outside the cabin door, where he could best keep his eye on the whole scene, stood Chief Flick; next to him was a state policeman from F Barracks in Bancroft, Sgt. Dusty Rhoades. There was some question about jurisdiction. Rhoades didn't believe this area of Woodland was in Winwar Township.

The chief said differently; besides, the W.P.D. was on the scene first, and that usually determined who was in charge. This last part, Oscar didn't say. It was understood. The main point of disagreement between him and Sgt. Rhoades was how best to pick up the fugitive.

"I can have dogs here inside an hour, we'll have him before dark," said the trooper, a thick, strapping man in his mid-thirties.

"You put that kind of tail on McManus, you'll never get him."

"He's wounded—"

"All the more reason."

"What are you telling me? Who is this guy?"

"Dusty, I'll bring him in," said Oscar. "I appreciate your help—"

A petite young woman in jogging shoes, raspberry cords and a red sweater walked up to the two officers. She gave Oscar a big smile. "Hi, chief. Haven't seen you for a while."

"Audrey. How you doing?"

"Just fine. Hello, Sgt. Rhoades."

The trooper nodded and walked away.

"What's his problem?" she said to Oscar.

"Ask him."

"What do we have here?"

"Sadie and Chuck Wojciechowski from Winwar Trailer Park—both dead."

She had out her handy pad and began writing. "What were they doing in Dwayne McManus' cabin?"

"Having a fight."

"Come on, chief."

"Wojciechowski came looking for his wife."

"Were Sadie Wojciechowski and McManus having an affair?"

Just then one of the sheriff's deputies, a skinny young man with skin problems, came out of the cabin. "The medical examiner's signed the release."

"Take 'em away."

"Where's McManus now?" Audrey Ryder asked the chief.

"We don't know."

"He's your officer, what do you mean you don't know?"

"I said I don't know."

Two black zippered bags were wheeled out and placed in the back of a waiting brown station wagon. Oscar gave his head a small shake.

"Were they?" Aurey asked again.

"Who? What?"

"Having an affair. McManus and Sadie."

"I guess they were."

"I saw a Winwar Rescue Squad ambulance on my way here—had to be doing seventy-five," Audrey said. "Any connection to this?"

"Yeah. Tony Bradley was in it."

"Leonard Bradley's son?"

"That's right."

"What was he doing here?"

"Getting the drop on McManus."

"Will he be arrested?"

"Arrested?"

"For 'getting the drop' on a police officer."

"We'll look into it. If he lives."

"How was he hurt?"

"Chief, come here," O'Shea suddenly called out.

Oscar walked quickly up to his sergeant, who was standing at the rear bumper of McManus' Chevy. A spare tire lay on the ground. "Yeah, Jim?"

"We need a witness."

Oscar looked toward the cabin. Sgt. Rhoades and his junior man were coming out, and the chief called them over and spoke to Rhoades briefly. The junior man couldn't have been a month out of the academy. It didn't look like he shaved yet. "Sure, whatever," said the big trooper.

O'Shea glanced at the rookie's nametag. "Shepherd, look inside the spare-tire well. If you see anything, sing out."

The young trooper clambered inside. "I see something!" he said after a moment.

"Come on out with it," O'Shea said.

The state trooper backed out of the trunk with his hand snugly closed.

"Give what you got to the chief," O'Shea said.

Shepherd dropped a gold wedding ring in Oscar's hand. The chief and Sgt. O'Shea exchanged a long, slow look. Then Oscar examined the inside of the ring, but in the failing light he couldn't make out the inscription. "Audrey, tell me what it says inside, will you?"

She took the ring. "It says, 'L. to P. 5/15/49.'"

Oscar looked at Sgt. Rhoades. "I'd like to take Shepherd along with us, okay with you?"

"No problem."

"What all is going on here?" asked Audrey Ryder.

"You wouldn't believe me if I told you," said Oscar, walking away. He hardly could himself.

O'Shea was already behind the wheel of Oscar's cruiser, and then, with the young trooper in back, they took off.

"Where to?" asked O'Shea as they rolled down the road, flashers going.

"Cooper County Courthouse."

Chief Flick then reached for his transmitter and pressed the speak button. "Signal 1 to base," he said. "Come in, base."

Chapter **29**

"No, *No*," William Woolever was raging. "I have not prosecuted Leonard Bradley to the full extent of the law just to let him go now, to say it's over. *No*, goddamn it!"

Besides the district attorney in the private dark-paneled chamber were Chet, the chief, Sgt. O'Shea, the young state trooper Don Shepherd, and of course Judge Cruikshank. On the long, rectangular table at which they were sitting, a broken string of bloody pearls and a gold ring were lying on a sheet of paper. Then Woolever was off again. "This is a conspiracy—the Bradley clan and the Winwar Police Department—to keep Leonard Bradley from going to prison. Justice is going out the window here—"

"Your Honor," Chet said, "What's going out the window is the *in*justice here. I've said from the beginning Mr. Bradley is innocent. But last fall the Winwar police found evidence that pointed to him as a suspect. He was indicted and we went to trial. We've had a trial, but we don't need a verdict—because Mr. Bradley didn't kill his wife! The police *now* know who killed Phyllis Bradley. Do you think it looks good for the chief to say,'We arrested the wrong person. The person who killed Mrs. Bradley is one of my own officers!' But here they are, saying it!

Naming Dwayne McManus. Why? Because Tony Bradley interrupted McManus as he was taking Mrs. Bradley's pearls from
Sadie Wojciechowski's neck and now McManus—"

"It hasn't been established these are the missing pearls," Woolever countered. "The onyx clasp, as an identifiable feature, is
not evident. I refuse to let Mr. Evers say McManus was taking
Mrs. Bradley's pearls from Sadie Wojciechowski's neck."

"Why was he taking them off her then?" asked the chief. "If
the pearls weren't hot, if they had no bearing on the case, he
would've left them on Sadie's neck. It's why he went back to his
cabin. McManus knows you don't tamper with the body of a
person who dies under unusual circumstances."

"He was removing the pearls because he was afraid they might
disappear in the morgue."

Oscar shook his head.

"How about the ring?" said Sgt. O'Shea.

"It was planted."

"Judge, as soon as I saw the ring I told Chief Flick about it,"
O'Shea said. "Then we had a third party come over. I asked
Trooper Shepherd if he'd crawl inside McManus' trunk and have
a look."

"What did you see?" Judge Cruikshank asked Shepherd.

"I crawled in and looked in the spare-tire well and saw that
ring." The young trooper pointed to the ring on the table. "Sgt.
O'Shea told me to bring it out—then I handed it to Chief Flick.
A reporter looked inside the ring and read the inscription."

"O'Shea dropped the ring in the tire well, Your Honor. It's a
conspiracy—"

"I just happened to have it, right? I've been carrying it around
in my pocket for the past seven months!"

"Chief, in your opinion, how did Mrs. Bradley's ring get inside
McManus' trunk?" the judge asked.

"When he took her to Brenner Heights in the trunk of his car,
she either slipped it off or it fell off her finger, rolling into the
tire well."

"McManus wouldn't have seen it in all those months?" Woolever shouted. "You find it in a spur-of-the-moment search, he
doesn't see it in half a year? No, the ring is planted. Mr. Evers

talked all about *my* bogus evidence. *There's* your real bogus evidence. The jury must be allowed, Your Honor, to deliver its verdict!"

"Mr. Woolever," said Chet, "*Dwayne McManus* killed Mrs. Bradley. The only reason you want a verdict on Leonard Bradley is for the political mileage you'd get out of it—"

"I could *lose*, Mr. Evers. Consider that before you accuse me of being so cynical."

"But it's a risk you'll gladly take, considering the alternative." Chet turned to the judge. "Your Honor, any verdict at this point would be a travesty, knowing what we know now. Do we let our egos and political ambitions dictate legal proceedings, or do we admit that, as it turned out, this trial was an exercise. If we want the verdict on an exercise, let the jury come in. Then we can see who 'won' or 'lost.' I have a good amount of sporting blood in me and used to enjoy moot court when I was in law school. But we're all beyond that now. I submit, respectfully, that all charges against Mr. Bradley be dropped, effectively terminating the jurors' deliberations."

"To do that, your honor, would be an unconscionable breach of due process!"

Wilbur Cruikshank glanced at his watch, for some reason conscious that under his robe he had on a red-flannel shirt. "I'll rule on this in twenty-four hours," he said. "If the jurors reach a verdict before then, I'll keep them sequestered—in fairness to both parties."

He stood up. "Chief, I'll take custody of the new evidence. Good night, all."

He found Leonard and Catherine in a small room on the main floor of the hospital at 9:20. Tony was still on the operating table, was all they could report. They were both looking drawn, anxious, tired, Catherine almost to the point of illness. As for the meeting with Woolever and Judge Cruikshank, Chet said, the D.A. had fussed and fumed. Woolever insisted that he had proved his case against Leonard and wanted the legal process to continue.

"What did the judge say?" Catherine asked.

"Not much, but it's my opinion the new evidence had its effect on him. How strong, I don't know. There are legal considerations for him to weigh and consider. To dismiss a sitting jury isn't an everyday courtroom proceeding."

"Now what?"

Leonard was listening but his thoughts were elsewhere. "We wait for the judge's ruling," Chet said. "The immediate question is, does Judge Cruikshank let the jury come in and render a verdict? Woolever argues yes. His reputation's on the line, it's an election year."

"But he *could* lose!"

"He knows that. Still, losing would at least be going down in flames. To have your whole case summarily tossed out—that's a terrible embarrassment."

"How long before Cruikshank rules?" Leonard asked.

"He said within twenty-four hours."

They waited, mostly in silence. Chet went out and bought sandwiches and coffee at ten o'clock, bringing the box lunch to the room. Then, shortly after eleven, a physician walked in, introduced himself as Dr. Lawrence Morton, and Leonard, Catherine and Chet all immediately stood up. Dr. Morton was a large, bald, pink-faced man of fifty, and he looked totally exhausted. When he learned what the relationships were, he spoke mostly to Leonard. His son Tony was resting, receiving transfusions. He had lost a large amount of blood. The bullet had entered the right side of his upper chest, just below the collar bone, then had veered slightly downward, tore through his lung and had stopped a quarter-inch from the heart. From the loss of blood and shock to his system, it was a wonder he'd survived at all. His son's physical condition was terrific—certainly one of the reasons he'd made it to the hospital. Credit also had to be given to the Winwar Rescue Squad. In any event, Dr. Morton said, he had removed the bullet, had sewn up a huge amount of torn muscle and tissue. Tony was now in intensive care with around-the-clock monitoring. Any number of things could go wrong at this point—it was a crucial period—the doctor was particularly worried about embolisms. Tony's vital signs were weak but steady. This last was extremely important. Dr. Morton saw no reason for them to sit up all night. If there were any developments the intensive-care staff would call them immediately. He, himself, would be returning first thing in the morning.

Dr. Morton went out, and for several minutes Catherine, Chet and Leonard simply stood quietly in the small room. Leonard then said he'd be staying. Catherine said she'd stay too, but Leonard urged her to go, she was exhausted, she needed sleep.

"I can't leave you here alone, daddy."

"I'll be okay, I want you to get some rest."

She hugged him tightly; then, drained, she left with Chet.

They were in bed in the guest room; it had a lime rug and high windows and white wicker furniture. Catherine lay on her side, Chet on his back. A quarter-moon hung in the sky.

She was dead tired; but he obviously needed to talk, so she listened. "Part of me would like to hear a not-guilty verdict. Part of me wants to beat Woolever on the turf we established and *then* have the judge dismiss the charges . . . But I think of Tony— while we talked and argued in the courtroom, he was out there, putting his life on the line. In light of what happened today, it makes the whole trial seem farsical."

"Don't say that. In my opinion, you beat Woolever. I thought you were brilliant. When you got Lt. Bock . . . to admit that point . . . about the shoe prints . . . "

"It was clever, Catherine; there's a difference."

Her eyes were growing heavy and then she was sleeping. Chet smiled and kissed her lips.

A phone was ringing next to the bed. It was just dawn, the earliest light. Catherine woke up with a start. Oh, God, no! she thought. "Hello."

"Is this the Bradley residence?"

"Yes."

"This is Mrs. Brownell. I'm sorry to disturb you so early."

"Oh. Oh, Mrs. Brownell. That's all right. This is Catherine."

"Hello, Catherine. Debby just had a baby boy—I'm calling from the delivery room."

She held the receiver, staring across the gray room.

"Catherine?"

"Yes?"

"Debby just had a baby boy—"

"That's wonderful."

"Sean Michael. Eight pounds. They're both doing just fine. Is Tony there? I tried reaching him in Mink Hollow—"

"No, he stepped out . . . he's not here."

"We were expecting him and then he never—"

"Mrs. Brownell—"

"Yes?"

Then she said it, right or wrong, she said it. "Tony's been hurt, he's in the hospital. I'm sorry to have to tell you. It just happened yesterday evening. Mrs. Brownell, he found out who really killed our mother and the man shot him—"

"Oh, my God—"

"Mom?" came Debby's voice in the background.

"Is Tony—?"

"He's in intensive care. It's why he stayed," Catherine said. "It's why he wasn't there."

"Mom, what is it?"

"I'll call again later," said Mrs. Brownell, needing to go to Debby.

Catherine hung up, looked at Chet, finally sleeping. She got out of bed and walked barefoot down the corridor to the door, opened it and crossed the driveway to the path leading to the pond. A fine mist was rising from the water. Her white cotton gown and legs were wet from the heavy dew but she didn't feel the chill. She continued past the pond to the big upper field where her brother had practiced golf shots as a boy. They had kept it short then. Now it was long. Catherine stood in the tall grass, looking at the line of trees at the far end of the field. When they were both kids he would sometimes ask her to shag for him. The balls would come high and deep and she would lose them in the sky and she was always afraid one might hit her, plus it was a pain picking up a hundred balls and dropping them in the canvas bag and toting it back to Tony. But now it was a memory of something between them and she saw herself by the trees picking up golf balls and dropping them in the green canvas bag. The sun was just coming up above the trees, and she stood there looking out at the sun and the trees and the grass, and a girl shagging balls for her brother.

At 7:25 that morning they went in together, Chet, Catherine and Leonard. Dr. Morton was already in the room, looking at charts, reading the reports. Tony was heavily bandaged across his chest, receiving plasma, and Dr. Morton said his vital signs were still holding, some improving. They stood a few feet from the bed. Leonard went up and was grateful to see his son's eyes were open. "Debby just had a baby boy—they're both doing fine," he said. "Sean Michael—eight pounds!" He stopped for a moment, he was finding it difficult to talk . . . "Tony, I'm choking up here—, but thank you, not just for what you did for me, but for all of us, the family."

He leaned over and kissed his son's forehead, backed away. Catherine told Tony how proud she was of him and that she had Buck at the house and was taking good care of him. And Chet, pressing his hand, said the next time Tony showed him a toothpick he'd pay attention. Outside in the hallway Dr. Morton said his confidence was building that Tony would pull through. As the threesome were going down a network of long hallways with noiseless green floors and entering the main lobby, Adam Pohl was coming in from the street.

"I just heard the news driving in. How is he, Leonard?"

"Holding his own."

"Thank God."

There was a small pause. "How's Danny?"

"He's doing well. It's going to be a new life for him. For Ruth and me too . . ."

"That's great. We have brave sons, Adam."

"They have brave fathers," said the priest.

Then emotion overcame both men and there were no more words needed. They stood, quietly holding each other, in the lobby of the hospital.

Chapter **30**

The cabin seemed different the next morning; in the early light it had a peaceful, quiet look. The sun, easing through the big hemlocks and oaks, gave the pair of little front windows a warm, hospitable glow. Oscar might almost have expected an old woodsman to open his door and invite him, Sgt. O'Shea and Patrolman Diehl in for a cup of coffee.

The three officers were dressed as woodsmen themselves: jackets, coarse pants, tramping boots. O'Shea buckled on a nylon belt pack and Diehl slipped into and adjusted a knapsack. All three had two-way radios on their belts and carried canteens. O'Shea and Diehl's sidearms were barely visible; what showed beneath their jackets were stubby brown noses. Oscar's gun rode on his hip. As a final piece of equipment, the chief slipped binoculars over his shoulder; over his, O'Shea tightened the leather sling of a .308 semi-automatic rifle.

They walked behind the cabin, glancing up at the steps leading to the deck. The door was open and the sill and boards were stained. The men started down, taking the flat stones that served as steps. Chodokee Creek always ran strong until late summer; it was running strong now. They reached the bank, stood on a

302

pair of big boulders—O'Shea and Diehl on one, Oscar on the other.

"I did this once as a kid," the chief said. "We left from Chodokee Forks. Took five hours."

"From here, then, maybe three and a half, four," said O'Shea.

"Except it was fall," Oscar said. "That made it easier, you could cross back and forth across the creek. Now here's what I want to say. What's a safe path for me may not be for you. We stay together but you don't have to follow in the other guy's steps. Any questions?"

There were none.

"Let's do it," said the chief.

Starting out, it wasn't really a climb, just hard slow going. They stayed near the water. A couple of times Oscar saw that the opposite bank would make for better going but the risk was too great even though it was only twelve or fifteen feet across. As they continued on, the creek bed began getting deeper, became an actual gorge and they were expending too much energy clambering over boulders—slowing them down. On top of the gorge the land looked steep but free of obstacles. O'Shea thought they should strike for the higher ground, Oscar agreed, so they turned away from the creek and struggled and climbed, pulling on trees and extending hands to each other. It was only eighty yards but they were exhausted when they reached the top.

"Let's take a break," Oscar said.

They sat with their backs against a huge mountain boulder and drank from their canteens. From his back pocket O'Shea pulled out a red bandanna and wiped his face and neck. Overhead, a hawk was circling, and above the now diminished roar of Chodokee Creek the men heard its cry. "Kreee-eeee, kree-eeee."

"Early morning warning system," said Diehl.

"You may not be wrong," Oscar said.

When he and Len had made the hike as kids, he'd been sore for a week. Now he figured he might be sore for the rest of his life. He glanced at his sergeant. "Was he holding his shoulder, Jim?"

"At first I didn't know he was hit," O'Shea said. "Then I saw blood soaking through his jacket. I think he reached up once..."

The chief nodded. "Come on, let's move."

"Kreeee-eeee, kreee-eeee."

"Hawk's giving me the creeps," Diehl said, looking up.

The terrain rose sharply and they climbed a hundred feet and had to rest, then another hundred and had to rest, always using a tree or rock to lean against. "Chief, we're gettin' away from the creek," O'Shea said.

They began heading more toward the gorge again in what was both a climbing and a falling off, like, Oscar thought, when you were a kid riding your bike uphill and the road had a high crown. When they reached the gorge, Chodokee Creek, below, came into view through the big evergreens. "I remember there's a falls where the creek comes out of the lake," Oscar said, "but you have to be on the far side to get there."

"When do you want to cross?"

"About now looks good."

They slid down, grabbing hold of trees, working their way slowly—sometimes not so slowly—to the water. Oscar's buns felt like he'd just busted a half-dozen broncos. When they reached the bottom of the gorge the water was only six feet across but fast and strong, and they took ten minutes finding a secure stepping stone in the middle so they could safely jump across. On the other side they trudged on, climbing again.

"If he was hit, how in hell could he do this?" Diehl said as they stopped to rest against the trunks of big trees. "I'm about dead."

"He probably went an easier way," said the chief.

"There's an easier way?"

"Isn't there always?"

"Why didn't *we* take it?"

"He didn't feel like hanging around," O'Shea said, "to tell us about it."

Oscar was about dead too and the hardest part was still ahead. Diehl passed around sandwiches and they shared the top to the coffee thermos. "Anyway, this is the most direct way," Oscar said.

"Suppose he ain't here," Diehl said.

"Look at it this way"—Oscar handed the empty thermos top to the patrolman—"you'll always be able to tell your grandchildren you made it to Kelly Lake. Okay, last leg—let's get going on it."

"Kreeee-eeee, kreee-eeee."

"Goddamn bird," said Diehl.

They scrambled up, half the time on all fours, digging in hard and hanging on when they rested, arms coupled around trees. Oscar just hoped his heart wouldn't quit on him, but they sure could say, if it did, he'd died with his boots on. Then they saw the falls; above, where the water first started plunging down, was all open, all sky. To get there they were faced with a rocky cliff, an up-and-down escarpment fifteen feet high. "There's a chimney along here, we got to look for it," the chief said.

"What's a chimney?" Diehl asked O'Shea.

"Just look for it."

Oscar pushed along the base of the cliff, then saw the opening. It resembled a small cave but the hole continued upward inside the escarpment like a tunnel. "Over here!" he shouted.

O'Shea and Diehl came up. "I'll go first," the chief said. "If you slip going up this thing you're in deep shit, so easy does it. And don't start up till I say okay from the top."

He went into the cave and looked up, then reached for his first hold. He remembered when Len and he had come on the chimney, the question was who'd go first. Oscar finally had and had made it OK and then Len started and when he was near the top Oscar had taken his hand to help him out, and then they had both sat there looking out at the lake, feeling like they were on top of the world. He stretched and heaved, looked for a footing. A jagged rock scraped his back. His foot slipped and a stone went crashing down. He kept on, grabbing hold and stretching and pulling himself toward the daylight, sometimes wedging his shoulders against the rocky walls for a rest. A stone dug into his thigh and he swore. The opening was wider across now, four feet, and he didn't look down. Maybe McManus would be right there, waiting at the top. Those were the chances you took. Maybe he wouldn't be anywhere. One more heave—one more scrape of the old body—and he was out. Oscar rolled over and lay panting in deep grass. He gave himself a minute to catch his breath, not long enough, then crawled over to the mouth of the chimney.

"Diehl, yo! Come on!"

They were about fifty feet from the shore. Sgt. O'Shea had taken a pretty bad scrape on his forehead and Diehl had used the first-aid kit, putting a bandage on the cut; all three officers were pretty beat up, a scruffy lot kneeling in the long grass looking out at the water. "What we're going to do is walk along," the chief said. "It's three miles around—more if you count the inlets and coves. We're going to walk nice and easy. He already knows we're here."

"He does?" said Diehl, his scooped-out cheeks looking hollower than normal.

"If he's here," the chief said.

They stood and began walking, limping. Patrolman Diehl's two-way radio was crushed. "Is he here or isn't he?" he asked Sgt. O'Shea.

"Who the hell knows?"

"I'm getting spooked."

"Just keep your eyes peeled."

They walked along the edge of the lake, roughly abreast—O'Shea, with the rifle on the left, then Diehl and the chief. It was a cool, perfectly clear day, and Oscar imagined last night the temperature had dropped to freezing or below. Snow was still in the peaks. A fish jumped far out. *Kersplasshhh.* "Man, oh man," said O'Shea. Closer in, several dome-shaped piles of sticks dotted the surface, and beavers were swimming about, carrying twigs and branches in their teeth, diving. Past the far shore the land

was very big and wild, valleys and ranges, and more valleys and
more ranges. Oscar stopped, and they all stopped. He pulled
out his binoculars and scanned the shoreline. Then they were
walking again.

"This would be a great spot to come camping," Burt Diehl
said. "Barbara would love it."

"Barbara, your girlfriend?" said O'Shea. "She'd get stuck in
the chimney, Burt."

"Fuck you."

Oscar's thigh was stiffening up, his whole body ached. They
moved along for twenty minutes and came to a cove. The chief
raised his glasses, moving them slowly along the shore of the
inlet, stopping; moving them slowly, stopping. Then he stopped
altogether.

"I see something."

"What is it?"

"Take a look. Next to that big log."

O'Shea used the glasses. "Somebody's layin' there."

"Who? Can you tell?" said Diehl.

"No."

"Come on," said Oscar.

They began moving into the cove. The shore was strewn with
rocks and driftwood and slanted slightly; between shoreline and
forest was a distance of some forty feet. Halfway in, the chief
lifted his binocs. The man was face down. When they were thirty
yards away from him Oscar put his hand to the side, low. "I want
you and Burt to move up the shore," he said to O'Shea. "Then
keep even with me."

"OK, Chief. Give me another look."

Oscar handed O'Shea the glasses.

"Sonofabitch looks dead to me."

Diehl asked for the binoculars and raised them to his eyes.
"You can see the flies buzzin' around him. He's gotta be dead."

The chief stowed the glasses and the sergeant unslung his rifle
and went up the shore with Diehl. Oscar walked along the shoreline toward the body. When he was twenty steps away he yelled,
"McManus!"

No movement. Chief Flick went in closer. He didn't see any sign that Dwayne was breathing. "McManus?"

"Easy does it, Chief," said O'Shea, nearer the woods.

Oscar loosened his gun but didn't take it from his holster; his eyes stayed fixed on the body—gore and swarming insects from shoulder to hip. Slowly he went in, thinking to roll McManus over—when he was maybe six steps from the body it came to life. Dwayne rose up, scrambling to his feet with blurring speed. His one arm hung low, crippled at his side. His other arm was weirdly raised, level with his head, fingers taut like spikes, and he came at the chief with his head partly down, angled, a wild animal glare in his blood-streaked eyes. He looked huge to the chief, who drew his weapon and stepped back. But he didn't fire. The next moment O'Shea's .308 barked in the cool mountain air and a bullet tore into McManus' body and still he kept on, and the sergeant's rifle cracked again and another high-powered bullet ripped into Dwayne and he fell on the shore of Kelly Lake. He did not move again.

O'Shea ran up. "Chief, what the hell?"

Oscar was staring at the body. Suddenly it seemed normal again, a man's.

"Where's his gun? He was pointing a gun at you!" yelled O'Shea.

Oscar rolled Dwayne over. His .38—blasted by one of the shots, blood-soaked—was in his holster.

"Sonofabitch," said O'Shea. "The way his hand was lifted, I swear to Christ—"

"You did what you thought you had to, Jim. Easy now," said the chief.

Coming toward them taking slow, measured steps, looking shaken and pale, was Burt Diehl.

O'Shea had a small flask in his emergency rations and Oscar said give Diehl a pull and Diehl took a good pull. Then Sgt. O'Shea used his radio. They sat on the shore, and no one spoke.

"How did you know he'd be here, chief?" O'Shea asked, calmer now, breaking the silence.

"Where else was there for him to go?"

They were quiet again. Diehl had a second tug of the brandy. Behind them, Dwayne lay on the loose stones, his right hand still raised, even with his head. And then there was a whirring, rumbling noise in the sky, and Chief Flick and Sgt. O'Shea stood up, waving their arms at the chopper.

Chapter 31

Leonard Bradley reached into his rural box and pulled out the day's delivery: a local newspaper, two or three bills, several pieces of junk mail and a letter in a light blue envelope. He got back in his car and continued past his farm, along the ridge.

It was three-thirty. He had spent an hour at the hospital, then had driven to Willow to have lunch with Chet and Catherine. How long-lasting the relationship between his daughter and Chet would be, Leonard couldn't say. He just knew they seemed happy together, and California hadn't come up once.

He parked, lowered the garage door and went inside the house, walking the length of the hallway to the living room and settling in the easy chair by the hearth. He tossed the mail on the brass coffee table, keeping the light blue envelope, which he opened. The letter read:

Dear Leonard,
I've had you constantly on my mind this past week. My God, all the terrible, bizarre things that have touched your life. I was so happy to read where the charges against you had been dropped. But was deeply troubled to learn your son was seriously wounded and in the hospital.
Leonard, I would like to see you, and hope, as I write this, it could

be tomorrow. But I'll leave that to you . . . maybe you're in a different place, after all you've been through . . . On my way home from Bancroft I drove down Main Street in Winwar. It's a pretty town and the countryside is beautiful. Do you think the raccoons and woodchucks thereabouts would tolerate this urbanite's visit for a weekend? I have so much I want to share with you. Until then (if granted a visa), all my love,

Diane

He read the letter again, then put it down. The paper was the local weekly, so the news was several days old, but Leonard knew a good number of folk in and around Winwar were reading about the abrupt end to the trial for the first time. One of the articles on the front page was a reprint from the Times-Herald. He'd read it a couple of days ago, and reread it again now.

Audrey Ryder had taken it upon herself to poll all the jurors and how they were leaning at the time Judge Cruikshank had thanked them for their efforts and dismissed them. Three were completely undecided; five were favoring acquittal; and four believed Leonard Bradley was guilty. Those four scared him. The foreman, Ron Zack, was one of the uncommitted. Leonard reread his comment: "The way things were going, it would've taken weeks for all of us to agree, if then. Probably we would've declared a hung jury in a few more days."

Even today, Chet had said, "Can you imagine, having to go through all that again?" Leonard had said he couldn't imagine it.

He put the paper down. The house was very quiet, empty, with Catherine gone—and Tony's dog too. Catherine had taken Buck with her to Willow for the time being. On impulse Leonard walked into the kitchen, sitting down at the low ceramic counter and dialing a number. When a woman announced, "Good afternoon, Bradley Corporation," Leonard said he wanted to speak to Eleanor Chapman. In a moment his secretary was on the line.

"Mr. Bradley's office," she said.

"Hello, Eleanor."

"Mr. Bradley! How are you?"

"Okay. I'll be coming in tomorrow."

"That's wonderful."

"It's time—either that or I retire."

"Young man like you!"

Leonard laughed. "Promise me something. No fanfare, no welcoming committee. I want it like any other day."

"I'll take care of it. How's Tony doing, Mr. Bradley?"

"It's going to take months of therapy, maybe longer," Leonard said. "But his spirits are good. Debby came today with Amy and the baby."

"You must feel so thankful," she said.

"I do. See you tomorrow."

He put down the phone. It was early but he thought he might make a drink and sit at the pond. As he finished mixing a vodka and tonic, there was a knock at the door. He walked into the hall. Standing outside was the chief. He hadn't seen his old friend for several days, and he slid open the glass panel.

"Len, how you doing?"

"Oscar. Not too bad. Come on in."

"Thanks."

"I just made myself a little drink—"

"I'll have a light one."

Leonard went back to his bar, made a bourbon and carried the two glasses into the living room. He and Oscar sat down.

"How's Tony?"

"Still critical but improving every day."

"That's good." Oscar gave his head a little shake. "When I saw him laying there, Len, I tell you—I thought he'd had it."

They were quiet for a few moments. "I'm turning in my badge," Chief Flick said.

Leonard frowned. "Resigning?"

"Stepping down, call it what you want. I've put this tan-and-brown uniform on long enough."

"You love that uniform."

"A man needs a change."

Leonard looked skeptical. "What will you be doing? Any plans?"

"Heading west."

Leonard thought, You never left the West. He said, "Going home."

"Yeah."

"Does Difficulty really exist, Oscar? After all these years, level with me."

The chief grinned. "It's a place and a half, Len."

"What's Sylvia say?"

"She isn't coming."

"Oh?"

"Nearest mall's 217 miles away."

They were quiet again. Then Leonard had to ask: "What happened at Kelly Lake, Oscar? Can you tell me?"

"I'll tell you this—it was weird," the chief said, taking a swallow of his drink. "Burt Diehl, a good everyday cop, isn't sleeping, hardly eats. He may quit."

Oscar set his glass down. "He was laying there on the shore, Len, in one of the coves. By the looks of him, he was dead for sure. Then when I was a few feet away he jumped up, lightning quick. He looked huge, way beyond normal size—don't ask me why, but I can't forget. He came at me, his one arm crippled, the other raised up, a crazy look in his eyes. O'Shea thought he was holding a gun—him and Diehl were covering me as I went in—and drilled him with two shots from his .308."

Leonard waited for more, just staring at the chief.

"It was almost like he wasn't human, Len," Oscar went on. "He once told me he could think like a deer or a bear, any animal. That was why he was the best hunter around. Something happened to him at Kelly Lake, laying there in the cold night, wounded, bleeding. His pain had to be god awful. Anyway, it's over now." He took a last taste of his drink and stood up.

Leonard walked him to the door, slid it open. "Come out and visit me," the chief said. "We'll get you a nice quiet horse and ride out to Rattlesnake Gulch."

"Couldn't we just sit in the Silver Dollar Saloon?"

"Whatever you want."

Oscar was looking at him pretty hard. "I'm sorry, I guess that's the last thing I want to say—why I really came by."

"For what?"

"For arresting you last fall—"

"You were doing your job. Like you said."

"I know what I said." He gave his old friend a rap on the arm, then ambled down the path.

Leonard, looking after him, could already see the spurs on his boots, the rowels spinning.

He woke up at 7:25, had breakfast, dressed in a gray suit with a faint blue stripe and a silk cobalt blue tie, backed his automobile out of the garage and drove to the village. The Corner Restaurant was packed; a lot of fishermen were in town hitting the Chodokee with hardware and minnows. He went another mile, entered the company's main gate and parked in his spot outside the executive wing.

It was a few minutes before eight and the employee lot wasn't even half full. Some workers were still coming in but they moved slowly to the plant entrance. Leonard felt a heaviness in the air as he walked along the flagstone path to the trio of glass doors. Everyone was worried; new layoffs were imminent.

Then he was inside the lobby. The receptionist was just getting settled behind her desk. "Good morning, Mr. Bradley!"

She was trying to sound cheerful, but Leonard didn't think she was feeling cheerful. "Good morning, Paula."

He continued past her desk. Through the glass doors leading into the executive offices he saw Bob Rakower stroll across to the coffee alcove—and there was Matt Summersell, snappily attired in glen plaid, chatting with production manager Bill Nero. Then, as he always did at the start and end of every day, Leonard directed his eyes to the bronze bas-relief head of his father.

He stopped and looked. It wasn't the usual quick glance he gave his father. Then he walked into the wing.

"Len, good morning."

"Good morning, Matt."

"I've got some interesting numbers to show you—"

"Give me twenty minutes."

He walked on. "Good morning, Mr. Bradley," his secretary said, looking up from her desk.

"Hello, Eleanor. Come in, please."

She followed Leonard inside his office. At his desk he pulled out his swivel chair. "Sit down."

Eleanor sat in the chair at the corner of his desk; she had on a tan suit and matching leather heels. "You're looking fine, Mr. Bradley."

"Thank you." He glanced at the packets of paper, neatly arranged in front of him. "Where do I start, Eleanor?"

"We'll figure it all out," she said.

"I'm glad you said 'we'."

She smiled. "Is there anything I can do for you, Mr. Bradley?"

"I want to run an idea by you," he said. "Just now when I walked in, the lobby seemed sort of dead—there's no color out there."

"I agree."

"Let's do something then. Maybe you could get in some plants, see about a fountain. We could hang a couple of landscapes."

"It sounds like a wonderful idea. I'll start it going."

"Good." He hesitated a moment. "Something else. I'd like you to call the plant engineer and have him take down the sculpture of my father."

"Excuse me?"

"I'd like the head of my father removed, stored somewhere. I'd like that done this morning."

She didn't say anything. She just sat in the chair looking at him.

"Why are you staring at me, Eleanor?"

"I'm sorry."

"Are you upset by that?"

"No."

"You seem upsct."

"I just never thought I'd see the day. I'm really *delighted.*"

"You are?"

"Mr. Bradley, I know how much you respected your father. I respected him—he cast a long shadow. He founded the company, he guided it through the depression and war years. Then you took over." She stopped; maybe she was saying too much.

"Go ahead. It's okay."

"For all your own achievements, I've always felt *he* was still in charge. Because *you* felt it, Mr. Bradley—I think until just now."

Eleanor excused herself, and Leonard sat still for a long time, alone in his office. Then he swiveled in his chair, looking out at the grounds, and beyond. An early May sun was rising over Winwar.